continued . . .

The Woman Who Heard Color

KELLY JONES

BERKLEY BOOKS, NEW YORK

THE BERKLEY PUBLISHING GROUP
Published by the Penguin Group
Penguin Group (USA) Inc.
375 Hudson Street, New York, New York 10014, USA
Penguin Group (Canada), 90 Eglinton Avenue East, Suite 700, Toronto, Ontario M4P 2Y3, Canada
(a division of Pearson Penguin Canada Inc.)
Penguin Books Ltd., 80 Strand, London WC2R 0RL, England
Penguin Group Ireland, 25 St. Stephen's Green, Dublin 2, Ireland (a division of Penguin Books Ltd.)
Penguin Group (Australia), 250 Camberwell Road, Camberwell, Victoria 3124, Australia
(a division of Pearson Australia Group Pty. Ltd.)
Penguin Books India Pvt. Ltd., 11 Community Centre, Panchsheel Park, New Delhi—110 017, India
Penguin Group (NZ), 67 Apollo Drive, Rosedale, Auckland 0632, New Zealand
(a division of Pearson New Zealand Ltd.)
Penguin Books (South Africa) (Pty.) Ltd., 24 Sturdee Avenue, Rosebank, Johannesburg 2196,
South Africa

Penguin Books Ltd., Registered Offices: 80 Strand, London WC2R 0RL, England

This is an original publication of The Berkley Publishing Group.

This is a work of fiction. Names, characters, places, and incidents either are the product of the author's imagination or are used fictitiously, and any resemblance to actual persons, living or dead, business establishments, events, or locales is entirely coincidental. The publisher does not have any control over and does not assume any responsibility for author or third-party websites or their content.

PRINTING HISTORY
Berkley trade paperback edition / October 2011

Library of Congress Cataloging-in-Publication Data

Jones, Kelly, 1948–
    The woman who heard color / Kelly Jones.—Berkley trade paperback ed.
        p. cm.
    ISBN 978-0-425-24305-3
    1. Art thefts—Investigation—Fiction.   2. Mothers and daughters—Fiction.   I. Title.
    PS3610.O6264W66 2011
    813'.6—dc23   2011020927

PRINTED IN THE UNITED STATES OF AMERICA

10   9   8   7   6   5   4   3   2   1

The Woman
Who Heard Color

CHAPTER ONE

Lauren and Isabella

New York City
August 2009

As Lauren O'Farrell hurried up from the subway on her way to visit Isabella Fletcher, she knew the moisture under her blouse, along her collar, and spotting her chest was as much the result of nerves as the heat that had invaded the city for the past several days. She had never done anything like this before. At times she had gathered information through slightly deceptive means, but she'd never lied in an attempt to find her way into someone's home. She reasoned that it was highly unlikely, if not impossible, that Mrs. Fletcher would have agreed to open her door to the accusation that her mother was a Nazi collaborator, a woman who had assisted Hitler in purging the state galleries of what he had dubbed *degenerate art*, then stood by as paintings, prints, and drawings considered unimportant were destroyed, while the more valuable pieces were moved about as political pawns in a game clearly headed toward war and the final solution. A woman who had possibly lined her own pockets with funds obtained from "disposing" of art, and who had most likely kept a painting or two for her own collection.

Mrs. Fletcher had sounded skeptical when Lauren called this

morning and explained she'd been hired to do a private investigation relating to a liability lawsuit being threatened by a property owner in the building and she was interviewing residents to gather information. All lies. When the woman asked for the particulars on the lawsuit, Lauren replied that she was not at liberty to discuss this, as it would possibly prejudice the results of her random interviews. She supplied the number of her state investigator's license, which she legitimately possessed, but she could hear the uncertainty in Mrs. Fletcher's voice when she said she'd like time to consider this and would call back later. Two hours passed as Lauren mentally chastised herself for thinking the woman would fall for such an obviously bogus story. Then her phone rang, and without bothering to inquire if her schedule was open, Isabella Fletcher informed her that they would meet that afternoon at two.

The doorman at the building located just blocks from Central Park, a beefy fellow with a burly voice, greeted Lauren with a tip of the hat, asked for her identification, examined it meticulously, and then sent her up, saying, "Mrs. Fletcher is expecting you."

As Lauren entered she felt that sudden, final rush of heat that often came over her when she stepped from outdoors on a hot summer day into an air-conditioned building. The lobby was deserted. A man and woman exited the elevator and Lauren got on. It ascended; her stomach dropped. She told herself once more that what she was doing was completely justified.

An elderly woman opened the door, security chain in place, and peered out with clear blue eyes set below stern-looking brows and asked, in a voice equally as firm, "You *are* the investigator, Ms. O'Farrell?" Isabella Fletcher had not a trace of an accent, something Lauren had noted during their call.

"Yes. Very pleased to meet you, Mrs. Fletcher."

Running her eyes over the younger woman as if having second thoughts, Isabella Fletcher asked to see her state-issued investigator's license, as well as her driver's license, which Lauren produced. For a moment she was sure Mrs. Fletcher would simply shut the door, but instead she said flatly, "You certainly aren't what I expected."

She'd heard this before, in a variety of ways. Generally it was, *You're much shorter than I thought*, as if her phone voice was several inches taller than her stature of five foot two. Or that she was much younger than expected, though she had just turned thirty-six, which she considered well into adulthood. Or, *I thought you were Irish*. Would it be that difficult to surmise that she had married an American man with Irish roots? She wondered why people seemed incapable of drawing this conclusion on their own. Often when a client, a museum official, or even the owner of a questionable piece of art met her face-to-face, she would catch a familiar reaction, seldom verbalized but easily read. She had her mother and grandmother Goldman's stature and profile; her grandmother Rosenthal's piercing dark eyes and thick, curly black hair. Or so her father said. She had never met her paternal grandparents.

Slowly, the door opened.

"Come in," Mrs. Fletcher said, motioning with an open palm, though her tone extended no invitation. She was beautifully dressed in a pale blue linen suit with a string of pearls. Her silver hair was styled as if she had just come from the "beauty parlor," as Patrick's grandma O'Farrell always called it.

A teapot whistled from the kitchen as they stepped from the foyer. "Would you like tea?" Isabella Fletcher offered. Lauren wondered if the woman had timed the pot to whistle precisely as they entered the living room. Grateful she had arrived on time, though she usually did, Lauren guessed that tardiness would have been frowned upon.

"Yes, please, that would be wonderful," she told Mrs. Fletcher, though a cup of hot tea wasn't exactly what she would have ordered.

Isabella gestured to the sofa and left the room to fetch the tea, allowing Lauren to sit and settle her large bag—which doubled as her briefcase—at her feet, and at the same time do a quick once-over of her surroundings. The room smelled of fresh-cut flowers—there was a crystal vase filled with yellow roses just inside the entry on a table—and something she couldn't quite make out, a mixture of lemon furniture polish and a familiar but unnamed scent, vaguely medicinal, that she often noticed when visiting older clients. The drapes were partially drawn, the room quiet and poorly lit. Her eyes darted quickly, taking in the marble fireplace and the built-in bookcases filled with hardcover books. A lovely upholstered sofa and chairs with silk and tapestry throw pillows were arranged over a hardwood floor spattered with an array of Oriental rugs, worn just enough to declare they were authentic. Though the furnishings were traditional, the art on the walls—numerous paintings, drawings, and prints, many not clearly visible due to the dim lighting—was all modern. Works by the Expressionists. The Impressionists. Paintings in an abstract style. Quick pen and ink drawings in a loose sketchy hand. Lauren's heart skipped a beat. Were they possibly originals?

She spotted what looked like a Franz Marc above the mantel, one of his colorful animal paintings. A Gabriele Münter, a bright village scene of Murnau. Maybe an Otto Dix etching, though it was too far away to make out the details. All German artists. All artists who would clearly have been among those labeled degenerate. She was about to get up and step closer when Mrs. Fletcher returned with a tray. There was an old-fashioned, well-schooled graciousness about the woman, even if her mannerisms were rather stiff and formal. Lauren guessed her to be in her late seventies or early eighties, which would be exactly right if she was who Lauren suspected she was.

"This is very kind of you, Mrs. Fletcher," she said as the woman placed the tray on the table. Cookies were arranged on a small dish, set out beside a teapot, china cups, cloth napkins, tiny spoons, and sugar. The cookies were perfectly round, obviously store bought.

"I seldom bake anymore," Mrs. Fletcher said, her words touched with the smallest hint of apology. She poured them each a cup of tea, offered sugar, which Lauren declined, and then lifted the plate of cookies. Lauren had eaten a late lunch and wasn't hungry, but she took one just to be polite and placed it on her napkin.

Then Mrs. Fletcher sat in a wing-backed chair, arranged at a comfortable angle to converse with Lauren, who found the sofa a little too soft for comfort. She adjusted herself, straightening her back, discreetly pushing one of the numerous throw pillows behind her. The woman added the tiniest amount of sugar to her tea, stirred, and then placed the spoon on her saucer.

"These pictures," Lauren started in casually, as if making small talk to warm up to the questions about her alleged investigation, "they are lovely."

Isabella nodded.

"Very modern," Lauren added, "and colorful." Stated as if she knew nothing of art. "Are they originals?"

"Modern." The woman laughed out the word. "Many are older than I am. And I'm no spring chicken. Many of these are more than a hundred years old."

Lauren shook her head in mock disbelief.

"Do you know how much they would be worth if originals?" Mrs. Fletcher replied to Lauren's second question with one of her own, clearly avoiding a direct answer.

She shrugged as if she had no idea, and then waited a moment, hoping Mrs. Fletcher would go on, perhaps volunteer more about the paintings. Lauren could almost imagine the conversation she'd have with Patrick this evening after her visit.

"Well . . ." Mrs. Fletcher finally said, smoothing her skirt with her hand. The single word was delivered as if she'd just instructed Lauren to get on with it. The woman lifted a cookie from the plate and set it on her saucer.

Lauren reached into her bag and pulled out a pen and a note-book, ready to talk about the purported reason for her being here. On the subway she'd rehearsed possible lines such as, *How long have you lived in the building?* She hoped this would open up a discussion about Mrs. Fletcher's background. Lauren smiled, but the woman's expression remained grave.

"I know why you are here," Isabella Fletcher said without preface.

Lauren gazed down at her notebook, avoiding eye contact, wondering if the woman could possibly know why she was really here. "Oh?" she said, as she pushed back a strand of hair and tucked it behind her ear. She looked up.

"I'd prefer you not take notes," Mrs. Fletcher said. She eyed Lauren's bag. "You don't have a recording device?"

Lauren shook her head and slipped the notebook and pen back in her bag.

"It's about the Kandinsky," Isabella said.

Lauren sat silently, so surprised at the woman's words that she was at a loss for her own. "The Kandinsky?" she finally asked, her eyes involuntarily moving along the wall again.

"No, no," Isabella Fletcher said with a little chuckle. "It's not here. It's much too large for the room." Then, before Lauren could reply, she added, "The art detective. You're the art detective."

Lauren felt a prickly sweep of tension brush over her at this announcement, and that was exactly how the words had come out of Mrs. Fletcher. An announcement. Neither spoke, but they exchanged a quick glance. The older woman was aware that she had just taken the upper hand—Lauren could see it in the purse of her lips—and was allowing the young woman as much time as necessary to digest this.

The art detective? There was only one place where that information could have come from, Lauren realized. A small article had appeared in her university alumni magazine a couple of years ago, describing how she helped locate pieces lost in the war, particularly paintings looted from Jewish families. Her searches included delving into private collections, even into inventories of reputable museums. Sometimes the museums would hire her to investigate an acquisition of questionable provenance.

Lauren had never called herself the art detective, but this was the heading on the article.

After completing her doctorate, working as a museum intern, and teaching a university night class one semester, she'd taken a position as Assistant Curator of Modern Paintings at the Cleveland Museum of Art. Her duties included cataloguing the collection and studying new acquisitions. In researching the history of a painting, she'd come to understand that you could learn as much from the back of a work of art as from the painting itself. She discovered seals, numerical markings, custom stamps, inscriptions, and inventory stamps. She learned that the Nazis were particularly adept at keeping detailed records.

Her pregnancy—unplanned but welcomed by both her and her husband—was followed by a job offer in New York City for Patrick, and Lauren decided she would go into business for herself, using these skills to locate lost art. She could set her own hours and arrange her work to allow more time with the baby. After Adam arrived, she often felt overwhelmed by it all, but she had persisted, balancing work with motherhood. Adam was now three, a bright, happy child, and she'd been successful in her work, recovering numerous pieces of lost art. Court action was pending on others.

"As an investigator," Isabella Fletcher finally said, "one might think you would do a more thorough background check. It seems we both attended the same university." A smugness laced around her words in a polite, well-bred tone. She picked up the cookie, took a small nibble, then placed it back on her saucer. Wiping her thin lips on the napkin, she left a small spot of pink lipstick on the white linen.

Lauren could feel a pulse directly behind her left eye and wondered if the woman could see this nervous twitch. "Wassily

Kandinsky, the Russian," she said, needing to find some words to fill the conversational void.

"Yes, he was Russian, but he studied in Munich. He did some of his most important work in Germany. If one is to look upon the artist's body of work, Germany should be given credit for his early training and inspiration."

She wondered why Mrs. Fletcher told her she knew Lauren was here about the Kandinsky. Lauren knew nothing about a Kandinsky. Could it possibly be one of the state-owned pieces confiscated by Hitler? There were large gaps in the inventories from Berlin, blank spaces regarding the pieces taken to Lucerne. Or did Mrs. Fletcher think she was here to recover looted art? This was the topic of the university article; the story was about Lauren's efforts to return stolen art taken from the Jews during World War II.

"Your family is from Munich?" she asked, guessing now that Mrs. Fletcher had invited her to present a defense for ownership of a painting Lauren hadn't even been aware of.

"My father was born there," Mrs. Fletcher told her. "That's where my parents met."

"And your mother?" Lauren asked. "Where was she born?"

"In Bavaria. My mother's family was engaged in dairy farming in a region known as the Allgäu."

It was really her mother whom Lauren was interested in learning more about. Would Isabella Fletcher possibly reveal information about her mother, unaware that this was exactly what Lauren was looking for? *Tread carefully,* she warned herself.

"They still make wonderful cheese in the area," Isabella said. "My aunt and uncle continued the business here in the States. Koebler Creamery?"

"Oh, yes." Lauren flashed her a quick smile. "They make wonderful ice cream." It was through the Koebler family that she had actually tracked down Isabella's mother, Hanna Schmid, a woman gone now for over sixty years, a woman who Lauren believed had attempted to hide her true identity the entire time she lived in America.

"The Kandinsky has been in the family for many years," Isabella said.

"Acquired in Germany?" Lauren asked.

Isabella blinked once, twice, and then glanced at a photo on the end table next to her. "Andrew and I never had children." A handsome man, most likely in his mid-fifties at the time the picture was taken. Andrew Fletcher, Lauren assumed.

The old woman's eyes took on a moist, glassy film. "There's no one left in my generation on my side of the family. My brother, my sister—half sister actually—all long gone. Years and years ago. All my cousins, those in Germany, those in America. All deceased. Andrew's sister is still with us, though not doing particularly well." Her voice had taken on a softer tone. "The younger Fletcher nephews and nieces—I don't know these young people coming up now. They've never even set eyes on the Kandinsky. Never even been here for a visit," she added with an indifferent shake of her head. "The business will be passed down to Fletcher family members. But the painting . . ." Her voice trailed off.

Absentmindedly, Lauren fingered the edge of a silk pillow, soft and soothing like the satin trim on a baby's blanket. She could feel her nerves on edge. Excitement over a possible discovery mixed with equal shares of anxiety and confusion. She was startled that Isabella Fletcher was sharing this information with her.

Mrs. Fletcher said, "I trust that your intentions are honorable, though I assure you the Kandinsky was acquired legally." Lauren detected a slight quiver in her voice. She offered a nod of reassurance, encouraging the woman to go on.

"I understand perfectly well that art was stolen during the war. We continue to hear such stories." Mrs. Fletcher's voice was even now, though the woman patted her chest with a nervous flutter and ran her fingertips over her pearls. "Valuable art that disappeared during the war, assumed destroyed by bombs or looted by the Nazis, turns up and suddenly families come out of the woodwork to claim paintings that the present owners believed were legitimately acquired. Why, the other day I saw an article about a Van Gogh purchased by a famous movie actress, and it seems it had been gained illegally—I assure you this is not the case here. Our Kandinsky was legitimately purchased by my family. There are no claims to be made, which is quite obviously why you are here."

After a moment, Lauren asked cautiously, "Your family purchased the Kandinsky in Munich?"

Isabella nodded.

Again Lauren studied the many pictures on the wall. "May I see it?" she ventured.

Isabella Fletcher laughed, a chuckle really, which transformed into a somewhat unladylike snort. Again, she wiped her mouth with the linen napkin. "No, I don't think I'm quite ready for that." She cleared her throat before continuing. "I'm not getting any younger, though I am still in excellent health. But soon, I must decide what will become of the painting. I could sell it, divide the sizable proceeds among family members. But as far as the world is concerned, this painting no longer exists." She gazed at Lauren, fully expecting another question.

Lauren was attempting to remain calm, receptive, not overly eager. She had so many questions, but didn't want to say the wrong thing, something that might turn off this flow of information. She picked up her cookie and took a bite, then took a sip of tea. Such delicate china. Hoping Mrs. Fletcher would go on, she remained silent.

"I should clear all this up before I'm gone," the older woman said, "or, heaven forbid," she added, with a dismissive wave, "before I lose my memory and senses. No one knows the story behind the Kandinsky. It would be difficult to sell the painting if the provenance was misunderstood." Abruptly she rose and went to the window, pulling the drapes open farther to let in more light. For a moment she gazed down as if studying something on the street.

"I have never shared the entire story," Mrs. Fletcher said, sitting again. "Perhaps it is time."

Lauren was struck by this, wondering if Isabella really intended to share something she had shared with no one else. Why would she trust a stranger who'd entered her home under false pretenses?

"Tell me a little about the painting," Lauren said, her voice tight, but calm.

"It's one of his earlier works, not that geometric . . ." Isabella paused and shook her head as if envisioning something distasteful. "His later work, produced during his Bauhaus period, all circles and squares. I'm not fond of this period of the artist's work. I much prefer the paintings he did in Munich." She let out a little laugh. "But to each his own. I'm sure that's what my father would say. My mother, too. Everyone should be allowed the freedom to choose what he or she likes or dislikes. Our Kandinsky was painted about 1910, long before I came into the world."

Again Lauren waited, hoping Mrs. Fletcher would add more, but the woman said nothing. Finally Lauren asked, "Will you tell me how this painting came to your family? When it was purchased?"

"Originally the year my brother was born, nineteen eleven. A gift to my mother from my father in celebration of my brother's birth. It hung in our music room. We called it 'Willy's Colors.' He loved it."

"Willy? Your brother?"

Isabella nodded. "Wilhelm. He's been gone many years."

"*Originally* purchased?"

"*Originally*, yes. It was actually purchased twice."

Twice? Lauren wondered. What did this mean? "You inherited the painting from your parents?"

"Yes."

"You came to America with your parents?" Lauren asked just to see what she'd say.

"My father died in Germany."

"Your mother?"

"She escaped."

"Escaped?" Lauren was intrigued by Isabella's use of this word. Left illegally, with false documents, her pockets stuffed with cash, her luggage with art—that would be a more accurate description. "Escaped with the painting?" she asked.

"It came later."

The woman's answers were becoming more terse. One moment Mrs. Fletcher seemed ready to share, opening up. Then she closed like a blossom deprived of light. Lauren waited patiently, busying her hands again along the edge of the pillow.

Isabella said, "To understand the history of this painting, my parents' story must be understood. My mother's story. Yes . . ." She let out a small, quiet laugh. "Mother always considered Kandinsky *her* artist." The woman fixed her eyes on Lauren, and once, then twice, she blinked, her wrinkled lids skimming moist, soft blue eyes. "The truth must be known."

"I have nothing against the truth," Lauren replied, the edge to her voice much sharper than she'd intended, so sharp it cut like a challenge.

Mrs. Fletcher nodded and her gaze, steady on the younger woman, did not waver. The firm set of her mouth, the slight lift of her chin, seemed to be telling Lauren that she was up to this challenge.

"Paintings by Kandinsky," Isabella said, "as well as work by other progressive artists, were considered elitist art by Hitler, as if one needed some kind of pedigree to understand it. His theory was that if the common man off the street didn't get it, it was crap."

Lauren swallowed a laugh, surprised at Isabella's use of the word *crap*. The older woman let out a small refined chuckle, as if she had surprised herself.

She continued, "He often associated the word *elitist* with the Jewish race."

Lauren touched the rim of her still-almost-full cup of tea, running her fingers over the fine, fragile edge. She could feel her breath going in and out with a quick, uneven rhythm.

"My mother," Mrs. Fletcher said, "she certainly didn't come from an elitist background, yet she had a great love for this type of art."

"You said she was born in the country, on a farm. How did she end up in Munich?"

Isabella pondered the question, as if deciding how to reply. "It began because she was unhappy. I guess she was probably searching for something."

"Like what?"

"Independence. Excitement. A better life. What do any of us search for?"

"Did she find it?"

"I believe there were moments of true happiness." A faint smile flickered across the woman's face. "She grew up as part of a large family with a strict German father. When her mother was alive she was very happy. After she lost her mother, her father remarried. I know my mother despised her stepmother, though later I think she might have had some regrets that they never established a real relationship."

"What year was that?" Lauren asked. "When she went to Munich?"

"She was just sixteen." Isabella thought for a moment. "Nineteen hundred."

"Turn of the century. She was just sixteen? She went alone?"

Isabella nodded. "Yes. Well, no, not exactly. My aunt Katie— Käthe, then—was already working in Munich. Mother hoped she too might find a position in the house where her older sister was employed as a cook. She used to write home to my mother—they were very close. Their home in Bavaria was set in one of the most beautiful landscapes in the world. As a child I often visited my uncle and cousins on the farm. Have you ever seen the Bavarian Alps, Ms. O'Farrell?"

"Yes, I have. They're beautiful." She'd spent a semester in Europe, studying art, taking advantage of every opportunity to travel, and she'd been back to Germany twice, going through Nazi archives.

"The Munich house was lovely," Mrs. Fletcher said. "Quite exotic, particularly for a girl from the country, but something you might expect to find somewhere on the Mediterranean rather than in the heart of a German city. Red tiled roof. Marble floors. Handwoven rugs. Sleek walnut banisters."

Isabella closed her eyes as if imagining this scene, as if returning in her mind to her homeland. And then her eyes opened wide and again she looked directly at Lauren. "The story must be told. The true story." These words were delivered with a heaviness that Lauren could actually feel, as if the older woman was about to hand over something of great importance, as if it were Isabella Fletcher now issuing a challenge.

CHAPTER TWO

Hanna

Munich, Germany
September 1900

Bright reds, then muffled tones of blue, flashed before Hanna's eyes—the train screeching to a halt, the rustle of passengers gathering bags and parcels. The man sitting beside her stood, lifted a small case from overhead, handed it to his wife, and nodded a farewell to Hanna, who had nothing to gather.

"Enjoy your visit, dear," the woman said sweetly, touching Hanna's arm.

Passengers filed down the narrow aisle of the train carriage. Hanna remained seated, pressing her fingers to her ears, closing her eyes, seeking protection in the muted light beneath her eyelids. When she opened them, the passenger car was empty, save for a young mother and child who had occupied a seat in the back. Clutching a bag in one hand, pulling her small daughter by the other, the woman made her way down the aisle. The girl looked back at Hanna, her eyes growing wide with concern as if to ask, *Are you not getting off?*

Hanna forced a smile, nodded, and then rose, walked down the aisle, out the door, down the steps, and planted one shaky foot and then the other on the wooden platform of the Munich Bahnhof.

What have I done? she asked herself as she threaded through the crowd and followed the bustle into the station. Gazing up at the wide expanse of ceiling, she nearly tumbled over a small boy stooping to pick up a pfennig.

"Entschuldigen Sie, bitte," she said, patting the child on the head. She continued past a family sitting on a bench sharing sausages and bread, around a man and woman engaged in lively conversation, and moved along with a collection of people leaving the station as an assortment of hurried travelers came in. Some were dressed as Hanna in Bavarian country clothes: women in dirndls, crimped skirts, and country shoes; men in lederhosen, jankers, warm woolen socks, and alpine feathered caps. Most wore dark city clothes.

She stepped out of the station into the busy Bahnhofplatz. Light reflected off the windows of tall stone buildings surrounding the square. Puffs of smoke rose from chimney stacks. Horses' shod hooves clicked heavily against the cobblestones, sending off a splash of color.

Moisture hung in the air, clouds dimming the pale blue sky. Hanna reached up and slid her hand down one braid, then the other, giving each a little tug to smooth out the frizz. As always, she had braided it that morning, after helping Dora and then Leni with their hair. Unlike her stepsister and sister, who both possessed agreeable, fine, straight hair, Hanna's hair was a mass of unruly curls, and even when confined to braids it seemed to protest. On a humid day her hair was most rebellious, red spirals and wisps attempting to escape.

She made her way through knots of carriages outside on the wide street. She had been to the city just once, four years ago when she was twelve and had come with her father, mother, and older sister, Käthe. Their mother had presented the trip to Munich as a grand adventure for her two eldest daughters, though Hanna had little recollection of the city other than that it was large and noisy with many sounds and colors. She had been preoccupied with fear for her mother, and the memory that stayed with her was the smell of the doctor's office, and then the long, silent train ride back home.

She dipped her hand into her left pocket, fingering her remaining coins. After the train fare she still had enough for something to eat. She imagined her family sitting down for dinner. By now her father and older brothers, Frederick and Karl, would have returned from the upper pasture where they had gone to check on the cattle. Her stepmother, Gerta, would be home from Weitnau, the fabric and notions she'd gone to fetch tucked into her shopping basket. Would Leni tell them when they asked—for surely they would notice the empty seat at the table—that Hanna had simply walked out of the house and left them? She shivered at the thought of what she'd done.

She reached into her other pocket for Käthe's letter. Perhaps Hanna, too, could find work in Munich. And then she chided herself for thinking such thoughts. She had not come to Munich seeking employment. She was just off for a little holiday in the city.

She walked, gazing into one store window after another, finally stopping at a bakery. Her empty stomach rumbled as she admired the cakes, breads, and tarts in the window. Buttery smells, the aroma of cinnamon and apples, wafted out as she opened the door.

"*Guten Tag,*" the woman at the counter greeted Hanna. Her plump round cheeks dimpled as she offered a smile.

"*Guten Tag,*" Hanna replied, surveying the fresh pastries. She bought a raspberry marmalade tart and stood as she ate. She licked the sugary jam from her fingers, then pulled the letter from her pocket again and asked where she might find the street address on the envelope from Käthe, which she showed the woman to make sure she understood.

"My sister Käthe Schmid is employed by Herr Moses Fleischmann," Hanna explained proudly.

"The Jew. His gallery is on Theatinerstrasse," the woman replied with a wave of the arm, as if the gallery might be just down the street.

Hanna nodded. "Yes, but she works in his home as a cook." She pointed again to the address on the envelope and then read it aloud, guessing from the woman's quick squinty glance that she could not read.

She instructed Hanna to go to the Marienplatz, which she described with gestures, her hands going this way and that. "Catch the tram with the number one hundred eighty-seven painted on the front, then get off at the fifth stop and walk left about two blocks."

"*Danke*," Hanna thanked her and stepped back out onto the street. She walked, following the woman's instructions until she arrived at a large square. Her eyes spun, first to the enormous Rathaus with its spiky steeples, then to the lovely golden statue of the Virgin on the tall pedestal in the center of the square. The Marienplatz—dedicated to the mother of Christ. People scurried about, stylish women in dark skirts and fitted jackets, hair arranged neatly in sophisticated chignons; men in long pants and tall city hats, hailing carriages, greeting friends. Busy people with events to attend, invitations to honor, business to deal with. Hanna felt a sudden rush of excitement. Surely this was the adventure her mother had intended for her in Munich.

Two sets of tracks ran along one side of the Platz and a cluster of single train carriages, attached to a line overhead, stopped and then started in an orderly fashion as passengers stepped off and others got on. Hanna walked between a line of horse carriages and the trams, until she spotted the car the woman had told her to board. She paid for a place with her remaining coins, sat, and watched the street signs as they passed, Käthe's envelope clutched in her hand. At the fifth stop she got off just as the woman at the bakery had advised her. Then she walked two blocks, and a small but ever-growing twist of delight turned in her stomach, pushing aside the shame and trepidation that had sat like two stones in her belly since she'd stepped onto the train in Kempton.

When she approached the large house with the red tiled roof she knew she had found the Fleischmann home. It was just as Käthe had described. A fountain with mermaids and sleek winged horses carved about the base stood in the garden in front of the house. The horses spewed water from their mouths, creating a lovely, colorful rhythm. The grounds still held a hint of late-summer bloom.

Hanna thought of Käthe's earlier letters, telling of the modern kitchen with the latest equipment, the rooms with electric lights, silk drapes, flocked wallpaper, marble and wood-carved moldings around the doors, upholstered furniture, and lovely paintings and drawings hanging on the walls. Her letters were filled with details of the beautiful gowns and jewels worn by the wife of the distinguished Herr Fleischmann, of dinners and parties, of entertaining wealthy and famous guests who stayed long into the evening, eating, drinking, conversing about topics of great interest, playing games, and listening to music. Käthe's letters were so descriptive Hanna could smell the dumplings and strudels as she read, and she could hear the music Frau Fleischmann played on her piano. Now as she walked along the street in front of the house, she tried to imagine which window she might gaze through to look into the kitchen, the dining room, the parlor, the music room. It was an enormous house with so many windows, so many rooms.

She walked around to the side of the building, staring up, wishing her sister's face might appear. A woman stepped out on an upper balcony, stared down, then walked back in. Finally Hanna decided she must go to the back, to the servants' entrance.

After several knocks an older woman came to the door. "*Guten Tag,*" she said, greeting Hanna with a smile.

"*Grüss Gott,*" Hanna replied.

"You've come to seek work?" the woman asked.

"I've come to visit my sister Käthe."

A smile of recognition spread slowly across the woman's face. "*Ja*, I can see you are Käthe's sister. *Bitte*, do come in." She stood back, holding the door for Hanna. There was a narrow hall just inside the door and two sets of stairs, one leading up and one leading down. She motioned for Hanna to follow and they started down the steps. The smell of roasting meat laced the air, and Hanna imagined Käthe at work, preparing one of the lavish meals she had described in her letters. The woman asked her to sit in a room that appeared to be a dining area for the help, as there was nothing fancy about it. Two long wooden tables with roughly hewed benches were arranged in the center of the room. A fireplace stood against one wall, and a door on the other. The woman went through the door, and the warm smells grew stronger as the aroma of dinner drifted out and into the room where Hanna waited.

Within seconds Käthe appeared, wiping her hands on her apron, brushing a dusting of flour from her cheek, a wide, surprised grin lighting up her pretty, round face.

"Hanna," she shrieked, throwing her arms around her sister. "Whatever are you doing here in Munich?"

"I've come to visit."

"You've grown!" Käthe exclaimed, still smiling as if this were a good thing.

Hanna realized that she was now taller than Käthe. Bigger, too, in every way. Over the past months Hanna's chest had gotten larger, as had her hips, causing her to question if she'd ever stop growing.

Käthe's grin turned to a look of concern. "Everything is fine at home?"

"Fine?" Hanna replied with a sharp edge, wondering if Käthe understood that nothing had been fine at home since their father married Gerta, the tailor's widow from Kempton, with her commands and demands and her whiny little daughter, Dora.

"You should have informed me that you were coming," Käthe said.

"I didn't know myself," Hanna replied, the words catching in her throat, "that I . . ." How could she explain that she had simply left? Without telling anyone, not even Leni. She had not planned this visit, so she could not have let Käthe know she was coming.

She could barely believe it was just this morning that she was digging potatoes and baking bread with Leni, arguing with Dora over bringing in wood for the stove, commending Peter for his helpfulness, an image playing in her head all the while—her stepmother sitting in a café in Weitnau, sipping a nice warm cup of tea, nibbling on a bakery-made pastry. Hanna had told Leni she was going out to pee, but had instead run upstairs to the girls' room, dug into the middle drawer of the dresser she shared with her sisters, slipped the coins—saved from her egg money and hidden under her pantaloons—into her pocket, placed Käthe's most recent letter in the other, and then quietly tiptoed down the stairs, stepped out of the house, hurried down the lane toward the main road, and caught a ride with their neighbor Herr Hinkel. She told him she was going to Kempton on an errand for her father.

"Father is well?" Käthe asked in a soft voice.

Hanna nodded.

"The others? The children?"

"Leni is fine." Leni was ten, still so much a little girl, the obedient daughter. Hanna doubted she would ever want to do anything other than tend to *küch* and *kinder*, kitchen and children, that she was perfectly content to peel potatoes, look after the little ones, and do exactly as she was told by Gerta. "Peter, as sweet as ever."

Käthe smiled. At five, Peter was a delight. He had been so young when their mother became ill that he had received much of his tending from the two older girls.

"Dora, as spoiled as ever," Hanna added. Their stepsister was just two months younger than Peter, but whined like a baby.

"Karl is almost as tall as Father, and Frederick is in love with Helga Merkel."

Käthe nodded knowingly. Käthe the romantic. Then she sighed with what Hanna perceived as homesickness. Neither girl mentioned their stepmother. "It is so wonderful to see you, to have news from home, but you have not chosen the most joyful time to come for a visit." She took Hanna's arm and led her down the hall. "The mistress," she whispered as they entered a tiny nunlike cell, one of many off the long narrow hall, "she is not well." She patted the quilt spread over the narrow bed butted up against the wall and the girls sat. Taking her younger sister's hands in hers, Käthe asked, "You've brought nothing with you?"

Hanna shook her head and lowered it, the excitement of this grand adventure again overtaken with the enormity of what she had done. "Father doesn't know," she said softly.

Abruptly Käthe released Hanna's hands, and her own rose to her mouth, reminding Hanna how everything had been so dramatic with Käthe. She wondered if life in the Fleischmann household was truly as exciting and lively as she'd written in her letters, and if her sister, who surely must have been confined to the kitchen, could really be aware of the activities she'd described taking place in the dining room, the parlor, and the music room.

"Oh, Hanna, you haven't run away from home?" Käthe squealed in horror.

Hanna nodded.

"Father will be so worried."

"If he should even notice I'm missing . . ." Hanna giggled nervously, but wondered how she could ever face her father again. She replayed the thoughts that had moved in her mind on her walk through the city. "Is there work for me here? Could I get a position like you?"

"You plan to stay?"

Hanna raised her shoulders.

"Perhaps," Käthe replied thoughtfully. "Brigitte has gone back home to tend her mother who is very ill. I will ask Frau Metzger, the head housekeeper. But first we must send word to Father. We must post a letter immediately to let him know you are safe, that you are here with me." Again she took her sister's hand and held it tightly, then touched Hanna's face. They had not seen each other for almost six months, since Käthe had come to visit last Easter. "You have grown into a lovely young woman. You look very much like Mother." She reached over and lifted a braid, wrapping it around Hanna's crown. "So very much like Mother," she said.

Everyone in the family had hair with a touch of red, from Frederick's dark auburn to Leni's blond, which in a certain light held a hint of ginger. But Hanna's, more than anyone else's, resembled their mother's, which was a fiery red. Hanna generally covered it with a good bandana because people stared, but she had neglected to cover it in her hurry.

Käthe planted a kiss on her cheek. "Oh, my dear sweet little sister, what have you done?" She studied Hanna for several moments, and then said, "I will speak with Frau Metzger, but first a letter to Father." She knelt on the floor, pulled a box from under the bed, and took out paper and pen. She scribbled a note and sealed it in an envelope. "I will ask Frau Stadler to post it when she goes to market early tomorrow morning."

Having brought nothing other than the skirt and blouse she wore, Hanna slept in her chemise and bloomers that night, snuggled against Käthe's side. She woke often, an excitement jumping inside her, anticipating this new life that she was about to begin.

The following morning, Käthe talked to Frau Metzger and came back with a long dark skirt, white blouse, and starched apron. "You are about the same size as Brigitte and these should fit perfectly." She handed the uniform to Hanna. "Congratulations, you are now an employee of Herr Moses Fleischmann."

* * *

The Fleischmann home was indeed as beautiful as Käthe had described, and over the next days, as she received instructions from Frau Metzger, Hanna was able to explore nearly every corner. Heavy velvet drapes hung in the formal rooms on the ground floor. The doorframes were made of smooth, rich marble from Italy, or carved wood, one in the shape of a mythical figure with the face of a lion and the claws and wings of an eagle. The walls in the parlor were covered with flocked paper in deep, rich red. The walls and ceilings in the library and music room were made from luscious dark wood. The fine carpets, Frau Metzger told Hanna, had been imported from the Orient. Pots of shiny green ferns grew inside, which to a farmer's daughter was very strange, and made her giggle, but they were also beautiful and exotic, as was everything in the Fleischmann home. Hanna had truly entered a new world. And the sculptures displayed on pedestals in various rooms, the pictures that hung on the walls—she had never seen anything like them. She had seen paintings of saints and angels and the Lamb of God in the church at Weitnau, but nothing like these. Scenes of nature done in the most unusual colors, and paintings and sculptures of women, slightly draped or completely nude. And mythical figures like those described in the books they had borrowed from the library.

A piano, shining and finely polished—Hanna knew because she polished it herself—stood in the music room, though it sat quietly without music. There were no parties, no entertaining of important guests as Käthe had described in her letters. The few dinners in those first weeks were attended only by Herr Fleischmann's bookkeeper or banker in very austere businesslike settings. Käthe said it was because of the mistress, but she was sure that she would get better, and soon there would be dinners and parties again, she promised.

Even after a full week, Hanna had barely laid eyes on Herr Fleischmann, who rose early to go to the gallery and returned late. He was a stout man with dark curly hair, who spoke in a slow, deliberate, thoughtful tone. His voice was the color of the deep violet-blue of the Alpine gentian.

Hanna did not see the mistress of the house. She did not clean her room just down the hall from Herr Fleischmann's room, which she cleaned and dusted and swept with a little sweeper with wheels and a moving brush that was much handier than the broom they used at home.

Frau Fleischmann took her meals in her room, delivered by Frau Hirsch, a kindly older woman with eyes as large and brown as the cows on the farm. Frau Hirsch was the only one who attended to Frau Fleischmann. Hanna was told by Freda, who worked as the laundress, that Frau Hirsch had been employed by Frau Fleischmann's family since the mistress was a child and had come with her when she married Herr Fleischmann just two years after the first Frau Fleischmann had passed away.

The second Frau Fleischmann, Hanna learned, was much younger than her husband. A daughter from the first marriage lived in Berlin and was married to a wealthy jeweler. She infrequently visited the house of her father. She did not like her stepmother. Even though Hanna had met neither of them, she, too, decided she did not like the stepmother. She understood how it felt to have a woman come, disrupt the entire household, and attempt to take the place of your mother. Hanna had also left the house of her father to seek a new life. Oh, that she would have had a wealthy jeweler from Berlin come to her rescue, to shower her with diamonds and love.

Hanna's duties involved a variety of tasks—dusting, sweeping, polishing, watering the plants, cleaning the lampshades, scrubbing the bathrooms, serving meals. The part she liked best was dusting the frames on the numerous pictures that hung along the walls in the hall and in every room. She was instructed not to touch the paintings themselves. Some were enormous in large gilt frames, others smaller drawings without color. Just as she was getting used to one, getting to like it, or deciding that she did not like it, it would disappear. Frau Metzger explained it had been taken back to the gallery to show or had possibly been sold.

One day, as Hanna was carefully running the cloth along the lower edge of the frame of a new painting that had arrived the previous afternoon, staring up at the colors, studying the thickness of the paint in one particular area, wondering how the artist knew how to do it like that, daydreaming a little, a voice from behind startled her.

"Cézanne."

Hanna easily recognized the voice as Herr Fleischmann's, and it frightened her because she realized that she was not dusting as efficiently as Frau Metzger expected. Though the woman had never scolded her, as her stepmother might have, she'd once told Hanna that she worked too slowly. But if the paintings had remained the same, perhaps she could have worked more quickly. And this one was so different from anything Hanna had ever seen. The colors were brilliant. The paint seemed to dance and vibrate. At first she was unable to determine exactly what it was, but the more she looked, she could make out the shapes of a mountain, a grove of trees. She discovered if she stood back, rather than examine it up close, the strokes of paint would blend together and it actually became a scene. Hanna wondered how the artist did that, and smiled at the thought that he had painted it with a brush twice the length of his arm.

After a long moment waiting for Herr Fleischmann, who still stood behind her, to speak, or to leave, she said, "It's lovely." She turned with a slight bow. "From Paris? A French painter?"

She knew Herr Fleischmann had recently traveled to Paris, and she imagined it was one of the paintings he had acquired during his visit. She also imagined it would soon disappear from the wall, so she was taking a slow, careful look.

Hanna found herself blushing now with embarrassment. Perhaps her curiosity made her go a step further than she should have in addressing her employer.

"Have you ever been to Paris?" he asked, a question that seemed absurd. She was a dairy farmer's daughter from Weitnau.

"In books," Hanna replied. "In dreams."

He smiled. "Ah, someday you will go to Paris. A girl who dreams of Paris will go one day."

She nodded politely, though Hanna thought he was again being ridiculous, maybe even mocking her. She continued her dusting and Herr Fleischmann continued standing behind her. Perhaps he was discovering something new, she thought, something he had not seen in the painting before.

"Every time I look, I see something new," he mused, "something different."

"Yes, yes," she said with excitement, again with more animation than she guessed Herr Fleischmann was used to seeing in a maid. She couldn't help herself.

Then he said, "Very good," and turned and walked down the hall.

During her third week of employment, Hanna learned that finally there were to be guests, a real party. Herr Fleischmann was entertaining several art instructors from the Academy of Fine Arts in Munich and half a dozen of the most promising students, an event the Fleischmanns hosted at least twice a year.

Hanna took wraps and hats at the front entryway as the guests arrived. The first to enter was a handsome man with wavy dark hair and a thick black mustache that curled in such a way as to make him look a bit devilish or at least dangerous. He was followed by a tall, distinguished man with a neatly trimmed goatee, intelligent eyes, a regal posture, and pince-nez glasses, then a younger gent in a tatty coat. A bald man with close-set eyes accompanied a young fellow with greasy hair and a nervous twitch who adjusted his tie as he glanced in the mirror just inside the entryway.

As they were greeted and welcomed by Herr Fleischmann, Hanna picked out one voice, that of the distinguished guest with the goatee. His tone was deep and melodic with an exotic lilt and such a lovely color of blue. He sounded like a foreign prince, and that is what she called him in her mind—The Prince.

Herr Fleischmann addressed the man with the thick mustache as Herr von Stuck. The name sounded familiar and Hanna remembered the signature on a painting that had hung in the parlor for several days. She found the painting intriguing in a dark, sinister way. It was done in deep colors, the flesh of a naked woman, her sleek body wrapped in a snake, catching the only light that appeared in the picture. Hanna studied this man carefully now. The man who wrapped a snake around a woman with his brush and paints.

The Prince was introduced by Herr von Stuck as Wassily Kandinsky. They were led into the dining room. There were no women in attendance at this particular meal, though Hanna thought from the chatter in the kitchen that Frau Fleischmann might appear. She had not yet laid eyes on her.

As Hanna served the guests, she was in a position to catch bits and pieces of the conversation as she came in and out of the dining room.

"It was in Moscow at an exhibition of French art," Prince Kandinsky said, and Hanna's mind worked quickly, remembering the lessons in geography her mother had taught her. The Prince was Russian, which explained the way he spoke. "The catalogue identified it as a work by the artist Claude Monet, and informed me that it was a haystack." The others listen with great respect.

"Yet I did not recognize it as such. The object itself seemed to be lacking in the painting, and I wondered if the identification of the haystack was essential to the picture."

"As long as we have color, Herr Kandinsky is satisfied," Herr von Stuck observed wryly.

"But perhaps the forms, the recognizable images, become less important. It was the color, the light, the feelings which drew me inexplicably to this painting," the Prince replied, as Hanna carefully placed the china plate with the second course before him. He glanced at her and with warm eyes nodded, which gave her a small start, as she had been instructed to become invisible as she served.

"Herr Kandinsky wishes the painting to be just that—a painting?" Herr von Stuck retorted.

"It is a concept to consider," Kandinsky replied.

The guests stayed long into the evening, talking of Paris, of Vienna, of artists named Gauguin, Seurat, Klimt, and Munch, of a young artist named P. Ruiz Picasso whose work had been chosen for exhibition at the Exposition Universelle in Paris that spring.

"I like to keep an eye on such artists," Herr Fleischmann said. His eyes swept over the men at the table, and Hanna wondered if some of these students would become famous, if their work would soon hang in the galleries in Paris, Vienna, and at the Fleischmann Gallery here in Munich. She felt a little prick of excitement along the back of her neck. What fun it would be to get a glimpse into the academy where they were trained, to observe the artists at work and say, *Yes, this is the one who will set the trend, who will sell at the prestigious galleries.*

"I'd love to go," Hanna said as she slipped off her skirt and hung it on the hook next to the bed that night.

"To Paris?" Käthe folded back the covers. "To see the artists who paint with light and color?"

Hanna had shared much of what she'd overheard that evening as she and Käthe cleaned the kitchen after the guests had retired to the parlor for a smoke and after-dinner drink. Somehow Hanna felt by repeating it she could hold on to it longer, and she was surprised that Käthe had been listening that carefully.

"Yes, Paris, and Vienna, too," Hanna replied, unable to hold her grin. She reached up and turned out the light so Käthe would not make fun.

"Where else, you little dreamer?" Käthe laughed as she slipped into bed. Käthe, Hanna feared, had no dreams other than marrying Hans Koebler, the cheesemaker's son from Kempton with whom she corresponded regularly. Her mouth would turn up into the most ridiculous smile when she received a letter, and her eyes would glow. When too much time passed between letters she could become rather grumpy.

"To the Munich Academy of Fine Arts," Hanna said.

"Women are not allowed. You want to be an artist?"

"Not as a student." Hanna sat on the edge of the bed, not quite ready for sleep. She was too excited to close her eyes. She did not want the day to end.

"As what?" Käthe's voice rose in the way it did when she thought her little sister had said something unrealistic or stupid.

"I want to look at the work of the different students. To see which ones will become famous. To see how they do the colors."

"To listen to the colors sing?" Käthe teased. "To hear the colors make music?" She stroked her sister's back. "Come, let's sleep."

Hanna crawled in beside her. She had been assigned her own small cot in the servants' quarters, but she wasn't used to sleeping alone, and it was so cold in the basement that most nights she slept with Käthe. "Not always music, but sound," Hanna said quietly. She didn't talk about it much anymore. Käthe knew. Leni knew. And, of course, her mother knew. The first time she told Käthe she laughed, and then told Mother. Hanna thought it was that way with everyone when she said, "The cows in the barn, what green sounds they are making today." She didn't realize that everyone didn't hear in color. She was only three, just learning the names of the different colors, and was very confused, as there were so many colors and not enough names to call them.

"You could go to the Academy," Käthe said, yanking the covers which she often accused her sister of hoarding, "if you are willing to take off all your clothes."

"Take off my clothes?"

"They must have models. Freda's cousin is a model at the Academy."

Often Herr Fleischmann brought a painting of a nude, such as that by Herr von Stuck, home from the gallery. And the sculptures were generally of nudes, both men and women. Hanna was more curious than embarrassed, and Frau Metzger said it was art, that the human form was one of God's greatest creations, and artists for centuries going back to the Greeks and Romans had taken inspiration from the human body. Hanna knew that the artists in the Academy must learn how to draw and paint the human body. Surely they would need real models.

"Freda's cousin takes off her clothes for the artists?" she asked.

"I'm tired," Käthe replied, her voice distorted by a weary yawn.

"Where is it?" Hanna asked after thinking this over for several moments. "The Academy of Fine Arts."

But the answer came back as a soft little snore, and she knew Käthe had already fallen asleep. Hanna was too excited to sleep, but she decided that night that somehow, someday, she would get into the studio of the Academy. Even if she had to take off all her clothes.

CHAPTER THREE

Lauren and Isabella

New York City
August 2009

Lauren O'Farrell had been sitting for over half an hour with Isabella Fletcher and had learned nothing more about a Kandinsky painting, if such a painting existed. She'd discovered nothing to confirm Isabella's mother, Hanna, had collaborated with Hitler in disposing of his degenerate art, though she could now almost smell the red geraniums hanging in the green wooden window boxes on the farm in Bavaria and feel the cool Alpine breeze blowing over her skin.

Mrs. Fletcher talked a little about her mother's going to Munich, but then circled back, evidently deciding Lauren needed a description of the farm, which necessitated Isabella's walking over to the bookcase and taking out several maps. Pulling a pair of reading glasses from a drawer in the end table, she settled them on her nose, unfolded the largest map, and spread it out on the coffee table in front of them. She pointed to the small dot designating the village of Weitnau, then the exact location of the farm, and traced the road to Munich with her finger. Lauren imagined she could now drive the route herself, though Mrs. Fletcher explained her mother had taken the train, as there were

no automobiles at the time. After the maps, Mrs. Fletcher produced a book filled with lovely pictures of the Alps, followed by
a heavy volume with scenes of Munich.

"My mother once told me that at home on the farm," Mrs.
Fletcher said, glancing at Lauren over her glasses, "the only things
hanging on the walls were a frying pan, an axe, and a crucifix. In
the Munich home, walls were covered with paintings and drawings.
Sculptures sat on tables and pedestals. The only art she'd known
was religious art in the church at Weitnau, the village where they
attended Sunday mass—paintings of angels, saints, Mary, and
Christ. But in Munich the art was like nothing she had seen before.
Mother truly fell in love with the concept that an artist could
express how he or she saw the world in so many different ways."

Isabella Fletcher's movements were graceful as she rose to find
the maps and books in the bookcase. Graceful and refined, yet
there was something intimidating about her, reminding Lauren
of Mrs. Kline, her eighth-grade English teacher. She and her girl-
friends used to call her the Nazi. Everyone knew you'd better stay
in line in Mrs. Kline's classroom.

And now Lauren sensed that Isabella Fletcher's expectations
were little different from Mrs. Kline's. Pay attention, she seemed to
imply. You might just learn something if you sit and listen. The older
woman was certainly leading the conversation. Even when Lauren
asked a question, which she was trying to refrain from as much as
possible, Mrs. Fletcher inevitably veered off. Lauren wasn't sure
where this story was going, but she guessed the less she attempted to
direct the conversation, the more information she might gain.

As Mrs. Fletcher carefully folded a large map of present-day Germany, then placed her glasses on the end table, Lauren wondered
again if she might be on the path to discovering something she hadn't
even considered. Or was the old woman simply playing with her?

Lauren had written her master's thesis on art, politics, and
cultural censorship, and had done extensive research on the art

trade in Germany just before World War II. She'd come across the names of dealers, particularly those in Munich and Berlin, who joined with Hitler to use the art to further the causes of the Third Reich, to fill the Nazis' war chest, and more often than not to increase their own wealth in the process. Lauren was shocked when she discovered the name of a woman among these dealers. She needed to know more. Over the past several years, in between working for clients or museums, she had attempted to find additional facts about this woman. As far as Lauren could determine, she had escaped, possibly to South America or North America, most likely going through Switzerland, then departing from France. Slowly, in her spare time, Lauren had put bits and pieces of information together.

Patrick had once accused her of becoming obsessed. "What will you do if you eventually fill in all these blanks?" he'd asked. "You know this woman is dead. She was born over a hundred and twenty years ago."

Lauren was used to dealing with such obstacles of time. In her search for looted art, the crime scene was often long ago destroyed, many of the victims in their graves for more than half a century, the perpetrators of the crimes mere remnants of history. She was generally working with descendents of the victims.

Lauren's eyes scanned the walls again. Could any of this art be real? Nazi censored? Nazi seized? She needed to get a closer look, perhaps even lift a piece from the wall and check the back for revealing inscriptions or numbers. She knew exactly how the paintings had been marked in Berlin.

After replacing the maps and books on the bookshelf flanking the fireplace, Isabella settled once again into her chair and offered more tea from the pot, though Lauren guessed it was now luke-warm at best.

"Yes, please," Lauren said. And then she asked, "Your mother adapted well to life in Munich?" She would attempt to keep the conversation centered on events in the city, those that might relate to the art.

"Oh, yes, she adapted very well," Mrs. Fletcher replied as she poured more tea for Lauren and then herself. The older woman, in her expensive-looking suit and pearls, might have been a society lady serving as hostess at some social gathering. Lauren felt underdressed in her slacks and simple cotton blouse.

"She saw it as a grand adventure," Isabella explained. "My mother had little formal education—well, *none* to speak of—but her experiences in the city, her exposure to the more modern movements, yes, it was in Munich that she became acquainted with the art. She certainly didn't get this exposure at the farm."

"She learned about art from studying the paintings in the home where she found work?"

Isabella nodded. "Yes, and later in the gallery."

"The gallery?" Lauren asked.

"Yes, the Fleischmann Gallery, of course."

Lauren felt an increase in the beat of her heart as well as her breathing. *Fleischmann.* Exactly the name she was searching for. She knew now that she was on the right track. She had so many questions, but feared if she spoke, Mrs. Fletcher could detect a change in her tone. It would be difficult to keep the excitement out of her voice. She took a sip of tea, gulped, and then coughed nervously, hardly believing this information had just been unceremoniously placed in her hands. Mrs. Fletcher asked if she needed a glass of water. Lauren shook her head and took another small sip of tea.

"Initially my mother learned by observation," Mrs. Fletcher continued, "and then she became involved in the *business* of art."

"The *business* of art?" Lauren asked, placing the same emphasis on the word *business*.

"Oh, yes, next to family, art was the most important aspect of my mother's life."

"This exposure in Munich eventually developed into a career for Hanna?" she baited the older woman.

"She was very much involved. She and my father formed a true partnership. She knew many of the artists," Mrs. Fletcher added, waving toward the painting that Lauren had earlier identified as a Franz Marc, a colorful mosaiclike piece with two horses in an unnatural shade of blue. "She became acquainted with most of these artists."

"Kandinsky?"

"Oh, yes."

"She purchased the Kandinsky," Lauren asked, "from the artist himself? In Munich?"

"Yes."

"You said the painting was purchased twice?"

"I did say that." There was a note of annoyance in Mrs. Fletcher's tone, as if she were warning the young woman to be patient. Lauren thought of all the documents she'd examined, German records, American immigration papers, all the hours she'd already spent on this project, how very close she felt right now.

"Yes, originally purchased from Kandinsky," Mrs. Fletcher said, "but we are getting ahead of the story." Lauren smiled and nodded, detecting a little shake of the finger in Isabella Fletcher's voice.

CHAPTER FOUR

Hanna

Munich
October–November 1900

When Frau Hirsch took ill, and was confined to her bed, Frau Stadler, the head cook, asked Hanna to take the tray in to the mistress, a request she eagerly accepted. She was curious to get a look at the wife who had sent her stepdaughter away, a woman Hanna had already decided she did not like.

Frau Fleischmann was sitting up in bed when Hanna entered the room. Her skin was soft and pale with the slightest blush in her cheeks. Long blond hair fell over her thin shoulders, and an oval-shaped locket lay in the hollow of her slender neck. As Hanna approached she noticed the woman's eyes, rimmed with dark lashes. They were the most unusual color she'd ever seen. They were not brown, or blue, or green. Her eyes could only be described as golden, and there was the softest, sweetest, saddest timbre in the color. Hanna could hear it clearly.

A book was folded across her lap. She looked up and smiled, and instantly Hanna knew she could not hate this woman who smiled at a stranger.

"Thank you, Hanna," she said, addressing her by name. "*Bitte,* the tray goes here." Her voice was nearly the same color as her eyes, which startled Hanna.

"You are Käthe's sister?"

"Yes, Frau Fleischmann," Hanna answered, placing the tray on the table beside the bed. She removed the lid, just as Frau Stadler had instructed her, poured coffee from the silver pot, added two drops of cream and a lump of sugar, and placed a spoon on the saucer.

"You look very much like your sister."

Hanna was surprised, again, that she knew her sister's name, that she knew what Käthe looked like. She had a thought lodged in her mind that Frau Fleischmann cared little about the household help. Hanna studied the cover on the book. A novel. The author Theodor Fontane.

"Do you read?" Frau Fleischmann asked, stirring her coffee. Her eyes rose up to meet Hanna's. She was much younger than Hanna had expected. She knew she was younger than her husband, but she looked barely older than Käthe, who at eighteen was two years older than Hanna. And yet there was a weariness about her, shadows under her golden eyes that made Hanna think she had lived for many years.

"Yes, I read." She had never officially gone to school, but her mother, who believed an education was important even for a farmer's daughter, had taught the children to read, or perhaps they had taught one another, as there were no grade levels, no tests, and everyone advanced at their own pace. Hanna was always curious—"my curious little bunny," her mother called her. And a dreamer. She loved the stories, but also the histories. She would read anything and everything she could find, and her mother would take them to the lending library in Kempton once or twice a month when she was well.

Frau Fleischmann asked that Hanna read from the book, then motioned that she draw the chair, which sat near the vanity across the room, closer to the bed.

Hanna sat on the soft pink cushion, opened the book, and began to read. She didn't understand much of what she read. Frau Fleischmann listened intently, tore pieces from her breakfast roll with nervous fingers, and drank two cups of coffee, then wiped her delicate, thin lips on the white linen napkin that Hanna had folded on the tray just as Frau Stadler had instructed her.

"*Danke,*" she said after a while. "Thank you." She placed her napkin on the tray and lay back as if the effort to eat had exhausted her. "Please inquire of Frau Hirsch's health. I hope that she is doing much better."

Hanna never had the opportunity to wish Frau Hirsch well. She learned when she returned the tray to the kitchen that morning that the old woman had passed.

This was how it began, how Hanna worked herself into the intimacies of the Fleischmann household. After Frau Hirsch's death, she became the personal maid to Frau Fleischmann. She was not in the least upset at giving up her role as assistant housekeeper, though at first she missed having time to study the paintings as she cleaned.

On the days when Frau Fleischmann was feeling well, Hanna helped her dress for dinner. She tired easily, ate little, and often left before the meal was finished, particularly when they had guests.

After dinner, as Hanna helped her prepare for bed, put away her evening gown, and combed through her long golden hair, the mistress told her stories—of those who had come that evening, their places in Munich society, the particular interest of each in the world of art. Sometimes she described the way in which her husband had made a sale on that particular evening. Hanna could see that she loved him dearly—for his kindness, for his skill, and for his ability to entertain, to make his guests comfortable, to put them in the mood to buy a valuable, terribly expensive painting, to convince them that a particular artist could change the world of art and carry them along as an investor to the top. Frau Fleischmann understood this was a business, though she also had a deep respect and love for the work of the artists themselves. And she knew them all, could describe in detail the specifics of their work. She lent Hanna books from her library that told about the art from the past, the classical sculpture of the Romans and Greeks, the lovely paintings from the Italian Renaissance, the Baroque art from Germany, Holland, and Spain.

Hanna read to her from the latest novels, from books of philosophy and religion, from the fashion magazines that came from Paris. Frau Fleischmann said that when she was feeling better, they would go to Paris with Herr Fleischmann to shop and to visit the galleries, to see the current trends in the very active, ever-changing world of art in France where artists were using colors and shapes in innovative ways.

Frau Fleischmann was delicate and feminine, and yet there was a quality in her that was almost like a man. She took an interest in everything, asking Hanna to read from the newspaper each day, commenting on the political situation. Her interests were not those associated with the kitchen or household but those of the world, which she seemed to embrace even from her small world that was often confined to her bedroom.

Her name was Helene, she told Hanna, after Helen of Troy in Greek mythology. The most beautiful woman in the world, the daughter of Zeus.

According to the custom of the day among the wealthy, Frau Fleischmann had her own bedroom. Hanna didn't know if Herr Fleischmann ever visited the boudoir other than to fetch his spouse and escort her down to dinner. Rumor was that Frau Fleischmann was too delicate for the activities and duties of a wife. There was also gossip that, on occasion, her husband visited the brothels, but Hanna could not imagine a gentleman as refined as Herr Fleischmann doing such a thing.

When Hanna saw them together, sometimes sitting in the parlor after dinner, she could tell that he loved her. She could see by the way he looked into her eyes, by the softness of his touch when he placed his hand on her shoulder, on the small of her back when he walked her up the stairs, and then kissed her on the lips before she retired to her room, he to his. How did Hanna see all of this? Because she was always on hand to assist her mistress.

Frau Fleischmann's moods shifted from day to day. Sometimes she was delighted with the breakfast Hanna brought in on the tray, and she would talk and talk, about the trips she had taken with her husband during the early years of their marriage, how they had visited the art studios in Paris. She told Hanna that the great family wealth had come more from the selling of antiquities and traditional art rather than modern-day paintings, but Herr Fleischmann, unlike his father who had started the business, had a particular interest in the modern trends.

"There is so much happening now in the world of art," she told Hanna, "all very exciting." Hanna could hear it in her voice, the enthusiasm, the desire to be involved in her husband's work.

Yet sometimes she barely spoke to Hanna, asking her to leave the room. When Hanna returned to check on her, the food on the tray would be untouched.

On a very good day, Frau Fleischmann would ask Hanna to walk her down to the music room and she would sit at the piano. She gestured for the girl to sit in a chair beside her, and she played the most beautiful music Hanna had ever heard. She told her the names of the composers—Bach, Handel, Mozart, Wagner. But, as the days passed, Frau Fleischmann's energy often failed, and her fingers refused to perform as she wished. There were days when she could not play the music. Sometimes she cried. One day she forced her fingers one by one into a ball and banged violently on the ivory keys.

After that particular outburst, they didn't return to the music room for several days, and when they did, Frau Fleischmann said, "*Bitte*, come sit here beside me." She patted the bench, and as Hanna sat, she placed her hands over the girl's. "Fingers here," she said, guiding with her own. "Press this key ever so slightly, then here with greater force. Yes, that's right; hold it for just a moment. Yes! Yes!" she exclaimed with delight.

Strangely, it came easily, as if Hanna had known all along— which key on the piano to touch, the exact pressure and timing, the rhythm. And always she could repeat the sounds in her head, even when she did not play. The colors—she would see. Oh, yes, such lovely colors that came with the music.

After another week, in which her mistress continually praised Hanna, telling her what a gifted musician she was, Frau Fleischmann offered, "Let me teach you how to read the notes on the music sheets. One day I won't be here to guide you."

Hanna didn't like these words, and she could see Frau Fleischmann was well aware of her discomfort. "Why, someday, my lovely Hanna, you will leave me. You will marry, and you will have precious little babies to tend. You will play a lovely lullaby, softly, sweetly. Don't you want to learn to read the music?"

"Yes, Frau Fleischmann, I do."

But Hanna did not learn as quickly as she had hoped, and she could see the frustrations building in her mistress. She wanted more than anything to please her, to become her fingers. She wanted to make her smile.

"*Nein, nein,*" Frau Fleischmann shouted one morning as they sat in the music room shortly after breakfast. Mornings were usually her best time of day, but it was now late November, the weather turned cold, and Hanna could see that the winter was especially hard on her. "What is so difficult about this?" Frau

Fleischmann took in a deep, exasperated breath. "Oh, Hanna, please forgive my impatience." Her voice trembled, as did her hands. "I don't understand why this is so difficult for you. You are such a bright girl, quicker than any I have known." She pointed to the note written on the music sheet propped on the piano stand, and with her other hand moved the girl's on the keys. There was a frightening jerkiness about the movement, and now Hanna was trembling, too.

Suddenly it came to her. She could see it—this note for the green tone, this for the golden yellow. "It's the golden sound," she exclaimed, realizing she had said it aloud, only after Frau Fleischmann straightened her back and stared at Hanna with disbelief, then puzzlement.

"Golden sound?" Frau Fleischmann asked.

Hanna didn't want to tell her about the colors. She didn't want her to think she was insane.

"What do you mean, *golden* sound?"

"Nothing," Hanna replied.

"This sound makes you think of gold?"

"Not think."

"But?"

"See," Hanna replied in a whisper.

"You see a color?" Frau Fleischmann's voice was soft.

Hanna nodded.

"And this?" Ever so lightly, Frau Fleischmann tapped a key on the piano, a deeper tone to the left of the keyboard. She seemed both amused and curious.

"Blue," Hanna said.

Frau Fleischmann tapped another key. "What color?"

Hanna didn't answer.

"Please," Frau Fleischmann wheedled in a gentle voice, "tell me. Do all of the notes have color?"

"Blue," Hanna said.

"Like this?" Frau Fleischmann repeated the first note the girl had called blue.

"But a different blue."

"This?" Frau Fleischmann pointed to a dark blue velvet pillow on the love seat.

Hanna shook her head. "No. A very soft blue, like on an early-spring morning, the blue of the sky nearest the horizon."

"Quite specific. Very interesting. And this?"

They worked through the keys on the piano, Hanna describing the colors. Then Frau Fleischmann combined several together. Hanna couldn't just say orange, or pink, or blue, because that wasn't the way it was. That wasn't what she saw. Every note had a particular shade or tone, some of them without any names that she could name, so she compared them to colors she knew, mostly in nature, not always getting them exactly right. If only Frau Fleischmann could see what she saw. How inadequate words are to describe what we see.

"Pumpkin, just before the harvest, and honey melon, ripe and fresh and sweet." Hanna could see the colors clearly with each note. And she could see Frau Fleischmann was testing her, repeating over and over to make sure she named the same specific color for the same sound.

"You really do see color in the music!" Frau Fleischmann said, her voice ringing with excitement.

Hanna nodded, delighted for the first time with this talent that seemed to please her mistress so.

Every afternoon, following her midday meal in her room, after Hanna had read to her, Frau Fleischmann fell into a deep sleep. The doctor who came often to the house—as an art patron and friend, as well as to attend to Frau Fleischmann—had given her medication to help her sleep. Hanna knew she was told to take it only in the evenings, but she also knew her mistress often took it during the day. Always she slept for at least three hours in the afternoon, often more. At first Hanna lingered in the kitchen with Käthe, visiting, sometimes helping out with dinner, but when she realized she had no obligation, she took to walking in the afternoon.

She started exploring the city and found her way quite easily. So many sounds and smells and colors. Hanna realized the way her senses were all mixed together, she had extra ways to remember places and names. She loved riding on the streetcars. She visited the art museums, the Alte Pinakothek, the Neue Pinakothek, and stood before the paintings of Dürer, Rembrandt, and the Italian Renaissance artists she had learned about from Frau Fleischmann's books. She studied the paintings up close, then from afar, and wondered how the artists had known to put a splash of color here, a shadow or patch of light there, and why some of the artists whose paintings hung in the Fleischmann home had decided to do it so differently. She could see that the way artists painted would change from time to time, from place to place, just as the fashions the women wore in Munich were so different from those her family wore at the farm. In Munich there were so many different possibilities. And were there not many possibilities in the way an artist might paint a scene? A human figure? She wanted to see how it was done. She wanted to go to the Academy of Fine Arts where the students learned how to do this.

One morning she asked Freda about her cousin, who did indeed model at the Academy. "It's very good money," she said. "A few hours a day and she makes what I make working for a full week."

"She takes off her clothes?"

"*Ja*, naked," Freda answered, putting her hand over her mouth to suppress her giggles.

"Do you know where it is?" Hanna asked. "The Academy of Fine Arts."

"On Akademiestrasse in the University District."

The following day, Hanna set out to find the Academy of Fine Arts. She took the tram to Leopoldstrasse near the Englischer Garten, and then walked but a short distance where she easily found the Academy on Akademiestrasse. She paced in front of the building, watching the students as they entered—first the young man with the greasy hair, a skinny young stoop-shouldered lad she remembered seeing that evening when Herr Fleischmann entertained the students and instructors. She watched for Herr von Stuck and Herr Kandinsky, but saw neither.

The next day, after Frau Fleischmann's eyes lowered and Hanna heard that gentle, rhythmic breathing that told her the mistress had fallen into a deep slumber from which she would not return for several hours, Hanna hurried down the stairs and out the back door. She dashed through the streets, hopped onto the tram, and then jumped off, running quickly to the Academy. She stood on the street outside, waited until she'd gained enough breath to speak, and then she climbed the steps, opened the door, and walked in. Quietly and respectfully, she moved along the hall, nodding to those she passed, trying to comport herself as if she belonged there. Finally she could see an open door and she entered and found a young man sitting at a desk.

He looked up from the ledger on which he was making an entry.

She was about to inquire if she might observe the students at work, but realized this request was unlikely to get the desired results. A young woman would not be invited into the studio, unless . . .

"May I help?" he asked.

"I'd like to inquire," she said, forming the words first in her head, "about a position here at the Academy of Fine Arts."

"A position?" he asked. His brows pressed together tightly, and then pulled apart in amusement. He had very dark eyes with long lashes, and brows that seemed too perfect, as if they had been painted on with a brush. "As . . . ?" he asked, holding out his hands dramatically.

"A human model," she said. The words sounded strange even to Hanna's ears.

The amusement deepened around his eyes. "Have you had experience as a *human model*?" There was a smile in his voice, almost as if he were making fun, but then his demeanor shifted and became very businesslike. "You've worked as an artists' model?"

Hanna nodded. She couldn't quite bring herself to put the lie into words.

He studied her for a moment, perhaps determining if she had the right proportions to be a model. This made her somewhat uncomfortable. She should leave now, immediately, she thought. But there is no shame in the body, Hanna told herself. *Temple of the Holy Spirit.* Why, it had been the subject of art for centuries, just as Frau Metzger had told her, just as she'd seen in the books that Frau Fleischmann had lent her, and in the museums of the city. She should not be ashamed of her body.

"How old are you?" he asked, his perfect brows pushing together in doubt.

"Eighteen," she replied without hesitation. She could become quite proficient at telling lies, Hanna realized as the number slipped from her lips with such confidence.

"Where have you worked?"

"At a private school," she answered, remembering a discussion at dinner the night the artists from the Academy came. Hadn't Herr Kandinsky said that when he first came to Munich he had studied at a private school? "Anton Ažbe," she added, remembering the name.

He nodded as though she had supplied the correct answers. For a moment Hanna wished that he had caught her in her lies. What was she doing here? Burying herself in her own deceit?

"You must be an angel sent to us today," the young man said. "We have a life drawing class starting in . . ." He glanced at his wrist. He was wearing what looked like a gold bracelet, but then Hanna noticed it was a clock. "Just five minutes from now," he continued, looking up at her, "and our model has not yet arrived." She was intrigued by this timepiece. Her father carried a pocket watch on a gold chain, as did Herr Fleischmann. She had never seen a man wearing a clock that looked like a piece of women's jewelry. "Would you be available today?" he asked.

"Today?" she said, thinking of no other words. This had not been her intention. She was merely inquiring. She wasn't even sure she could do this. "Today?" she repeated.

Again, he glanced at his wrist. If she'd had her own clock she would have looked at it, but Hanna told time the old-fashioned way—by observing the sun, by listening to those internal rhythms telling her the mistress would be waking from her nap and require assistance in dressing for dinner.

Take off her clothes? In front of a group of strangers, a group of young men? Yes, in the name of art, she could.

"Yes," she said.

"Come, angel," he replied. There was nothing salacious in the tone of his voice. She might have described it as sweet, or kind, but Hanna felt nothing like an angel. Yet, now as she followed him, she felt only a trickle of guilt, which seemed oddly disproportionate to what she was about to do. Was she about to commit a mortal sin? *Temple of the Holy Spirit.* Taking her clothes off for complete strangers?

The young man led her back to the studio. It looked different than she thought it would. She wasn't sure what she had expected, but for some reason she thought the walls would be covered with paintings and drawings, like the Fleischmann Gallery on Theatinerstrasse where she had once accompanied Frau Fleischmann on one of their few outings. Hanna had only a quick glance into the gallery, as they had just stopped by for a short moment. She had been disappointed then because she had no time to look about, and now she was equally disappointed by what she saw.

The walls were white and stark and bare. The floor was simple wood with no rugs as in the lavish Fleischmann home. Wooden chairs were scattered about the room, as were stands, similar to those she'd seen in the parlor used to hold paintings that Herr Fleischmann brought home to display when guests came for dinner. He had called them easels. An odor hung in the air, a smell that reminded Hanna of pine trees in the forest near home. It was a good, clean, comforting smell. The windows were without drapes, letting in abundant light. There was a small area curtained off where the young man said she could undress. He presented her with a silk dressing gown that looked very much like a cheaper version of the one that Frau Fleischmann threw over her nightclothes when she felt well enough to take her breakfast at the table by the window in her room. Hanna thought it strange that she was allowed a special room for undressing, when he called it the dressing room. It seemed everything was backward, and it was only now that she was overcome with that expected sense of guilt and apprehension. If she'd had more time to think, surely she would have fled from the room.

She took off her shoes, her skirt, her blouse, and her underclothes, and hung them on the brass hooks attached to the wall. She put on the silk dressing gown and wrapped her arms around herself, feeling a chill. Now what? Should she go out into the studio? Or wait for someone to come get her? She decided to wait. She could now hear a shuffling of papers, moving about of chairs being dragged across the floor. Voices of students. All men, she thought, and felt a rush of heat come over her. What if she took off the dressing gown and her body was covered with red bumps of embarrassment? She heard laughter coming from the studio now, young men carrying on the way they do, like her brothers and father, the men at the dairy farm. What was she doing here? Could she still change her mind? Throw on her clothes, run from the studio? Was Frau Fleischmann waking from her nap?

Hanna heard a man clearing his throat on the other side of the curtain. "Fräulein, are you ready? The students have arrived."

She stepped out.

He smiled, not in a suggestive or deviant way, but in a way that said welcome. Yet at the same time a line of surprise formed across his forehead. Hanna recognized Herr von Stuck, the handsome art instructor with the dark curly hair and thick black mustache. The painter who wrapped snakes around his naked women. She felt a tightening about her throat, and for a moment she thought she might faint, or perhaps burst into tears.

"I was expecting Magda," he said.

"I fear Magda hasn't made it today," she replied, regaining the small amount of composure she'd once possessed, sounding very official, as if it were Magda herself who had sent Hanna in her stead.

"Well, fine, you will do fine." He pointed to a chair in front of the dressing room with the curtain as a backdrop. After several moments of hesitation, slowly, her hands trembling, she removed the dressing gown. In a businesslike manner, he instructed her to sit, asking her to place her arms folded across her lap, to angle her shoulders back just a bit. "Are you warm enough?" he asked thoughtfully.

Hanna knew she was visibly shivering. "Yes, thank you, sir."

She couldn't look out toward the students. She lowered her eyes. When finally she glanced up she could see they were all busily at work. There were no lecherous stares, no rude comments about her body. It seemed she had become invisible as a person. She might have been a cluster of grapes, an apple, a bottle of wine set upon a velvet cloth. Hanna listened to Herr von Stuck as he walked about the room, moving from pupil to pupil. She couldn't see any of the art, as everything was turned toward the artists and away from her. "The light source," he said, motioning to the window on the left, "always consider your light source. How can we have a shadow here"—he pointed at the drawing—"if the light comes from there?"

She recognized several as those who had come weeks ago for dinner. The young twitchy artist with the greasy hair that kept falling into his face, the distinguished gentleman with the lovely accent, who she now realized was not an instructor as she'd then thought, but merely a student himself.

"Ah, Herr Kandinsky, I test your patience," Herr von Stuck said as he stood behind the Prince. "Or, perhaps, it is you who test my patience."

Kandinsky smiled, but said nothing.

"The color will soon come, but first we must become aware of the values of the color, and we must learn these values by doing it all without color."

Even though Hanna could not see the art, she could see that they were not painting as she'd hoped, but merely drawing with pencils. The redness that she was sure colored her entire body from head to toe would not show up in a drawing in black and white.

"It is indeed my patience you test," Kandinsky finally replied, "because the colors are singing in my mind. How do I draw in black and white a woman whose hair shouts with color?"

Hanna felt a warmth deepen within her as he spoke of her as a woman. She no longer felt like an inanimate prop, a model for the artists. She was a woman.

The room was soon filled with smoke. Must every artist feed his creativity with tobacco? she wondered. The greasy-haired young man opened a window. They took a quick break about halfway through. Hanna put on her dressing gown and walked back behind the curtained area and stood by herself until she was summoned once more by Herr von Stuck.

When they finished the second half of the class, she dressed hurriedly, but even so, when she went back into the studio, the students had left, the easels were empty. She would never see the drawings, she thought with a strange sadness. It wasn't that she wanted to see these images of herself, but just how they had put in the light and shadows, how they had made her hair, her flesh, in black and white.

The young man at the desk thanked Hanna and asked, "Will you come again on Friday?"

Hanna wondered if she could arrange this. Frau Fleischmann napped each afternoon, and as long as she continued with this schedule, Hanna should be able to come. She wondered about Magda, if she would show up and take her place. Hanna laughed a little at the thought—not that Magda would return, but that in her mind she was already claiming it as *her place*.

"Yes," she replied, "I will come on Friday."

O n Friday, as Frau Fleischmann napped, Hanna ventured out and hurried to the Academy. She was greeted by the same young man, who motioned her back to the studio. Again she undressed and waited for Herr von Stuck to announce they were ready for her.

By the time he came for her, the students had arrived and set up their equipment and, fortunately, it appeared that Magda had voluntarily given up her career as an artists' model. Or perhaps, Hanna thought with an inward laugh, Josef, as the clerk had asked her to call him, had turned her away, thinking Hanna made a much better muse.

She sat and arranged herself again the way Herr von Stuck had instructed her on the last visit to the Academy. He seemed pleased and did not request any adjustment. Hanna knew if she were to pass herself off as a true model she would have to show that she understood how it was done. It seemed very simple—

remember the pose from day to day, ask no questions, remain silent, speak only if spoken to.

She glanced quickly about, again aware that several of these students had been present the evening Herr Fleischmann hosted the dinner. Herr Kandinsky had smiled at her as she presented him with a veal cutlet! And now she sat before him completely naked. Did he recognize her? And there was Herr Alexej Jawlensky, also a Russian—she'd learned from the students' banter—and also one of the dinner guests. He looked at her through his squinty eyes, his way of concentrating, she decided, as she was sure he didn't know her. Perhaps she looked very different when she was fully dressed, with her bright red hair piled up and under her little maid's cap. Of course, no one would take notice of a maid, she reasoned. And the thought came with a true sense of relief.

A second quick sigh of relief escaped her body, and then she sat, perfectly still, daydreaming, as she found it the best way to hold a pose. She envisioned a painting by an Austrian artist that had recently hung in the Fleischmann home. Although Hanna was no longer cleaning and dusting, and did not linger before a painting to study it as she worked, she now had time to view the paintings with some leisure. Having been taken under Frau Fleischmann's wing, so to speak, becoming her assistant—Hanna no longer considered herself a maid—she felt a new boldness and, daresay, entitlement as she strode about the house. Often Herr Fleischmann appeared out of nowhere, almost as though he had been waiting for Hanna to place herself before one of his paintings. And she did believe he enjoyed their discussions about the art.

One day he asked, "Fräulein Hanna, what do you think of this painting by Gustav Klimt, my latest discovery from Vienna?" The colors vibrated with a rich, deep cacophony of sounds. Somewhat daring, she thought, the shapes and angles on the figures like nothing she had ever seen, and the music she heard was a quick, sparkling, jumbled but delightful blend from the highest notes on the scale.

"I think it is quite moving," she replied.

"Moving?" he asked with a lightness in his voice.

Why did she always describe things in such a way, using absurd words that no one else understood? she wondered with embarrassment.

"It stirs something within me," she said, trying to explain.

"Ah, stirring the spirit," he came back with a chuckle, and she was not sure if she amused him or if he understood and shared this feeling. "Yes, it also moves me," he added agreeably. "Good art will always stir the soul." He touched her lightly on the shoulder, as her father did when she had accomplished a task and he was pleased. And Hanna felt another stirring, deep within. But this assuredly was not in her soul, as it was clearly something moving deep within her body.

She felt herself blush and grow warm now at the thought of Herr Fleischmann's touch, and forced herself to clear such thoughts from her head. The students were moving about now, taking their mid-session break. Hanna slipped on her dressing gown and retreated to the area behind the curtain. She stretched her arms, wiggled her shoulders and legs to get the blood flowing, to prepare herself to sit once more. She wondered if it would be permissible to go out into the studio and look at the work of the students. This was why she had come—to see how it was done, taking what was real and putting it first through the artist's mind, then onto paper or canvas. But if she ventured out, might one of the artists question her? Would they speak to her as if she were a person now? Probably not. She was but a young woman, a body, the subject for a drawing lesson. By the time Hanna had sorted through all this, the artists were back at their easels, ready to continue.

After the class, again the students packed away their supplies and were out of the room before she returned. She had yet to catch a glimpse of any of the drawings. She received her pay from Josef at the front desk, just as she had after the last session, and tucked it in her pocket. As she walked out of the building and turned toward Leopoldstrasse, Hanna's heart leapt up to her throat. Coming from the opposite direction, clearly moving toward the Academy, was Herr Fleischmann. She turned her head, tilted her hat over her eyes, angling her body away from his. He passed by unaware of her. Hanna watched as he climbed the stairs, opened the door, and entered the building. This should not have surprised her, as she knew Herr Fleischmann had many friends at the Academy, that he often met for drinks or dinner with professors, and always showed an interest in the work of their students, always on the lookout for the next movement or trend in the art world, attempting to catch it before the other dealers.

Hanna hurried toward home, secure in her belief that he had not seen her.

The following week Hanna returned to the studio at the Academy of Fine Arts on Monday, and again on Wednesday, and then Friday. It was beginning to feel like a real job, though she loved going. She daydreamed when the studio was quiet, the students deep in concentration. She listened when they engaged in conversation, particularly when they discussed the concept of color. Several were now painting, rather than just drawing. Herr von Stuck and Herr Kandinsky often went back and forth about the teacher's insistence that Kandinsky finish each piece, and that, for now, he work in black and white, as it was important that he understand underlying tones, tints, and shades before advancing to color.

Through the conversations at the studio, in her position as the invisible mind, the visible body, she learned much about the artists themselves. Wassily Kandinsky was a musician as well as an artist. He spoke of how the colors had actual connections to specific notes. She perked up considerably when he said this.

Alexej Jawlensky said, "Ah, my friend Herr Kandinsky not only sees the color, he *hears* the color." He had come to Munich about the same time as Kandinsky, though they had not known each other in their mother country. Hanna learned that he had also studied with Anton Ažbe, and she guessed that the two had become acquainted then. They were older and seemed more mature than many of the other students. Jawlensky had had a career in the military; Kandinsky was educated as a lawyer in Russia, and both were now embarking on new careers as artists.

"A concept explored by the Greeks," Kandinsky replied in response to Jawlensky's comment, "as well as more modern musicians such as Beethoven and Schubert. This blending of the senses." He went on to speak of an opera he had attended in Moscow where he had heard the colors along with the music, how he had experienced similar sensations, a mixing of sound and color during his childhood, opening a paint box to discover a symphony. "But, alas, I must now complete my drawings and paintings without the colors." He shot a glance toward his instructor, Herr von Stuck.

Though Hanna was eager to hear more, the conversation went no further that day after several of the younger students requested silence in the studio for concentration.

"You might hear the color, Herr Kandinsky," one of them politely joked, "but others require silence for their creativity."

She continued thusly, tending to Frau Fleischmann, practicing her music to the delight of her mistress. Hoping each day to have a small conversation with Herr Fleischmann about art, rushing off with a true sense of excitement to the Academy three afternoons a week.

One might think that Käthe would be jealous of Hanna, becoming Frau Fleischmann's little lapdog, as she'd overheard Freda whispering to herself one morning as she gathered the laundry. But Käthe was consumed with what was going on in her own life. They would both go home for Christmas, something Hanna was looking forward to and dreading at the same time, as she had not yet written to her father, and neither of them had made any apologies. But she knew Käthe would not return to Munich with her. Hans Koebler was to ask for Käthe's hand in marriage on Christmas Eve. So, Käthe felt no jealousy and was quite delighted that, when she left, Hanna would be in such a favorable position.

CHAPTER FIVE

Hanna

Munich
December 1900

"You should have seen her dress," Hanna told Josef, the clerk at the Academy. She had just tucked her pay into her pocket and, as she often did now, she lingered for a short time to visit. "Blue silk, so obviously expensive."

"The jewels," he came back, urgency coupled with curiosity in his voice. "Her husband's a jeweler in Berlin, so there must be jewels."

"Covered with them," Hanna replied with a laugh.

Strangely, Josef Bloch and Hanna had become friends. They frequently visited as she came in and out of the studio. He was a sweet man, rather flamboyant in his dress, but he had a way of making Hanna feel comfortable, and he loved to chat.

"Oh, yes, her neck was covered with diamonds set in gold, accented with sapphires to match the color of her dress. Enormous diamonds hung from her ears, and a tiara glistened on her head set amidst her dark curls." This woman does not dress herself for the evening, Hanna had thought when she peeked into the music room, observing the guests; she decorates herself like a Christmas tree. She giggled now at the image. "She looks much like her father, with dark hair and eyes. Now, this is very strange"—Hanna could feel her voice, as well as Josef's interest, rise—"her name is the same as her stepmother, who incidentally isn't much older than the daughter, and much more beautiful with her golden colors. They are both named Helene! They call the daughter Young Helene."

"How awkward," Josef replied. "The two Helenes—Frau Fleischmann, the wife; Frau Kaufmann, the daughter—did they get on?"

"I sensed the party was intended to keep her stepdaughter occupied, to ensure Frau Fleischmann did not have to spend a long evening conversing with the Young Helene." Frau Fleischmann had stayed at the party much later than Hanna thought she should, considering her health. But she could see she had done this for Herr Fleischmann, that she made every effort to make this a pleasant visit for his daughter and her husband.

"Then all went well?" Josef inquired.

"From what I could see," Hanna replied, "but you understand I'm just the maid. I didn't join them at the party."

"Someday you will," Josef said seriously, and she shot him a look of genuine doubt. "Oh, yes, little girl," he replied shaking a finger at her, "someday you will have a wealthy husband, and you will entertain your own guests, you'll be invited to grand parties. Perhaps your husband will cover you with jewels," he added with a grin.

Hanna liked this idea and she smiled at the thought. "Young Helene's husband, Herr Kaufmann, is a handsome man, and the little boy is named the same as his father. They call him Little Jakob. He's just over a year—so sweet."

"You like children?" Josef asked.

"Yes, of course. I come from a big family." Hanna thought of how resentful she'd felt over her stepmother's demands that she watch after the younger children, but she missed Leni, and she especially missed little Peter. It had been fun having a child in the house during the Kaufmanns' visit. Frau Fleischmann, and thus Hanna, had spent as much time with Little Jakob as Young Helene would allow. Hanna could see her mistress would have loved a child of her own.

Everything about this visit—the potential of tension between stepmother and stepdaughter, the little boy—made Hanna think all the more about her impending return home for Christmas.

"I'm rather nervous about going home," she confessed to Josef. He was an attentive listener and he offered good advice when she had a problem. "I haven't written my father," she explained. "He sent a letter addressed to Käthe, and his biggest concern appeared to be my lack of consideration in leaving during the busiest time of the year, right before the harvest, before the cattle were brought down from the highlands. And Gerta, my stepmother—she's a witch," Hanna added with a shaky laugh. "So, I'm not sure how it will all go when Käthe and I return home. I'm not even sure that I should go. Sometimes I feel more at home here in Munich with the Fleischmanns. Maybe I should just stay here."

"What?" Josef squealed. "And celebrate the birth of Christ with your new Jewish family? No, no, no, little girl, you must go home." Hanna knew that Josef was Jewish, too, that he didn't celebrate Christmas, and she knew he was right—she had to go.

"And gifts!" he said, raising his arms in the air dramatically. "You must take gifts for everyone."

Hanna laughed. "Do you think this will make everything fine with Father?"

"It couldn't make things worse," he said with a sympathetic smile. "Take the old witch a pretty gift from the city. Show your father how well you are doing."

Hanna had tucked away the money she'd earned at the studio, because she didn't want anyone to know what she was doing. Even Käthe was unaware of how Hanna passed her afternoons while Frau Fleischmann napped. She certainly had money for gifts.

"You've been to the Christmas market?" Josef asked. He pulled paper from his desk, drew a map, and handed it to Hanna, then placed several marks to show her where to find the best stalls.

The following afternoon, she took off as soon as Frau Fleischmann was asleep and, based on Josef's instructions, as well as her nose, she easily found the market. The air was thick with the sweet perfume of pines, decorated lavishly with candles, cranberry strings, cookies, popcorn, and handmade ornaments. The scent of gingerbread mingled with the smell of the woods brought into the city to celebrate the holidays and reminded her of home. Hanna wandered through rows and rows of merchants' booths, selecting a colorful marionette for Peter, a china doll for Dora, musical boxes for Leni, Käthe, and their stepmother. For her older brothers and father she found finely crafted tobacco pouches.

On the way home she purchased a beautiful silver-framed mirror for Frau Fleischmann that she found in a shop on Maximilianstrasse. She would wrap and leave it on the side table in her bedroom the morning of her departure for home. The Fleischmanns did not celebrate Christmas, but she would leave it as a gift of thanks for her mistress's many kindnesses.

One evening, just days before Hanna was to return to the farm for the holiday, Herr Fleischmann left word that he wished to see her in his room. Hanna knew he kept an office just off the bedroom, but she couldn't imagine why he would call her in any official capacity as an employee of the household. As a housekeeper she had reported to Frau Metzger, and then as Frau Fleischmann's assistant she took instructions only from her mistress. She'd had no real conversations with Herr Fleischmann, other than those when their paths crossed as she stood entranced before a painting or sculpture. Strangely, this had given Hanna an unspoken intimacy with her employer. Perhaps he wished to speak to her of Frau Fleischmann. Her health was still irregular, alternating good days with bad. Yes, she decided, he wished to have a conversation about his wife, as Hanna was the one who looked after her every need.

She sat in the kitchen, munching on a slice of apple as she visited with Käthe, who was preparing dessert for that evening, giddy with excitement about their return home. She spoke about the plans she and Hans had made for the big day. Hanna told her sister about her scheduled meeting with Herr Fleischmann, and Käthe suggested that he was going to give her additional duties, as her position now allowed too much idle time.

"Perhaps," she said with a grin, as she arranged the sliced apples in a baking pan, "you will take over my duties here in the kitchen." Hanna knew this was preposterous, as did Käthe, for Frau Stadler supervised the kitchen help, and Herr Fleischmann couldn't care less about who did what as long as there was bread on the table. Käthe covered the apples with fresh dough, pricked it with a fork, and slid the pan into the oven. "What should I wear?" she said. "Hans will meet me at the train station in Kempton." Ah, Käthe had other things on her mind.

Hanna paced in the downstairs hall and then climbed the stairs, arriving a few minutes before the designated time, eager and nervous to know why Herr Fleischmann wished to see her. It was just before dinner, and he had returned early from the gallery. When Hanna knocked, he called her in. He stood before a mirror, his face half-lathered as he scraped a blade across his face with a smooth gesture, and then wiped it on a towel. He had a heavy beard and Hanna guessed that he shaved twice a day, as he often returned with a shadow darkening his chin in the late afternoon, and then appeared for dinner with a smooth, clean-shaven jaw. A basin of water sat on the vanity. She should have waited until the appointed time, but she feared being late, which resulted in her being early.

He was wearing no jacket or tie, his shirt unbuttoned with a thatch of heavy black hair clearly visible, a towel wrapped around his neck. Hanna felt terribly uncomfortable.

"Please sit," he said, motioning her to a chair from which she had a full view of his face in the mirror. She felt herself blush, yet the intimacy of the encounter seemed lessened by the fact that she was not staring at him face-on. "I have something . . ." He motioned to the office, just off his bedroom. Hanna knew about the office because she had dusted the bookshelves and the desk and swept the carpet when she was a housekeeper.

"Sit while I finish," he said.

Hanna folded her hands in her lap and stared down. Waiting. For what seemed like a very long time, neither of them said anything. He cleared his throat and patted his face dry with the towel, then his neck. He buttoned his shirt as he turned and reached for a tie on the bed, put it around his neck, and deftly looped it into a knot, straightening and pulling here and there, gazing in the mirror.

"Tell me, Hanna, are you happy here?"

"Here, sir?" The question struck her as strange, and then she realized he meant working here in the Fleischmann home. He surely didn't mean sitting here in his bedroom.

He smoothed the tie into place, and turned back to her as if she had hesitated because she wished to consider his question, rather than because she hadn't understood what he was asking. Hanna felt her palms grow damp, as they often did when she was in Herr Fleischmann's presence. She longed for opportunities to speak with him, to catch him as he stood studying a work of art, to hear the exquisite color of his voice. And, yet, at the same time, when she found herself in his company, she felt silly and girlish. And now, here she sat in the privacy of his bedroom, stuttering over her words.

"Yes, Herr Fleischmann," she finally answered. "I'm very happy here."

"Frau Fleischmann tells me that Käthe will not return after

Christmas?" He looked as if he were asking if Hanna, too, would fail to return after their visit home.

"She's getting married," she said, then wished she hadn't. Even their father did not know yet about Hans' intention to ask for Käthe's hand.

"A local boy from your village?"

"The cheesemaker's son from Kempton."

He nodded as though this were pleasing news. "Käthe is very happy?"

"She is floating in happiness."

"Your father is pleased?"

Hanna didn't want to explain that their father didn't yet know. "Yes, very pleased."

"Good news for a father when his daughter makes an agreeable match."

She wondered if he was thinking of his own daughter, covered with jewels, gifts from her husband.

"You enjoy your work here, then?" he asked, and she guessed their conversation about Käthe's future was nothing more than a politeness and had nothing to do with the reason for which he had called her.

"Yes, sometimes it barely feels like work at all," she answered without hesitation.

"Very good, then. You find the pay adequate?"

She wondered now if he had called her to negotiate an increase in pay, and immediately regretted admitting how much she enjoyed the work. In truth she would have done it for nothing more than food and a bed. It was much better than working for a small part of the egg money at home.

"Perhaps an increase in your wages would be in order after your return," he said before she could formulate a reply.

Hanna grinned. Herr Fleischmann smiled with approval. She

felt very important, that he found her so valuable he would offer more pay.

"Frau Fleischmann has been talking about a trip to Paris in the spring. She'd like you to accompany us. You've been a great help to her, Hanna."

"*Danke*, sir." She now felt ready to burst with joy. Paris! She could have leapt off the chair and bounced to the ceiling. "Oh, thank you, Herr Fleischmann."

Abruptly now, he walked to the desk in the adjoining room, which Hanna could see from where she sat. She didn't move.

"I have something for you, Hanna," he said, returning with a rolled paper in his hand, tied with a string.

He handed it to her. "*Danke*, Herr Fleischmann." What was this? A Christmas gift? As far as she knew he had given no one else in the household a gift, and Hanna knew he didn't celebrate the holiday.

She turned the rolled paper over in her hands. They felt damp from her nervousness, and she didn't want to stain the paper. Her curiosity, along with the excitement of the announcement about Paris, made her shake with excitement and anticipation. Was she to open it now?

"Perhaps with the raise in pay," he said, "you will no longer find it necessary to take on additional work."

What did he mean? He looked her directly in the eyes now, and Hanna forced herself not to look down. "Additional work?" she asked innocently, and wished again she had said nothing. He knew. He had seen her that day at the Academy. She couldn't dare ask. "Thank you, Herr Fleischmann," she said, still turning the paper over in her hands, wishing not to continue the conversation regarding additional work. "This is very kind of you."

"Then it is agreed," he said, the inflection in his voice requiring no answer. "If you are bored during the afternoons when

Frau Fleischmann naps, Hanna," he added with a warm smile, "perhaps we can find additional duties for you."

"Then the raise in pay is contingent on my performing additional duties?" What was he asking? There was something almost seductive in his smile now, and she thought of what Freda had said, the gossip about Herr Fleischmann frequenting the brothels, and now the possibility that he knew she had worked at the Academy as a model. No, surely he did not think that because she would take off her clothes . . . Without thinking, she glanced at the bed.

"Oh, no, no." He shook his head, as if he were reading her thoughts. He laughed, not unkindly, but it made her feel ridiculous that she was thinking of herself as a woman, that he would have such thoughts about her. That she would have such thoughts about herself. Hanna wondered if her entire body was now the color of her hair.

"Something that will be very good for you, for your future, I assure you, Hanna. We'll speak more of this when you return."

He reached over to the wooden valet for his coat and put it on. "I must go down for dinner now."

She took it this was her invitation to leave, her dismissal. She stood, did a small curtsy, and left the room, gift in hand, hoping that her natural color returned before she ran into anyone else. What would they think if they saw her coming from Herr Fleischmann's bedroom, all flushed and nervous?

Hanna carried the gift down to the servants' quarters. No one was present. The kitchen help was all busy making preparations for dinner, and the housekeeping girls were in the dining room, setting the silver and china. She entered her room and sat on the bed. Carefully, she slipped the string from the paper, wondering if it might be a gift from the gallery, a drawing, perhaps a watercolor or print. As she unrolled the paper, she took in a deep breath, which she held until it was completely smoothed out and visible.

Hanna gasped.

It was a drawing. She knew it was done by a student at the Academy. She had longed to see one of the drawings; now here it was. What a strange sensation to gaze upon an artist's vision of oneself. Hanna could feel herself positioning her arms, her legs, forcing herself to sit still and steady, maintaining the same pose for almost an hour per sitting. And she could feel herself shiver—she was in fact shivering at this very moment, feeling again as if she had removed every piece of clothing, as if she were bare. Herr Fleischmann did know; he knew about Hanna's going to the Academy, about her posing naked for the students. Was this not a gift, but his way of saying, fine, but no more? No more posing at the Academy of Fine Arts.

Or was his gift more?

CHAPTER SIX

Hanna

Munich
January–February 1901

After Christmas, Hanna was more than eager to return to Munich. While her gifts had been well received, particularly by the little ones, her offerings were overshadowed by her older sister's announcement on Christmas Eve. Her stepmother avoided her, and the harsh words she expected from her father were never spoken. His lack of attention was almost more hurtful than if he had taken a stick and beaten her.

Hanna took an early-morning train back to Munich by herself, leaving Käthe and Hans wrapped tightly and securely in their love and enthusiasm for the new life they were about to start together. Their stepmother was surprisingly excited about the prospect of planning the wedding and sewing a lovely dress for Käthe. Hanna's curiosity about Herr Fleischmann's plans for her had occupied a good deal of her time while away, and a nervous energy, mingled with anticipation, had kept her awake through most of her last night at the farm.

She had left the drawing in Munich, tucked safely in a box under her bed. She didn't dare take it home with her, as there was little privacy. What would she have done or said if her father—or, worse yet, her stepmother—had discovered it? She had studied it carefully the evening Herr Fleischmann had given it to her, trying to guess which one of the students had drawn it, placing them in her mind at the studio, guessing from the angle of the drawing that it had to be Herr Kandinsky or perhaps Herr Jawlensky, though it was not signed. She wondered if Herr Fleischmann had chosen it at random, or if he had picked this artist above the others because there was something special in the work. How did one know which artist was best? Hanna wondered if this was a talent that came naturally—the ability to see the potential in a particular artist, even as a student, the skill to judge the value of a painting or drawing. Or could this be learned? Could she possibly ask Herr Fleischmann? No, surely not.

As the train pulled into the station, the familiar sounds and colors of Munich welcomed her, and Hanna's thoughts turned to Frau Fleischmann, who had also been much on her mind. She was eager to see her again. At times she worried that her mistress could not survive without her, that she was essential to the woman's well-being, that no one understood her as Hanna did.

She dropped her bag in the servants' quarters in the basement and climbed the steps to find Frau Fleischmann just finishing breakfast in her bedroom.

"Oh, Hanna, I've truly missed you," she said as Hanna entered. "Thank you for the gift. It is lovely and so very thoughtful of you. Now, come here, my darling. Why, I think you've grown even more beautiful during your visit home." She reached up and touched her face. "The fresh air of the country is good for you." Hanna had spent little time outdoors, as it had been very cold. It had snowed most of the time she'd been gone, but the way Frau Fleischmann carried on, one might think it had been June or July and she'd come back with sun-kissed skin and a new batch of freckles scattered across her nose.

"Sit," Frau Fleischmann said, patting the empty chair at the table by the window where she sat. She looked well, which both pleased Hanna and made her wonder how important she really was to her mistress. "Herr Fleischmann has spoken to you?"

Hanna had yet to see Herr Fleischmann as he had left for the gallery. She realized Frau Fleischmann must be talking about the conversation they'd had before she left for the farm. Surely he hadn't spoken to her of Hanna's extra activities in the afternoons when her mistress napped. She felt herself grow warm with the thought that she might have seen the drawing.

"Paris!" Frau Fleischmann squealed with delight. "We're going to Paris."

Hanna smiled, relieved that she was talking about Paris, excited once more at the thought. She felt sure that Frau Fleischmann knew nothing of the drawing or her business at the Academy of Fine Arts. "I appreciate this," she said softly.

"Oh, I couldn't do it without you, Hanna. You've truly been a blessing for me. A short while ago, the trip would have been nothing, but now, ah, my strength is not what it once was. But, you, Hanna, you are the angel sent to look after me. Frau Hirsch was a dear to me, but very frail and hardly had the strength to keep up with me herself toward the end. But you, Hanna . . ." Frau Fleischmann laughed, and her words and the slight sarcastic ring of the laugh stung Hanna. Surely she meant this as a compliment, but at the same time, Hanna wondered if she was thinking—what a big, healthy farm girl you are, so capable of helping me down the stairs; why, I think you could carry me if need be.

Later that morning Frau Fleischmann asked that Hanna help her down to the music room. Though she looked refreshed, she walked with an uneven step and needed assistance going down the stairs. Hanna thought of her comment again, and was thankful that she was a big strong farm girl, for if she had been as tiny and delicate as her mistress, or as old and feeble as Frau Hirsch, she would most likely still have been dusting the furniture and mopping the floors.

Frau Fleischmann asked that Hanna play for her and she spoke of the concerts they would attend in Paris, about the opera, the exhibitions in the famous Musée du Louvre. "Perhaps later we will go to Vienna."

"Oh, that would be lovely," Hanna exclaimed.

That afternoon as Frau Fleischmann napped, Hanna went out for a walk. She knew she could no longer go to the Academy, but she wanted to let them know she would not return. The school had closed for the holidays, but would be reopening the following week. She didn't know if anyone would be present.

She took the tram and then walked to Akademiestrasse. The door was locked. She peered in the window and found not a hint that anyone was in the building. As she turned she literally ran into Herr von Stuck.

"The Academy has closed for the holidays," he said as if he did not recognize her. She was wearing a hat Frau Fleischmann had given her. She adjusted it, pulling it up to show her face.

"I'm the model, Hanna," she said.

"Yes, of course."

"I'm afraid I won't be coming again."

"*Nein?*" He sounded disappointed, which made her feel her work at the Academy had some value.

"*Nein.*"

"You've found employment elsewhere?" he asked, a wrinkle forming across his brow.

"Yes," she answered. "I've taken on new duties."

"We'll miss you, Hanna," he said sincerely. "Best of luck in your new endeavors."

My new endeavors, she thought as she took the tram back to the Fleischmanns', wondering what Herr Fleischmann had in store for her, curious to know if she would be assigned additional duties. But she soon learned from Frau Metzger that Herr Fleischmann had gone to Vienna and would not return for a week.

She waited, anxiously. Often in the afternoons when Frau Fleischmann slept, she went to the library and read, or to the music room to play, sitting alone with the piano. The rest of the staff seemed more relaxed during Herr Fleischmann's absences. The mistress required very little and meals were not prepared for guests nor served in the dining room. Hanna grew impatient. She needed something else to occupy her time. She should have kept her job at the Academy. Herr Fleischmann might not even remember his offer when he came back home.

Two days after he returned, he called her to his room. This time he sat at his desk, making entries in a large book. Hanna knew he also kept an office at the gallery, where she assumed he did the business connected with the art, but running the large household must have been a business in itself.

He motioned her to sit on the chair in front of his desk. He closed the book, set the pen aside and looked up at her. His eyes were dark and serious, the tone heavy and deep. "What is it that you wish to do with your life, Hanna?" he asked.

Surely he was continuing the conversation they had started before Christmas. "I'm happy here, sir." She laughed out of nervousness and felt very much like a child. "Well, when there is more to do. I find the time during which I do nothing quite boring."

"Is this why you went to the studio to be a model at the Academy of Art?"

She didn't want to talk about this. She couldn't really explain in words why she went to the Academy, but she had given it up for him, and she thought it unfair of him to ask her to explain.

"I wanted . . . I wanted to see how it was done."

"You want to be an artist?"

She shook her head. "There is no room for women at the Academy."

"A woman might enroll at the Women Artists' Association. Is this what you wish?"

Hanna knew she had no talent as an artist, but she wanted to know more about how it was created. She wanted to see more paintings, more drawings and sculptures. She wanted to see it, not to create it.

"No," she said, "I have no desire to be an artist. I have no talent."

"Then music? Frau Fleischmann would like you to develop this skill. She tells me you play the music by color."

Hanna felt strangely betrayed by this, that Frau Fleischmann would share with her husband what she'd told her in a very private way. But perhaps this was how it was with husbands and wives.

"I enjoy the music, but . . ."

"Yes." He motioned with his head, coaxing her to go on.

Why does he take such an interest in me? she wondered.

"You think because you are a farmer's daughter, because you are a woman, you cannot make use of your talents?"

It was because of Frau Fleischmann, she thought. He is doing this to please his wife. "Perhaps I should just marry well," she came back, with surprising harshness in her voice, and regretted it immediately. Why should she have anger toward Herr Fleischmann, who had been nothing but kind to her? But why did he, as well as Frau Fleischmann, have such an interest in her future?

Herr Fleischmann smiled. "I'm not sure how much help I can be there," he said. "I've always believed it is the heart that should lead in such matters. But in other areas, Hanna, Frau Fleischmann and I are prepared to help you. You are a woman of many talents."

He was calling her a woman. Why should she feel this a greater compliment than his telling her she had talent? But she did. Hanna blushed and gazed down at the book on his desk.

"What are your dreams?" he asked.

She had never been asked this question before, had never seriously thought of it, though her mother had always called her a dreamer. What *were* her dreams? What would she like to do with her life, if she could do anything she wanted?

"My dream," she said slowly, "is to be like you, Herr Fleischmann . . ." She couldn't believe she had said this, and when her
eyes rose to his and did not waver she could not believe her own
boldness. But she wanted to catch his reaction, to see if she
shocked him terribly. He said nothing, gave no indication that he
thought she had spoken foolishly. He nodded as if he wished her
to continue, and so she did. "To travel the world, to go to the
studios of artists, to galleries, and museums, to see what is new,
to find what will attract the eye of the collector, to discover art
that will last and become part of history."

Now he laughed, a deep, deep laugh. "You want to be like me?"
he said with a grin. Well, there it was, she thought—he thinks me
ridiculous.

He was silent for several moments, his expression pensive. He
stood, gazed across the room, and then thoughtfully looked down
at the parquet floor as if he wished to choose his words carefully,
as not to hurt her feelings any more than he obviously had.

A woman art dealer? she thought. An artist perhaps, or a musician, surely just for the entertainment of men, to produce a nice
little show, to display some delicate, feminine watercolors in the
parlor, then take a bow and go back to the kitchen, or perhaps the
dusting.

He continued to stare at the floor, which caused Hanna to
look down, too. He cleared his throat. When they both looked up
she could see the slightest movement on his face, almost a smile.
In his eyes, not yet on his lips. "This is what we will do. Each
afternoon while Frau Fleischmann naps, you will come to the gallery. Perhaps you will find your initial duties rather dull, but
surely you don't expect to become me without some work." He
shot her an amused, yet at the same time satisfied, grin.

Hanna was smiling now, too. She could not have thought of
anything she would rather do.

The next afternoon, per Herr Fleischmann's instructions,

Hanna walked to the gallery on Theatinerstrasse. Herr Fleischmann was not there, but his assistant, Herr Engle, whom she had
never formally met, but who had come to the house on occasion,
greeted her warmly and said that he was expecting her and had a
list of tasks for her to complete.

As she learned over the next several days, she was, indeed, not
to become Herr Fleischmann without some work. Her duties
were much like those she had been assigned at the Fleischmann
home when she first arrived in Munich. She was little more than
the cleaning lady—dusting frames, straightening up in the back
room where frames were assembled, sweeping the carpet, preparing tea and coffee in the small kitchen. But, oh, just to be at the
gallery each day, to see and hear the wonderful colors, to witness
the comings and goings of both the art and the patrons. Artists
came in, some to gaze, others to deliver paintings, to talk with
Herr Fleischmann. Customers and collectors sat to discuss a purchase, sipping coffee, partaking of little pastries.

Though her contact with the customers was limited to making
them comfortable, offering coffee or tea, she observed carefully as
they came in and out of the gallery. She began to see how the patrons'
tastes were different, which particular pieces they might favor, who
preferred which artists, and how each artist had his own style.

She learned quickly, through overheard conversations, those
who were truly in a position to buy, those who had the greatest
resources. The banker, Herr Ostner; the factory owner, Herr
Hummel; the brewer, Herr Adelmann. They were looking to the
future, as most astute businessmen, purchasing works to adorn
their mansions, their country homes, to show them off, to display
their good taste, to offer evidence that they had money enough to
hang it on the wall for guests to admire. But also to possess works
that would one day be sought by others. The rich, Hanna soon
learned, intended only to become richer. Art was art, but also a
business. And there was a profit to be made.

Each morning she attended her mistress at home, then left for the gallery where she spent the afternoons. At night, in that hazy, uncertain time before slumber, she constructed her own dreams. Someday, she would become an art dealer herself. She would travel all over Europe, discovering new talent. She would meet with important clients. She would be the most famous and the most wealthy art dealer in all of Germany.

CHAPTER SEVEN

Hanna

Paris and Munich
March–April 1901

Frau Fleischmann was feeling exceptionally well. The weather was beautiful, as if Paris had just awakened from a long winter slumber. The rain and wind they had expected had been pushed aside by bright sunny days, and an early budding was beginning to color the dark skeletal trees lining the boulevards, a melody skipping along the branches.

They visited the fashion houses, as Helene was always interested in the latest designs. Before leaving for France, they had pored over the magazines and catalogues of Callot Sœurs, Raudnitz, Jacques Doucet, and now in Paris, they spent several days placing orders with the designers on the most elegant streets in the city.

With Herr Fleischmann, they went to the Louvre.

"This is what you must learn," Herr Fleischmann said as they strolled through the rooms displaying the Greek sculptures, then the Italian Renaissance paintings. "Always we must go back to the classical art. We must study the past to approach the future."

They visited private studios, young artists who had yet to make names for themselves, and exhibitions in the city, particularly those that had been recommended by the many Parisian dealers with whom Herr Fleischmann kept in touch from Munich. There was a friendly sense of camaraderie as well as competition among the dealers, as Hanna learned when she attended dinners and evening events, sometimes with Frau Fleischmann and Herr Fleischmann, sometimes just as Herr Fleischmann's assistant. She often wondered what these men and often their wives, the Fleischmanns' friends, thought her position was, though she could only imagine. Through overheard conversations at the gallery in Munich, she was aware of the delight some of their patrons took in sharing personal details, sometimes quite scandalous, regarding others' lives. She laughed a little at this realization—that the wealthy were really no different from the common folk when it came to a juicy bit of gossip.

Though sometimes bitter, Frau Fleischmann was realistic about her health, and knew when not to extend beyond her limits. When she did not accompany them, on their return Hanna would describe everyone they had met, the women's gowns, what had been served, the conversations that had taken place. Herr Fleischmann, while not unkind, was at times impatient, and left the retelling to Hanna. As his wife pointed out, he did not remember the little things that Hanna always noticed. Oh, how her mistress enjoyed the stories. And Hanna realized that this was of great benefit to her also, as she learned to listen, to see, to pick up the smallest details.

They went to an exhibition at the Bernheim-Jeune Galerie, a retrospective of a Dutch artist named Vincent van Gogh. Helene wanted to go, but she was not feeling well, and conceded that she should stay at the hotel and rest.

Hanna's heart thumped wildly, her pulse jumped about in her ears, as they moved slowly through the gallery—so much color, such sounds, such music. Bright patches of color—one could even see the brushstrokes, brilliant swirls of paint. Hanna was tempted to reach out and touch them. The simple pictures of flowers and villages and starry skies looked nothing like real scenes, and yet they were alive!

The brochures, the chatter in the gallery, was all in French, which Hanna did not understand. She guessed that some of these admirers were also artists, that others—from the way Herr Fleischmann, who had a good command of the language, chatted with them as they examined the work—were also dealers.

As they left, Herr Fleischmann asked, "What do you think, Hanna?"

"I've never seen such lovely combinations of colors, of shapes, and textures," she said, "but I want to know more."

"About?"

"The artist."

"But, you like the work? The work should be taken on its own merit."

"Yes, it should," she agreed. "But as dealers of art, should we not have knowledge of the artist himself?"

Herr Fleischmann nodded, and she detected a small smile playing about his mouth. He was pleased with her reply, and she guessed amused that she seemed to be including herself as one of the dealers.

"This artist will become very important in the development of twentieth-century art. Unfortunately the man himself did not make it to the twentieth century."

"He's dead?" Hanna asked.

Again Herr Fleischmann nodded.

"He died a wealthy man?"

Herr Fleischmann laughed. He raised a hand to hail a passing hansom cab, which stopped. The driver jumped down and held the door for them.

As they sat, Herr Fleischmann continued, "No, the truth is he died, it is believed, at his own hand. Very poor. It is said he sold but one painting in his lifetime."

"How sad," Hanna said. "Perhaps if he had had a good art dealer, his work would have made him wealthy."

"Perhaps he was too advanced for his own time," Herr Fleischmann came back. "But, I believe at last his time has come. We must return to the exhibition when Helene is feeling better. She will love this work."

The following day they went early, as mornings were best for Helene. After a second slow walk through the gallery, Frau Fleischmann as entranced as Hanna and Herr Fleischmann, Hanna listening carefully to their whispered conversations, she knew they would be returning to Munich with a painting or two by this poor, dead, brilliant Dutch painter.

And she realized something that might have been obvious— once a painter had died, his work could actually become more valuable. A simple matter of the number of paintings available for purchase and the number of buyers desiring the work. A dead artist could create no further paintings, and thus if his work became desirable, it could make the dealer who had realized his value very, very wealthy.

Shortly after their return home, Hanna was assigned a new duty, assisting Herr Engle in the bookkeeping at the gallery. She was amazed to learn how little of the proceeds from the paintings went to the artists. When she asked Herr Fleischmann about this, he replied, "What would the artists be without the dealers? It is the creativity of the painter that will sell, but if it is not presented to those with the money, those who can pay the price, what is the use of the artist in the world of economics?" He explained that many artists had very little business sense, that they were creative spirits. Many of them cared little for the money, but they needed it to live. "Some artists struggle," he told her, "not only with their creativity, but with the simple aspects of life to make ends meet."

He's speaking of Vincent van Gogh, Hanna reflected.

"That's why a good artist needs a good dealer," Herr Fleischmann went on. "We are not here to take advantage, but to nurture, to encourage, to give the artists the means to continue their work."

"And a little profit for ourselves," she said.

Again she could see that Herr Fleischmann was pleased with her reply. She wanted to touch him at that moment. She wanted him to reach out and take her hand and smile into her eyes the way he did with Helene.

"You learn very quickly, Hanna," he said. And that was all.

One afternoon, as she was adjusting a painting that hung in the first gallery, she turned and Josef, her friend from the Academy of Fine Arts, stood before her.

"Why, Hanna," he said with a wide grin, bringing his hands together as if he were about to applaud her, "what a delight to find you here. You are no longer modeling for the artists, but selling their creations?" He wore a bright blue tie. He dressed differently from the other men she saw in Munich, and his colorful clothing made him sound much livelier, too. Even the way he spoke, his inflection, the way he moved, so dramatic and animated, was different. Sometimes Hanna didn't know quite what to think of Josef, though she had always found him delightful and warm.

"How good to see you, Josef. You've come to buy a painting?" She grinned now, too.

"I've come to speak with Herr Fleischmann. I hear there is a position available."

"Why, yes." Herr Engle was retiring soon, and there had been several gentlemen in and out over the past several days. What fun it would be, she thought, to have Josef here at the gallery.

She escorted him to Herr Fleischmann's office and then went back to the gallery where she waited with anticipation.

"Did it go well?" she asked when he returned.

"Yes, I believe it did. It is my dream to work at the Fleischmann Gallery."

She reached out and gave his hand a little squeeze. "Oh, Josef, it would be such a pleasure to have you here."

"Do you have any influence"—he motioned with his head back to Herr Fleischmann's office—"with those who make the important decisions?" His perfect eyebrows rose in a comical way, almost independently of each other.

"I'm little more than the charwoman around here." That wasn't exactly true—she had been given much more responsibility and training since their return from Paris. But she didn't want Josef to think she might be able to persuade Herr Fleischmann to hire him.

After Josef left, Herr Fleischmann came out of his office and approached her.

"This Josef Bloch, he is a friend?"

"Yes. I became acquainted with him when I . . ." She felt her face grow warm. They hadn't talked about her work as a model at the Academy since their conversation after Christmas. "He was a clerk at the Academy. He's good with numbers." She didn't know that this was true, but she assumed, because of his previous position, it was. "But he is also very knowledgeable about art, and he likes people. He could do just about anything here at the gallery."

"Meet with clients and sell paintings?" he asked with a grin.

"Yes," she said, "but I had hoped that might be my future position."

He laughed and patted her on the shoulder. "You know, the business is growing. We're doing very well. There will be opportunities."

Hanna took this to mean an opportunity might be available for her as well as Josef. She was delighted when she learned the next day that he would be starting the following week.

Having him at the gallery made it all the more fun. He made her laugh, and they giggled over the silliest things. One day Frau Ostner wore a hat adorned with feathers, though it appeared as if the entire bird had been placed upon the woman's head. Josef said he feared it might take flight. Herr Adelmann was one of their most valuable clients, but Hanna and Josef often exchanged expressions of comical dismay after he left. The brewer was among the wealthiest men in Munich, yet he had the speech and manners of an uneducated man and he said the most outrageous things, as if there was nothing to sift his coarse thoughts from his mind to his mouth.

But Josef also had a serious side, and he loved the art as much as Hanna. They would often share their thoughts on particular artists, suggest which client might be interested in the various work in the gallery.

Since Käthe had left Munich, Hanna had no one to talk to. There were other girls employed in the house, but it seemed their interests had more to do with people and rumor and scandal, not ideas about business, creativity, or art. Josef loved a good bit of gossip, too, but there was more to their friendship than that. He had become her best friend.

Hanna still spent her mornings tending to her mistress, and she had noticed since their return from Paris that Frau Fleischmann's health had declined. The doctor visited more often; he made adjustments in the medication. Her afternoon naps often ran into the evening. Several times, Hanna witnessed Dr. Langermann whispering to Herr Fleischmann outside his wife's bedroom door. At the gallery he seemed distracted, turning major decisions over to Josef.

One afternoon as she helped Frau Fleischmann with her lunch, of which she ate very little, a memory crept back to Hanna in the form of a hard, cold, colorless scent. She recognized it as the smell of her first visit to Munich with her sister, father, and mother.

All the way to the gallery that afternoon on the streetcar,

Hanna sobbed, the woman sitting next to her offering concern and a hankie. "I'm fine," Hanna told her, but she was not fine.

When she walked into the gallery, Josef looked up and instantly asked, "What is it, little girl?"

"She's getting worse."

"Frau Fleischmann?"

She wiped her face with the borrowed hankie and nodded. "She seemed to be better when we went to Paris, but since we've come back—I know she's not doing at all well. Dr. Langermann has been there almost every morning this week."

Josef put his arm around her. "Frau Fleischmann is a young woman, and Dr. Langermann is the best doctor in Munich. I'm sure she will get better."

And though she wanted desperately to believe him, Hanna knew it wasn't true. She knew that Helene would not get better— a familiar realization that came with an odd and unfamiliar mix of anger, fear, and something that she dared not name, because the emotion was so evil and selfish she didn't want it pushing its way into her head. She knew Frau Fleischmann's death would also be the end of many opportunities for her—the trips to Paris, the possibility of Vienna, the lessons in music, style, and manners.

But, perhaps the most wicked thought of all was that it might present new possibilities.

CHAPTER EIGHT

Lauren and Isabella

New York City
August 2009

"I should heat more water for tea," Isabella told Lauren as the older woman stood and lifted the tray.

"More tea would be wonderful," Lauren replied, thinking this would provide another opportunity to look around while Mrs. Fletcher was out of the room.

Reaching for her bag as soon as the woman left, Lauren grabbed her BlackBerry, stuck it in her pocket, pushed herself up from the soft nest of sofa and throw pillows, crossed the room, and stood before the fireplace. The colorful Franz Marc, really the centerpiece of the room, hung above the mantel. It appeared to be a copy, though it had the texture and look of authenticity. Lauren knew you could order a painting on the Internet with thick layers of paint that closely resembled an original. Made in China, she guessed, and could imagine an assembly-line creation—one artist filling in blue horses, another dabbing in red hills. She was aware that Franz Marc had done a number of paintings based on the blue horses theme and that at least one had disappeared during the war. Mrs. Fletcher's faux painting was similar to an original now in a Minneapolis museum, though hers was not nearly as large. Lauren pulled the BlackBerry from her pocket and snapped a photo.

Glancing at a small piece on the wall to the left, her mind filled with a jumble of colliding thoughts about what Mrs. Fletcher had told her over the past hour. The woman had spent an inordinate amount of time going over the history of Germany during the late-nineteenth and early-twentieth centuries, speaking of Prussian emperors and Bavarian kings as if this information were essential to wherever Isabella intended to go with this conversation.

As Lauren listened, she tried to seem interested, though she had a fairly good grasp of German history. Several times the woman had shot her a stern look. Finally Isabella said, "To understand the history of art in Germany, you must understand the history of Germany itself."

This was all fine, but Lauren wanted to know more about Hanna's later activities in Munich and Berlin. Mrs. Fletcher had barely moved on from her mother's life on the farm to her early work in the Fleischmann household, her developing interest in art, and her training at the gallery. If Lauren hoped to learn anything important, they needed to fast-forward to the thirties, and they had barely progressed from Hanna's arrival in Munich in 1900.

As she stepped closer to the small picture, she studied it carefully, quickly snapping another photo. It appeared to be an original etching. A scratchy signature and the edition numbers in pencil were visible along the bottom. Lauren had never held herself out as an expert in authenticating or appraising art—though she felt she could generally tell by a close examination if a painting was authentic—and often, after she had done the legwork, the historical research, she advised her clients to have a professional appraiser verify the work. In a sense it was like getting a second opinion.

"I believe it is going to be a nice afternoon," Isabella Fletcher called from the kitchen. "It was so cloudy this morning, and earlier this afternoon I thought we might have some rain, but the sun is peeking out from the clouds."

"That's good," Lauren called back, but she was thinking that the rain might be nice, might actually cool things down.

The etching, a group of maimed war survivors, was certainly in the style of the artist Otto Dix. The signature appeared to be authentic, little more than a scribble just as Dix would have signed it. She was about to lift the picture off the wall and take a quick look to see if there was any identification on the back when Isabella returned from the kitchen with a fresh pot of tea. She said nothing about Lauren having approached the etching.

Both women sat again and Isabella poured a cup for each of them.

"Mother loved working in the gallery," Mrs. Fletcher began. "She enjoyed the travel immensely, seeing works by various artists. She learned so much during those early years at the gallery. But she really developed her own tastes, her own ideas about art."

Now the woman's arm arched gracefully toward the gallery on the wall, speaking of one artist, moving quickly on to another as if she were giving a lecture in an art history class. Two gold bracelets on her left wrist slid down as she motioned, the slight click of gold upon gold. Lauren had noticed earlier that Mrs. Fletcher still wore a wedding set, two thin gold bands with a small diamond. A gift from a young man, Lauren wondered, a promise of things to come? On her right hand she wore a second ring, another diamond, much larger. Promise fulfilled?

Her hands were spotted with age, but elegant and carefully manicured with a pale frosted pink. Lauren glanced down at her own hands, her wedding ring with a respectable-sized diamond, a hastily filed nail that she'd chipped early this morning on the kitchen sink as she was rushing to feed Adam before dropping him off at day care.

"My mother," Isabella Fletcher said, "had a special talent—

some might call it an affliction—that was probably quite helpful in her ability to judge art, to appreciate it."

"What was that?" Lauren asked.

"Synesthesia. Do you know what that means?"

"Yes, I do," Lauren replied with interest, wondering what other unexpected facts the woman might come up with. "It's a—"

"Neurological condition," Isabella broke in, "in which perceptions normally associated with the senses become blended. Sight might produce a sound, taste may provoke a sensation of touch, the sense of hearing might result in the visualization of color. My mother could actually hear color, and conversely, she would see colors produced by specific sounds. I think it enhanced her appreciation of both art and music. My mother was also a musician—did I tell you she played the piano beautifully? You've heard the expression 'play by ear'?"

"Yes, I've heard that," Lauren replied, intrigued by this new information about Hanna.

"In a way my mother played not by ear, but by eye. She saw a specific color associated with each note and tone."

"That's amazing."

"It's said that Wassily Kandinsky was also a synesthete. He enjoyed music as well as art, often naming his paintings after musical terms—Improvisations, Compositions. There were ten *Compositions* in all. Ours is Kandinsky's *Composition II*."

Lauren's heart nearly jumped out of her chest. The old woman continued to carry on about the artistic blending of sound and color, elaborating on her personal belief that Kandinsky's was more an emotional or psychological sensation, rather than a physical experience as was her mother's synesthesia.

Composition II? Lauren wanted to ask. *Are you sure?*

"My mother actually *heard* color," Isabella explained, "and had a visual perception of sound. It wasn't just an experience of emotions. Oh, you know how people say, I'm blue, meaning feeling sad, or green with envy, or he's a yellow coward." She laughed. "It was not metaphor, or emotion, but a physical, visual sensation with Mother."

Could this painting possibly have survived? Lauren wondered.

"Perhaps this combining of music and color," Isabella said, "contributed to my mother's love for Kandinsky's work. He was one of her favorite painters. They became friends as well as professional colleagues. She generally didn't talk about her synesthesia—it made her feel odd. But with Wassily Kandinsky, because of this shared ability, she felt a kinship. She handled much of his work during his tenure in Germany." Isabella sighed. "His earlier tenure in Munich."

Lauren had seen a Kandinsky sketch of this *Composition* in the Guggenheim here in New York. The artist did numerous preliminary sketches for paintings. Though his finished canvases often appeared to have come from a spontaneous, unplanned effort, Lauren knew that much thought went into everything Wassily Kandinsky created. Though a sketch for *Composition II* had survived, it was believed that the original had been lost in the war, destroyed by bombings in Berlin. If Isabella was correct, if she really possessed Wassily Kandinsky's *Composition II*, this would be an enormous find in the art world.

Lauren attempted to form a picture in her mind, to visualize the sketch. Still some representational elements, she recalled—robed figures of women in bright colors; leaping animals that brought to mind giraffes and horses; towers and steeples and mountains in the background in vibrant reds, yellows, blues, and greens.

"*Composition II?*" she finally asked, feeling that nervous twitch behind her left eye.

"Yes," Isabella replied flatly.

"That's . . . well, that's amazing," Lauren stumbled over her words, stunned at what Mrs. Fletcher had just offered her.

"I have something I'd like to show you," Isabella said abruptly. She rose without further explanation and left the room.

Lauren sat, unable to move, her breathing coming in and out rapidly, every sensible thought removed from her head. She placed a hand over her chest; and the rhythm seemed to be counting off minutes. She glanced around the room for a clock, unable to find one, but knowing she'd been here much longer than anticipated. Yet Isabella had confirmed none of the facts Lauren wanted to verify concerning Hanna. And now this! *Composition II*? She reached in her bag and pulled out her phone, checking the time and then quickly punching in a text to Patrick, telling him her meeting was running later than expected. Could he please pick up Adam? Again she thought of the conversation she might have with him this evening. *Well, how was your day?* she thought with a grin, slipping her phone back in her bag.

Earlier, before Mrs. Fletcher had revealed that her Kandinsky was one of his *Compositions*, she'd said the painting was too large for the room. Lauren knew the surviving sketch was more than 3 by 4 feet, that the original painting was believed to have been twice that size.

Isabella returned carrying a cardboard tube. So much for Lauren's thought that she might haul out the Kandinsky, which, considering the size, would be impossible for one old woman anyway.

"Much was lost when the family left Munich," Mrs. Fletcher said, her voice low. "Just about everything." She clutched the tube protectively to her chest. "I have so little to remember my family by." One arm swept across the room with a flutter, and then dropped to her side. "Most of these are reproductions, copies, and prints, but original paintings by several of these artists did hang in our home in Munich."

"The family was unable to bring them to America?" Lauren asked, her eyes gliding again from wall to wall.

Mrs. Fletcher said nothing as she sat, removed the plastic cap from the tube, slid a rolled paper out, and smoothed it flat on the coffee table with her hands.

It was a simple pencil drawing of a young woman—nude at that.

"My mother," Isabella said.

"She's lovely," Lauren replied, and she was.

"Yes," Isabella said.

The young woman in the drawing sat in a wooden chair, her hands folded demurely in her lap, her posture straight and alert, hair loosely braided and coiled on her head, curls escaping to frame her face. A subtle expression of tentativeness emanated from her eyes, the set of her lips. Yet something about her conveyed a certain confidence known only to the young who have yet to experience the fullness of life. Lauren realized that she had never seen a photo, a drawing, or any image of this woman. But Lauren had created her own. Hanna was a frumpy old woman of fifty-plus-years with thick ankles set in sensible leather shoes. Her graying hair was tied up into a matronly knot, often set under a proper old-lady hat. But, even having created this image, Lauren never truly thought of the woman as having flesh and bone.

Now, as Lauren studied the drawing, Hanna seemed very real. She looked young, maybe still in her teens, and a little unsure of herself, despite the affected composure. Lauren had never considered Hanna as anything but an old woman. She'd certainly never thought of her as an innocent girl.

"My mother was a beautiful woman," Isabella said. "I wish this drawing were in color. I wish I had a photograph of my mother at this age, though, of course that would be in black and white. She had the most gorgeous red hair. With age it faded somewhat, lost its luster. We all tend to do that," she added with a tepid laugh, "fade with age and lose our luster. But at this time, her hair would have been a brilliant, showstopping red."

"How old was your mother here?" Lauren asked.

"Honestly, I'm not sure. I wasn't even aware of this drawing until after she passed away. I know little about when or by whom it was done."

"A beautiful young woman," Lauren said.

"Yes, she was. I wish I could tell you more about this time in her life," Mrs. Fletcher added softly, gazing at the drawing and then up at Lauren. She released her hands and the drawing seemed to roll up on its own. Isabella adjusted it carefully and slid it back in the tube.

So do I, Lauren thought, wondering how much Isabella could possibly know about this young Hanna. Often while doing her research, when talking to people who hadn't been personally involved in the history she was attempting to trace, she wished she could speak with those who had lived the experience. What she often needed—wanted—was an interview with a ghost.

"How much do you know about your own mother's youth?" Mrs. Fletcher asked. Her tone was flat and unreadable, yet Lauren felt as if Isabella had just read her mind.

"I'm not aware that she ever posed in the nude," Lauren replied, unable to resist, and then immediately wished she'd held her tongue.

Mrs. Fletcher offered her a quick smile, and Lauren felt both grateful and relieved. When the old woman emitted a soft laugh, Lauren sensed the possibility of a growing trust. Taking a deep breath, she hoped to hold on to whatever rapport they had established and move forward at the same time. "Your mother," she started in slowly, "got her initial art training at the Fleischmann Gallery in Munich . . . Your mother's name was Hanna Schmid?" *Among others,* Lauren thought. She knew this wasn't her legal name, but . . .

"Yes, she did go by Hanna Schmid," Mrs. Fletcher said. "It was, of course, her maiden name, not her married name. It's a little confusing I know—" She stopped abruptly, paused for a long moment, her eyes moving quickly and nervously around the room, finally settling on the window. The light falling into the room had shifted. "And I'll get to the explanation for that."

CHAPTER NINE

Hanna

Florence, Italy
April 1904

"Why, it looks like the Feldherrnhalle in Munich!" Hanna exclaimed, moving quickly through the Piazza della Signoria, maneuvering around pigeons pecking seeds and insects off the cobblestone, and vendors with small wheeled carts hawking post-cards and trinkets.

"Our loggia," Moses explained, attempting to catch up with the young woman, "was inspired by the Loggia dei Lanzi. Munich's Feldherrnhalle wasn't built until the mid eighteen hundreds by Ludwig I as a memorial for the heroes of Bavaria."

Hanna stood and studied the three arches of the building, her eyes moving from one sculpture to the next displayed in the open arcade. "Fourteenth century," she guessed aloud, turning to Moses, who nodded and smiled with approval. She had so much more to learn, but she had a wonderful teacher, if she could just listen and absorb.

"Giambologna," Moses said, pointing to the sculpture under the third arch. *"Rape of the Sabine Women."* His finger moved from the three figures twisting and wrapping around one another in a pose both beautiful and disturbing, to the figure holding the head of Medusa. "*Perseus* by Cellini . . . *Ajax and Patroclus*, a copy of a fourth-century B.C. Greek original." He pointed out the Roman statues, along the back of the arcade, all inspired by Greek originals.

Along with Roman sculptures, in these past days in Florence they had seen hundreds of paintings and frescoes created during the Italian Renaissance. Hanna had studied such art at the museums in Munich and Paris, and in books, but here she felt so much closer to its creation, and with Moses by her side it was like having a private tour guide. He challenged her to really look, to examine technique and style, to decide for herself what she liked and did not like, and why. She could see how the technical skills had advanced from the earliest work they had seen in the lovely Uffizi—flat-faced, two-dimensional Madonnas—to the finely sculpted, shadowed, nuanced creations of the High Renaissance.

She thought of paintings she had seen by nineteenth- and twentieth-century artists in Paris and at home in Germany, and reflected on the fact that many of them were so realistic they could have been taken with a camera. Where were the modern artists headed from here? Was it a mere matter of advancing in technique? Surely there was more to it than that. If it could all be done with a camera, would the artist become obsolete? She thought of the very "modern" paintings they had seen in Paris and many of the contemporary pieces they were showing at the Fleischmann, creations where form and shape and color seemed to be as important as recognizable images and subject.

They had been away from Munich for just over a month now, and Hanna was still walking about as if in a dream. They had gone down through Austria, spending a week in Vienna, then on to Italy. She had fallen in love with the dark, moody canals of Venice, the city's reflected light and color, and then the amazing pure light of Florence. One of the patrons at the Munich gallery had referred to sunny Italy, and now Hanna understood, though her own experience of Tuscany was enhanced by the stunning arrangement of harmonious tones. Her first encounter with Brunelleschi's bright red Duomo against a sun-drenched sky of brilliant blue had created such a magnificent sound, Hanna felt as if her heart had stopped. Then the soft, sweet tones of the faded Italian frescoes, the shimmery, silvery sounds of the church bells, and the lovely melody of a sunset viewed from Fiesole.

It had been almost three years since Helene's passing, and even now as she felt such joy, Hanna's memories of those days after Frau Fleischmann's death were vivid. She'd wandered about, feeling without direction, without connection. Though Helene had had little contact with members of the household other than Hanna and Moses, it seemed as if the very life, the air they all breathed, had been sucked out of the house and every living person who remained.

Hanna had continued to sleep on the small cot that had been brought into Frau Fleischmann's room during those last weeks. No one told her to move back to the servants' quarters. No one told her anything. Hanna would wake in the night, go to the closet, and take in the scent of Helene, pressing her beautiful gowns to her nose. She would sit at her vanity, open a bottle of perfume, then another, to bring her back.

Sometimes she went to the music room and played. The sounds and colors were discordant and out of harmony, though these were the same notes she had been playing before. Some afternoons she could barely make her way to the gallery. When she arrived, she went to the back room, sat, and wept.

Moses seemed to be in his own world of grief, and barely spoke to Hanna. One day, Josef said to her, "This isn't what Frau Fleischmann would want, Hanna. You must come to the gallery in the morning now." Hanna realized that Josef had taken over the day-to-day management of the business, that Helene's passing had put Herr Fleischmann into the same unproductive state as Hanna herself.

She started arriving early. Josef pointed out what needed to be done at the gallery. She began to take pleasure in her work again.

Late the next week, Herr Fleischmann said, "You are arriving in the morning now?" He seemed truly surprised.

"For almost two weeks." Hanna sensed that this realization had just come to him, that he hadn't been aware that she was now spending full days at the gallery.

He looked confused, a faraway, distant look in his eyes, but he said no more.

"Josef said—" she started to explain.

"Yes, of course," he broke in. "How fortunate we are to have Josef."

After several more weeks Herr Fleischmann said, "Hanna, you have also been very helpful," as though they were continuing a conversation they had started just moments before.

"Thank you, sir."

"Helene would be proud of you." He smiled and it was the first time she had seen him smile for so very long, the first time she had heard him speak his wife's name since her passing.

After that, there were days when he spoke to her, others when he did not. He traveled often, sometimes leaving Munich for months. Hanna moved back to the servants' quarters, though she was no longer an employee in the household. She worked only at the gallery. No one told her to move out.

Josef relied on her, particularly when Herr Fleischmann was away from the city. When Moses returned from these trips, he had new art and stories about when and how they had been acquired. She listened intently as he spoke with Josef, with patrons at the gallery. Gradually she became involved in these conversations, and then Moses began to share ideas with Hanna and ask her opinion as if he valued what she had to say.

She knew she was in love with him; perhaps she had been in love from that day he stood behind her, his lovely voice speaking the word *Cézanne*. They were connected, drawn together by this love of the art. But was this the extent of his affection for her? And could she dare have these feelings for her employer, for the husband of her precious Helene, whom she had loved so dearly? Sometimes the guilt overwhelmed her, but how could she contain or deny such emotions? One had little control over a passion as strong as love.

Sometimes he would touch her lightly on the hand or the shoulder, or offer a smile, a glance that made her ache inside. Words were never exchanged concerning their feelings for each other, but she sensed something was growing, a spark ignited within Moses as well as herself.

One day, several months after her nineteenth birthday, he said to her, "Hanna, I'm planning a trip in the spring to Vienna, and then down south to Italy. It would be a wonderful opportunity for you."

What was he suggesting? That she accompany him? She had longed to go to Vienna, and Italy was a wish that came only in her dreams. "But, would that be . . ." She searched for the proper word, which she decided was the word *proper* itself.

"Proper?" he said with a grin, as if he had plucked the word out of her mind. "Yes, if you were to accompany me as my wife."

She was silent for a long, stunned moment. Was he professing his love for her? He had never told her he loved her, never courted her in a traditional sense. And yet, there were moments when they worked side by side that she imagined it, that he did love her.

"Are you asking me to marry you?" she'd asked with disbelief.

"Your acceptance would be my greatest happiness," he had replied.

The following day, they crossed the lovely Ponte Vecchio, over the Arno River, and ventured into the Brancacci Chapel in the Church of Santa Maria del Carmine. It was early and they had the chapel to themselves. The walls were covered with frescoes, scenes depicting biblical themes, many from the New Testament, Christ and the apostles, all with halos that looked to Hanna like hovering golden plates.

"This fresco by Masaccio," Moses said, pointing to a small section with two simple figures, "had enormous impact on Florentine art. Even the great Michelangelo came here to study. Masaccio's work was considered innovative for its time. Can you imagine why?"

Hanna studied the two figures, obviously Adam and Eve. She glanced quickly around the chapel again at the biblical figures, strangely garbed in Renaissance costumes, placed in fifteenth-century Florence from the appearance of the buildings.

The Adam and Eve were unclad, save for the leaves placed in strategic positions. Moses had earlier told her how such leaves were often added later to some of the sculptures that were created gloriously nude.

There was some advancement, she observed, in technique from earlier works—the angel foreshortened, and the light was skillfully, realistically presented. Though hadn't she seen such efforts in the work of Giotto?

"The emotion!" she burst out. This Adam was clearly distraught, burying his head in his hands. And the Eve—why, Hanna could nearly hear her wail. And they were such plain-looking folk, peasants, not royalty. "The emotion," she repeated, "as if they are real people with real feelings."

Again Moses nodded, as if to say, *You are a very good student, my dear.*

"How does that happen?" Hanna asked, and then realized she probably sounded stupid. "We've gone through the museums and you've pointed out work from a place, a particular time, and there seems to be a similarity in style, in manner, as if each artist is learning from the others, sometimes merely copying. And then suddenly, one artist decides, 'I'm going to do it differently.' "

Moses laughed and Hanna felt her face flush.

Slowly, thoughtfully, he said, "I don't know if *suddenly* is precisely how it all happens."

Hanna laughed, too. "Can you imagine if Cézanne, or perhaps Monet or Renoir, or even Van Gogh, had lived in the fifteenth century and painted a fresco here at the Brancacci Chapel, an Adam and Eve, perhaps a Saint Peter, with their bold brushstrokes and bright, thick splashes of color!"

"Yes, now that would be *sudden*!"

"It's all gradual," she announced. "It's artistic evolution. The changes come slowly."

Moses touched his chin with his hand. The line between his brows deepened.

"But do you think at times these changes might move more quickly?" Hanna asked. "Like the technology in this century— the development of the automobile, the way factories are now producing what used to be made strictly by hand. Is the art world moving, changing more rapidly now, too?"

"Oh, Hanna, you give one much to ponder." He smiled and added, "Some interesting ideas, Frau Fleischmann." She loved it when he called her Frau Fleischmann, but on occasion she was overcome with an urge to turn and look to see if he were speaking to someone else. To see if Helene was standing beside them. Often the feeling was accompanied by guilt, as if she were attempting to take the place of Helene. She would and could not. She tried desperately not to think of herself as the third wife.

"Though it is not completely the artist's vision," Moses commented as they continued to look up at the fresco. "Something has been added." He tilted his head toward her as if she were to guess. It seemed a little learning game he liked to play with her.

"The leaves," she answered. "The leaves covering the . . ." Hanna blushed. She was standing here with her husband, a man who had now seen and touched, it seemed, every inch of her body, who had actually marveled over it their first night together. And here she was, blushing over the private parts of two painted figures.

"Yes, the leaves were added later," Moses said, "by Cosimo III."

"The king?"

"A Medici. Not royalty, in the strictest sense, but the family ruled over Florence."

"Yes, the Medicis." A name she was very much aware of during her days in Florence. "The power to censor?"

Moses nodded.

"Do power, wealth, and nobility give one the right to determine how an artist paints, or who is allowed to view the painting as the artist created it?"

"Power, yes," Moses replied without hesitation. "Yes, power has been known to dictate art."

"What do you think Masaccio would have to say about that?" she asked. "The defilement of his work?"

"He would not be pleased," Moses said. "An artist is never pleased when his work is compromised."

CHAPTER TEN

Lauren and Isabella

New York City
August 2009

"An enormous chandelier hung in the entry of the Munich house," Isabella told Lauren. "An original blown-glass piece created on the Venetian islands of Murano. My father purchased it for my mother on their honeymoon and had it sent ahead so it would be installed by the time they returned home. They went to Austria, then Italy, a two-month trip. People used to do that back then—particularly the wealthy, and my parents were very well-off. That chandelier would be worth a fortune had it survived."

Had it survived, Lauren thought, picturing an intricate Italian chandelier with its scrolled glass branches and pastel florals, sparkling with reflected light. Had this lovely piece been looted? Or had it come crashing to the floor in a wartime bombing, sending shards of glass everywhere? As she imagined this disturbing image, Lauren wondered when Isabella would get back to the *Composition,* a painting believed to have been lost in World War II. At moments she questioned if the old woman was fabricating parts of her story, particularly those relating to the Kandinsky.

"Andrew and I could barely take two days when we married," Mrs. Fletcher went on. "We spent one night at a little inn in

Upstate New York. But those were different times." She gazed over at the photo of her late husband, emitting a restrained sigh.

They sat quietly for a moment, Lauren wondering how she could encourage Mrs. Fletcher to continue revealing Hanna's story as well as more about the Kandinsky, without seeming overly eager. And how could she keep her from veering off on another tangent without appearing disrespectful? Yet she knew now that Hanna Schmid *was* Hanna Fleischmann, a fact that Isabella had provided without prodding.

Listen, she told herself once more. *Be patient.*

"My parents waited several years to have a child," Isabella said. "I don't mean wait in the sense that young people wait now—I believe that they truly wanted a child, but their inability to do so right away allowed my mother to establish a career. She was definitely ahead of her time. A woman with more than just husband and children." Isabella Fletcher's face shone with unmistakable pride.

Then she stood, picked up the drawing in the tube, and again left the room.

Lauren reached for her BlackBerry to check if Patrick had replied to her text. He hadn't. She needed to know soon if he could pick Adam up from day care. If she didn't hear from him, she'd have to leave. She felt that familiar tug of maternal conflict and guilt.

She left a message asking that he send a text to let her know. Would Mrs. Fletcher invite her again, Lauren wondered, if she had to leave? The woman had never had a child; she wasn't a mother, and Lauren didn't know if she would understand. Hearing footsteps, Lauren slipped the phone back into her bag.

Mrs. Fletcher held a photograph, which she placed on the table as she sat.

It was black and white, fairly old, Lauren could see, and protected in an ornate frame that appeared equally as dated. The girl in the photo was about eight or nine, the age of Lauren's niece, Amanda, her brother Aaron's daughter. She wore a white frock, a big bow in her hair. From the thirties, Lauren guessed. The girl was sitting in a wicker chair. A boy stood next to her wearing a suit and tie. The girl looked very serious. The boy was smiling. Lauren couldn't even guess how old the boy was, but it was obvious that he had Down syndrome.

"I was almost nine in this picture," Mrs. Fletcher said. "My brother was twenty-five."

Lauren studied the photograph, attempting to come up with appropriate words. The girl, a young Isabella, was a beautiful child. Very pale, with soft blond curls, evident even in the black-and-white photo. There was a sadness about her. The boy looked happy and proud and innocent, unaware of what was troubling the girl.

"There was a fair gap in your age," Lauren finally said.

"Yes," the older woman replied, staring down at the picture as she ran her fingers over her skirt. She looked up at Lauren and a slow, hesitant grin lifted her lips. "I believe I was an unexpected surprise for my parents." Her smile softened. "And, yes, he was mentally challenged, intellectually disabled—isn't that what they call it now? That's not what they called it back then. Not in Germany, anyway. And I believe the Americans would have said *retarded* or *Mongoloid*. My parents were advised to put him away. That's what they did with children like Willy back then. But Mother refused."

Lauren couldn't even think of what to say now so she said nothing. She thought back to her own pregnancy, the day Adam was born, the relief she felt after every toe and finger was counted.

"He was a dear, sweet boy," Isabella said. "My mother and father adored him, as did I."

Remembering what Mrs. Fletcher had told her earlier—that her father purchased the Kandinsky as a gift to celebrate her brother's birth in 1911—Lauren guessed this photo would have been taken about 1936. And she knew exactly what was happening in Germany in the mid-thirties.

She picked up the picture of the two children, carefully examining the details as if there was something hidden within that might give her a clue as to where to go from here.

Yes, Lauren knew what was coming. She knew what was happening in Germany at the time of this portrait. A new government had begun to take shape, a government that would control every aspect of German life. A society in which a premium was placed on physical perfection. A society in which a boy such as Willy Fleischmann would be regarded as disposable rubbish.

Lauren felt a sudden, sharp heat prick at her chest. She was a spectator, positioned more than seventy years from the day the son and daughter of Hanna and Moses Fleischmann sat for this portrait, and she was aware of what history had now revealed.

She also knew, as Isabella had said, that children with such disabilities were usually sent to institutions back then, yet here Isabella sat along with Willy. Brother and sister. A Jewish father. A Christian mother. Children born into a world that would turn so very unkind.

As Lauren was about to set the photo back down on the table, her unsteady hand bumped her teacup, and in an attempt to catch it, she dropped the photo, which crashed against the leg of the table. She heard a crack. A fist of tension clenched around her heart, and then an enormous weight dropped to the pit of her stomach. Bending to pick up the picture, she exchanged a wide-eyed look with Mrs. Fletcher, who had risen, napkin in hand, to lap up the spilled tea.

"I'm so sorry," Lauren said, turning the framed photo over, seeing that, just as she suspected, the glass had broken. None of the pieces had fallen out of the frame, and thank God it didn't appear to have scratched the photo. "Mrs. Fletcher, I'm so terribly sorry." Her voice was unsteady, her tone anxious as well as apologetic. She took her own napkin, dabbing as she glanced down at the table leg, grateful to see no visible damage.

The woman gazed down at the photo of her young self and her brother. "It's just the glass. *That* can be fixed."

"I'd like to take care of it, replace the glass. I must apologize for my clumsiness."

"I'll take care of it," Isabella answered sharply, gathering the cup—fortunately and miraculously unbroken—and the sopping napkins and plopping them on the tray. "Now, let's continue, please."

"Yes, please," Lauren replied, though she felt on the verge of tears.

CHAPTER ELEVEN

Hanna

Hanna sat at the piano, little Willy on her lap. At two and a half, he was finally starting to talk, though his words were undecipherable to anyone other than his mother. But what a joy this child was to both herself and Moses.

The little boy looked up at his mother with a grin. This was their magic room. Each morning after breakfast they came here and Willy sat on her lap as she played. He was always very still until she had finished, and then he would play his own tune, tapping the keys with his chubby little fingers, his mother guiding him along, the child delighted with the sounds he created.

When he was born, she didn't know if he would survive; she didn't know if her marriage would survive. Those early years had been happy, though interspersed with Hanna's thoughts of Helene, her guilt over having married her mistress's husband—having coveted her husband, even as Helene lay on her deathbed. Often Hanna struggled with the thought that Moses did not love her as he had loved Helene, that she was competing with a dead woman, and she questioned how she could possibly be jealous of a woman who had been gone from this earth for years. But she was not Helene, and she had made a new place in Moses' heart. They worked together at the gallery, shared their thoughts about the art as they sat for supper, entertained collectors and art patrons in their home where Hanna, unlike Helene, could act as hostess. Sometimes she'd catch a glance from Moses as she spoke with one of their guests about a particular painting that she knew they would love, and Hanna could see the admiration and respect in her husband's eyes, in his subtle smile.

They talked about having a family. They had assumed they would. Hanna was young and healthy. But then it didn't happen. A year passed, then another.

When finally Willy arrived, Hanna often felt that Moses hated her, as if this defective child were her fault. The doctor said they should put him in a mental facility where he could receive proper care. She remembered clearly shouting at Dr. Langermann, "No, I will not. He is my child and you cannot take him away from me." She'd hated Dr. Langermann then and, at times, she hated Moses because he had not one comforting word to offer her.

She thought back further to the great happiness she had felt when she realized, finally, after almost seven years of marriage, she was with child.

She knew by then that Moses and Helene had wanted a child but she had been unable to conceive. And Hanna thought that if she could only give him this son, he would love her as much as he loved the beautiful Helene, perhaps even more. She knew when they married he did not love her as he had loved his second wife, perhaps even his first, so Hanna set out to earn his love. She would present him with a son.

At first, when she suspected she was with child, she didn't tell Moses. She told no one. She'd had such a difficult time conceiving, she wanted to make sure, and she feared she might lose the baby in those early weeks. Even after she missed her second month, she did not tell Moses. Then, into what she believed was her third month, her husband was so preoccupied with work, she was unable to find a perfect moment to share her joyous news.

The Fleischmann Gallery was about to open one of its biggest and most controversial exhibitions, featuring the work of the Neue Kunstlervereinigung München, with artists Kandinsky, Gabriele Münter, Alexej Jawlensky and Marianne Werefkin. The group had stirred up debate concerning their artistic validity, particularly the Russian, Kandinsky. He was showing several pieces, among them two lovely paintings he called *Composition I* and *Composition II*. They were said to be inspired by his music. Hanna knew they would leave the critics baffled and confused. What did these strange shapes represent? Was that a horse? Were those figures people? Water? A tree? She wondered if it truly mattered.

Moses was completely engaged in preparations for the show and did not notice the expansion of her waistline. Josef did, but he promised to tell no one until she was ready.

On the day before the exhibition opened, as Hanna helped Josef hang Kandinsky's *Composition II*, she felt it—the first movement. It was not the tiny burst of a bubble that her sister Leni had described. It was as if the child were leaping in her womb, as if the bright, vibrant colors of the Kandinsky, which were creating a beautiful mixture of sounds, were stimulating the child, as if he could see and hear it, too. A verse from the gospel of St. Luke came to her: "The moment your greeting sounded in my ears, the baby leapt in my womb for joy."

After the opening of the exhibition, she told Moses that she was with child.

"How far along?" he asked with concern.

Hanna took his hand in hers and placed it over her belly.

"How did I not know?" he replied with disbelief.

"You've been very busy with the exhibition."

"Yes," he said. She could hear the worry, the fear and caution in his voice.

"I felt the first movement," she said, "as I stood before Kandinsky's *Composition II*, and I sensed that I had been given a sign. It was as if he were leaping. Oh, Moses we must buy this painting!" she exclaimed.

"Of course," Moses replied, his voice rising now, attempting to share in her exhilaration. "Yes, of course we will buy the painting."

The painting was hung in the music room, and during those months of her pregnancy, each time Hanna entered and sat at the piano in the still of the room, it would begin—a concert with trumpets and cymbals and oboes and flutes. And the baby inside her danced to the colors.

Now, as she sat with little Willy, she felt that same joy. He ran his fingers over the piano keys, delighted with the sounds, then reached up for his mother, patting her gently on the cheek.

After Willy was born, Young Helene, Hanna's stepdaughter, came to visit and stayed for two weeks. Little Jakob, now thirteen, remained home with his father in Berlin. Hanna wondered if Helene feared his presence might remind her that she would never have a normal boy. She'd always been kind to Hanna. When she married Moses, Hanna feared his daughter would not accept her, as she had never gotten on with her first stepmother. Yet Hanna, being the younger, could never see Young Helene as a daughter. She soon discovered she enjoyed the woman's companionship immensely. Was it because they were more like sisters? Or was it because they both knew what it was like to live in the same shadow—the shadow of Moses' second wife, the beautiful golden-eyed Helene?

Hanna appreciated Young Helene's coming to help with the new baby. Her sister Käthe, her husband and family, were now in America, and her younger sister, Leni, was living in Kempton with her husband, too large with child herself to be of any help. Helene said nothing about the baby being different, which was both a comfort and an irritation. She said only, "What a sweet baby you have, Hanna."

For months after the baby's birth, Hanna rarely saw her husband. He rose early and spent all day at the gallery. She stayed in her room all day, tending to Willy, imagining he was a perfectly normal child. Moses returned home late. They did not take their meals together. He did not come to her room. He did not visit the nursery—she knew because she asked the nurse. Hanna ate alone before feeding Willy and putting him to bed. Had she, like Helene, become a wife who slept alone in her room? A woman too weak to face the world?

That spring, as the seasons changed, the cold wind of winter alternating with a teasing breath of warm air, Hanna took ill. It started with a slight rattle in the chest and then seemed to overtake her entire body. She could barely breathe. She could barely get out of bed to attend to little Willy, whose own breathing had become hard and labored.

He cried and cried, and then he stopped as if he had no strength to continue. His tiny body took on a pale, frightening color. Hanna screamed and sent the nurse to fetch Dr. Langermann. She picked up Willy and prayed and prayed to a God to whom she had not spoken since the day her son was born. "Please," she pleaded, "please do not take this child from me."

Moses had not yet left for work, as it was early morning, and he ran to the room, his eyes filled with fear. "What is it?"

"Willy," Hanna cried. Then for the first time, not aloud but in her heart, she said, *He is my child. I want him as he is. I want Willy. Please, dear Lord, spare my child, this imperfect, flawed little child.* This was how she made her bargain with God. Willy was her child, and she would accept him just the way he had been given to her, if God would forgive her for wanting him any other way.

Miraculously, before Dr. Langermann arrived, the child's color had returned and he was breathing again.

Then Hanna noticed the change in Moses. Though they never

spoke of it, she knew he, too, had made a bargain with his own God. Moses had entered the same pact as she.

Every day after that, he came into the room and picked up their baby, and Hanna could see the smile, the father's love. Finally, Moses had accepted this child. The beautiful, imperfect little angel, the product of their imperfect love.

Now, after two years, neither Hanna nor Moses could imagine their life without Willy. Hanna kissed the top of his head as they sat at the piano, then lifted him and carried him around the room to look at the paintings, another part of their little morning ritual. She had hung her favorites here in their magic room. The large colorful Kandinsky *Composition*, a smaller piece by Franz Marc, a lovely little Chagall with its floating figures.

She set him down on the floor now, and immediately he toddled over to the Kandinsky.

"Bla, bla, bla, rot, rot, rot," he sang, raising his arms in the air, then patting his ears. Hanna wondered if he was naming the colors, and she often wondered if Willy, too, shared her blending of the senses, as he would sometimes touch his ears and smile when he viewed a painting. He was just now beginning to communicate in words, but there was clearly something in this painting by Wassily Kandinsky that he loved.

Sasha, a young woman who helped out with Willy at home, entered the room, and Hanna handed him over to her. Sasha was a tiny little thing with an enormous heart. She had been with them since before Willy's birth, and Hanna knew she loved him dearly. Hanna would not have dreamed of continuing her work at the gallery without someone as reliable and loving as Sasha to look after her son.

Hanna had an appointment at the gallery that afternoon. When Willy was an infant she often took him to work with her.

She kept a crib by her desk. When he was awake she'd put him on the floor with his toys. But now that he was starting to toddle about, it was difficult. She worked part days only, or if she had an appointment. Today she was meeting with Herr Kandinsky. She'd asked him to come by the gallery, explaining she had a business proposition for him, the offer to purchase several of his works. She had discussed it with Moses in great detail, but she was to make the offer on her own. Moses, too, loved Kandinsky, but always teased Hanna that the Russian was her artist.

Herr Kandinsky was beginning to make a name for himself internationally, having shown his work throughout Europe and at the Armory show in America earlier in the year, which exposed him to a whole new world of collectors. His prices had risen considerably over the past two or three years, and Hanna wanted to acquire several paintings now, as she knew their value would continue to increase.

He came in as he always did, greeting her warmly, telling Hanna how lovely she looked that afternoon, inquiring of Herr Fleischmann and young Willy.

Hanna told him how much her son loved the large *Composition* that hung in the music room at home. She thought of the pseudo-intellectuals who visited the gallery, who would object and complain, "But what is it? What is this rubbish? What am I to think of this Kandinsky who believes he can break the rules?" If they could but approach these paintings with the openness of a child, they might be touched.

"When I take him to the music room," Hanna told Herr Kandinsky, "he points to your *Composition* and smiles and sings." Hanna had tried to separate the emotional connection she had for this particular artist from her professional vision, which at times was difficult. But even as a collector, a dealer of art, she realized emotion would always be part of it. As Kandinsky himself might say, "What is art without emotion?"

Hanna called for refreshments, inviting him to sit.

"I'd like to purchase these three paintings, Herr Kandinsky." She made her offer. He hesitated for a moment, and Hanna wondered if he would attempt to draw a higher price, perhaps feeling that as his agent she could not play both sides of this venture. She felt the price more than reasonable. After some discussion, his suggesting a higher price, Hanna's coming up a little, he accepted her offer, and she immediately went to the office.

"Please, will you write up a bill of sale and a check?" Hanna asked Josef with a grin.

"You made the deal?" he asked with a smile of his own.

"Yes."

"All three paintings?"

"He's reluctant to part with them, but yes."

When she returned, Herr Kandinsky was standing in front of one of the paintings, as if he were saying a final farewell.

He thanked Hanna for the purchase and for the Fleischmanns' support over the years, as he tucked the papers in his pocket. "Please, extend my sincerest gratitude also to Herr Fleischmann. And my love to little Willy."

Hanna watched as he walked out, down the street, around the corner. He had such a regal posture, so impeccably dressed. The Russian Prince, she thought, remembering what she had called him when he came for dinner with his teacher Herr von Stuck. He had advanced beyond so many of them now, creating his own work and style.

They never spoke of those days in the studio, but she remembered how he had exclaimed to Herr von Stuck, "How can I draw this young woman in black and white when her hair sings with color?"

She smiled as she thought of those early days, and of how much had happened since then for Herr Kandinsky, for Moses, and for herself.

She sat, wondering if somewhere in Munich another bright, innovative artist might be waiting to be discovered. And then, pulling out of her reverie, she heard the door open. As if her musings had produced him, a young man walked in.

He wore a nicely tailored suit, which appeared to be new, the fabric showing no wear, yet it hung poorly on his thin frame. He held a leather portfolio, and she knew immediately he was an artist, probably a student. It was not unusual for such a young man to appear without invitation at the gallery, portfolio tucked under his arm. Sometimes they would take on a haughty attitude, as if a show of confidence would increase their chances. Sometimes they would enter like this young man, a timid mouse. Attitude seldom predicted the quality of the art.

"I've brought some of my work," the young man said, his eyes downcast, unable to meet Hanna's. His German carried the slightest regional accent. Austrian, she guessed.

He stood shivering—from nerves, surely, as the gallery was not cold—waiting awkwardly for an invitation to show off his work. He wore his hair rather longish, disregarding the accepted style of the time, his only outward sign that he wished to proclaim himself an artist. He reached up with his free hand and pushed it back over his ear. Hanna wanted to put her hand on his shoulder to steady his quivering body. Finally he looked up. He had steel-blue eyes, like crystal-clear pools of water, the depth somewhat deceiving. There was something a bit frightening about them, in both color and sound, the resonance of a heavy thumb pressed and held stubbornly to a single piano key. The movement of his body showed no signs of confidence, but there was something very determined in those eyes.

"*Bitte,*" she said. "Let's sit, so I might go over your work with you." It was a small portfolio, so she guessed he had brought drawings, watercolors possibly. She motioned him to the area between the two larger galleries, where she and Herr Kandinsky had sat minutes earlier, where a sofa, chairs, and tables had been arranged for guests. He followed her back like a shy, lost puppy. She called to Berta, a young woman they had recently taken on to do the small odd jobs Hanna had undertaken when she first came to the gallery. Berta also helped with Willy on the days Hanna brought him to work. "Please, for the young man and myself. Coffee?" Hanna turned to him.

He shook his head as if she'd offered him a cup of poison, and held the portfolio to his chest.

"That's fine, Berta. No need." The young woman smiled and did a little curtsy.

Hanna took the portfolio and placed it on the table. She opened it slowly, trying to engage him in conversation as she looked at the first drawing, a nude done in pencil. "You've studied?" she asked.

"At the Academy in Vienna," he replied in a soft voice. He sat stiffly, expectantly, on the edge of his chair, his hands folded in his lap. In this intimacy, sitting closely, she caught a scent—he smelled freshly scrubbed, like a little boy, yet tinged with nervousness, the sweat of a grown man.

"Ah, I thought perhaps you were from Vienna."

The drawing looked like one done by a student who had taken a drawing class, perhaps on a secondary-school level, but Hanna doubted a prospective student presenting such a drawing would be admitted into first year at the Academy in Vienna. She suspected that he was lying to her about his studies.

If Herr Fleischmann had been there, Hanna would have called him into the gallery to examine the student's work. She took no pleasure in sending them away. Moses was much more honest. "Better crush their hopes now," he would tell her after the artist tucked his drawings and canvases back in his portfolio, hung his head, and left with hopes destroyed, ego forever bruised.

But this afternoon, Hanna was alone.

Carefully and respectfully she turned the drawing over and

placed it to the side to reveal the next. It was another drawing of a woman. The angle of her arm made her look distorted, but unfortunately Hanna didn't believe this was the artist's intent. She laughed inwardly, making every effort not to show how terrible she thought this drawing was. They had recently shown work from the cubists, and Hanna loved the way the figures were purposely distorted. Picasso was a master at this. But Picasso could paint a human figure so real one might believe it could step out of the canvas. Picasso had moved beyond a mere imitation of life. It was particularly sad when, as in this young man's case, the artist had attempted a realistic drawing of a woman and had failed so miserably.

Hanna could sense, and then actually feel him take in several deep breaths, and for a moment she thought he might pass out right there on the table. She wanted desperately to say something kind.

She turned to the next drawing. Nicely done. The Opera House in Vienna. Ah, his talent lay not in a representation of a living body, but in a structure made of stone. He had quite skillfully reproduced the building. His perspective was flawless, the composition commendable. "This one is quite nice," she said.

He let out a relieved breath, so she quickly added, not to get his hopes up, "Nice, though it's not the type of work we're showing here at the Fleischmann now."

"But, you like it?" he asked hopefully, reaching out with his voice.

"You show a definite skill for this type of drawing. Perhaps your talent lies in the design of buildings."

"I've often been told I show great talent in this area, that I might be an architect. I earned a living in Vienna with these drawings. Then various commercial work, doing posters, travel brochures and postcards. I've been doing some paintings. I'd like to bring them in, but I thought perhaps if you saw the drawings first."

He struck her as one who, once a small compliment was paid, became like a wound-up mechanical toy. As if the energy of a kind word could provide the momentum for him to go on and on. And, of course, these young artists, they all wanted to be recognized for their paintings, and so few of them would ever gain the praise they so desperately sought.

"We're really not showing this type of work now," she repeated, regretting the encouragement she'd given him. Oh, how she wished Moses had been here for this one. For a moment, she thought about going to the office and asking Josef to come attend to this young man.

They sat for a few more moments, and then finally, realizing she had no more to say, no further encouragement to offer, he gathered up the drawings, his fingers moving with fanatic fervor. His lips pressed together tightly, and his face took on an almost ghostly pale. When he looked up at her, Hanna felt that had his lips parted at this point, he would more likely have taken a bite out of her than have spoken to her. His pale blue eyes shot through her.

"Thank you for bringing them in," she said. "I wish you the best of luck." They both stood.

He said nothing more, as if he were a spoiled child who could respond only to continuous adoration. Hanna felt almost like his mother, as if she had just disciplined him for bad behavior.

He walked quickly toward the door without looking back. The tip of his shoe caught on the carpet, and Hanna feared he would fall, but he caught himself and continued. He pulled the door open with a quick jerk. It closed slowly and quietly behind him without the slam she was sure he would have wished for her ears. She watched as he marched down the street, and it seemed his posture suddenly straightened. He held his head high as if to say, *You're not getting me down, you old witch. I know who I am. You won't destroy me.*

I will hear from you again, Hanna thought as she watched

him disappear into the crowd on Theatinerstrasse. He was not an artist, but he had an almost frightening determination about him. Then she felt a chill, as if the air in the room had cooled, and it was she who shivered now.

Hanna walked back into the second gallery and asked Berta to fetch her a cup of tea to warm herself. She sat, unable to get the image of this man out of her mind, unable to shake the feelings of impending doom that he had left behind.

He had not told Hanna his name. He did not introduce himself. But the drawings were all signed—A. Hitler.

CHAPTER TWELVE

Lauren and Isabella

New York City
August 2009

"Picasso, Cézanne, Matisse, Chagall, Klimt, Schiele, Van Gogh, Kandinsky, Münter, Jawlensky," Isabella said. "Yes, paintings by all of these artists hung in the gallery and in our home in Munich." She closed her eyes, and Lauren imagined the old woman was seeing these paintings along the hallway, in the music room and parlor, rooms she had described to Lauren with a clear and detailed memory.

"Your mother and father knew these artists, but did *you* know any of them personally?" Lauren asked.

"Many of these artists were before my time, but there were others I met, at the gallery, as guests in our home. Making acquaintance with one of these artists back then didn't seem like an event—it was just what my parents did. I never met Wassily Kandinsky, but I do remember meeting Ms. Münter, who was Kandinsky's girlfriend—his mistress, some might say, as he was married when they took up with one another. She was friendly with my mother, and I do have a vague recollection of her. I guess the memory sticks because most of the artists back then were men. A few women, but not many.

"The Fleischmann Gallery was particularly known for exhibitions of a group of artists founded by Kandinsky and Franz Marc. The Swiss artist Paul Klee later joined them. Their name originally came from the name of an almanac edited by Kandinsky and Marc. *Der Blaue Reiter*."

"The Blue Rider," Lauren translated.

"Yes, both Kandinsky and Franz Marc incorporated horses, sometimes men riding horses, into their work. And they both seemed to favor the color blue."

Lauren thought of the lovely colors used by both artists, Wassily Kandinsky and Franz Marc. Blues and yellows, pure and bright, presented in the most unusual ways. Animals in tones never found in nature. Exciting shapes on canvas, often without any correlation to true, real images. She glanced again at the painting of the blue horses, and then envisioned the lively colors and mysterious forms of Kandinsky's *Composition II*.

"What was happening in Germany was rather progressive," Lauren said. "So many associate these new art movements with France—you know the Impressionists and Postimpressionists. Few are aware of what was taking place artistically in Germany during the early part of the twentieth century."

"How true, how true," Isabella said, shaking her head, but smiling at the same time. "Yes, it was very progressive. My mother felt privileged to be a witness to this creativity and originality. A participant, in a sense, really. As you know, those who are dealing art can have an enormous influence, as can collectors and patrons, those who support these artists."

"Without this support, many of these artists would have been unable to continue their work," Lauren said, thinking how exciting it would have been for both Hanna and Moses to be part of this history. She wondered if they realized how influential these artists would become.

Being a dealer or patron of contemporary art was always a bit of a gamble.

"At the same time," Mrs. Fletcher told her, "a group of equally innovative artists, including Fritz Bleyl, Ernst Ludwig Kirchner, Erich Heckel, and Karl Schmidt-Rottluff, known as *Die Brücke*, had formed in Dresden, then moved on to Berlin."

"The Bridge," Lauren said, her eyes resting on a painting of a street scene, houses in golds, reds, and greens, a boxy composition that had seemed familiar, though earlier she was unable to identify the artist. Now she realized it was a Schmidt-Rottluff. She caught Isabella's eye. The woman's chin, as well as her lips, lifted in a subtle gesture of respect and acknowledgment.

It was exciting to speak with someone who had such an understanding of German art during this period, though Lauren was aware that Isabella Fletcher hadn't even been born at the time. Had she learned this from her mother or father? Had her mother taken her by the hand, approached the various paintings in the gallery, in the home, and explained to the child who each artist was, which particular circle of artists he was associated with? Lauren smiled at the thought.

Isabella appeared to be enjoying this conversation, too, as if she appreciated Lauren's knowledge of a time that many had forgotten as a black cloud began to gather over Germany.

Then, as if this cloud had descended over the room in which the two women sat, Isabella Fletcher's face suddenly shifted, taking on a grave pallor. She held her hands in her lap, one upon the other, shuffling restlessly as if suddenly, she did not want to continue.

Lauren sat quietly, attempting to gather some careful words to keep the conversation flowing, when Mrs. Fletcher said, "Then everything changed. When the war started."

"In the late thirties," Lauren said.

"Oh, no, no, no," Isabella answered, a touch of anger in her tone as if she were scolding a naughty child. "Why is it you young people think there was just one war?"

"You're talking about the First World War." Lauren was offended that Mrs. Fletcher thought she had so little understanding of world history. Given the way the old woman was jumping around without regard to chronology, anyone might have trouble following her story.

"Yes, I'm speaking of what we called the Great War." Isabella closed her eyes briefly, as if attempting to rid her mind of the horrors. "Millions of young soldiers died, almost two million of them German. I had two uncles—my mother's brothers Karl and Peter—whom I never even met. They both died in the war. Helene, my father's older daughter, lost her son, Little Jakob. I never even knew him. He was barely nineteen, a beautiful young man, from photos I remember—in his uniform, so dashing. Jakob wanted to be an airplane pilot, lured by the romance of it all. He would never fly, never have the opportunity for that and so much more that should have been his." Isabella's eyes met Lauren's. "You wonder how something that happened years before I was born could have had such a profound effect on my life."

Lauren understood that the events during and after the First World War, particularly in Germany, had much to do with the origins of the second. And she knew many young Jewish men, such as Jakob Kaufmann, had given their lives for their country in the Great War.

"Honestly," Isabella said, "many in Germany would claim it was just one long, uninterrupted war. Life wasn't much better for many Germans between the two wars. Even when the fighting was over in November of 1918, when Germany accepted the armistice, the suffering went on." Her tone was bitter. "Blockades set up during the war remained, starving much of the population. People were forced to eat pinecones and nettles and flour made from chestnuts."

Lauren sat without words, waiting for Isabella to continue, again fingering the silk edge of the throw pillow.

"Oh, yes, life was unkind to so many Germans," Mrs. Fletcher said with a sigh. "My parents were wealthy enough that they weathered the storm, but there were others who barely got by. My mother's younger sister, Leni, and her husband, Uncle Kurt, would have starved if they and their children had not moved in with my parents for a while. Leni was my mother's younger sister. She had a stepsister, Dora, whom she couldn't stand. She married a Nazi."

Lauren realized how many had been caught up in these times, young men sent off to war, never to return, people dying of starvation. Everyone in Germany had been affected in some way, even the wealthy.

"I suppose I'm boring you with this family history," Isabella said. "Most of it I know only from stories, many I overheard from the grown-ups when I was a child. Everyone said I looked just like Leni, which I always took as a compliment, as she was stunning. She was the blonde in the family. The most beautiful, but I think there was always some jealousy, at least from what Aunt Katie said, because Leni didn't make as favorable a marriage as her sisters. She married a factory worker in Munich—well, actually no, I think they married in Weitnau, then came to Munich to work. This was very typical back then—farmworkers coming to the city for factory jobs. Munich in the years before the war had grown to a large metropolis of over half a million citizens and much of the middle class was made up of rural folks like Leni and her husband. The pay was good, well, before the war, before the terrible inflation . . ." Isabella emitted a feeble laugh of resignation. "Excuse me again, Ms. O'Farrell. I do sound like a very old lady, carrying on like this."

"Please," Lauren said, "I'd like to know more. This history of your family as well as your knowledge of Germany's history, it's sad, but fascinating. I find it very interesting, and it is too important to forget."

"Yes," Isabella replied, "it is. I remember my aunt used to go on and on, talking about this family member or that one, jumping from here to there, talking about people I never met. But sometimes I wish I had listened better. So much family history is lost just because no one listens. It is shameful when such history is lost. Or when it's never even told."

Lauren nodded in agreement, thinking of how little she'd known of her father's early life when she herself was a child. How she had been hesitant to ask, seeing even in her innocence how reluctant he was to share the details of his childhood. She knew now that her father had grown up in London, that he'd come to America to teach at UC Berkeley in the sixties. He and Lauren's mother met through friends, though she knew very little about that. Her father, Felix Rosenthal II, taught chemistry; her mother was an artist. An odd match, she always thought. Her father spoke with a British accent, which made everything he said sound intellectual and important, though he spoke little of things that mattered. Lauren's mother, Ruth Goldman Rosenthal, was an artist, yet during the time she was raising her children—Lauren and her brother, Aaron—she seldom painted.

"This all happened," Isabella said quietly, twisting the ring on her finger, "before I was born. But you hear stories. You know how sometimes you look back on your life, at things that happened or things you might have heard as a child, and in retrospect they suddenly make sense?" Isabella shook her head and her thin lips slowly curved into a half smile. "Well, maybe you're too young yet."

"No, I do understand," Lauren replied. "There are times when you can look at things more objectively from a distance."

Isabella said no more, as if this sudden openness and outpouring had emptied her of words. Her eyes moved along the wall, again settling on the window, and then she glanced thoughtfully down at the tea tray. For a second Lauren thought she was going to pick it up, stand, and announce they were finished. She searched desperately in her mind, trying to come up with the right observation or question, and finally said, "How did all this—the events and aftermath of the first war—affect business at the gallery?" She hoped she didn't sound insensitive, that her interest would provide a gentle nudge for Isabella to continue.

After several moments the old woman replied, "During the war, business was practically nonexistent." She took in a deep breath, and paused. "Many young artists were called up to fight. Young Franz Marc was killed in battle." She motioned toward the painting of the plump blue horses. "Even for those who didn't go to war, supplies were difficult to find. And many of the foreign artists working in Germany were forced to flee. Suddenly, these men had become enemies. Wassily Kandinsky, though he'd lived in Germany off-and-on for almost fifteen years, was given but twenty-four hours to remove himself when Russia became involved in the conflict." Again she stopped before going on. "The aftermath of the war brought a whole new era of creativity—Max Beckman, Otto Dix, men who had served and come back home. Some of it is very gory, very depressing. But it certainly expressed a darkness, a despair, a sense of loss that had fallen all over Germany after the war." Isabella's eyes rested on the small etching of the distorted, injured soldiers.

"You asked if any of these are originals," she said. "Yes, a few. I know it may seem strange but the etching by Otto Dix was a gift from Andrew. He found it here in New York at a private gallery and bought it for me as an anniversary gift. A painting of war as a gift of love." She shook her head and a quiet laugh escaped. "A form of self-expression." She looked directly at Lauren. "That's very important, you know, that an artist be free to express his or her inner feelings."

"Yes," Lauren agreed, "free artistic expression is essential for creativity."

"A few of the others are originals, none of the paintings, but a few etchings and drawings." Again Mrs. Fletcher smoothed her skirt with a nervous hand. "And yes, there is documentation to verify ownership." There was a little snip at the end of the sentence, Mrs. Fletcher telling Lauren she could not challenge the ownership of any of these.

"After the Great War, the First World War," Mrs. Fletcher continued, "Germany was a political and economic mess, even an emotional mess you might say. The citizens of Germany felt as if they had been betrayed by their own leaders who signed the hated armistice. *Stabbed in the back* was the saying." The woman gave off a little shudder, as if she could feel it, a physical rather than metaphorical sensation. "You've heard that phrase, Ms. O'Farrell?"

She nodded.

"Germans thought they were winning the war, if you can believe that, but then with the treaty they were forced to admit guilt, take responsibility for damages. They were saddled with enormous reparation payments and forbidden to rebuild the military. Territories and colonies were taken away—divvied up by the victors. A republic was formed, but many Germans were not ready to give up their kings and monarchs. Women were given the right to vote. Women in Germany gained the right to vote before American women."

"American women gained the right to vote in . . . the early twenties?"

"Nineteen twenty, I believe," Isabella said. "But in Germany it was a year earlier. This new government, the German Republic, though hated by many, was also surprisingly supportive of art, literature, and music. Berlin became the center of a cultural life of theaters and nightclubs, of jazz, and other entertainment which many considered indecent, including nude performers and transvestite balls. Some thought it was little more than pornography, depravity, and perverted behavior. The Bauhaus, the school of architecture and applied arts in Weimar, where Kandinsky had taken a position, was supported by the Republic."

"He came back to Germany after the war?" Lauren asked, though it was a fact she was well aware of.

"Germany, yes. Munich, no. His paintings took on a new form of expression, geometric shapes, lines, forms, completely abstract now, still plenty of color."

"His most commonly reproduced work probably—paintings from his Bauhaus phase." Lauren remembered that Mrs. Fletcher had expressed a dislike for this period of the artist's work. "He'd gone completely abstract by then."

"You know Kandinsky is often called the father of abstract art?"

"Yes," Lauren replied. "He was a great influence on those artists stretching beyond realism."

"The pieces in our gallery were all from before that time. He and my mother had a bit of a falling-out."

"Oh?" Lauren asked with interest, leaning forward.

"His invitation to exit from Germany was so sudden that he had to leave many of his paintings with Ms. Münter. When he returned he wanted them back. By then they had broken up—not cordially, as I understand. Kandinsky asked my mother to act as a go-between, as she was friendly with Ms. Münter. He implored her to persuade the woman to hand over his paintings, but Mother wrote and told him that it was between the two of them." Isabella laughed. "My mother had good sense, in that respect. He'd already married a young Russian woman, half his age—he'd divorced the first Russian wife. Ms. Münter was heartbroken. She refused to return many of the paintings."

Lauren was aware of this, also aware that in a sense the story had a happy ending—at least for the paintings that Gabriele Münter refused to return. "Your Kandinsky *Composition*? Still in the family then?" she asked.

"Yes," Isabella replied.

"This was during the mid-twenties," Lauren said, wanting to make sure they were both situated in the same time period. "Between the two wars, a period when there were still some innovative things taking place in the German world of art."

"Oh, yes, definitely. With the open views of the Republic, modern art was shown in the galleries and state-funded museums. Artists were once more free to paint, free to express themselves, and supplies were readily available. Eventually even the general economy picked up somewhat, particularly after the Americans helped in rewriting the terms of reparation. Though the $33 billion debt that had been dictated by the Treaty of Versailles was not forgiven, the terms of payment were rewritten. This did not make the injustices of the agreement acceptable to the Germans, but it did ease the pain.

"Both of my parents believed this might be temporary. The Americans and Germans had fought on opposite sides in the Great War, and I think my mother understood it might not last— this *peace built on quicksand*, as the American president Woodrow Wilson called it—so she went to visit Käthe and her family in America. My father remained in Germany, feeling the business needed his full attention."

"What year was that?"

"Nineteen twenty-six."

"So, you were . . . ?"

"Not yet." Isabella held up a finger, again telling Lauren to be patient. "This was the year *before* I was born. "Willy accompanied her. He was in his teens then, but in so many ways still a little boy."

Both Isabella's and Lauren's eyes moved together toward the photo with the shattered glass—the young Isabella, now an old woman, and the young man who would never grow old.

CHAPTER THIRTEEN

Hanna

America
Summer 1926

It was a long journey on the boat. Willy loved it. He went about visiting with the other passengers, taking part in any recreational activities available, looking out onto the vast expanse of water with childlike delight. Sasha had accompanied them, and was kept busy following Willy about the large boat, making sure he didn't bother the other passengers.

Hanna was not particularly fond of this mode of travel—the lack of scenery, the dearth of color, made her feel melancholy. Yet she questioned whether the gloom she felt within her had perhaps begun before their departure. She planned to stay in America for the entire summer, the longest she had ever been away from her husband, but he had expressed little concern over this lengthy separation. She understood he could not leave Munich. Business and the general economy were much too fragile now. People were convinced there would be another war. Nothing had been stable for years.

Often, particularly in the evenings, she found herself alone, reflecting on her life, her marriage. She and Moses had celebrated their twenty-second anniversary in April. She felt herself grinning as she recalled his unexpected proposal, their trip to Austria and Italy, the years that followed, their travels in search of art, the life they shared as they worked so compatibly, so happily at the gallery. Back then she had felt so close to him, so connected through their shared passion for the artists' creativity.

Moses often teased her that he had no choice but to marry her. He'd taught her everything he knew about art, about the art of dealing art, and he couldn't let her go now.

It was always presented in a lighthearted, loving way, but now at times Hanna wondered if this *was* the reason he had married her—because of the art. It had always been a big part of what had drawn them together. She knew that. But for the past several years, it seemed that this was all that was left—the art, the business. Yet, hadn't their feelings for each other ebbed and flowed many times throughout these past twenty-two years?

When Willy came to them, imperfect as he was, this change in their lives, this baby who was not at all the child they had prepared for, created an enormous chasm between them. Yet it was the threat of losing him that had brought them back together. Then the war, the turmoil in Germany that followed, both their efforts thrown into ensuring the gallery's survival. Business was bad, then things improved. Artists were inspired, not by images of the imagination, but by the despair, and a whole new form of art emerged. Their marriage, Hanna reflected, was not unlike Germany itself—joy followed by despair, interspersed with hope, and then newness emerging, then back to uncertainty.

As she stared out onto the vast expanse of colorless ocean, she reflected on how it might represent the current state of her marriage. Flat and dull. Yet, didn't this very body have great depth? She and Moses had a relationship that ran very deep over the expanse of many years, many shared experiences. They loved each other and they would be fine. And maybe this time apart was exactly what they needed.

* * *

Hans and Käthe lived on a dairy farm in New York, which confused Hanna at first because she didn't understand how they could have a farm in the city. But they were in the *state* of New York, in Onondaga County, a short distance from a small village south of the city of Syracuse. They had established a creamery where they produced their own cheese, based on family recipes Hans' father had developed in Germany.

Hanna had not seen Käthe for more than seventeen years, and though they had written, there was much to catch up on. The early-summer mornings were filled with talk and laughter. Hanna helped with the cooking and cleaning, finding amusement in the fact that in America, even in prosperous families, everyone had chores. Käthe teased Hanna about bringing along her maid, though she explained Sasha was as much a friend as an employee.

Each day, Hanna rose and helped Käthe with breakfast—an enormous amount of food—bacon, eggs, potatoes, toasted bread.

"My husband needs a big meal to get him through the morning," Käthe said, giving Hans a little peck on the cheek as he returned from the early-morning milking. He grinned as he sat, jabbing with enthusiasm at a large pile of potatoes. He was a quiet man, but Hanna could see there was still great affection in the way Käthe and Hans loved each other. She wondered, If she and Moses had been sweethearts from their youth, as her sister and her husband had, might their marriage have had this tenderness? She could not escape the fact that she was Moses' third wife, that he had loved two wives before Hanna. And she could never escape the thought that she was second best at that, perhaps even third, as she had never known his first wife, Young Helene's mother. Perhaps all married couples have these ups and downs, she reasoned, and she should be grateful for what she still shared with her husband. And perhaps, she reflected, we see in others only the surface. As with the ocean, much lies beneath.

One morning as the two sisters walked along the lane next to the pasture, Käthe took Hanna's arm in hers. "It's so good to have you here," she said. "I wish you could stay." Earlier in the visit Hanna had described some of the difficulties facing the people of Germany, the distrust many held for the Republic, and Käthe had suggested—more than once—that the Fleischmanns move to America.

The two women stopped as they approached the corral. Hanna propped her elbows on the fence and watched as Käthe's daughter Ella led the horse with Willy astride, grinning and waving at his mother and aunt. Sasha stood on the opposite side of the corral, her face scrunched up in an expression that told Hanna she was concerned that Willy might tumble off at any time. Sasha was a small woman, and Hanna guessed that if her son took a fall, Sasha would be incapable of getting him up. Though Willy was short of stature, he was much heavier than Sasha now and of equal height. Hanna nodded at Sasha, as if to say, *It's fine.* She tried not to deny Willy the fun that other boys might enjoy.

"Look at me, Mama," he called out.

"You look like a cowboy," Hanna called back. At fifteen, he was still a child, bubbling with excitement.

"Could you ever live like this again?" Käthe asked. "In the country?"

"I'm having a wonderful time," Hanna replied. She was, but she missed the excitement of the gallery, the city, and she missed her husband. "Willy would love it."

"If you decide to move here," Käthe suggested, "Moses could open a gallery in New York City. I hear the art scene there has begun to compete with that in many cities in Europe."

"Moses would resist such an idea, I'm sure."

"We'll take you for a visit," Käthe said. "You can see for yourself and then tell Moses."

* * *

The following week Käthe and Hans took Hanna to visit New York City. She found the pace of life exciting, much more like home, and even the colors and sounds of the city reminded her of Munich. She was tempted to write to Moses and suggest he come join them, that they move the family to America, the land of opportunity where democracy worked, where one determined one's own future. But she knew he would never leave Germany.

Moses wrote often. The political instability they had witnessed for many years continued. Why was it so difficult for this republic to work in Germany? Hanna wondered.

They stayed through the summer. Käthe and Hans had a large family and they tended one another as they had in their own big family in Weitnau. Hanna often felt as if she had returned to her youth at the family farm in Bavaria, and she realized how much Willy had missed, being an only child in the city.

Willy loved America. He loved the country, the horses and cows, dogs and kittens. He loved his cousins and second cousins, and one day he asked his mother, "Mama, may I have a sister or a brother?"

"You love your cousins, don't you, dear Willy?" Hanna replied, giving him a hug.

"I want my own so when we get home I will have someone to play with."

Hanna was now forty-two and had longed for another child, but she knew it would not be.

"We'll come back to visit again someday," she offered.

She thought Willy's heart might break when they said their farewells, but she reminded him he would see his papa after they got off the big boat.

No sooner had they embarked from New York than Willy took ill. It started with the familiar cough, moving into his lungs.

Within a day he was so ill, Hanna feared that she might lose him. She called for the ship's doctor, but longed for Dr. Langermann in Munich, or even a specialist in America. She asked the captain if he could turn the ship back, so impaired was her thinking.

"There are other passengers, a schedule," he said kindly.

"Yes, of course, I understand."

For two days, Hanna barely slept. She stayed beside Willy, having meals brought to the cabin.

On the third evening, Sasha said, "Please, Frau Fleischmann, I can sit with Willy. Some fresh air would do you good."

"*Danke*, Sasha. Perhaps you're right." She threw on her wrap and hat and went up on deck. The sea was calm, the sky clear, the sounds soft and subdued. She thought of how much Willy loved the water, running about the big boat, visiting with the other passengers. She thought of Moses and wondered how he would survive if they lost him. How would she survive? Hanna closed her eyes and prayed that God would protect her son and bring him home safely.

"*Guten Abend*. It's a lovely evening."

She had not heard the man approach, nor had she seen anyone on the deck nearby, and for a moment Hanna thought she was hallucinating because the voice sounded like Moses.

When she turned, she must have had a startled look on her face, for the man said, "Pardon, I didn't mean to frighten you."

She could see now, the voice, the color had a touch more red than Moses', and the man, who was tall and slender—almost too thin—looked nothing like her husband. The moon, full and ripe, provided enough illumination that she could make out his face, which was angular, catching the light in the most interesting way, a highlighted cheekbone, a slight cleft in the chin. His hair appeared to be blond and he wore a full, well-groomed mustache. The softness of his colors, the sharp angles of his face and form, created an intriguing contrast. He was one of the most physically appealing men she had ever seen, and Hanna was overcome with bewilderment, tainted with shame that she would notice this, when she was so fraught with worry over her son's health.

"Excuse me, sir," she said, and turned and left, returning to her cabin.

The following morning, there was still no improvement in Willy's condition. Frantically Hanna called for the ship's doctor.

"Rest and liquid," he offered. "Make sure he does not become dehydrated." She sat with Willy all day, lifting his head from the pillow, helping him to swallow. Seeing her mistress was exhausted, Sasha said she would sit with him while Hanna got some sleep.

But she couldn't sleep, so Hanna threw on her wrap and left the cabin. She returned to the same place she'd met the stranger the evening before.

This time she was aware when he approached.

"*Guten Abend,*" Hanna said.

"*Guten Abend,*" he replied. "I must offer my apologies for frightening you last evening."

"And I for my abruptness," she said.

"Perhaps I should also apologize for my approaching a woman standing alone," he added, and Hanna smiled inwardly. Was he expressing regret for something that he had done again this evening?

They stood silently, gazing out to sea, and she felt a welcome comfort in the quiet, the gentle sway of the boat, the mere presence of this man.

Finally he said, "I haven't seen you in the dining room. You are traveling alone?"

"With my son. He's taken ill, and I'm not inclined to be very sociable."

"Again, my apologies." He turned to leave. He seemed to misunderstand that she was only explaining why she was not taking dinner with the other passengers, attempting to account for her rude behavior the evening before. But what excuse could she offer to herself for having returned, for wishing that she might see him once more?

"No, please," she called out, "stay."

He made no further movement, said nothing, but then slowly he walked back toward her.

"A woman in my employment for many years has accompanied us," Hanna told him. "She's sitting with Willy now. I wouldn't leave him alone." She felt a need to explain this to the man—that she was a good, loving mother. "We've been visiting my sister and her family in America." Suddenly Hanna was overcome with an urge to talk—about anything, nothing, everything. "My husband was not able to accompany us. His business . . . It's not a good time for him to leave for an extended period." Hanna knew it was the fatigue manifesting itself in this chattiness. She didn't want the man to leave.

"It is difficult," he said kindly, "so difficult when you feel helpless. If there was something I could do."

"Thank you for your concern."

"How old is your son?"

"Fifteen," Hanna replied, "but in many ways he is much younger. He doesn't learn as quickly as other children. He requires special care. But such a sweet boy, such a pleasure to . . . I'm so frightened that we might lose him." She was crying now, the man standing beside her, obviously not knowing what to say or do. What an uncomfortable position she had put him in. She rubbed the back of her hand against her eyes, and then gazed up at him. An anxious look pressed his brow, and she sensed he wanted desperately to console her. If he had taken her in his arms at this moment, Hanna would not have protested. He reached in his pocket and took out a fresh handkerchief and handed it to her.

"Please," she said with a sniffle, "forgive me."

"Forgive me for having so little comfort to offer," he said. "I, too, have children."

"*Danke,*" she said. "Thank you. I must go tend to my son."

"I wish you both well," he said.

The following morning, finally, Willy began to show improvement. By afternoon, he was sitting up, chatting, eating, asking if he might go outdoors to see the big ocean and the other people. "Perhaps tomorrow," Hanna told him, overjoyed with Willy's renewed energy and enthusiasm, yet still taking precautions to ensure his full recovery.

Now she felt as if she had an obligation to share this good news with the man.

Again that evening she returned to the deck and found him, as if he were waiting for her.

"So wonderful to hear of your son's recovered health," he said after Hanna told him how well Willy was doing now. "I thought about you and your son all day." He smiled. He had a lovely, generous smile, and she felt as if he had been saving it up for this good news.

"Thank you." She reached in her bag and produced the freshly laundered handkerchief. "For being kind, for listening, for the use of your handkerchief." She handed it to him, and then formally, awkwardly, she said, "Hanna Fleischmann." It seemed strange that they had spent the past two evenings in each other's company and had yet to introduce themselves.

"Johann Keller," he said, placing the handkerchief back in his pocket. "You are returning home?"

"Yes, Germany," she replied. "Munich. And you?"

"Zurich."

For several moments they stood without words, as if both were attempting to determine what to say next. Hanna's message had been delivered, she had returned the handkerchief. Should she excuse herself now?

He said, "Your husband was not able to accompany you because of business?"

She nodded.

"What is your husband's business?" he asked with interest.

"Art."

"Your husband is an artist?" His brow rose as if he couldn't imagine Hanna as the wife of an artist. His eyes ran over her, discreetly, her fine clothing, the latest fashions purchased just before her departure for America. Without doubt, he was thinking if this woman is married to an artist, he is a very successful artist.

"No, not an artist, but a dealer of art."

"I see," he said thoughtfully. "In Munich. A rather lively place for art in the last several decades."

"You have an interest in art?"

"Coincidently, yes," he said, offering now a delighted smile of discovery. "I work for a private gallery in Zurich."

"Why, how interesting. Do tell me about your gallery."

Again, he studied her, and then his lovely smile widened as if he had just come upon a great treasure. "Hanna Fleischmann?"

She nodded.

"Your husband is Moses Fleischmann?"

"You know him?"

"Of him, yes, of course. Anyone dealing art in Europe is aware of Moses Fleischmann, of his eye for what has often set the trend in the new movements. The proprietor of the gallery in which I'm employed has purchased several paintings through the Fleischmann Gallery."

"Oh, please tell me," she said, her voice jumping with excitement, "which artists?"

"Beckman, Kirchner, August Macke, Kandinsky—"

"Kandinsky is my artist," she cut in, "not Moses'."

He looked startled, but intrigued, perhaps even charmed, though this was certainly not her intention. "Your artist?" he asked with a grin. "How is it that you might claim the Russian Kandinsky?"

She went on to tell him of her own personal interest in the art chosen by the Fleischmann Gallery, the paintings that hung in their home, the Kandinsky *Composition* that had brought such pleasure to both herself and Willy.

"I understand he's up to eight *Compositions* now," Herr Keller said. "How many do you predict?"

"Who could even venture a guess," she replied with a laugh. "The first have little resemblance to the last, and the man continues to reinvent himself."

"Which makes him all the more interesting," Herr Keller observed.

"Yes," Hanna agreed.

They spoke of artists who had been painting in Germany since the war, surrounded, they both admitted, by substantial controversy, and of Swiss artists who were being shown at the gallery in Zurich, of Paul Klee, whom the Fleischmanns had represented in Munich.

The evening passed so quickly that the sky was beginning to lighten when finally she said, "My goodness, I must return to my cabin to check on Willy. It has been a pleasure visiting with you, Herr Keller."

"The pleasure has been mine, Frau Fleischmann."

The following evening, without having spoken of the possibility, they met again, as if they had scheduled this meeting place and time. They talked more about art, artists and creativity, and self-expression. He told her that he, too, had been visiting his sister who lived in New York. His wife and children, three sons, had remained home in Zurich. He asked about her sister and brother-in-law and she told him about their dairy farm and business.

"Koebler Creamery," she said, "established before the war, using old family recipes developed in Germany. They are just now beginning to make ice cream. You'll have to try it the next time you visit New York City, where it should be available soon. Hans Koebler is a savvy businessman."

"Koebler. I'll keep that in mind. Fine German cheese in America. Now, ice cream," he added with a warm smile, "can always win my heart."

A smile warm enough to melt ice cream, Hanna thought, feeling her own heart jump as if through a ring of fire.

He said, "You have told me about your husband, your involvement in your husband's business, your family in America. Tell me now more about Hanna Fleischmann." He seemed genuinely interested. She told him of growing up on a dairy farm in Bavaria, about her many brothers and sisters, her father, mother, and stepmother.

"Ah," he said, "yes, you have the wholesome, fresh look of a girl from the country."

"Wholesome?" she asked with a laugh and a blush. She had spent much of her time at her sister's outdoors and her naturally pale complexion had taken on some sun, a splatter of freckles across her nose.

"I didn't mean to offend you," he said. "You appear very healthy, as if you have spent time outdoors."

"This you believe is what a woman wants to hear from a man?" She could not believe they were speaking so freely, so intimately. She was a married woman, he a married man. Surely this was not proper behavior. "Do I take this as a compliment," she continued, unabashed, "or an insult?"

"A compliment, of course. Health and vitality is a desirable quality in a woman."

Desirable? she thought. They were flirting with each other. How could she allow herself to carry on in such a manner?

"But," he added, "when it is combined with the sophistication of an educated, cultured woman of the city, how could any man resist." Finally he blushed a little, too, but did not hesitate to continue. "How was it that you came to Munich, that you became the wife of Moses Fleischmann?" They were veering the conversation back to this—the fact that she was a married woman, as if they both realized the inappropriateness of such talk.

She told him about the day she had simply walked out of the house, down the lane, away from the farm, and taken off for Munich alone.

He grinned. "A young woman with a great sense of adventure, unafraid of the unknown world."

Was she venturing forth once more, Hanna wondered, into an unknown world?

She spoke of becoming an employee in the Fleischmann home, how she was taken into the family. She even told him—much to her own astonishment—about going to the Academy of Fine Arts. About the drawing Moses had given her as a gift.

They spoke of the difficult times that came from the war, of her personal challenges in caring for Willy, in keeping up with the developments in the art world over these past years. She told him about the colors, something she had shared with so few. Other than this stranger Hanna met on the boat, the only man with whom she felt she could speak openly was Josef, but he was a man with whom a woman could have nothing more than friendship.

Hanna woke the next morning, thinking of Johann, eager to see him again, wondering how she could bear waiting until evening. The day moved slowly as she presented herself one reason, then another, to justify her actions. At the beginning she was vulnerable, lonely, and concerned for Willy. She needed comfort, then someone with whom to share her joy in Willy's recovery. Now the thought of Johann made her hands warm, her head light, her pulse quicken. By late afternoon, all attempts at defending this friendship had broken down, because Hanna knew it had become more than mere friendship. She was behaving like a foolish, silly, lovesick girl. She was a woman of forty-two, a married woman at that, and yet she was acting like a smitten adolescent.

She loved Moses, but if there had ever been this excitement about it, she did not recall. He was a good father, a good husband, but he had never loved her as he had loved Helene. She had been his one perfect love and perhaps in life we are allowed but one. These feelings for Johann Keller could not be denied; perhaps they were meant to meet. Unable to dismiss these growing emotions, Hanna pushed aside her good judgment and went to him again.

That evening, without any warning, he placed his finger under her chin, tilted her face to his, and kissed her. She did not resist. She could not deny that she had participated fully in this unexpected kiss.

I must stop here, she told herself. But she knew she had already gone too far. She returned to her own cabin, but the following evening when he invited her to come to his cabin, she did.

She was discreet, waiting each evening until Willy was asleep before she went to him. When she told Sasha she was stepping out for some fresh air, the woman said, "Yes, Frau Fleischmann," and nothing more. Even if she were aware, Hanna trusted that Sasha would never betray her. Yet Hanna would not have thought herself capable of betraying Moses, and here she was, going willingly, gladly, happily, to a man who was not her husband.

"What are we to do?" she asked one evening as he held her in his arms after they made love, both fully aware this journey was about to end. She would soon return to her own cabin as she did every night, and they would have but one more together.

"Could you give up your life in Munich?" Johann asked.

She knew she could not leave her husband. She knew she could not leave her son, or take him away from Moses.

"Could you?" she asked. "Give up your life?"

"Oh, Hanna darling, why could we not have met at a different time?"

"It must end here," she told him.

"Yes," he replied softly, pulling her closer.

They agreed that when they arrived in Europe the affair must end.

"How I have missed you both!" Moses exclaimed when he met their train at the station in Munich. He hugged his son and then took Hanna into his arms. Though Moses was always affectionate with Willy, he seldom displayed feelings for his wife in public.

"I was very sick on the boat," the boy told his father.

Moses shot Hanna, then Sasha, a concerned look. Sasha had been extremely quiet on the train ride home.

"He's fine now," Hanna reassured her husband. "Though he did give me quite a scare. It was a difficult crossing. He's fine. We're both fine." She glanced at Sasha as if to say, *It's over. We're home now.*

"I'm so happy to have you back safely again," Moses said.

Seeing Moses, hearing the comfort of his voice, stirred Hanna once more, and she realized how fortunate she was to have him in her life, what a good and kind man he was. She felt great shame over what had happened on the boat from America. She would remove any trace of Johann Keller from her mind and heart.

Her body was less cooperative. Hanna was overcome with fatigue. At first she thought it was the onset of the flu, a virus she had picked up on her crossing but had kept dormant, truly believing as a mother she could quiet a bodily invasion to remain strong to tend to her poor Willy.

When Moses came to her the night following her arrival home, she was too exhausted to respond to his affection and he was content to hold her in his arms as she fell into a fitful sleep.

The following morning at breakfast, he asked, "Are you ill, Hanna?"

"Just very tired," she replied. "It was a long journey."

He did not come to her again, and she knew he was waiting for her. But she was so very tired, and very ashamed.

The next week when she noticed the tenderness in her breasts, and then the following when she missed her monthly bleeding, Hanna knew she was with child. She was a married woman, carrying a child that was not her husband's.

The following night she went to Moses.

CHAPTER FOURTEEN

Lauren and Isabella

New York City
August 2009

"I was born in Munich in 1927," Isabella informed Lauren, who did the math quickly in her head. Isabella Fletcher was eighty-two. For a woman her age she seemed very agile in both body and mind. Lauren was about to offer a compliment, when Isabella said, "I'm told I was eager to come into this world, as I arrived several weeks early—a tiny wrinkled red little thing, with a mop of black hair, and dark blue eyes, as my mother described me. But within weeks, my skin lightened to a translucent ivory, and that dark fuzz was replaced with pale blond curls. My eyes, which the doctor said would darken, turned an even softer blue. Papa used to tease me—saying he would have loved me no matter what, but he was quite delighted that I turned out to be a true beauty." Mrs. Fletcher gave her head a modest little shake. "Oh, dear, Ms. O'Farrell, I do apologize. For a young woman perhaps this is near impossible to imagine."

"Not at all." It struck Lauren that even at eighty-two, Isabella was an attractive woman; when she was young, she would have been stunning. "You are still a beautiful woman," she added, hoping Isabella didn't find this to be patronizing.

"Thank you," Isabella replied with a nod. "It's not as easy keeping things up as it used to be." She laughed lightly.

Lauren smiled. She was definitely caught up in the story and she'd enjoyed speaking with Mrs. Fletcher about the art in Germany and throughout Europe, but they were moving very slowly toward the reason she was here. In fact, now she wasn't even sure why she was here. Learning more about Hanna Schmid Fleischmann's involvement with the Nazis' purge of art was her original intention, but now Isabella Fletcher had introduced a whole new aspect to Lauren's project—the Kandinsky *Composition*. Lauren wasn't sure why Isabella was being so open, but she didn't want to say or do anything to discourage her.

As they sat, Lauren was turning around in her mind the new facts that Isabella Fletcher had revealed, placing them beside what she already knew, attempting to see how they all fit together. According to Isabella, Kandinsky's *Composition II* had been purchased about 1911, shortly after it was created in the early part of the century. It had been Willy Fleischmann's favorite, as well as one of Hanna's favorites, and the woman had an affinity with the artist Kandinsky because they shared this affliction of synesthesia. Or perhaps it was a gift, considering how both of them made their living. But Mrs. Fletcher had said the family purchased the painting twice. Lauren wanted to know when and how that had happened. Had they purchased it a second time from the man in Berlin who owned the painting during the war? Lauren couldn't remember his name. How did *Composition II* get from the Fleischmann collection in Munich to the family in Berlin in the first place? *If* it was true that Moses and Hanna Fleischmann were the original owners.

"Ms. O'Farrell, would you like more tea?" Isabella rose.

"Yes, please," Lauren said, sensing that as long as Mrs. Fletcher kept filling the teapot, she'd keep talking. After the spilled tea incident, she was especially grateful for this offer. But with all this tea drinking, she really needed to use the restroom.

She glanced toward the hallway and asked, "May I use the powder room?"

"Second door on the right." Isabella motioned with her head as she carried the tray to the kitchen.

Lauren stood, gave her shoulders a little shake to release some of the tension and stiffness, and then grabbed her bag. She needed to call Patrick again. She'd glanced repeatedly in her bag and still hadn't received a text. If she didn't hear from him soon she'd have to leave.

She started toward the hall, but then stopped, gazing up at what appeared to be a Chagall. Quickly, she pulled her BlackBerry from her bag and snapped a picture and then, walking slowly toward the hall, she took a photo of a small Picasso drawing. Perhaps an original? Then another—the Gabriele Münter—a village scene that was very similar in style to the Kandinsky paintings from the early part of the twentieth century when the two artists were working together. Finally a Monet, one of his water lilies. How many of those had the artist painted? Lauren guessed this one was a copy.

Isabella used the half bath in the laundry room off the kitchen, deposited the wet napkins in the hamper, then walked slowly back to the stove, lifted the teapot, filled it with fresh water, and returned it to the burner. Then she sat at the table, waiting for the pot to whistle, questioning herself as to the wisdom of having invited this young woman into her home.

When Lauren O'Farrell had phoned this morning, Isabella recognized the name from an article she'd read a year or so ago. After the call, she'd found the clipping in a drawer in the bedroom and concluded then that the woman had come to inquire

about the Kandinsky, somehow having become aware of its
survival, knowing it was a painting that disappeared during the
war. Did she think Isabella had obtained it illegally? Was this
the reason for her initial lie as to why she wished to speak with
Isabella?

This was something she needed to clear up—that she was the
rightful owner of the Kandinsky. In deciding to meet with the
young woman, Isabella had reasoned that it might be beneficial
to share this information with a knowledgeable person, particularly one whose profession involved verifying ownership of art
whose history had intersected with the Nazis' reign in Germany.

But as soon as Isabella mentioned the Kandinsky, she could see
from Lauren's guarded reaction that her call was motivated by
more than a search for a missing piece of art. Isabella had been
warned many years ago that questions might arise about what her
mother had done in Germany before World War II, and she had
lived in fear of this—that someone would come to her with questions about Hanna Fleischmann. But then, nothing—no questions, no inquiries, no accusations. And even Lauren O'Farrell
yet to throw out any allegations. But, from the way the young
woman sat so politely, so attentively, prodding Isabella to open
up, to speak of her family, Isabella guessed that she was searching,
not for a specific painting but for information to condemn Hanna.
And this was why Isabella was speaking of memories she had
pushed back in her mind for many years. She wanted Lauren to
know what a beautiful, lovely, talented woman her mother had
been, how much she loved her children. She wanted to control this
conversation, to offer her side of the story—Hanna's side. Though
in truth, because of her mother's reluctance to speak of many
things, there were parts of her life that Isabella knew little about.
Did this young woman know more about Hanna than her own
daughter? And did Ms. O'Farrell think that Isabella didn't know

what she was up to? She was snooping about right now. Did she think Isabella wasn't aware of this?

Should she send her home? But she knew she'd already said too much, and now she must continue. If Lauren O'Farrell even suggested that her mother had done anything dishonorable, Isabella would defend her. If these accusations were made later, after Isabella's demise, no one would remain to stand up for Hanna.

Isabella stood and opened the drawer where she kept the table linen and lifted out two fresh napkins.

Lauren could hear Mrs. Fletcher shuffling around in the kitchen. Water running. Filling up the tea kettle. She stepped out of the living room and started down the hall toward the bathroom, glancing into the first door to the right to see an impressive dining suite with large upholstered chairs. Windows ran along the far wall, curtains drawn. A lush Oriental rug in dark reds and golds spread over the hardwood floor. Her eyes moved along the wall to the left, noting several small pictures. She stepped in and quickly snapped a photo of what looked like a Matisse, then another Chagall, then a simple line drawing that she was certain was a Picasso. Three large pictures hung above a buffet on the wall opposite the windows, all obviously prints, not paintings, all expensively framed under glass. A Van Gogh. A Klimt. A Cézanne. Each a floral motif in the artist's distinct style. None of them German, but artists who would have been rejected by the Reich's Commission of Propaganda and Public Enlightenment. All degenerate. As she stepped back, she noticed a vague rectangular shape, a darker tone than the rest of the wall. As if something else, something quite large, had at one time been there. A large rectangle, unfaded by light. Could a painting have once hung in this very spot? Kandinsky's *Composition*?

She continued down the hall into the small powder room. Her eyes darted along the walls, more paintings and prints. She easily identified a Franz Marc—a colorful composition of cats. Obviously an Isabella Fletcher favorite. And an Alexej Jawlensky, this one a drawing of a face with simple lines. Perhaps an original. She looked closely. Yes, it appeared to be authentic. Quickly, she took several pictures.

After using the bathroom, Lauren washed her hands with a delicious-smelling vanilla soap, dried them on a thick, lush, bright yellow towel, and then called Patrick, who answered right away and told her he was just about to send a text. He'd been in a conference for the past hour.

"Where are you?" he asked.

"With Mrs. Fletcher. Well, right now she's in the kitchen and I'm—"

"So, your little ploy worked out?" She could hear the smile of approval in his voice.

"I'm not sure," Lauren replied. "But, yes, I guess it did. She invited me to her home. I've got so much to tell you, but I can't leave right now. You'll be able to pick Adam up at day care?"

"No problem," he said.

"Thanks so much."

"She's Hanna's daughter?"

"Yes, and I've learned so much. I'll tell you all about it tonight."

"Can't wait," Patrick said. "See you then."

Lauren rechecked her phone to make sure the ringtone was still off before sliding it back in her bag. She'd learned from interviewing older people that they started to distrust you as soon as you pulled out some miniature electronic device, so she generally kept it out of sight and silenced. As she stepped out into the hall she heard the shrill whistle of the teapot coming from the kitchen. She moved quietly, taking several steps to an open door, and peered in. The room didn't look lived in, and from the twin beds she thought it was possibly a guest room. She glanced back to another door off the hall—the master bedroom? She could hear footsteps, Mrs. Fletcher shuffling from the kitchen toward the living room. As much as she was tempted, Lauren refrained from a closer look into the second room. Again she passed the dining room and it seemed now, as she stepped through the door for just a second, that it was only her imagination that had created the image of that darker tinted shape. The light falling into the room had changed in the time it took to boil water for tea, to use the toilet. The colors on the wall didn't even look the same as they had just a few minutes ago.

Mrs. Fletcher was setting the tray on the table when Lauren entered the living room. She'd replaced the soggy napkins with fresh ones. After they had settled down again, cups filled with hot tea, Isabella said, "You know what happened to the Kandinskys that Gabriele Münter kept when the Russian left Germany? Some of them she was forced by legal rulings to return. The others she took very good care of, hiding them at her country home in Murnau during the first war, then the years of the Nazi rule, through the destructive years of the second war. On her eightieth birthday she donated them to the city of Munich, where they are now housed in a public gallery."

"That's lovely," Lauren replied, though she knew this history. She'd visited the Lenbauchhaus in Munich where many of these paintings were displayed. "She saved them for the world to enjoy. It would have been dreadful had they been destroyed by a jilted lover, or war, or anything else."

Isabella nodded in agreement and the two women sat in silence for several moments, sipping tea. Lauren felt more relaxed, now that she'd talked to Patrick, but there was still so much more she wanted to know. About Hanna. About the Kandinsky *Composition*. About the art in the Fletcher home.

She asked, "The Kandinsky painting hung in your home in

Munich when you were a child? During the late twenties, early thirties?"

"Yes. And I have wonderful memories of those years," Isabella replied, "though I suspect my parents tried to protect me from what was going on. It's common knowledge now that these were horrific times. The stock market in New York crashed just after I turned two, and of course affected the economy of the entire world. With Germany still grappling with the aftermath of World War I, it wasn't a pleasant environment. But I had no idea. When I look back, when I read about that period of history, I can hardly reconcile it with my childhood. I was so very happy and so very loved. But yes, the country continued to struggle. Everyone was looking for something to save us. Or someone—a superhero who could restore the glory that Germany once knew."

"And that's when Adolf Hitler came into the picture," Lauren said.

"Yes," Mrs. Fletcher answered. "The perfect storm. I think that's the way they say it now—when all the conditions are exactly right for something terrifying to happen. That's when Adolf Hitler entered the picture."

CHAPTER FIFTEEN

Hanna

Munich
February–March 1932

Willy and Isabella ran up, then down, then up the stairs, checking through the hall window where they could get a better view of the street.

"I don't see them yet," Willy called in a loud voice, clearly audible to Hanna and Helene, who sat downstairs visiting in the music room. Moses and Jakob, Helene's husband, were in the library. Talking politics and business, Hanna suspected, though she had requested they refrain from such discussions for the day. It was Willy's twenty-first birthday. He had been exceptionally healthy that fall and winter, and Hanna was extremely grateful. Despite the dire conditions throughout Germany, today she felt a particular joy.

"I can't see them yet," Willy called down again.

"He's been waiting for days," Hanna told Helene. "I hope they're not much longer."

"Leni," Helene replied with a shake of her head. "Perhaps she can no longer rely on mere nature for her beauty, and it would be unfair to ask that she arrive on time without sufficient preparations." Helene, with all her jewels and expensive clothes, could not compete with Leni's beauty. The woman had gained considerable weight since Hanna had first met her, yet Leni, who'd been pregnant for what seemed like half of her life, was still as trim and slender as a teen, and she always looked beautiful.

"They're coming, they're coming," Willy's voice echoed from the top of the stairs.

Within seconds he was shouting with excitement, "Mama, Mama," as he and four-year-old Isabella came rushing in, the little girl dragging him by the hand. "We must begin the music. Baby sister says we must begin the music."

Hanna smiled, observing that Isabella was hardly a baby anymore. But to Willy she would always be his "baby sister." She recalled those early walks in the park in Munich, Willy pushing the baby in her pram, inviting everyone they met to take a peek, declaring, "You must look. She is the most beautiful baby in the world!"

Some turned away with disgust, and Hanna saw the underlying disbelief in many, questioning how this strange young man could lay claim to the most beautiful baby in the world. But those who accepted his invitation and peeked into the carriage would always exclaim, "Why, yes, your little sister is the most beautiful baby in the world!"

Now it was Isabella leading Willy, tugging him up and down the stairs, instructing him on how his party should be conducted. It was Isabella who had suggested they celebrate in the music room because this was where Willy was happiest. Though she often took over the decision making for her much older brother, he was always agreeable, and oh, how she loved him. Willy, of course, thought this precious little girl had been created just for him.

"Isn't she the bossiest child you've ever seen?" Hanna asked Helene with a laugh.

"She knows what she wants," Helene replied with a proud smile, as if this beautiful little girl were her own.

From the beginning it was quite evident that Isabella had a mind of her own. The child spoke early, her first word *Papa*, her second *Baba*, her baby word for her brother, Willy. She was a busy little girl with an independent spirit, and demanded everything just so—always her way—which at times could be a test for both mother and child. If Hanna gave her an apple, she would insist on an orange. If her mother chose a satin ribbon for her hair, Isabella would pick velvet.

Leni, who popped out babies faster than one could count them, assured her sister that this was all very normal, when Hanna knew what she really meant was, *You've never had a normal child*. "It's perfectly natural for a child to challenge a parent," Leni had said with authority. And challenge Isabella did. But there was also a softness, a sweetness to her. In the evening when Hanna put her to bed and they settled down to read a story, talk about the events of the day, and share a prayer, thanking God for Papa, Willy, Helene, Sasha, Aunt Leni, and an enormous list including all her uncles, cousins, and just about anyone who had touched her life in any way, she would always beg her mother to stay a little longer. As Hanna tucked her in, the child planted kisses on her forehead, her nose, her cheeks, and her chin, and Hanna felt Isabella was the true completion of her life.

Each time she smiled, Hanna saw Johann Keller. Yet the guilt she felt was tinged by the enormous joy and gratitude for the gift of this beautiful child. Moses adored her, and never once questioned that she was his own flesh and blood.

Hanna rose from her chair and looked out the window. The yard was dappled with late-winter sunlight and faded colors, creating a muted melody. Often this time of year she longed for the sounds and colors of spring. One of the boys was unlatching the gate, and then they were all running toward the house, the smallest stooping to pick up a stone and tossing it into the fountain, turned off for the season. One of the girls carefully balanced a gift. Leni and Kurt followed, along with their eldest daughter, her husband, and their new baby.

Leni was wearing a suit that Hanna had given her, one of her own that would have been out of style if Leni had not made some alterations. Her little sister had obviously paid attention to their stepmother's instructions in sewing. She looked stunning.

"She looks so much like her aunt Leni," Helene observed, glancing toward Isabella, who was arranging the sheets on which she'd had her mother write out the words for the songs, Willy's favorites. Not yet five, she could already read.

"She does," Hanna replied.

"How fortunate," Helene remarked quietly with a little toss of her head, "that she got her beauty from your side of the family. The intellectual aptitude from her father."

Hanna flinched a little at that, but turned and gazed back out the window. She did not dare take insult, as she was thankful that Helene attributed the child's cleverness to her father, Moses Fleischmann. And yes, she was grateful that Isabella resembled Leni, and equally as grateful that she did not inherit Leni's intellect. Her sister was easily led, and at times Hanna wondered if she even had a mind of her own.

The cousins were entering the room, hugging both Willy and Isabella, greeting their aunts, placing the gifts on a small table that was decked with a festive cloth. Leni reached out and gave each of the women a quick kiss on each cheek. "Why, Helene, you are here again! One would think you might move to Munich, but I suppose it would be impossible for your husband to leave his business in Berlin." She eyed Helene's ruby broach. "You look very lovely on this happy occasion!" she exclaimed, turning to her older sister.

"The children are so excited," Hanna said, surveying the lively little group. "Isabella, please go to the library and tell Papa the party has begun." Isabella tugged at her favorite cousin's hand, instructing her to come along.

As Willy greeted his guests, then as they sat for music and games, enjoyed refreshments and gifts, Hanna thought how completely happy she could be if her family could be swept up and deposited in a different place, a different time. Since Isabella's arrival, she felt a renewed companionship and shared love with her husband, and she could hardly recall the sense of despair that had invaded her during her voyage to and from America. Being here with Helene and Leni, their husbands and the children, Hanna felt content.

Yet even though she had admonished Moses to refrain from such conversations, no one could ignore what was going on all around them in Germany. Moses said it would get better, but Hanna feared this instability, this uncertain economy, could swallow them all. The stock market crash had reverberated around the world. The German Republic had yet to earn the people's trust, and they had barely time to catch their breath and regroup after the war and daunting ills that followed. Germany defaulted on the repayment plan. American loans, which were basically supporting the economy, were recalled, and once more Germany was compelled to look for a rescue.

Hanna could feel and see the tension all around her in Munich.

At home, she heard the fear and worry in talk among the servants. Spouses working in the factories had lost their jobs.

"Germany, the most powerful nation in the world?" she overheard Frau Weiss, the cook, say one evening as Hanna was about to enter the kitchen. She paused a moment at the door.

"Now it is mere survival," the woman declared, resignation in her voice.

The cook's young assistant said, "I'm grateful for the work here, but how long will Herr Fleischmann be able to keep us on? When even the rich no longer have money, who will be spending it on pretty pictures and statues?"

Over the past weeks, Hanna had repeatedly heard a name that had been moving throughout every circle in Munich for the past two years, gradually gaining momentum.

Adolf Hitler.

One morning on her way home from the gallery she stopped by the market to pick up a treat of fresh fruit for Willy and Isabella's lunch, and she overheard a conversation among strangers.

"My husband went to the beerhouse last night to hear him speak," a woman said as she surveyed a bin of apples. "Herr Hitler wants to make life better for us working folks. He supports the unions. There will be pensions for the old, free education for the young."

"He's going to build up the army again," a plump young woman joined in.

"But the treaty prohibits that," another woman said as she asked the vendor for a kilo of apples.

"To hell with the treaty," the vendor jumped in as he placed several bright red apples on his scales. "Nothing but a betrayal by the Republic, that French treaty. What we need is someone, a real German, to say the hell with that piece of rubbish. To hell with the Republic that does nothing but stab us in the back."

Again on the streetcar ride home, Hanna heard the same.

"He's going to restore Germany's military strength," an old man with gray whiskers said to another in a quiet voice.

"His Brownshirts are nothing but bullies," his companion replied. "They were over there at my neighbors' last night throwing rocks at the window."

"Jews?" the other man queried in an even lower voice. "Maybe they deserve it. Those Jews are the cause of this whole mess."

Hanna shivered, and then the man sitting next to her, obviously also eavesdropping on the conversation, interjected, "Hitler's Brownshirts?" The man had but one good leg, the other a stump, and Hanna guessed he was a war veteran. "Bullies and thugs, they've been called, but maybe that's what it will take. I'm tired of being pushed around. Let's do a little pushing of our own."

She could hardly reconcile this Adolf Hitler with the timid artist who had come to the gallery years ago. She had seen him

once after that, showing his paintings on Leopoldstrasse near the
Academy of Fine Arts. Artists often displayed their paintings
along the street, hoping to attract customers who thought they
were enrolled at the art school and might be seduced into believing they could discover a student before he made a name for himself. Some shoppers were simply looking for a pretty picture.

Hanna had stopped for a moment to look. He was helping a
customer, and she didn't think he noticed her. He was showing
his architectural pieces, which, Hanna remembered from his visit
to the Fleischmann Gallery, were probably his most appealing
work. They were nicely done, but she saw nothing innovative or
original. She hoped he was doing well, as she did not wish any of
the young artists the fate that would generally be theirs. She sincerely hoped he might find a way to use his talent.

Then he was gone. As were all the young artists. All the young
men. The Great War had begun.

She might have forgotten him, but then some years after the
war, as Germany struggled to find itself, as they were falling deeper
and deeper behind with the reparation payments, she saw his photograph in the newspaper with an article describing an event that
took place in Munich on the evening of November 8, 1923.

The article described Adolf Hitler jumping up on a table at the
Bürgerbräukeller, a beer hall on the outskirts of Munich, where
Bavarian government officials were meeting with a group of businessmen. He'd fired off two shots in the air and shouted, "The
revolution has begun!"

He actually got the leaders into a meeting of sorts and threatened them with the supposed army he had ready to storm the
place. The uprising was put down, though several of Hitler's followers were killed. Hitler went into hiding in Munich and was
apprehended within days. His unsuccessful attempt to overthrow
the government was almost laughable.

This "Beer Hall Putsch" was attributed to a party called the

National Socialist German Workers' Party. Adolf Hitler, the leader, was described as a veteran of the Great War.

He received a short prison sentence and then again he seemed to disappear. But now he was back.

Hanna attempted to push such thoughts from her mind, the very concerns she knew the men were discussing earlier in the library. Today was her son's twenty-first birthday, and each year with Willy was another cause for celebration. She glanced over at Helene and could see a quiet sadness within her as she watched the children. Hanna knew she was thinking of the boy who had not lived to celebrate such an occasion. They seldom spoke of Little Jakob, and Hanna would never put into words what both women knew—that she would never lose her own son to the devastation of war. He would always be a child.

"Could we possibly elect this man as our next president?" Hanna asked one evening as she and Moses walked home from seeing a film. One couldn't venture down a street in Munich without passing political posters plastered on every building and wall endorsing the Nazi candidate. Trucks with loudspeakers motored through the city, blasting his praise, sending off a spark of sharp color. Even in the movie theater that evening, a short film was shown before the feature—Adolf Hitler's face larger than life, enormous flags with swastikas flying against a cloudless sky.

"No, never," Moses replied. "The people hold much respect for President von Hindenburg. They look up to him as a war hero, defender of the German people."

"But Hitler is playing to the same sense of patriotism and nationalism," Hanna said, "representing himself as a war hero, too." When he began his campaign, the opposition brought up the fact that he wasn't even a German citizen. The party immediately responded by calling up his war record, his service in the

German Army. In a skillfully orchestrated political maneuver, Hitler was named attaché of the legation of Brunswick in Berlin, and was thus granted citizenship.

"Frederick is convinced that he'll make things better for the farmers," Hanna told her husband, "assure them that food prices allow a decent living, that they aren't overtaxed." She had recently returned with the children from a visit to the farm that her older brother had inherited after her father died. "The Hinkels have been forced to sell. The farm has been in the family for generations. Frederick is frightened the family will lose everything. And now all this propaganda . . ." Hanna motioned as they passed a line of posters with Hitler's face staring out at them with determination. "I'm just frightened," she said. "So many are being taken in by his promises. Leni among them. She's concerned if things don't improve they'll be moving in with us again."

"God protect us from that," Moses said with a laugh. Moses loved children but the thought of Leni's brood moving in again was enough to have him talk about setting up a cot at the gallery.

"I'm just frightened that this Adolf Hitler will be our next president."

"No," Moses told her emphatically. "President von Hindenburg will be reelected."

Her husband had a way of putting her at ease, yet Hanna feared the leader of the Nazi Party had enough support that he could actually win the election. "I hope you are correct."

"Now, tell me, my dear, when have I not been correct?" he said with a gentle tease in his voice as he wrapped his arm around her protectively.

CHAPTER SIXTEEN

Lauren and Isabella

"Despite the Nazis' efforts, neither candidate attained the required absolute majority," Isabella said. "In the runoff election, voters chose to retain President von Hindenburg."

"Then he turned around and appointed Hitler Chancellor," Lauren added.

"Yes," Isabella replied. "I'm afraid he did. By then the Nazi Party was the most powerful in the Reichstag. Some said the appointment was an attempt to keep the Nazis under control, to bring them into the fold, to keep an eye on them." Then, surprising Lauren, she laughed. "Others said the old man was senile."

"How old was he?"

"Oh, let's see . . ." Isabella threw the younger woman a self-mocking, squinty-eyed look, "Much older than I. He was eighty-six, but very tired. He'd been president for eight years, through the worst times in Germany's history."

But, the very worst, Lauren knew, the most horrendous years, were yet to come.

"Shortly after this," Isabella said, "the Reichstag, the Parliament building in Berlin, was set afire and gutted. The Communists were blamed, a Dutch man of limited mental capacity tried and convicted." She glanced at the picture of herself and her brother, Willy, under the broken glass. "All of this played out in the public eye, the photos of the poor man in the newspaper, helpless, unable to understand the charges against him. Everyone knew it was really the Nazis. Mother never talked about it, but can you imagine how frightened she must have been at that? To see this mentally challenged man put on trial and then convicted?"

"She was afraid for Willy," Lauren said.

"Yes, of course, and she was married to a wealthy, successful Jewish businessman. That was about the worst thing you could be at the time. A national boycott of Jewish businesses was proclaimed less than three months after Adolf Hitler became Chancellor. My father decided to close the gallery. By then, most of the business was conducted during private appointments with regular clients. Few sales were made to customers who walked in unexpectedly, and it had been months since they'd had an exhibition."

"A terrible environment in which to run a business," Lauren said, aware of how much life had changed for so many.

"If you were a Jew," Isabella replied.

Lauren thought of what Mrs. Fletcher's parents must have been going through at the time, and then she thought of her own grandparents, her father's mother and father. Felix Rosenthal was a physician in Leipzig, Germany. A respected doctor. The Rosenthal family history had come to Lauren mostly through her mother, not her father, and much she'd filled in by studying history itself.

She was aware that after Hitler was appointed Chancellor, Dr. Rosenthal continued to treat his patients, both Jews and non-Jews, though Lauren had learned that state-supported health insurance refused to reimburse Jewish doctors. She imagined her grandfather treated many without pay. He stayed in Germany, feeling an obligation to those he cared for.

"In ways, it came about gradually," Isabella went on, "or

that's what many claim. As though it just sneaked up on them, this government takeover of virtually every aspect of German life. Yet, after Hitler was appointed Chancellor, in those first few months the changes were substantial. The Reichstag fire was followed by the rescinding of civil liberties; the Enabling Act was passed." She paused for a moment and cleared her throat. "That was basically the end of the Republic. Hitler seized power. On a temporary basis, of course, to protect the people from this Communist revolution. Oh, Communists were considered nearly as low as Jews. An equal threat to the people of Germany. According to some, there was no difference."

Mrs. Fletcher might have been reciting facts from a history book, yet Lauren knew how deeply these events had touched Isabella's family. And Lauren's family, too.

"By the summer of 1933 all political parties," the woman explained, "except for the Nazis, were banned. The government continued to go after the Jews. Again, to protect the people." She ran her fingers along the side of her neck, and then clasped her hands together in her lap. "Government positions were available only to Aryans. Jewish professors were dismissed from the universities. Books were burned and cultural chambers were set up to control the arts—instruments of propaganda. Oh, yes, the Nazis were especially skilled at that. I'm not even sure that President von Hindenburg knew what was going on." Isabella's body stiffened as she leaned back in the large winged chair. "A concentration camp was set up outside of Munich. A place to send political foes of the German government. And who could object to that?" She breathed deeply and exhaled. "This government that promised to restore Germany to its proper place in the world." Her tone was hard and cold. She picked up her napkin and wiped a spot of moisture that had formed at the corner of her mouth.

The room seemed very still and quiet. Now and then, during their conversation, Lauren had heard a low whir or hum that she guessed might be the air-conditioning. No street sounds climbed up to penetrate the stone walls or sealed windows.

"Then, in the summer of 1934," Isabella said after several moments, "President Paul von Hindenburg passed. Hitler declared himself Führer. That was the official end of the German Republic, though the Germans were by then living under a dictatorship anyway."

"The Republic," Lauren said quietly, "that was so supportive of the type of art your parents sold in the gallery?"

"Yes," Isabella replied.

Lauren knew that in 1935, the Nazi reign now fully under way, Hitler in charge, Felix Rosenthal sent his wife, Miriam, and his two-year-old daughter, Mimi, to London to stay with Miriam's sister and her family. He was to join them later. At the time Miriam was one month pregnant with their son. Lauren's father, Felix Rosenthal II, was born in London in 1936. He would never know his father.

"Hitler was quite adept," Isabella said, breaking into Lauren's thoughts, "at removing any obstacle that might stand in the way of his ultimate plan. In a night of murder, sometimes called the Night of Long Knives, often the Blood Purge of 1934, he did away with a number of fellow Nazis, those who might challenge his authority or impede his rise to even greater power. It's all in the history books." Waving toward the bookcase, her hand rested for a moment in midair before dropping to the arm of her chair. "I wasn't yet six when Hitler became Chancellor. The summer President von Hindenburg passed away, I celebrated my seventh birthday. We had such a lovely life in Munich. I had no idea what was going on. Much of what was happening then I learned later." Her voice was soft, almost a whisper. "Much later."

CHAPTER SEVENTEEN

Hanna

Munich
March–May 1935

One afternoon Hanna and Leni took the children on an outing. Leni, her husband, and children had just moved into a new, larger apartment. "Things are improving. Life is much better," she told Hanna.

They had bundled up the children to take them out for some fresh air. It had been a long winter and they had all been confined by the weather. But today the sun was out, the sky an exquisite-sounding blue, and Willy had been begging to see the mechanical jousting knights and dancing coopers in the clock tower. Leni and Hanna watched the children as they giggled and pranced in the square to the tune of the chimes. Despite the lovely, cloudless sky, a substantial chill hung in the air, and little puffs of breath escaped from their mouths as they hopped and skipped joyfully to the music. Observing them, Hanna felt a shiver come over her, and she thought how great a contrast this scene of happy children was to the emotions that were roiling inside her.

While there was but a small crowd gathered in the Marien-platz that afternoon, there were several soldiers in starched uniforms with shiny boots and swastikas on their arms, weapons at their sides, surveying the square. Hanna sensed that Leni felt more secure now that Hitler was rebuilding Germany's forces, but these men terrified Hanna. When she went out, she often turned the other way and took a longer route to her destination, just to avoid them. At times it seemed they were everywhere.

"I'm frightened," Hanna told her sister in a low voice. "The Nazi government claims they are making life better for all Germans, yet their definition of Germans has become rather narrow." Hanna stared at her sister, knowing full well that Leni knew what she was talking about.

"We'll get through it," Leni assured her with far too much brightness in her voice.

How could she be so cheerful? Hanna wondered. At least she had sensitivity enough not to say, "Things are so much better now that Hitler is running the country." But she had heard it from others, overheard conversations in the shops, from the servants speaking about family members who had finally gone back to work—that for the majority of the middle-class Germans, the economic situation had improved.

She felt herself grow warm with anger toward her sister. Could Leni not remember that it was Moses who had taken care of her family through the hard times, that it was not Hitler? Hanna wanted to turn and slap her and tell her to wake up and see what was true, that what she was seeing as good times would not last either. That there was evil in the air.

"Mama, mama." Willy ran to his mother with a big grin. "Can we have ice cream?"

"Ice cream!" Hanna said with a laugh, patting Willy's bright red cheeks, pulling his wool cap, which was flapping about, down snuggly over his pink ears. "It's much too cold for ice cream!"

"Then chocolate cake?" Little Isabella had now joined them and took her big brother's hand. "And warm milk with chocolate, too!" she exclaimed.

"Yes," Willy said with a clap of his gloved hands, "chocolate cake. And the cousins, too?"

Hanna had had enough of her sister for the day, but she knew how much Willy and Isabella loved this time with the cousins.

"Chocolate! Chocolate!" Willy shouted, throwing his arms in the air.

"Yes, of course," Hanna said, tapping her finger to her mouth, her way of telling him not to talk so loudly. "We'll go by the bakery on our way home."

The women said nothing more as they gathered the children and headed for home. But Hanna thought of an earlier conversation she'd had with her sister. Leni had declared that Hitler was a great supporter of the arts, that it was his intention to make art available to the common people. She presented this as if it would please Hanna.

It was true that shortly after he became Chancellor, Adolf Hitler had laid the cornerstone for a national art museum. The government's Ministry of Public Enlightenment and Propaganda soon established a series of chambers to oversee film, radio, music, theater, literature, journalism, painting, sculpture, and graphics. But Hanna knew that the Nazis' definition of art was as narrowly defined as their definition of a true German. These chambers were merely a way of controlling creativity.

Directors, even non-Jews, had been dismissed from state galleries for showing art that the Reich did not approve of.

Literature had taken a hit with mass burnings of books in Berlin.

Would the paintings be next? she wondered.

When they arrived at the bakery, Hanna took Willy inside the small shop while Leni, the others in tow, headed toward the Fleischmann home to request the kitchen girls heat water for tea and warm the milk and chocolate.

A man and woman stood in front of the display case. "*Guten Tag*, Frau Fleischmann," the woman said.

"*Guten Tag*," Hanna replied. They looked familiar, but she could not recall who they were.

Willy pressed his nose up against the display case filled with lovely cakes and pastries.

"Which one?" Hanna asked.

"Can we pick two whole cakes?" he asked, glancing back at his mother. She noticed he'd left a little smudge on the glass.

"One should be enough," Hanna replied, and then she heard it, barely a whisper, but it might as well have been shouted.

"*Mischling*," the woman said in a quiet voice to her husband. "The little retarded half-breed."

Hanna turned, her eyes boring through the woman, who quickly lowered her gaze toward the pastry display as if the words had not come out of her mouth.

Hanna stared down at the lovely assortment of sweets under the glass case, and in her mind's eye she imagined herself saying, *Yes, two. I'll take the chocolate cake, and yes, this lovely crème pie.* And then she pictured herself turning around and smashing the cream pie into the woman's face. She placed her hand on the edge of the display case, to steady herself. She was shaking with rage.

She knew she could not exhibit such behavior with her son here by her side, so instead she took a deep, deep breath, grabbed Willy's hand, and said, "We'll go to the bakery down the street." Quickly, she pulled her bewildered son toward the door.

"Then what did you do?" Moses asked her that evening.

"We went and got the cake at a different bakery. I didn't want to confront the woman with Willy right there. He didn't hear or maybe he didn't understand, and I just didn't . . . Oh,

Moses, what are we to do? Hitler has stirred up so much hate—toward those who are different, toward the Jews."

"Hitler did not invent anti-Semitism," he answered calmly.

Hanna knew this was true and Moses had survived in this world for many years, and perhaps learned from his father, that in such a hostile society one must strive for personal satisfaction, hold one's head high, take care of family, and remain principled, not hateful.

"Hate met with hate accomplishes nothing," Moses replied with his familiar mantra.

"But it isn't right."

"No, of course it isn't. But we'll get through it."

Hanna stared at her husband. This was exactly what Leni had said that afternoon.

They tried to live their lives with as few changes and interruptions as possible. They didn't talk about what was going on in Germany when the children might overhear. Isabella was too young to understand, and Willy too innocent. They continued with their outings, though these were less frequent, and Hanna was always careful, with a watchful eye.

One fine spring day, she said to Sasha, "Let's take the children for a picnic lunch."

So they packed a basket with fruit and cheese, bread and pastries, and took off for the Englischer Garten.

When they arrived they spread a blanket to relax in a little wooded area.

Isabella shouted, "Butterflies, Mama! Look at the lovely butterflies!"

Willy asked for an apple and requested to cut it himself. Within seconds, he had sliced into his finger, and it oozed a deep red. The two women each grabbed a napkin. Hanna reached for Willy, pressing the linen to his finger to stop the bleeding.

"I'm sorry, Mama," he apologized.

"It will be all right, darling," she reassured him. "It was an accident." The napkin had turned a scarlet red, and Sasha handed her another. Finally they were able to stop the bleeding. Hanna turned back to check on Isabella, and a panic far worse than one caused by the sight of blood surged through her. She was gone!

"Isabella!" Hanna shouted as she stood. "Sasha, where is she?"

"After the butterflies?"

"How could she have disappeared so quickly? Stay here with Willy."

Hanna took off, sprinting across the path, looking up, then back, then down. A hot, uncontrollable fear rushed from her heart and invaded every part of her body.

"Have you seen a little girl?" Hanna asked the first person she saw, a young man walking a dog. "She's seven, almost eight, with long blond hair."

He shook his head.

Hanna flew down the path shouting, "Isabella, Isabella." She glanced over at a nearby pond and would not allow herself to believe her daughter might have gone near the water. She threaded in and out of the wooded areas along the main path, asking everyone she saw, "Have you seen a little blond girl?"

When she saw a group of soldiers coming toward her, Hanna's heart dropped to her feet. In a panic, she turned, walking quickly— afraid to run, thinking they might chase after her. Quickly she moved in the opposite direction, and then after glancing back, realizing they were not following her, again she ran.

It might have been five minutes before she spotted Isabella, standing in front of a man who was sitting on a bench. But it seemed like a day, a month, an eternity.

"Isabella," Hanna panted, out of breath, as she rushed up to her. "You have frightened Mama terribly. You must never do that again." She pulled the child to her and hugged her tightly.

"A little girl shouldn't be wandering about by herself," the man said flatly.

Hanna released her from the hug and took her hand. She could not defend herself, but with the shame came relief that she had found her safe.

"Particularly a little Jewish girl." His words came out more threat than warning. Hanna had always felt Isabella would be protected by the way she looked—her blond hair, her very blue eyes, but now this man . . . How did he know? Hanna stared at him, but said nothing. She had never seen him before. He was neither young nor old. His hair was a light brown and his eyes the color and tone of mud. A slow grin spread across his face and there was a small gap between his two front teeth. He reached up and ran a tobacco-stained finger along his lower lip.

Hanna turned and, holding firmly to her daughter's hand, she started to walk. Quickly.

"Never talk to strangers," she said when they were well away from the man.

"Yes, I know," Isabella answered with a quiver in her voice.

"What did he say to you?"

"He asked me if I was lost, and I said, 'No, Mama and Willy and Sasha are in the bushes,' and he said, 'Where is your father?' and I said, 'He is at the gallery,' and he said, 'What is your father's name?' and I said, 'Moses Fleischmann,' and then he said, 'Oh, the Jew,' and I said, 'Yes, and I am a Jew, too, just like my papa.'" The quiver was gone now, her voice filled with confidence and pride.

Hanna stopped and knelt down beside her daughter. "Isabella, you must never say that. You must never say you are a Jew."

"But I am," she answered, almost defiantly. "I am a Jew, just like Papa."

"No," Hanna said, "you must never say that."

"I am a Jew."

"Isabella, please," Hanna whispered.

"But I am a Jew! I am a Jew, just like Papa!" She was shouting now, and people walking along the path stopped abruptly and stared.

Hanna picked her up and held her close, her little form stiffening the way it did when she was in a fit of temper, every muscle in her body tense. Hanna could feel Isabella's heart beat rapidly against the ever-increasing beat of her own, and then she felt the child loosen, everything go limp. Isabella was sobbing now, and by the time they got back to Willy and Sasha, who had spread out the picnic lunch for all of them, so was Hanna.

CHAPTER EIGHTEEN

Lauren and Isabella

New York City
August 2009

The old woman looked exhausted, and Lauren wondered if she should suggest they continue tomorrow. She knew she wasn't even close to gathering the information she'd set out to find, and her mind was flipping back and forth regarding the validity of what Isabella had told her about the Kandinsky painting. Lauren's greatest immediate concern: if she left now, would Mrs. Fletcher extend another invitation?

She'd just given Lauren a summary of Hitler's first years in power. One moment she was accusing every non-Jew in Germany of being involved. The very next minute she was bent on convincing Lauren that not everyone jumped on the Hitler bandwagon, though there were many who did, she told her, and for many it had nothing to do with hating the Jews. Lauren wondered again what it would have been like in Germany to be a child with a Jewish family on one side, an Aryan family on the other.

She thought of her own child's mixed heritage. Even in a loving, peaceful environment it presented obstacles. She and Patrick had decided to expose Adam to both families' traditions, if not yet the full expanse of either religion. They celebrated Christmas as well as the

Jewish holidays. Lauren's family was not particularly religious. Patrick came from a long line of Catholics. His grandmother O'Farrell was especially devout—the prayer-book, rosary-carrying old-fashioned Catholic. When Adam was born, she gave them a medal of a guardian angel to hang on his crib from a blue ribbon. Lauren liked the idea of an angel specially assigned to look after her son.

Once more she thought of Felix and Miriam Rosenthal, the grandparents she never knew. Miriam had died in London, though Lauren had never been told exactly how. Her father was just five when he lost his mother.

"I honestly have no personal memory of any unhappiness," Isabella said, "though I know times became very difficult for my parents, for Jewish businesses in general, particularly for art dealers who were dealing in the less traditional forms of art. The German Republic was receptive to such art, but let's just say, well, Hitler and his crew were not terribly open-minded." She gave off a little snort as she adjusted herself in her chair, straightening her already-regal posture. "Many intellectuals, artists, and writers left Germany for countries more accepting of various forms of self-expression. Many of my parents' friends and business associates felt neither welcome nor safe in Germany anymore."

It seemed to Lauren they'd been over this already, and she, too, was feeling emotionally drained. She was about to suggest they meet again the following day when Mrs. Fletcher said, "There was a man who was very friendly with my mother."

Lauren perked up and Isabella waved a finger. "No, not like that—a friend, a dear, true friend. He worked at the gallery. His name was Josef, and even as a child I could see he and Mother were very close. He would show us the paintings and tell us about the different artists. I couldn't have been more than six or seven then. Josef was always delighted to see us. When I think of Josef, I smell peppermint." She took in a little sniff as if the scent hovered in the air that very moment. "He kept a crystal bowl of candy on his desk, and Willy and I always filled our pockets before leaving the gallery." Her lips moved as if verging on a smile, but Lauren could see they were trembling. "The whole idea of looking back on something and seeing it in a completely different light . . ." Her voice trailed off as she ran her fingers over the brim of her teacup. Lauren had given up on the tea long ago, but Mrs. Fletcher seemed to find comfort in having something to keep her nervous hands busy.

"Helene came often from Berlin," she continued, "and we used to go on outings with Aunt Leni and her family—so many cousins— to the park, the beautiful Englischer Garten. I remember one beautiful spring day we went to the park for a picnic. It was just Mother, Willy, and Sasha, a woman employed in our home. I wandered off by myself and then suddenly realized I was alone. Lost. My mother screamed at me when she found me. I thought she should be happy. Do you have children, Ms. O'Farrell?" she asked abruptly.

"Yes," Lauren replied with a smile. "Adam. He's three."

"A son. That's nice." Mrs. Fletcher glanced at the photo of her husband. "Andrew and I would have liked children, but life doesn't always turn out as one might have planned." She turned back to Lauren and asked, "You're married?"

"Yes."

Isabella laughed lightly. "I didn't mean to be rude. But, with young women these days you never know. It seems a husband isn't a prerequisite anymore for having a child."

"True." Lauren smiled and nodded in agreement.

"To an Irish boy, I gather," Isabella said. "So, it's Mrs. O'Farrell, not Ms.?"

"Lauren is fine," the younger woman replied.

"Being a mother, you understand my mother's reaction when she finally found me after searching the park. Her anger."

"Yes, I do understand," Lauren said, recalling the time she'd taken Adam with her to a sale at Macy's. A one-day sale. She'd had her eye on a particular blouse and hoped to find it at a bargain price. She was shuffling through a rack, searching, when she turned around and he was gone! Even now, more than a year later, she could feel that knot of panic tightening low in her gut. How could she have been so inattentive? Her first, and worst, thought was that someone had taken him. Her prayer was that he'd merely been curious and set off to explore, that his tiny hand was now slipped into the kind, warm hand of a grandmotherly salesclerk who would bring him back to his mother with understanding. Or even reprimand. Yes, she would gladly have taken a severe scolding.

She'd found him within minutes. He was hiding behind a rack of clothes as if they were playing a game of hide-and-seek. He was giggling when she pulled him out, her hand trembling all the way up her arm to her shoulder. She still remembered how furious she was with him.

No, she was furious with herself.

"You do understand that fear can often masquerade as anger," Isabella said, and again Lauren found herself nodding in agreement. Yes, she understood this. But then, she wondered, was Isabella Fletcher talking about something more than this incident in the park?

"I know now how frightened my mother was," Mrs. Fletcher said. "I remember when she found me, I was talking to a man. I knew I shouldn't talk to a stranger, and I knew I was lost. He asked me my father's name, and asked me if he was a Jew. I adored my father—he was so confident, so brave, so smart." Again, the woman's posture became more erect. She smiled. "Of course, I said yes, he was a Jew. Then I announced that I was a Jew, too. I wanted the man to know that I was brave. I had no idea what it meant then to admit you were a Jew. I was sure it was a very good thing." She laughed a little at the sad irony of the thought.

"And I understand now," Mrs. Fletcher said, "why my mother decided to take us to America. My father remained in Germany. Mother explained he had business to attend to before we could all be together. It was her intention to move the family like Aunt Katie and Uncle Hans, but I truly didn't understand at the time about Hitler and the Jews." Isabella stared directly at Lauren and asked, "You're Jewish?"

Lauren nodded. She thought that Isabella was going to ask about her family, but she didn't. They sat without further conversation. Finally Lauren asked, "You said your father died in Germany? He never made it to America?"

"He became very ill. Mother left Willy and me in America with our aunt and uncle and went back to Germany for him. I never saw my father again." She set her teacup on the end table and then ran her fingers over her throat, touching the pearls, gazing out as if she were looking far beyond the confines of the walls of the room.

"I'm sorry," Lauren said.

Isabella continued to stare, but said nothing.

Once more a heavy silence invaded the room. Lauren waited several moments before asking, "Your mother was able to make it out of Germany?" The word *escaped*—a word Mrs. Fletcher had used earlier—kept coming back to Lauren. She wondered what Isabella meant by this, if she did indeed know the true story of her mother's escape.

"Yes, much later. She was forced to stay in Germany for quite some time before she was able to come to America."

Lauren's grandfather, Dr. Rosenthal, too, had intended to reunite with his family.

"The painting, the Kandinsky *Composition*," Lauren said, "you mentioned earlier that she didn't bring it with her. It came later?"

"Yes, it came later."

"Am I right that you also said that it was purchased twice by the family?"

"Yes," Mrs. Fletcher replied slowly, her body shifting with fatigue, "and I am getting to that."

But Lauren wondered if either of them had the energy to continue.

CHAPTER NINETEEN

Hanna

Munich
September 1935–June 1936

Hanna's nerves were tender and on edge as she embarked from New York to return to Munich, and she felt as she had during those last months in Germany, as if she were always looking behind her, in front of her, and to her side for something that was so evil it didn't feel real. When she heard from Helene and learned of Moses' failing health, just weeks after she had arrived in New York with the children, Hanna immediately made arrangements to return home. She left Willy and Isabella in America with her sister, and planned to bring Moses back with her when he was well.

He was heavily medicated to fight the pain and at times delusional. Sometimes he called her Helene, though Hanna didn't know if he thought she was his dead wife, Helene, or if he was mistaking her for his daughter, who had come from Berlin as soon as she heard her father was ill.

Sometimes, in the mornings after breakfast, Hanna sensed that she and Moses were actually speaking to each other, carrying on a real conversation, and then as the day progressed, his words would shift from complete clarity to utter confusion. She feared it was the medication as much as the illness. She wanted to speak with Dr. Langermann, whom she trusted completely. But Dr. Langermann, who had been their physician for many years, was now living in Switzerland. It was almost impossible to find a doctor who would tend to Moses, the Jew. The medicine to ease his pain was ten times the cost it would have been just a few years ago. Pharmacies were instructed not to sell to the Jews, and it was difficult to legitimately get what was needed. Hanna felt there was no one left in the country that she could trust.

One morning, feeling the comfort of the music would ease her pain and help her nerves, she wandered into the music room. But before she could sit at the piano, she noticed how eerily quiet the room was, and then she realized that the large Kandinsky, the *Composition* they had purchased years ago, no longer hung on the wall. In a panic she fled from the room, rushing through the house searching for it, soon realizing that other paintings were missing. Consumed with tending Moses, worrying about her children, Hanna had not noticed that many of the paintings in their home had disappeared. She hurried through the house, going into rooms she had not set foot in since her return. In a flurry of frustration she went to the guest room where Helene was staying.

"What is it?" Helene said as she opened the door.

"It's . . . the paintings," Hanna said. "So many are missing. Do you know where they are?"

"The paintings?" Helene said in a faraway voice, telling Hanna that she had not been aware, that she, too, had been preoccupied with concern for Moses. After several moments she said, "Perhaps they have been taken back to the gallery."

"Yes, of course." She guessed that Helene was correct. They had closed the gallery, though they still owned the building. She knew Moses was unofficially dealing art, or rather had been before he took ill. Paintings were being stored in the building on Theatinerstrasse. Surely he'd taken them there as he was getting business in order before joining his family in America. She would ask Josef, who came to visit several times a week. He was running the business as well as the household finances, since Moses had become incapable of doing so.

"Josef, where has my lovely Kandinsky gone?" she asked the following morning.

"Fled to Paris," he replied with a wry smile. He still had his humor intact even in such dire times. And Hanna loved him for that.

"Yes," she said with a laugh that felt so good, as it seemed she'd not laughed in years, "I know the artist Wassily Kandinsky, along with just about anyone else with any sense, has fled."

The Bauhaus, which had been substantially supported by the liberal German Republic, had moved from Weimar to Dessau and then to Berlin, attempting to keep one step ahead of the Nazi Party. It had now closed down completely.

"But what of the painting? The Kandinsky *Composition?*" she asked. Hanna wasn't yet concerned about the smaller Kandinskys, the Picasso drawings, the Matisse, the Chagall, which she'd also noticed missing.

She could see now, Josef was reluctant to answer her.

"They're being stored at the gallery?" she asked.

"Yes . . . well, some."

"Some? What of the others? The Kandinsky?"

"Sold," he said quietly.

"Out of the country?" She tried to calm herself.

"Unfortunately, no."

Hanna wasn't sure why Josef said this—*unfortunately*—but she guessed because he realized the art, as well as the Jews, would be much safer outside of Germany. Hitler often referred to the "modern" art as Bolshevik art, or Jewish art. Anything he found distasteful was labeled Jewish, even if the artist who had created it had not an ounce of Jewish blood.

"Where?" she asked.

"In Berlin."

"Botho von Gamp?"

Josef nodded.

Botho von Gamp, an artist himself, was a great admirer of Kandinsky and owned one of Kandinsky's earlier pieces, *Composition III*. Hanna knew he had attempted to add their *Composition* to his collection earlier, but Moses had turned down a very generous offer because he knew how much both she and Willy loved this painting.

"How can this be? Moses knows it has a special meaning for me."

"It's difficult now," Josef explained, "financially. With the gallery closed, the less-than-favorable conditions for a Jewish business."

Hanna tried to understand. She didn't ask Josef the price, as she guessed it was much less than had been offered several years ago. She also suspected that they needed the money.

She did not ask her husband about the paintings. Hanna knew he would not have done this if there had been any other way.

Hanna waited at Moses' bedside. She seldom went out. The news of what was happening in Germany came to her through Josef, through the help in the house, though several had been let go since Hanna had left Munich. She'd released Sasha herself before she took the children to America, encouraging the woman to take a position with a non-Jewish family. Hanna prayed that Sasha understood she was trying to protect her.

In September a law had been enacted designating Jews as "subjects," which meant they were no longer considered citizens of Germany.

Jakob, who on occasion came along with his wife from Berlin, said, "It's not just the Jews, all German citizens have lost their rights." And Hanna could see this was true. The Republic was long gone. They were living under a dictatorship, though there seemed to be little protest from many. People were working again. For most there was food on the table, and the promise of a brighter future.

Hitler was building a new highway system, the Autobahn, which he described as the greatest network of roads in the world. Leni told Hanna that she and her husband would soon be able to purchase an automobile, that Hitler intended for all citizens of Germany—which meant only those he considered Aryan—to own an automobile. Of course, the Fleischmanns, the wealthy Jews, had had an automobile for many years.

Hanna could see that Hitler had taken control of every aspect of the economy, the culture, the educational system, the press. There was no way to truly understand what was going on, as there was nothing that was not controlled by the Nazis.

On occasion, when Hanna went out—to the market, for a walk to breathe fresh air—she could feel it, a tension moving about these people who claimed to be so content. On the streetcar, she heard whispers of camps, places set up by the Nazis to house political enemies.

"One morning, he was gone, simply gone," a woman said in a low voice.

"You think he's been taken prisoner?"

The woman nodded.

"What had he done?" another asked.

"He was Jewish," she said, the words spoken so quietly Hanna wondered if she had misheard. Though she knew she had not.

Hanna could hardly stand being around Leni anymore, and there were many friends who would no longer socialize with her. Most of their Jewish friends had left or were living their lives as quietly as possible.

But Leni was family, and Hanna would not allow these differences to tear them apart. She invited her sister to come by one afternoon for tea. Leni's two youngest accompanied her—as a good German mother Leni had a total of eight, patriotically reproducing as German women were encouraged to.

After they had been served in the parlor, they visited, carefully avoiding any controversial subjects, stepping cautiously in their conversation. The children finished quickly and went upstairs to the nursery.

"They've grown so much," Hanna said.

"*Ja*, they grow up so fast," Leni replied lightly.

Hanna knew they were both thinking of Willy and Isabella in America. It was an uncomfortable topic. Sometimes Hanna wondered if Leni even understood why she was afraid to bring them home.

"Would you like more tea?" Hanna offered.

"*Bitte*," Leni said. "The almond cookies are delicious."

Max, the smallest, stood in the doorway, rubbing grubby hands to moist cheeks.

"What is it, my precious?" Leni asked as the boy approached. She wiped away a tear with her napkin.

"Albert says that Uncle Moses is bad, that he is a Jew and that's why he is sick."

"No, Moses is a good man," she replied.

"But Jews are bad."

"Run along, now." Leni handed him a ginger cookie, and he seemed pleased, no longer unhappy.

Had she not heard these words from her child? Hanna wondered.

After Max left, she asked, "Why didn't you correct him?" She was shaking with rage.

"I told him Moses is a good man," Leni said defensively.

"But you left it at that, as if you want him to believe that Jews are bad, that Moses is a bizarre exception."

"I'm only protecting him, Hanna. Surely you understand. If I defend the Jews . . ." She reached up and rubbed her hand across her cheek. "He's just a boy, and he will repeat this at school. He will be ridiculed, perhaps bullied and beat up. I want my children to have an education, not to be afraid. Later when he's older—"

"Ideas put into a child's mind are difficult to dislodge," Hanna said, feeling a twitch at the corner of her mouth.

Leni nodded in agreement, but Hanna knew they could not continue this conversation. She was thankful that her own children were not there to witness the increasing strain between herself and her sister.

That winter they found a wonderful doctor who adjusted the medications and it seemed at times that Moses' health was improving. Hanna dreamed that they would soon leave for America to be with the children. In moments of even grander delusion, she dreamed that she would awaken one morning and learn that Hitler was gone, that the country was once more restored—the economy good for all, not just those designated worthy to claim Germany for themselves. The children would come home.

Moses missed his children terribly, and on occasion he apologized as if both his illness and the dire conditions in Germany were his fault. Some days he was extremely confused and Hanna wasn't sure he understood anything. On a good day, he would request that she take him to the music room and play for him. Wrapped in a blanket, he would lie on the divan, close his eyes, and request a piece she knew had been his wife Helene's favorite.

"Tell me about the colors," he asked one morning. "Tell me what you see."

His own sight had become dim, a *haziness*, he called it, which was especially unjust for Moses, a man who made his living in what he saw, a man whose true love all along might have been the art rather than the women who had come in and out of his life—his three wives. This saddened Hanna greatly, that her husband's sight had diminished so. Yet in the saddest, most selfish way, it pleased her that he would ask about the colors, because it was she who saw the colors in the music. It was Hanna to whom Moses now spoke.

"Tell me the colors," he asked again, his voice a strained whisper. "Tell me, my dearest Hanna."

"Blue," she said as she played.

"The color of the sky?"

"Looking straight up," she replied, "on a clear, summer day." Hanna knew Moses loved this—for what did one mean by the color blue? There were thousands, perhaps millions, of blues in nature, in art, in the paintings he loved—myriad different ways in which God presented them with the color blue, an abundance of shades in the painter's mix of pigments. What was blue? What did it look like? What did it sound like?

"Yes, the cerulean of the summer sky," he said. "I can see it." He laughed. "Now I can hear the color."

Hanna laughed, too. "No," she teased him, "I don't believe you."

"Hanna," Moses said, "what a gift you have been to me."

She waited anxiously for the letters from America, tearing the envelopes open excitedly, nervously, for news of the children. Käthe always assured her they were doing fine, though they missed Mama and Papa. In fear, Hanna did not write of Hitler. Käthe sent a photograph of the children. Hanna studied it carefully. Willy looked the same—with his wide, open grin. Isabella had grown. She looked taller, older, and her smile, unlike Willy's, held an undeniable touch of sadness.

Willy sent lovely painted pictures. Isabella wrote letters in her pretty, even hand. She was now attending an American public school and had started writing in English. "Mama and Papa, you must practice your English for when you come to live with us in America," she wrote. Hanna's heart dropped at the word *us*—as if she and Moses were no longer Isabella's family.

During one of Helene's frequent visits, she and Hanna sat in the parlor, each held within the quiet emptiness of their own thoughts. The time crept so slowly, so deliberately, that Hanna imagined she could hear each tick of the clock in the hallway upstairs. Or perhaps it was just the tick of her heart, counting out each minute.

"He's built an enormous new stadium." Helene looked up from the cross-stitch on her lap.

They were continuing a discussion they had started at breakfast. Hanna closed the book she was attempting to read. She was well aware that Hitler had invited the world to come visit. Germany was hosting the Olympics in Berlin. The bid had been taken before the Nazis came to power, but now Hitler saw this as the perfect opportunity to show the world how healthy, happy, and athletic his people were. A massive Olympic stadium had been constructed in Berlin. Hanna had not been to the capital city, but knew of the stadium from news accounts praising the Führer's impressive preparations for this world event.

"It's a hideous, monstrous construction," Helene said, jabbing the needle into her cross-stitch.

Hanna also knew that Hitler had plans for architectural monuments all over Germany, particularly in Munich, where the Haus der Deutschen Kunst, the national art gallery, was still under construction. It, too, could be described as hideous and monstrous. Hanna couldn't help but think of the encouragement that she had given him to pursue his talents in architecture.

"Surely symbolic of failings in personal areas of his life," Helene added dryly. "The bigger, the better, he seems to think." She gave off an unladylike snort, followed by a harsh laugh. "The shriveled-up little . . ." And then she used a word Hanna had never heard come out of Helene's mouth—a vulgar word to describe a man's body part, a word unsuited for a woman of good breeding. Hanna shook her head and blushed with embarrassment, though she couldn't help but smile. Helene repeated the word slowly and deliberately and they both started giggling, which was sad and funny at the same time. "Huge monoliths marking the entrance," she said, describing with her hands. "Oh, but those will soon fall, will go over with a . . ." She made a sound like the deflating of a balloon, the air being released, or perhaps it was the sound of a bodily function, which made them both laugh even more. Oh, how they needed something to break through the heavy darkness that hung over them all, Hanna thought, and if it could be at Hitler's expense, all the better.

"Do you know the signs are coming down?" Helene's mood shifted abruptly. "All the signs that say, 'No Jews served here,' 'Non-Aryans not admitted.' As if the world cannot see what Hitler is doing to the Jews. He wants the world to think he's leading a very progressive, tolerant society."

Hanna wondered—could the world truly not see? During her short time in America, she had talked to Käthe and Hans about what was going on in Germany, but they had little knowledge of Adolf Hitler. Since she had not sent for her children, surely they now understood.

Hitler asserted that Germany would once more claim its position as a world power. The military was growing with the introduction of conscription, openly defying the terms of the Treaty of Versailles. Certainly those outside of Germany could see he was setting up for world domination.

Josef told Hanna that they had an offer on the building on Theatinerstrasse and should take it. She was relying on Josef to attend to the finances for the business, as well as the household. She knew she could trust him.

Josef let the remaining household help go, save for one cook and one housekeeper, though many might have left on their own, as there were few who wished to work as maids and servants in the home of a Jew. Laws had been enacted forbidding employment of Aryan women under a certain age in Jewish households. As if the Jewish master would seduce or rape the nubile young women. Hanna remembered how kind Moses and Helene had been to both her and Käthe, how they had taken such good care of them as well as the others in their employment. And the implication that a young German girl would not be safe in a Jewish household made her so angry she could not even speak of it.

Hanna didn't know if Moses understood what was going on. She didn't know if he had any understanding of the state of their personal financial affairs.

And, as it would turn out, neither did Hanna.

CHAPTER TWENTY

Hanna

Munich and Berlin
September 1936–March 1937

On a cool fall morning at the end of September, Moses passed away. It was a peaceful passing, for which Hanna was grateful. Both she and Helene were by his side.

He was buried in the Jewish cemetery in Munich, where his mother and father and his two previous wives now rested.

Hanna had little time for mourning, for the shedding of tears. There was much to attend to before she would be able to leave. She needed to make arrangements for the care of the house so that she might be away for an undetermined time. She had to get the gallery cleaned out for the new owner, close bank accounts, and arrange for her travel. She would make a new life for herself in America with their children, and when the political situation was better they would return to Germany.

The following week, she and Josef spent several days at the gallery, packing up the few remaining paintings and sorting through financial papers. Just days before she was to sign the contract, Josef stayed on to finish boxing up business records. Hanna suggested he come by for dinner.

She waited. An hour passed, then another. Finally, she put on her wrap and took the tram to the gallery, fearing something had happened to him.

When she arrived on Theatinerstrasse, she saw dark smoke rising—obviously not from a chimney—and, as she got closer to the gallery, she could see it was coming from their building. She dashed down the street, her heart pumping, a pulse throbbing in every part of her body. The door was locked, and she couldn't get in.

"Help, please, someone help!" she screamed as she yanked and pulled and kicked on the door. No one answered. She pounded on the window, but had not the strength to break it. She glanced around, looking for something with which to bash in the window, but could find nothing. Finally, a man rushed up carrying a walking stick, the golden face of a lion on the head. He raised the stick and smashed the window, stepped over broken glass, and unlocked the door.

Hanna rushed inside. The air was thick with smoke. She put a hand over her nose and mouth. A pile of smoldering paper and canvases sat in the middle of the first gallery. The man attempted to smother it. She could make out a fire in the second hall, and rushed in, took off her coat, and immediately began slapping at the flames. But then she realized—Josef! She screamed, "Josef! Josef!"

Hanna dashed into the office still shouting his name, her cries the color of what she now saw—Josef lying in a crimson puddle. Her beautiful, beloved Josef, lying in his own blood. Across the wall, two words screamed out at her, matching the high-pitched wails that Hanna knew were coming from deep within her own body.

Scrawled across the white wall in deep, dark, blood red—JEWISH FAGGOT.

Hanna remembered nothing more of that day. And the next few days were but a fog. The following two weeks were lost. She would have only vague memories, but she knew she did not cry. She could not cry.

When finally she began to piece her life back together, she realized what a tangle of financial problems she would have to deal with. The final papers for the sale of the gallery had not yet been signed, and the buyer demanded repairs now be completed. Hanna also learned the insurance policy had lapsed. Much of their remaining art had been destroyed in the fire. The pile of rubbish that she found in the smoldering heap in the gallery must have contained some of the business records as well, and it was almost impossible to put all the parts of her financial and emotional life back together. It soon became evident that she would have to sell the house. A buyer was easily found, at a ridiculously low price, and after taxes and bills were paid she had far less than she had expected. Though many of the pieces in the gallery were owned by the Fleischmanns, there were several artist-owned paintings, and Hanna felt obligated to pay for those destroyed in the fire.

She went to Berlin and stayed with Helene and Jakob. They knew it was her wish to return to America to be with her children, but it soon became evident that, as she had waited for her husband's health to improve, the ease with which she had once left Germany had all but disappeared. There was now talk of quotas, enormous emigration taxes to be paid, and the amount of money that could be sent out of the country was limited. And yet, at the same time, one was required to show sufficient income to prove there would be no burden to the country of immigration, that jobs would not be taken from the true citizens. The entire world was still recovering from the Great Depression, and it seemed no one wanted these Germans who were looking for a new life.

Hanna went to the American Consulate in Berlin and stood in line with others who were attempting to leave the country. She realized that her children were living in America on visitors' visas and feared if she mentioned them, they might be forced to return. She knew she would be asked if she had relatives in America who would sponsor her, and she feared that if she used her sister's name, somehow the American immigration authorities would become aware of her children not having returned, and oh, she didn't know what to do. She was very much afraid. She had prided herself on being an independent woman. She had traveled to America twice without Moses, but now Hanna felt as if she could accomplish nothing on her own. She wished to have her husband to advise her, to hold her in his arms and comfort her.

She was given information on the requirements for emigration. The list was long and included a request for multiple copies of multiple forms, including tax documents, bank account affidavits, statements of sponsorship and support, certificates of good conduct, and proof of physical examination. She had none of these and was told to come back with the proper forms.

She stayed several more weeks with Helene and Jakob, attempting to get the papers sent from Munich, but the accountants and bankers with whom Moses had worked were either gone or would not respond to her inquiries. She could not spend her days waiting in Berlin. Helene and Jakob continued to offer their home and hospitality, though it was quite evident that business was not going well. They had but one servant in the house, and the meals were not the lavish offerings Hanna remembered from the pre-Hitler days. They, too, were feeling the financial burden of attempting to run a Jewish business in Nazi Germany.

"I can't sit here waiting," she told Helene one morning after breakfast. "I must return to Munich."

"Where will you go?" she asked, knowing they had sold their home, the home where she'd grown up.

"Leni," Hanna said. "Leni will help me."

As she was preparing to return, she knew she must make one more visit before leaving Berlin.

Hanna went to call on Botho von Gamp.

He was very proud of the fact that he now owned two large works by Kandinsky.

"You know our Führer would not approve," she said as she stood before Kandinsky's *Composition*, touched by the colors of a familiar melody as well as the memories evoked by this painting. Hanna wanted desperately to reclaim it. And again she felt that ache of betrayal on Moses' part, and the once-joyful sounds seemed oddly muted and dulled.

"He sees little value in the modern," Botho agreed.

They did not speak of it, but they both knew the Führer was stripping the state museums of anything he considered modern. While he touted himself as a lover and supporter of the arts, he abhorred the "modern," which he'd said was more suited for junkyards.

"Hitler is mounting an exhibition of German art," Botho went on. The Haus der Deutschen Kunst was near completion, and Hanna had heard that the Reich Chamber was still in the process of collecting pieces for the opening.

Hitler's original intention was to fill the halls of the new art temple with cultural treasures, the traditional state-owned paintings by artists such as Dürer, Holbein, and Grünewald. But then, abruptly, he'd shifted and declared that the Haus der Deutschen Kunst would be filled with new German art, though it was very confusing to those attempting to gather the art, as no one understood what he meant by "new German art."

"Quite the lover of art, our Führer," Hanna replied, barely attempting to hide her sarcasm, though she knew it was becoming increasingly more dangerous to say anything against Hitler, even as a joke, unless well aware of the company one was keeping. Even children who were educated in state schools were known to report their parents for anti-Hitler remarks.

"Yes, it will be interesting to see what graces the walls of his new temple," Botho said with what Hanna detected as a wince.

"I would like to purchase the Kandinsky," she came back abruptly.

"I'm sorry," he said, his voice laced with sincerity, and Hanna thought for a moment that he was going to say—so sorry I stole your painting. But instead he said, "For the loss of your husband." The way he said it, he might as well have said, *I know Moses left you with little more than the hat you are wearing. How can you possibly purchase this Kandinsky from me?*

"It has become an important piece in my collection," he continued. "I wouldn't consider selling it."

He offered Hanna coffee and they sat and visited about nothing really, perhaps both of them afraid to speak their minds, maybe even fearing they had already said more than caution might have advised. Hanna wondered if he knew how desperately she wanted to leave Germany, if he was aware that her children were no longer here.

Hanna returned to Munich alone. Completely alone. Without her children, her husband, her painting. She stayed with Leni. She missed the life they had in Munich, and the days when they lived and breathed for the art, for the artists whose vibrant colors brought her such joy, and even the dark, brooding colors of the artists who expressed the sadness left from the Great War. There was nothing but emptiness now. Some days, Hanna wished she had died along with Moses.

CHAPTER TWENTY-ONE

Hanna

Munich
April–June 1937

With great frustration Hanna looked for work and soon discovered that for a woman her age with limited skills, there was nothing.

She applied for a position as a seamstress's assistant, but when she was asked her name, the position was suddenly filled.

Then she answered an ad for a millinery shop that called for a Christian lady.

"I have experience working with customers," Hanna told the owner.

"Where have you worked?"

"At an art gallery here in Munich."

"Selling art is hardly the same as selling women's hats and gloves," he said. "I'll let you know."

Of course, he didn't.

She visited Ernst Hausmann, the new owner of the Fleischmann Gallery, now the Hausmann Gallery. He was a small, thin man with a soft lavender voice. Hanna had met him once after he'd expressed his initial interest in buying the business. Josef, and then a man from their bank, had handled the actual sale of the gallery.

Herr Hausmann graciously offered her tea, getting up to prepare it himself.

She gazed about the room. A client stood with Moses, and she could hear her husband's low, even voice, though she could not make out his words. The walls were covered with color, and then Moses along with the colors evaporated before her eyes and ears. Now Josef moved in a quick flash about the gallery, his voice rising and falling with excitement.

She was hallucinating, of course. She understood this much. Did this, the realization that it wasn't real, mean she was not going crazy? She felt a tightness in her throat, and then she felt as if she was about to stand up and scream. Holding her hand to her heart, she took a deep breath, attempting to pull herself together. Again she studied the room, and now she saw that it looked and sounded nothing like it had when it was the Fleischmann Gallery. Could she spend her days here again with memories of how it was then, how much everything had changed?

"How may I help you, Frau Fleischmann?" Herr Hausmann asked as he placed a tray with tea, milk, and sugar on the table, and then sat.

"I'm looking for work."

"I was under the impression that you had left the country." He poured her a cup.

Would he be less inclined to offer her work if he knew how desperately she was attempting to leave? Hanna shook her head, but felt any words she might utter were stuck in her throat. She gulped a drink of hot tea, feeling it burn as she swallowed.

"No," she replied. "I'm still here in Munich."

"I'm looking for someone . . . well, to help with various menial tasks around the gallery," he said, waving toward the tray, his words almost apologetic. "I'm afraid this is all I have to offer right now."

Once more, Hanna found herself back in the gallery, again as little more than a charwoman—sweeping floors, washing windows, preparing tea. Yet she was grateful to have this, as it gave her some income and placed her back where she felt comfortable—with the art.

The paintings in the gallery were mostly traditional. A few new artists were represented, but there was nothing one would consider "modern." Hanna was not fond of these "new" German artists, as there was no creativity or personal style. Everything was done in such a way as not to offend Hitler, which meant it was often pretty, and while it was meant to reflect reality, it represented in no way what was real in Nazi Germany.

Eventually, having saved much of her salary, Hanna was able to rent a room of her own. She now had little left, not even her piano or the music to comfort her in the absence of those she loved. The art was gone, save for the drawing of her that had been done long ago at the Academy. She had found it stored away in a box while cleaning out the home that Moses and she and his two wives before her had shared for so many years. The image of this innocent country girl brought a smile and sweet memories. *Was that really me?* Hanna wondered.

As the days and weeks dragged on, she was informed of additional tax forms that had not been filed. Papers arrived from the bank, and she realized her lack of financial resources would be the greatest roadblock in her attempt to go to her children.

Her job at the gallery created a rift with Helene and Jakob, who could not understand how she would consider becoming part of this Aryanization of Germany.

How can you work, Helene wrote, *in a business that right-fully should still belong to the family?*

It wasn't difficult to see that businesses owned by Jews were being forcibly sold to non-Jews at ridiculously low prices, that the owners had no other choice. Helene said they would take care of her, though Hanna knew she did not understand how much she needed her independence, and Hanna realized the Kaufmanns' own resources must be dwindling.

You're nothing more than a servant, Helene said, *a maid, cleaning up after the Aryans.*

She wrote as if Hanna were a Jew who had betrayed her people. Did Helene not recall that Hanna had started out as a maid in her father's home?

Ernst Hausmann was an agreeable man and Hanna was grateful for the work. Her employer soon realized she had considerable knowledge of art and had been very much involved in her husband's business. Within a short time she was taking a more active part in running the gallery, arranging displays and meeting with clients when he was not available.

One morning he approached Hanna and said, "A representative of the Chamber of Art will be visiting the gallery this afternoon, Frau Fleischmann, and I would like you to attend to him as I will be off on other business."

"What is the reason for this visit?" she asked.

"I'm sure you will be informed when he arrives."

Hanna was aware that the Chamber of Art, a division of the Reich Chamber of Culture, was still attempting to find additional work for the grand opening of the Haus der Deutschen Kunst, which would take place in just weeks. Pieces that were considered Aryan were pulled from the various government museums to be part of the exhibition. Dealers and gallery owners were being enlisted to make the Chamber aware of any new and talented artists who were celebrating the German people. They were all to be included in this event, which Hanna took to mean pieces might be "donated" from private galleries. It was presented as a contest, the coveted reward being the display in Hitler's temple of art.

On the other hand, modern pieces continued to be removed from state-supported museums, not for display in the German House of Art, but because Hitler did not want what was now being called *entartete kunst*—degenerate art—shown in Germany.

Hanna wondered if perhaps this representative was coming because the prior gallery, the Fleischmann Gallery, had been particularly known for its forward thinking and for showing the modern.

But a "modern" piece was not to be found in the new Hausmann Gallery.

A small number of paintings in the gallery were actually quite nice. Hanna was very fond of two Franz von Stucks that had been brought in by a Jewish collector who wished to sell them in his efforts to do what Hanna was also attempting to do—leave Germany. Word was that the officials in Berlin were known to make an unofficial deal to put a name at the top of the list. With quotas filled in many countries, the visas were often going to the highest bidder.

At precisely 4:00 P.M., the designated time, a well-dressed gentleman, accompanied by two young men in uniform, entered the gallery.

"I am Herr Brandt from the Chamber of Art," he said stiffly. "I am to meet with Herr Ernst Hausmann."

"I'm afraid Herr Hausmann is not available," Hanna explained.

"Why was I not informed of this?"

"I would be more than happy to help you," she said.

"And who are you?"

"Herr Hausmann's assistant," she replied, though she had been given no such title.

"Frau . . . ?" He motioned with his head for her to supply her name.

"Hanna Fleischmann."

The man's eyes darted about, but he said nothing more. Hanna offered him wine, coffee, or tea, all of which he declined. Without explanation, he started through the first gallery, as the two young soldiers stood by the door in military stances.

After a quick walk through the second hall, Herr Brandt marched into the parlor and, without a word, he sat, again gazing about, his eyes flickering with irritation. Hanna asked if he would like something, a glass of water perhaps, and he nodded a yes.

She went to fetch it herself, handed it to him, and stood, waiting for him to speak. She wasn't sure what it was that he wanted. She guessed that he was here to examine the art, perhaps confiscate it, or perhaps receive a gift for the Führer's exhibition. But she didn't know how this next step was to be conducted—remove the art, have Hitler sort through it to claim what he liked, perhaps even destroy what he did not?

"*Bitte,*" the man said, with a touch of resignation, motioning for her to sit. She did.

"Herr Brandt, what may I do for you?"

He gave off an exhausted sigh and then he said, "Sometimes it is impossible to know what the Führer wants. He speaks of true German art. I bring him a painting by Franz Marc. No truer German has ever existed. Born in Munich, educated in Germany. He served his country well, a true soldier, a true German. He gave his life for his country, and yet the Führer rants and raves, 'What have you brought me, but rubbish.' I once brought a lovely painting for him to examine and he became so enraged he kicked a hole through the canvas and stomped out of the room."

Hanna shuddered, and her stomach turned at the thought of Hitler kicking a hole through a painting. Particularly a Franz Marc.

"It is not a simple task to determine what the Führer means when he says German art."

Hanna didn't know why Herr Brandt was sharing this with her. It was not a wise move to speak any words other than adoring praise for their dictator. And though he was not actually criticizing, he was expressing some frustration. He took a deep, cleansing swallow of water, adjusted his back, stiffening his posture, then rose as a brave soldier about to do battle. "Tell me, Frau Fleischmann, if you were to choose five paintings from your gallery to display in the Haus der Deutschen Kunst for all of Germany to see what lovely art we have produced, which five would you choose?"

She was slightly taken aback by his request. Was Hanna to choose, or was he trying to catch her in some kind of betrayal? She wished only for him to gather his paintings as quickly as possible and leave.

Herr Brandt motioned Hanna to accompany him, and then quietly they walked about the gallery, the man stopping for a moment before a painting, then moving on to another. He said nothing, and Hanna tried to watch his facial expressions to determine which he found agreeable, which paintings he might consider presenting to the Führer for his approval.

German art is what the Führer says is German art, she thought, as they continued through the gallery. There were no guidelines other than these. It was not the artist, unless of course he was Jewish, which would automatically rule him out. German art was whatever Hitler decided it was. This was the way all aspects of culture were determined now, in music and literature as well as art.

And then she realized how easily she could do this. She had spent years at the Fleischmann Gallery working with clients, generally the most difficult, as Moses always said she had a way with them.

Hanna would suggest they browse, and she would watch carefully—the movement of the eyes, a twitch of a brow, a lift of the lips or a disapproving downward tug of displeasure. On a second stroll through the gallery, she would point out subtleties in the works they seemed to favor, offer what she saw as the most striking aspects of the work. She would ask questions. Is this for your personal collection? Do you wish to buy the painting as a gift? An investment? Where will it be displayed? If the situation felt right, she might suggest that the value of a particular painting would surely increase. But always she considered that a choice must be based primarily on personal taste, rarely admitting that she preferred some artists over others.

At times she would go outside the gallery to other dealers, even scout out a particular work. Once she was even asked by Frau Hummel to match the drapes in her music room, another time to find something complementary to the hues of the marble fireplace mantel. She was delighted with the painting Hanna found by a young German artist she knew would slip into obscurity. Yes, Hanna knew her clients. She knew what they would like.

And somehow she knew what Hitler would like.

She thought back many years to the day he had come to the gallery. A mama's boy, Hanna thought now, remembering how the young man had stomped out of the gallery. A little boy always seeking the approval of his mother. And she thought of how Leni carried on about Hitler's respect for motherhood and German wives.

"This painting," she said, pointing to a rather precious portrait of a blond woman, who actually looked a little like Leni—Hanna had noticed when it was delivered to the gallery how much it resembled her most beautiful sister. The woman sat on a simple wooden chair with her perfect little brood of three gathered adoringly around her. They all wore traditional German folk costumes, had a healthy glow about them, and Hanna had no doubt that it would find favor with the Führer.

"This one," she told Herr Brandt.

He examined the work for several long moments, during

which Hanna held her breath, and then he motioned to one of the two young men who stood silently at the door. The man was blond and brawny, the ideal German soldier.

Hanna let out a relieved breath, and then decided she should choose something representing the land, a scene with farmers. She picked one of workers during the harvest and looked to Herr Brandt for his approval. He smiled and nodded, first at Hanna, then the soldiers.

Ah, she thought, as the larger of the two young men lifted this one off the wall and placed it aside with her first choice, she must choose a nude—the Führer must have a nude. Inwardly, Hanna laughed a little, because she was actually having some fun here, the most fun she'd had in a long time. She could rid the gallery of the most distasteful art, have it carried off to be displayed before all of Germany in the new house of new German art.

"A good, wholesome, healthy Aryan woman," she said out loud. It was known that the mediocre artist Adolf Ziegler, who specialized in painting nudes, was a Hitler favorite. He had recently been appointed as President of the Chamber of Art. Oh, that she would have had one of Ziegler's beautiful nudes hanging in her gallery at this very moment! So she picked a portrait of three young women, surely done in imitation of Ziegler, as many of the young artists were painting to imitate what had already been approved. There was no originality. Originality had become *verboten*.

The three women in the painting sat in the most distorted and unnatural poses, on a stone bench—oh, cold bottoms, Hanna thought, and tried not to smile. In imitation of Ziegler, the artist hadn't been able to get those women to appear fully sitting. Perhaps a bit of a shadow here could have improved the situation, could have done away with that floating-bottom look, could have settled those three perfect posteriors down on the bench, she mused, trying to repaint the canvas in her mind, trying not to giggle.

"Two more," Herr Brandt encouraged her.

Surely they must represent the Aryan man also. A soldier, Hanna decided, looking around the gallery. Hitler loved anything depicting soldiers, wars, even mythical battles. Ah, there, a nice painting of a young soldier with his square—verging on cartoonish—Aryan jaw, his look of determination. "Here," she motioned, feeling quite confident now.

And for her final choice . . . Hanna walked slowly about the gallery, and realized for this one she might have to make a sacrifice. She stood before one of the few paintings in the gallery that she truly loved, for the creation itself, for the memories it brought, for the man who had painted it. Surely not a product of Nazi Germany, as the painter had died years ago. But she knew Hitler would love it, and she knew he could claim credit for anything he wanted.

It was a lovely Franz von Stuck entitled *Spring*, a mythical figure of a woman with flowers in her long flowing hair. Hanna knew Hitler loved the work of Franz von Stuck, who in his day, before the Kandinskys, Jawlenskys, Picassos, had been considered very modern and avant-garde. And perhaps this was where those attempting to choose the perfect Aryan art were confused. There was a modern art nouveau look about the artist's work, yet he favored mythical, allegorical, and classical themes. And Hitler identified with the classical. Hanna remembered that after the Beer Hall Putsch of 1923 he had hidden at his friend's home, Ernst Franz Hanfstaengl, and she knew the name because they had sold him a Franz von Stuck, *The Medusa*. Oddly, Hitler later said that it reminded him of his mother. And it was said his own personal style, his physical appearance—the square little mustache, the hair combed forward—was influenced by a von Stuck painting, the Norse god Odin.

"The Franz von Stuck," she told Herr Brandt, and here Hanna had to keep her inner laughter from turning to tears.

"Yes," he agreed, delighted. Then something in his eyes, about his brow, shifted. "Ah, yes." He, too, seemed almost sad, as if he

understood that this was now ripping her heart out. She wondered if he had been forced, as so many citizens of Germany, to
serve the Führer when he did not believe in the man's cause, or
perhaps his cause—to resurrect Germany—but not in the hateful
way he wished to accomplish it.

Herr Brandt collected his paintings, and they were taken away
by the two young strapping soldiers, who Hanna was sure had no
idea about the origin or quality of the art, had no idea if the dictator of all things cultural and otherwise would be pleased, or if
he would smash the paintings or kick holes in them.

After they left the gallery with the five paintings, Hanna felt
drained. She walked around, examining the bare spaces on the
walls where the paintings had hung just moments before. She was
shivering, though the gallery was not cold. Finally she sat. Again
she looked around the room, remembering when it had been
called the Fleischmann, thinking of those bold days when they
had hung the likes of Picasso, Klimt, Munch, Marc, and her
beloved Kandinsky. She could see the colors, vivid and pulsing.
She felt it again—an excitement and sense of innovation that
vibrated in the air, a time she feared would never exist again.

And then she could hear the colors, dancing on the canvases
that had covered the walls, now so drab and lifeless.

Hanna laughed out loud, a nervous, frightening sound coming forth from her own body.

And then the tears came. Slowly at first, and then profusely,
her entire body shaking. She could not stop herself, as she trembled, as the tears fell, until it seemed every ounce of moisture and
life had been drained from her, as if she might collapse and fall to
the floor. Yes, she wept for the art, for her children, her beloved
Josef, her Moses. Hanna wept for Germany.

One week later she received word that the Führer wished to
meet with her.

CHAPTER TWENTY-TWO

Hanna

Munich and Berchtesgaden
June–July 1937

"I am Herr Berger," the handsome young man introduced himself. "I will serve as your escort, Frau Fleischmann." Hanna had been informed of the time and date on which she should be prepared for her journey, but she was given no reason for the meeting, which had been arranged at the convenience of the Führer. All of Germany was operating on Hitler time now. Why shouldn't she? She was advised that she would travel by train, and though Hanna was not told where she would be going, she had been told to pack a bag.

A driver was waiting out front of the gallery. Herr Berger held the door for Hanna as she slipped into the backseat. Surely if she was being transported to one of Hitler's camps, she would not be taking a bag, and she would not be provided with escort, private car, and driver.

She was surprised at the courtesy of the young man and the respect with which he addressed her. He didn't explain why the Führer wished to meet with her. Perhaps he didn't know. Hanna guessed that he was sent to escort her to the train, but when they arrived at the station, unloaded the car, and the young man handed two tickets to the conductor, it appeared that he would accompany her the entire way. The thought had come to Hanna on several occasions as she prepared mentally and physically for her trip that the Führer had remembered her from years ago when he'd come to the gallery with his drawings and she had sent him away. But so many years had passed; surely he would not recognize her. Some days when she gazed in the mirror, Hanna hardly recognized herself. Her flaming red hair, now interwoven with strands of silver, barely contained the embers of fire. Her once-youthful figure had rounded and plumped. Hitler would not recognize her. But might he recognize her name?

They traveled south from Munich, Herr Berger asking several times if he could get her refreshments, if there was anything she needed.

"*Nein, danke,*" Hanna replied each time, too nervous to entertain the idea of eating or drinking anything.

They arrived at the train station at Berchtesgaden, which Hanna knew was near the Austrian border. Another young man came to fetch them in a late-model automobile and they drove silently up into the mountains. It was a beautiful part of the country in the Bavarian Alps, and under different circumstances Hanna might have felt at ease, even at home, yet her entire body was now shaking with fear. A lovely chalet perched on the hillside came into view, and Herr Berger told her this was where the Führer came to relax from his trying days. "He's often seen in the village, dressed in the costume of the *Volk*." It was a word that was now bandied about by Hitler and his followers—as if they were part of the common folk.

Herr Berger showed Hanna to a private bedroom and said that supper would be served at 8:30. She was to be prompt. Dress was informal.

"Perhaps you'd like a walk about the grounds before supper," he offered.

Thinking it might help rid her of the tension, Hanna said, "*Danke.* That would be very nice."

She asked for a few moments and the young man left. She studied the room—a bed, dresser with water pitcher and mirror. Several small paintings hung on the walls, watercolors of country scenes. She stepped closer and noticed the signature. *A. Hitler.*

Shortly, Herr Berger knocked on the door and asked if she was ready for a walk.

Hanna stepped out of the room and was led down the hall and out the back door. As Herr Berger escorted her about the grounds, she thought of how much Willy would love this setting, and it struck her that Herr Berger was about the same age as her son. Once more she was grateful that her children had escaped, even if she never saw them again. Hitler had taken the best of the youth, and with his propaganda had convinced them that he was the only hope for Germany, to revive the economy, to return the nation once more to world power.

The air was fresh and clean and reminded Hanna so much of the farm where she grew up—the beautiful mountain pastures and lush green meadows with the tranquil resonance of home, the imposing majestic Alps that could still send a wonderful shiver through her very core. Oh, what a lovely place, our Bavaria, she thought. And this, Hitler could not change. Memories of her childhood flooded back, then her trip to Munich, becoming part of the Fleischmann family, her lovely Helene, Moses, Young Helene and Jakob, Little Jakob. Is this how it is just before one's life is to end? she wondered. This stream of places and people from one's past?

Two large Alsatians, enclosed within a fenced area, barked and nipped at each other playfully. They looked very familiar, as Hitler was often photographed with his beloved pets. Hanna stopped and they came up to the gate, slapping their tails in a friendly greeting. Again she thought of her family home in Bavaria, the animals both Willy and Isabella loved. She wondered if her children would ever again visit their uncle Frederick in the country.

"Frau Fleischmann," her young escort interrupted her thoughts, "perhaps you wish to return to your room. Dinner will be served in half an hour."

Hanna returned to her room and combed through her hair, freshened her face with a quick dab of lipstick and rouge as if she were off to a social affair. She used the bathroom down the hall, returned to her room, and waited for a knock.

She was escorted to a dining room and left alone. The room was decorated in quaint Bavarian-style mountain furnishings. Hanna stood, wondering what she was to do. She glanced around, studying the paintings on the walls, one a pastoral setting and another a profile of Hitler in his military uniform.

As she stared at the portrait, the man himself walked in, and the first thing she thought was how different he looked and yet how very little he had changed since he came those many years ago to the gallery. At the time, a young artist, stiff and proud, and determined. Now older, the hair shorter, combed in a slightly different fashion, the mustache added since that day. He wore not the military uniform he was most often photographed wearing, and in the portrait on the wall, but the casual dress of the country—short pants, heavy stockings, and gray woolen jacket. *Like my father, my brothers,* Hanna thought. So intent on showing that he was one of them. His eyes, still the same—very pale blue. Deep, but empty. The tone as intense as anything she had ever heard.

"Frau Fleischmann," he said, "a pleasure." His voice sounded sincere, accommodating, another gentleman, like the young man he had so graciously sent to accompany her from Munich.

Hanna lowered her head, feeling fear, discomfort, incredulity, and then shame that she could offer this gesture of respect to such a man.

When she looked up, she sensed that he did not recognize her, and she felt some of the tension release itself from her body.

He invited her to sit. It appeared there would be no others partaking of the meal, which quickly reinstated Hanna's discomfort. A familiar scent, one from long ago, entered her nostrils. Soap and sweat, now tinged with a slight smell of country leather.

A pretty young blonde, in local dress and apron, presented them each with a bowl of soup, a basket of hearty brown Bavarian bread. The Führer passed the bread as if they were a little family of two sitting down for supper. They ate, at first without words. Her hand shook as she brought the soup to her mouth, as she broke off a small piece of bread. She could barely swallow.

"You find the accommodations agreeable?" he asked.

"Yes"—she started to say Herr Hitler, but then realized she didn't even know what to call him.

"I find it a relaxing atmosphere," he said, "to get away, to pursue pleasures away from my duties of caring for my people and my country."

A lump of bread caught in her throat. How could he speak such words? *Caring for my people?* She swallowed it down with a drink of water.

"You have children?" he asked.

"A son and daughter."

"Grandchildren?"

"Not yet." She knew this was Hitler's entire view of women— propagators of the Aryan race. And Hanna realized he saw her as an older woman, and was treating her with respect as he would his elderly aunt. He was just a few years younger than Hanna but regarded her as much older, which she took as both an insult and a great fortune for her under the circumstances. It was known that romantically Hitler favored younger women who would not dare to challenge his intellect. Respect for women and motherhood was deeply rooted in party propaganda, but what would he think if he knew Hanna had produced two children with a Jewish father, one by deception, one who would not fit Hitler's concept of a human being in any way.

"My condolences on your husband's passing."

A heat passed through her—not fear, Hanna realized, but indignation and anger. How dared he speak of her husband. This man was not worthy to polish her husband's shoes. Was he merely informing her that he knew she was the wife of Moses Fleischmann, the Jew? Yet, he now treated her with kindness. Was this the charm so many spoke of? Hanna saw it as nothing more than masterful manipulation and despicable duplicity. She imagined Hitler would say whatever necessary to draw one in, to gain a person's trust or to secure for himself whatever it was he wanted from them. But what did he want from Hanna? She said nothing in response, and prayed he would ask no more about her children.

They continued eating in silence, and then the young woman removed the bowls and brought in two plates with sausage, potatoes, and vegetables for Hanna, nothing but an enormous mound of potatoes for the Führer. Hanna waited. He nodded for her to continue. She ate several bites, and then realized she did not have the stomach to eat anything more. Her insides were rumbling and turning and tossing, and she felt that she might not be able to hold it down.

After some time, the young woman returned and removed Hanna's plate. Hitler asked that she wrap the remainder and save it for the dogs. Ah, yes, Hanna thought, Hitler, the animal lover.

The woman soon came back with dessert—slices of a Viennese torte, layered with fruit and cream, topped with an enormous mound of whipped cream for the Führer, a reasonable-sized dollop for Hanna.

He ate with great relish, wiping a lathering of the cream from his face. He asked if she'd like coffee, and remembering his refusal the day he came to the gallery, she said, "No, thank you."

The young woman cleared the table.

"I've been impressed with your selection for the German Art Museum," he said, staring directly at Hanna. His blue eyes were filled with approval, though if he knew what she really thought of the paintings, other than the sacrificial Franz von Stuck, it would surely turn to condemnation.

"Thank you," she managed to say.

"You were born in Bavaria?" he asked.

"In the Allgäu on a dairy farm."

He nodded affably. "Your father is a man of the land."

"Yes, a farmer."

"You learned of art from your husband?" he said.

"Yes," she replied, fearing she was treading on shaky ground. Was he attempting to get her to deny she had been married to a Jew when he obviously knew? Perhaps he wished Hanna to declare that she had been converted to his cause, that with the loss of her husband she was now able to reclaim her Aryan roots.

"We must work together, we Germans," he started in, "those with knowledge of the true German art, for the art must represent the beauty of our country and people. Above all, the subject matter should be understood. The art must be for the people. The art must represent the true beauty of nature, of that which is real and good. Art must always use the true forms seen in nature. Don't you agree, Frau Fleischmann?"

Hanna nodded a yes.

"Healthy art must be uplifting, noble, idealistic," he exclaimed, and held out his arms as if asking her to contribute to this conversation.

"Yes," she agreed, "art must be noble."

"There is no value in vile representations by scribblers and canvas scrawlers," he barked, overcome with emotion now, his eyes fixed on Hanna. She nodded and said nothing, as though she agreed with every word that came out of his mouth.

"Paintings and sculptures created by cultural Neanderthals and mental defectives? This is art?"

Hanna's back stiffened, fearing he knew about Willy.

The man continued, carrying on in a diatribe that made little sense. He spoke of the contemptibility of "unfinished work," paintings that distorted the beauty of nature and the German people. He spoke of art that could not be understood by the common man. "Elitist art," he railed, raising his clenched fist in defiance, "we must rid Germany of this elitist art. Art must be for the people."

Hanna sat quietly, her shoulders aching, her head throbbing, nodding now and then, as if someone else, someone who agreed with this madman, had entered her body. A sense of shame washed over her, but she could not speak.

He placed his napkin on the table and then said, "It is refreshing to find an art dealer who has an understanding of true German art, a dealer who celebrates the artistic accomplishments of the German people, one who possesses the proper sensitivity for art. How vile the artists who turn the beauty of Germany and its people into garbage, distortions, the foulest representations of life." Hanna knew he was referring to the very art they had shown at the Fleischmann, the art that now had no place in the museums and galleries. At any moment, she felt he might condemn her for being a traitor to the people and government, or perhaps grind her up and feed her to his dogs.

He rose and walked toward the window. Hanna remained seated, nervously wringing her hands under the table, wondering why she was here.

He looked out. "A beautiful view."

"Yes," she said, thinking this was possibly the only thing in which she could find common ground with Hitler—the beauty of Bavaria, the majestic mountains. She realized from the window he could see the country of his birth—Austria.

"We will have a grand opening of the Haus der Kunst in July," he said. "I would like to invite you as my guest."

"*Danke,*" she said, swallowing what felt like a stone. She didn't know what else to say.

"In conjunction with the Aryan exhibition," Hitler continued, "it has been decided to show the art that the Republic—" And here he practically spat out the word *Republic*, as if it were as vile as the art it had endorsed. "All of Germany must see how the Republic wasted the people's money. This rubbish will show in another exhibition so the people can compare the Aryan art with—" He couldn't, or chose not to, finish the thought in words, so overcome with irritation. "I wish you a pleasant return to Munich," he said, and then he swiveled abruptly in military-like fashion and left the room.

Hanna didn't know what to do. She remained seated for several moments, turning these thoughts over in her head. She had been invited as a guest to Hitler's art exhibition. And there would also be an exhibition of *entartete kunst*—the very art she had loved, the art that Moses and Hanna had introduced to so many in Munich, in Germany, and throughout the world. Now the Führer was going to put it forth for the people of Germany to ridicule..

After some time she decided she should return to her room. As soon as she stood, the young Herr Berger entered and escorted her down the hall.

"We will return on the seven A.M. train to Munich tomorrow," he told her as they reached Hanna's room. "Breakfast will be brought to you at five thirty A.M. I will call on you at six A.M." He wished that she sleep well and left.

Hanna did not sleep well, thoughts of what had just transpired pushing and spinning and burning inside her. Had she won the Führer's approval? She had been invited as his guest to attend the grand opening of the German Haus der Deutschen Kunst.

Three days after returning to Munich, Hanna was released

from the gallery, though she was given no explanation as to why. She knew it would be but a short time before she would no longer be able to pay the monthly lease on her room. Again, she went out looking for work. She felt every eye was upon her, that someone was watching her every move. Once more she attempted to gather the proper papers to go to her children, though she knew she did not have sufficient funds to do so.

The following week she received an official invitation to be an honored guest at *Tag der Deutschen Kunst*, The Day of German Art, in Munich on July 18, 1937. It was an invitation she knew she could not refuse.

And, strangely, Hanna now realized it was the art itself that had become her greatest obstacle to fleeing Germany.

CHAPTER TWENTY-THREE

Hanna

Munich
July 1937

Sculpted eagles clutching swastikas perched atop tall pylons along Prinzregentenstrasse. Hundreds of poles displaying bright Nazi flags, as shrill as the color of blood, lined the route from the railroad station to the center of Munich. A parade of more than seven thousand—soldiers in military uniform, performers in colorful costumes, garishly decorated animals, and motorcars—wound through the streets, moving with a great sense of celebration to the temple of German art.

Hanna was given a place of honor on a large dais, along with dignitaries and several other women, mostly widows of men whom the Führer had admired. Men dressed as Renaissance artists and Nordic gods marched triumphantly, intermingled with Viking ships and scale models of Hitler's architectural wonders, in this bizarre pageant to celebrate the artistic achievements of Germany. If Hanna had been one of the *volk* lining the street to view this spectacle, rather than an honored guest, she might have laughed. But as she looked down toward the cheering crowd she could do nothing but tremble with fear.

The highlight of the Day of German Art was the opening of

the Haus der Deutschen Kunst with the *Grosse Deutsche Kunstausstellung*, the Great German Art Exhibition.

From those still bold enough to make light of Hitler's grand accomplishments, Hanna had heard the building described as the Palazzo Kitschi, as well as the Munich Air Terminal. She had even heard a group of young people on the street referring to it as the *Bratwürstelgalerie* because the pillars that ran along the front of the building looked like sausages hanging from a butcher's shop. It was a monstrous, ugly building, constructed of sandstone and wasted, sacrificial marble, designed by one of Hitler's favorite architects, Paul Ludwig Troost, who had since passed on. His widow, Gertrude, was one of those being honored that day.

The Führer stood before his new temple, microphones set in place, as the parade concluded. Hanna, as a guest, was assigned a position so close she could see the twitch in his cheek as he prepared to address the crowd. He looked over the mass, his eyes moving slowly, though they appeared glazed—he was not seeing individuals, merely a throng of entranced followers.

He began his speech, praising the art of Germany.

"The artist does not create for the artist, but for the people," he declared, beaming with pride. He went on speaking of the valuable enrichment of Germany's cultural life. And then, abruptly, his tone and even his face shifted, and words like *purification* and *extermination* flew frantically and fervently toward the adoring crowd. "With the opening of this exhibition has come the end of artistic lunacy and with it the artistic pollution of our people," he shouted. From where Hanna stood she could see the spittle spraying from his mouth.

As Hitler had told her just weeks earlier, in conjunction with the grand opening of the Haus der Deutschen Kunst, another exhibition would take place. The following day the exhibition of *Entartete Kunst*, Degenerate Art, would open, and Hanna knew that today Hitler was just warming up the crowd for what was to follow.

After the speech, Hanna and the other guests were escorted into the building. They waited, standing together in the vast entrance, an enormous hall lined with red flags, potted laurel trees, and busts and paintings of the Führer. No one spoke, as if they were in a grand cathedral waiting for the services to begin on a sacred holiday.

After some time, Hitler appeared, dressed in a newly pressed uniform. Hanna had noticed he was dripping with sweat by the time the parade and speech finished, and he had obviously kept them all waiting while he freshened himself.

He loved a grand entry, Hanna observed, and she guessed that he enjoyed keeping his audience waiting, arriving late. He allowed a moment of silence to fill the room, giving his mere presence an air of importance, as if the words that were about to come out of his mouth were the most important ever uttered. And Hanna knew there would be more words.

Frau Troost, the architect's widow, who had spoken to Hanna earlier as they watched the parade, expressing a truly sincere regret that her husband had not lived to see this day, glanced over at Hanna as if to say, *How fortunate we are to be here in this man's presence.* Hanna could not help but think of her own husband.

She lowered her eyes, wishing not to reveal her true feelings as Hitler began to speak—another lengthy diatribe, enhanced repetition of what he'd said to the general mass gathered outside. Hanna shifted from one foot to the other on the hard stone floor, her legs weary from standing so long, wishing that she, too, had had time to refresh herself.

The guests began their personal tour of the Haus der Deutschen Kunst. A portrait of Hitler, standing proud in his military uniform, greeted the observers who moved silently into the first exhibition hall. The marble floors sparkled. Large skylights brought abundant light in to illuminate the paintings and sculptures.

The art was nicely spaced, giving viewers an opportunity to contemplate and study each piece. Hanna stood before one of the many large nude male sculptures that dominated the exhibition. When she heard one of the admirers whisper, "Such lovely classical lines, surely inspired by the Greeks," Hanna prayed that she would not burst into nervous laughter. She thought of Helene's describing Hitler's coliseum built for the Olympics, and her comments about how the man must believe that bigger is better. There was nothing at all elegant or classical about this sculpture. It was simply large.

Hanna took a deep breath, knowing it was more terror than humor that might drive her to hysterics. She continued on, moving along with the crowd.

Paintings of German mothers with perfect blond children hung beside portraits of healthy Aryan families. Muscular, square-jawed soldiers appeared alongside mythical heroes. Idealized pictures of farm laborers greeted the visitors. And there, among the art, Hanna found paintings that she herself had selected for the Führer.

Hitler strutted about the gallery. Cameras flashed. And Hanna was there, her photo taken, recorded for all. Yes, she was there, standing alongside the chosen, smiling as if she approved, smiling to keep from crying.

The next day the *Ausstellung Entartete Kunst*, the Exhibition of Degenerate Art, opened for a special group of supporters and officials to be followed by admission for the general public. The art was housed in a run-down building in the Hofgarten, a short distance from the new art museum. The Führer did not appear. Hanna surmised that the theatrics and drama of the previous day had drained his energy completely.

The opening speech was delivered by Adolf Ziegler, president of the Chamber of Art. In words reminiscent of those Hitler had spoken just the day before, Herr Ziegler described this art as the monstrous offspring of insanity, imprudence, ineptitude, and sheer degeneracy.

Entry to the exhibition was through a dark, narrow stairway. As Hanna stepped onto the landing in the upper level where the exhibition began, she was struck by the wood carving of Christ on the cross that hung in the entrance. The figure was sharply and unnaturally angled, stark and thin, the carved nails hammered through feet and hands, the ribs in the chest protruding, the distorted head crowned with thorns tilted toward the viewer. Terribly disturbing, surely as the artist Ludwig Gies had intended. But here, made even more so by the fact that it hung to be ridiculed, with the caption: *This horror hung as a war memorial in the Cathedral of Lübeck*. Hanna knew, particularly after seeing the exhibition the day before, that Hitler wished to portray war and battle as heroic, not disturbing.

The lighting in each small, narrow room was poor, the display space so cramped it was impossible to properly view the art. Hanna thought of the vast, well-lit rooms of the Haus der Deutschen Kunst. Here one piece, one artist, was forced upon another, and words of insult and hate, vile descriptions, were scrawled on walls between the paintings.

Insolent mockery of the Divine under Centrist rule, on the wall beside Emil Nolde's *Leben Christ*, Life of Christ, in Room 1.

Revelation of the Jewish racial soul, in Room 2, which contained only works by Jewish artists, Marc Chagall, one of Hanna's favorite, among them.

Insult to German womanhood, alongside nudes by Ernst Ludwig Kirchner and Otto Mueller in Room 3.

The ideal cretin and whore, scrawled in black on another wall.

A red sticker had been placed below many of the paintings. *Bezahlt von den Steuergroschen des arbeitenden deutschen Volkes*, paid for by the taxes of the German working people. Hitler was determined to show how the Republic had misused their money on the degenerate art that did nothing but defile the German people. The prices that the liberal Republic had paid for the art were often noted. It didn't take a fool to realize that these were prices that had been paid during a time of extreme inflation, when a loaf of bread could be obtained for no less than a dozen buckets of near-worthless marks, when people were burning money to warm themselves in the cold Munich winters.

Hanna lingered before a cluster of paintings, trying to imagine each hanging individually with room to take in the colors and forms without the distraction of half a dozen others forcing their way into her line of vision.

A watercolor by Paul Klee, *Der Geist des Don X*, The Spirit of Don X, was mislabeled—attributed to Kandinsky.

Two of the paintings by Wassily Kandinsky, who was described as "teacher of the Communist Bauhaus," were hung vertically when Hanna knew they were meant to hang horizontally. The pieces were totally abstract, with geometric lines and shapes easily identifying them as those from Kandinsky's Bauhaus period. But with the way they were hung, the balance and composition was upset, causing Hanna great distress. What an insult to the artist.

As Hanna walked through the narrow halls, the colors pushed and shoved in every direction, a dissonance of sounds blasting in her ears. It was a harsh melding of sound and color. Too much all at once. And this was indeed the intention—to create a claustrophobic confusion, an assault on the senses, which for Hanna came not only in what she saw, but also in what she heard. For a moment she sensed that she might faint or empty her stomach on the finely polished shoes of the president of the Chamber of Art. But she held her head high and continued through the gallery, silently bidding farewell to Chagall, Mondrian, Jawlensky, Kandinsky, Klee, Marc, Dix, Beckmann, and so many more.

Leaving the exhibition, knowing she could not tolerate the confinement of the streetcar after what she had just experienced, Hanna walked. Her head throbbed, a pounding in her left temple as she attempted to sort out what she had seen over the past two days at the two very different exhibitions.

There were several smaller pieces in the German House of Art that she rather liked; a small sculpture by Max Esser of wild ducks, a painting of a farm that reminded her of the Allgäu and her own family farm. But overall she found the larger pieces, particularly the sculptures, lacking in originality and creativity.

In the Degenerate Art Exhibition, there were pieces she thought were poorly done. There were others that caused her great discomfort, among them drawings by Otto Dix depicting sexual mutilation and murder that some critics believed were allegory and social or political statements. She wondered if he had witnessed such horrors during the war and felt a need to express this through his art.

Children were not allowed to attend the exhibition of the degenerate art because it was considered too disturbing and obscene. Some pieces might require a thoughtful discussion or a decision to bypass such works, but should that not be the parents' choice? Hanna was offended and saddened that the state itself had become the parent, dictating what a child was to see, to hear, to believe.

She thought of her own children in America. Willy loved colors and would have been delighted with some of the *entartete kunst*, particularly the Kandinskys and Klees. Isabella, on the other hand, could be rather moody about her art, and the thought made Hanna smile. Even at eight she might like a particular painting one day and choose something completely different the next. She would always express why she did or did not like them. Hanna knew her daughter would love the paintings by Franz Marc with cats and horses and birds.

Bicyclers sped by on the street, pedestrians walked briskly as Hanna continued on. She passed a young family with two children, a girl about four and a boy of seven or eight.

"Can we go for ice cream?" the boy asked, tugging at his mother's hand.

Moments like this, seeing other families, intensified Hanna's loneliness, her anger. How unfair that she could not take her own children for ice cream.

It was a warm afternoon and the walk was much more tiring than she had anticipated, particularly when she forced herself to take the longer route to avoid going by the Feldherrnhalle where Hitler had installed a memorial to honor his followers who had died at the hands of the Bavarian police the night of his attempted Putsch. Two SS guards in black uniforms were stationed there at all times and, out of respect, passersby were required to raise their arms in a salute.

Hanna's head continued to throb and perspiration dripped from her forehead. She stopped and took a handkerchief from her handbag, gazing around as she removed her hat and wiped her brow. Decorations for the German Day of Art still lined the streets, which were busy with late-afternoon traffic.

What would Moses think of all this? she wondered. For the past several days in particular she had felt the presence of her husband's spirit. She was grateful that he was not here to see this, but at the same time wishful that he was so they might talk. How sad Moses would be to see how the Reich Chamber of Art had chosen to display the art, separating it into two specific categories—approved, not approved.

As Hanna made her way back to the small room where she now lived alone, the images of the paintings, sculptures, and drawings, continued to flash and settle, and then disappeared in her mind.

She thought of what Josef had said many years ago after the Putsch, when Hitler was first attempting to gain control of Germany. When Hanna saw his photograph in the newspaper, she told Josef, "Why, he was here years ago, presenting his drawings in hopes that we might show them in the gallery." And Josef had replied lightly, as if making a joke, "Now, that's the kind of leader Germany needs, one with the sensitivity of an artist."

At the time no one knew what he really stood for.

She thought of Leni telling her how this man intended to bring the art to the people.

As she entered her room, she sat on the bed and Adolf Hitler's own words came back to her: "Art is for the people. The people will be called on to judge their own art."

Yet, in the very way it had been presented to the people, they were being told what should be labeled as art.

Hanna slept little that night, and restlessly the following. Several days later, while out looking for employment, she passed the House of German Art. It appeared almost deserted. Later she walked past the Hofgarten building. The line of those who wished to view the *entartete kunst* stretched on and on. She wondered if many others, as she did herself, felt it might be their last opportunity to see this art.

Unable to find work, again Hanna went to stay with Leni. The dissonance she had felt between herself and her sister had all but disappeared. Leni had no kind words for Hitler, no unkind words for Hanna. There were no arguments. The sisters barely spoke. Leni provided her with a home, with food, and family. For this Hanna would always be grateful.

She had little time to consider what she should do next, when again her life was interrupted. She received an official letter, forwarded to her from the Hausmann Gallery. Her expertise was required by the Ministry for Public Enlightenment and Propaganda. She was to appear in Berlin within the week and report to the Reich Cultural Chamber.

CHAPTER TWENTY-FOUR

Lauren and Isabella

New York City
August 2009

"By the time Mother told me that Papa had sold the Kandinsky *Composition*," Isabella said, "much worse things were happening in Germany."

They sat silently, enclosed it seemed in a world far removed from this lovely apartment in New York. The light in the room had shifted again; the bright colors of many of the paintings along the walls appeared shadowed and dimmed.

"I can only imagine how devastating that must have been for her," Lauren finally said, thinking of both the sale of the Kandinsky and the horrors that were to follow. With this thought she realized that she believed what Isabella Fletcher was telling her about the painting, though she had produced no evidence. Lauren, who always made every effort to set her emotions aside, to rely on logic, on facts, on proven history, believed her despite the fact that everything she'd read about Kandinsky's *Composition II* stated that it had been destroyed during the war. Would history have to be rewritten?

"Not only the Kandinsky," Isabella said, "but much of the art owned by the family. My father sent the money from selling the art to begin a new life in America. It was his intention to join us. Then we would all go home; at least I always believed that was my father's plan. I'm honestly not sure about my mother's. No one believed Hitler would be in power for long. But, well . . ." Mrs. Fletcher gave off a shudder and then her shoulders slumped as if a physical weight was bearing down upon her. "Well, everyone knows how that turned out." She stared at Lauren, but her eyes seemed blank and the younger woman knew the statement required no reply.

Was this her grandfather's thought, too? Lauren wondered. Had he, like Moses Fleischmann, assumed that Hitler would not last? Dr. Rosenthal had also sent his family away. Had it been his intention to bring them all back to Germany?

"The money arrived," Mrs. Fletcher continued, "evidently just after Mother left New York to return to Germany. She wrote Uncle Hans and told him not to send it back, though she surely could have used it. She instructed him to invest the money for me and my brother in America. Eventually it was used to pay for my university education."

"The Kandinsky painting was sold to someone in Berlin?"

"Yes, it was."

Lauren looked toward the bookcase. She could make out the words on the spines of several of the books. Large coffee table books with titles such as *Expressionism, German Art of the Twentieth Century, Kandinsky in Germany, The Birth of Abstract Art.* She wondered how much Isabella really remembered, how much she'd read in these books.

"This is where the known history of the painting generally stops," Isabella told her. "Anything I've read about *Composition II* refers to the German owner in Berlin, the belief that it was destroyed in bombings."

"Your mother purchased it back from the buyer in Berlin?" Lauren asked.

"It wasn't my mother."

Lauren raised her shoulders as her eyes widened as if to ask—who?

"I assure you it was a legal purchase," Isabella replied.

"You have documents to verify this?" Lauren asked, instantly wishing she'd stopped to steady her voice, to rearrange her words, to strip away the sharpness. She sounded so eager, so ready to launch accusations, when she was merely excited that this might all be true.

"Yes, there are documents to verify the family's ownership." The pitch of Mrs. Fletcher's voice ascended with irritation, and Lauren prayed the woman would continue. It seemed they were just now getting to the heart of the story. Lauren took in a deep breath, aware that her own emotions were drained and tattered.

"Your father didn't live to see the painting returned?" she asked quietly.

Isabella shook her head.

"Your mother stayed on?"

"Not that she had much of a choice." Rage wrapped around the woman's words as the circles of pink on her cheeks deepened against her pale skin. Lauren wondered what it would be like to carry such anger for more than seventy years. She thought of her own father, who seldom spoke of his parents. She was amazed at times that he went about his life without expressing any harsh feelings regarding his past. Surely there was anger. But he didn't talk about it.

Lauren knew her grandfather had died in Dachau, but she had never visited the camp during her trips to Germany. She had never visited her ancestral home of Leipzig. She'd never examined the Nazi death camp documents that were being opened up as the years passed. She had never seen the name Felix Rosenthal entered in any official record.

Her efforts had gone into her research on the lost art. She could not bring her grandfather back. But the art. A canvas, a drawing, an artist's creation could outlast him by centuries. Creativity could live on long after the creator was gone.

She'd been accused of having a vendetta. One modern-day art collector—who even Lauren would admit had been a victim, too, as there had been no knowledge that the painting was anything but a legal purchase—had said there was as much revenge as reclamation involved in her tireless efforts. She'd ruffled at the accusation. Yet, at times she wondered if this was true. And now she questioned why she had become so *obsessed*, as Patrick put it, with tracking down Hanna Fleischmann in the form of her heirs. Hanna's only remaining heir was Isabella Fletcher.

What did she hope to gain? The recovery of stolen art? The discovery of a lavish life that had been supported by the selling of confiscated, degenerate art?

"I didn't understand," Isabella said, her voice calmed, fatigue subduing the fury. "She wasn't a Jew, but she'd been married to one. I'm not sure that was a factor, if her difficulty getting out of Germany was related to this. By that time just about anyone applying for papers had trouble. Quotas had been filled for emigration to many countries that were willing to take Germans—Jews or otherwise."

Isabella motioned to the photo with the broken glass, the picture of the young girl with her brother. "This picture was taken in America. Aunt Katie took us to a studio to have it done to send to Mother. I remember how proud Willy was as we posed for the photographer, as he gave us instructions." Isabella smiled faintly at the memory. "I thought it was so she wouldn't forget us. It was very difficult for me to understand why she wouldn't come to us, particularly after Papa died. Or why she didn't send for us to come home. I didn't realize at the time that she—we—had lost everything; the art, the gallery, our home. She didn't write about any of this in the letters she sent to America. After a while she quit writing. I thought she was dead." The old woman's lip quivered.

Suddenly Lauren saw Mrs. Fletcher as a hurt, frightened little girl, waiting for her mother. She was the child in the photograph. The old woman blinked away the tears. Then she leaned back into her chair and it seemed her physical form had shrunk as if the large winged chair was about to swallow her up.

"I have never spoken of this," Isabella said, her voice so quiet Lauren could barely make out her words. "Never spoken of any of this to anyone other than Andrew." She let out a faint, sad laugh. "And now, here I sit, revealing all this to a stranger." She picked up her cup from the end table and took a small sip of what by now must have been cold tea, and then she cradled it protectively in her hands.

Both women remained silent, until finally, Lauren spoke quietly. "How did Hanna, your mother, survive with no home, no means of support?"

"Family. She lived with my half sister, her stepdaughter, Helene, who was really more like a sister, and her husband, Jakob, in Berlin, and then with Aunt Leni in Munich." Isabella set her cup on the table and resumed her formal posture, though Lauren sensed she had not regained her composure. "Eventually she found work for a short while. You must understand, speaking of this was painful for her. So much of what happened to her I don't really know. Eventually she returned to Berlin and—" Abruptly Isabella stopped. The words ceased to flow. Lauren could see her hand, running over the arm of her chair, was trembling. The woman closed her eyes. Her shoulders shuddered.

"Berlin?" Lauren asked. "She returned to Berlin?" Had they finally come to Berlin in the story? This was, as far as Lauren was concerned, where the story she was originally searching for really began. There was something revealing in this hesitation.

The two women's eyes locked for a brief moment, and then Isabella looked away, her gaze resting on the grate of the fireplace, as if staring into a fire, hoping it might provide some warmth for a room that had suddenly cooled.

"Did she move in with Helene again?" Lauren asked. "When she went back to Berlin? What did Hanna do in Berlin? Was she able to find work?" Inside she was telling herself to slow down, to shut up, to give the woman some space. Patrick said she tended to talk too much when she was nervous or excited or tired. Yet now she felt as if she were running out of time, as if she would never know what had really happened in Berlin. After Hanna's husband had died. After she'd sent her children away.

"I'm very tired, Ms. . . . Mrs. O'Farrell," Isabella corrected herself. "Could you return tomorrow?"

"Yes, I . . . Of course. I appreciate your talking to me." Lauren sat, waiting, though she wasn't sure what she was waiting for. Slowly, she reached down for her bag, glancing once more at the photo of Isabella and her brother, Willy. She picked up her teacup, placed it back on the tray, then offered to carry it back to the kitchen, but the woman held out her hand to stop her.

"I can take care of it," she said as they shared a cautious laugh, both aware of Lauren's earlier clumsiness, and the result of that. Perhaps both needing something less daunting than the events Isabella had just spoken of to end Lauren's visit.

"I'd feel much better," Lauren said, "if you'd let me replace the broken glass on your picture. I could bring it back tomorrow."

Isabella shot her a look as if to say, *Do you really think I'd let you take off with one of my most valuable possessions?*

"The glass, yes," the older woman finally said. "If you'll bring a new piece of glass we could replace it."

Quickly Lauren pulled a small measuring tape out of a zippered pocket in her bag, along with her notebook and pen, and Mrs. Fletcher nodded as if she approved of her organization, her being prepared. The younger woman took the measurements of the frame, jotting the numbers down, realizing it wasn't a standard size and she'd have to have the glass custom cut. She knew it would be better to take the photograph and frame and have it reassembled in a frame shop, but she didn't want to suggest this unless Isabella herself brought it up. Which she didn't.

"Thank you, Mrs. Fletcher," Lauren said as she placed measuring tape, pen, and notebook back into her bag. She stood. "I'll see you tomorrow, then."

"Yes," Isabella said. "We will talk more tomorrow. Sometime after lunch. One o'clock?"

"Yes, that would work for me," Lauren said, mentally rearranging her schedule, hoping Adam's day care would have an afternoon drop-in spot.

Mrs. Fletcher escorted her to the door. "Please," she said as they stepped into the foyer, "I'd request that you speak to no one of what I've told you about the Kandinsky *Composition*, about my family." The woman's voice had lost its strength.

The smell of the roses on the table in the crystal bowl intensified as they stood in the foyer, but as Lauren glanced over she felt as if they had begun to wither. And she had the feeling that Mrs. Fletcher was now having second thoughts about agreeing to this conversation, about the information she had revealed. Had she given Lauren more than she'd originally intended? Was the offer of tomorrow just a ploy to get her out of the apartment?

Lauren nodded in agreement. "Thank you," she said. "Thank you for talking to me."

"Tomorrow," Mrs. Fletcher repeated as she opened the door and Lauren stepped out, wondering how she could possibly go home to Patrick and Adam holding all of these thoughts, these emotions, these new revelations inside her.

CHAPTER TWENTY-FIVE

Hanna

Berlin
September 1937–May 1938

When Hanna arrived in Berlin, she was taken immediately to a large warehouse on Köpenickerstrasse by the young man who had been sent to accompany her from Munich. A quick glance informed her that the building was being used to store art, most likely that which had been confiscated from government collections. She was introduced to the supervisor, Herr Strasser, a tall, thin man with an unruly head of hair that he kept slicking back with his long fingers.

"What is it that is required of me?" she asked.

"The warehouse is filled with art owned by the Reich," Herr Strasser told her. "It must be catalogued, and because of your expertise, particularly in the area of"—and here he cleared his throat—"*the modern*, you are recognized as one most highly capable of this endeavor. There are others who are assisting, but your judgment and knowledge will be a great asset in determining the worth of this type of . . . Dare we call it art?"

So this was the reason she was here, because her knowledge and experience might be of value. The Commission was well aware that she had some usefulness.

Herr Strasser escorted her about the building. As Hanna moved down one aisle, then another, she could smell it, see it, and hear it. She stared in disbelief. Never in her life had she seen so many canvases, drawings, and sculptures gathered in such disarray in such a place. Quietly, she walked about the cold, dark building, which she guessed had been used at one time to store grain, as there was a thin dust of it on the floor, a scent hovering in the air. Paintings were stacked against the walls, one layer upon another. Sculptures sat on shelves, in no particular order. All of it appeared to be what Hitler would call *entartete kunst.*

Forcing herself to hold back the tears, Hanna continued through the warehouse, feeling as if she had been sent to identify bodies in a morgue, as she gazed upon pieces they had at one time shown at the Fleischmann in Munich. Picasso, Klimt, Munch, Jawlensky, Kandinsky. The colors were vibrating, bouncing and jumbling, and sounding about before her eyes and in her ears. She swallowed hard, and wondered, "What will become of the art once it has been catalogued?"

Only when the man replied, "Perhaps the Führer alone knows the answer to that," did she realize she had asked the question out loud.

Surely, Hanna thought, if he wished to destroy it, he would not go to the trouble of having it catalogued.

Herr Strasser gave off a snort of disapproval, and then laughed. "Have you ever seen such grotesque representations in your life?"

Hanna smiled as if she agreed, said nothing, and then once more walked through the maze of paintings and sculptures. She felt a warmth surge through her entire body. Her knees were about to give out. She swayed and dabbed the perspiration on her upper lip. The man noticed her distress, found a chair for her to sit, and asked, "Water?"

Hanna nodded.

After fetching a drink, Herr Strasser grimaced as he handed her the glass. "Such art does make one nauseous, does it not?"

She could not reply.

Hanna was escorted to a small, run-down hotel a short distance from the warehouse. She had not mentioned that she had relatives in Berlin. She did not want to call attention to her Jewish family or put them within harm's reach, though Jakob was in no way attempting to hide the fact that he was a Jew, as many of those remaining in Germany were. Some had escaped but, as Hanna was learning through her own frustrations, it had become increasingly more difficult.

The following morning she reported to work at the warehouse on Köpenickerstrasse. Records had come in from the various museums. She was to combine these and catalogue the art according to subject, artist, nationality, date of creation, size, medium, previous ownership, and suggested value.

Hanna knew she must initially review the contents of the warehouse. She was assigned a pockmarked youth named Ulrich to assist her. They started through the rows, Hanna taking notes as she examined individual canvases, prints, and drawings, Ulrich carefully moving or rearranging pieces for her to view. The task before them was overwhelming.

When Ulrich tapped her on the shoulder and asked if they had completed their work for the day, Hanna was amazed that it was already 6:00 P.M. She was returned to her hotel, dinner was delivered to her room, and she slept more soundly that night than she had in years.

The next morning, Herr Strasser—who Hanna had learned, after just one day, knew nothing about art—informed her that they were to identify individual pieces by putting the assigned inventory numbers on each.

"If we paint the number in a noticeable color," he suggested, "perhaps blue, but of course very small, on the front, lower right-hand corner, pieces could easily be matched to the inventory lists."

"What?" Hanna cried out in disbelief, unable to hide her horror. "How can you suggest such a mutilation? Surely this method of identification has not been suggested by your superior."

Herr Strasser looked startled at her outburst, then almost fearful. "Y-y-yes, yes, of course," he stuttered. "We must devise a better system." Nervously he combed through his hair with his fingers.

Anyone with any sense would know these paintings should not be marked, as it would severely decrease their value. She questioned how such an idiot had been put in charge. He was nothing more than a warehouse supervisor.

Finally, after she calmed down, Hanna said, "The numbers should be affixed in a manner that will not damage the art."

Herr Strasser nodded. His Adam's apple slid up and down his throat.

"Numbers could be recorded on the wooden stretchers of the canvases," she suggested, "with blue wax pencils, and on labels affixed to the backs of the prints and drawings. This way they could easily be removed or changed without causing harm."

"Yes, yes," he replied agreeably, almost thankfully, as if he understood that she had just saved him from doing something extremely stupid. "I will see that the proper materials are ordered."

After this particular incident, Hanna was even more determined that Hitler and his imbeciles would not defile or destroy the art.

As one week turned into another, the world outside the warehouse began to disappear. Hanna's life existed only for the art. Contentment enveloped her as she passed the days in this old building with the colors and music of her paintings. Strangely, she felt that she had some purpose and she imagined herself as a protector, the devoted mother tending to her children. There were moments of true joy, joy that Hanna could not defend in any way.

Rarely did she allow her thoughts to drift away from Köpenick-erstrasse and think of Willy and Isabella in America. She no longer had communications with her children or with Helene or Jakob in her attempts to protect them, and she had neither the money nor the emotional stamina to escape. Waiting it out seemed the only option, and in the process at least she might play a small role in caring for the paintings. She barely allowed herself to question what would happen to the art, or to her, after she had served her purpose.

At the end of the month, she received a paycheck, and only now did she admit what she had become. She was an employee of the Reich. She was working for Hitler!

Within two days she received a bill for lodging and meals, which her wages would barely cover. Though she had not been sent to one of the camps, she was virtually being held prisoner.

She continued the meticulous process of inventory and assigning numbers to the paintings. The records that had come from each of the museums came with great detail of provenance and ownership. None of these pieces had been taken from private owners, though many had been donated to the museums by wealthy individuals, some having been the Fleischmanns' clients. Hanna guessed that at some point the Commission would begin looting private collections. But these, according to the records, were all legitimately owned by the government, be it state or municipality. The government, of course, was now Adolf Hitler and those who did his bidding.

She began to make her own lists. When she went to the toilet, she pulled a pen from her pocket and recorded information she had collected during the day on a thin slip of paper she kept hidden inside her stockings, abbreviating, using initials and symbols to place as much information on each small sheet as possible. Every evening when she returned to her room she finished recording information from memory. She knew that her mind and heart would forever hold the colors, the images, and the sounds, but she would record the numbers here. She hid the lists under a loose floorboard in her room.

Herr Strasser, her supervisor, addressed her with respect, asking her opinions, requesting specific information from her about the artists' work. One day, feeling very brave, she said to him, "Perhaps the Führer should consider trading these paintings for those he finds more agreeable." Hanna immediately wished she had used a different word—*agreeable* made it sound like she was not in agreement with the leader of the Reich. "Or perhaps selling them outside the country. Some of these artists"—she pointed to a Picasso—"might find favor outside of Germany. Perhaps if they were sold, funds would be available to fill our galleries with true Aryan art." The word *Aryan* left a bitter taste on her tongue.

Herr Strasser pursed his lips, tapped a finger to his mouth as if considering passing this suggestion on to his supervisor, but he said nothing.

There were soon other visitors to Hanna's museum, as she had come to call it in her mind. Herr Franz Hofmann, the chairman of the confiscation committee, visited often. Herr Strasser became very nervous when Herr Hofmann appeared and always asked Hanna to escort him and explain what they had accomplished. After several visits and numerous conversations with Herr Hofmann, she sensed that he liked her and understood that her knowledge was of immense value. He began, in an almost teasing way, to call her the "Curator of the Degenerate."

Herr Joseph Goebbels, Minister of Public Enlightenment and Propaganda, appeared more than once. Hanna easily recognized him, as she had seen many photos in the newspaper and had been just an arm's length from him at the grand opening of the Haus der Deutschen Kunst. He was a thin, pale man with hollow cheeks and a slow, sinister smile. She knew at one time he had actually liked the "modern," but as soon as he realized Hitler had formed an unfavorable opinion, he immediately declared it abominable.

Herr Hermann Goering, who came from wealth and married into wealth, a man who was accustomed to being surrounded by fine art, stopped by on several occasions.

"Frau Fleischmann, you are well today?" he always asked with warmth. In stark contrast to Herr Goebbels, Herr Goering was a massive, energetic, friendly man, who often visited with Hanna when he stopped by. He had been a war hero, a decorated pilot in the German Air Force. He had once served as the president of the German Reichstag. If Hanna hadn't known that he was one of Hitler's closest advisors, one of the top-ranking officials in the Nazi Party, she might have found the man charming.

One day he asked, "This artist Van Gogh? His work is very valuable?"

"He's considered by many to be one of the greatest influences on contemporary art." Hanna didn't even know what this meant anymore. Contemporary art? In Germany it had taken on a much different meaning. "It's believed that he sold but one painting during his life, but yes, now his work is considered very important."

"My tastes run more to the classical art and decorative pieces. What do you think of medieval and Renaissance tapestries? I've collected several to decorate my estate here in Berlin. You should come visit me sometime."

Hanna had to catch herself from laughing at this invitation. She was as likely to visit Herr Goering's estate as she was to go to a grand ball in a gown designed in Paris.

"They are lovely," she replied, remembering a beautiful Renaissance tapestry Moses had purchased in Paris for their own home. Of course, it was gone now. "As a professional I know little about tapestry, as this is not my particular area of expertise, but yes, I find them quite lovely."

Herr Goering was known to entertain, and came one afternoon to borrow a piece for a "State" party, as he called it. Hanna guessed it would not be returned, particularly when Herr Strasser made a little adjustment to the inventory.

One afternoon Herr Goering chose a lovely Cézanne, then one day he arrived to claim a Munch, then a Marc. All, he explained, for Reich affairs or state-owned buildings. Again adjustments were made to the records. Hanna knew that he did not particularly favor this type of work, that Hitler would never allow one of them to hang in a government building. She guessed that Herr Goering was trading them for something he found more appealing. Perhaps even something for that lovely estate he had described to her with such fondness.

He was always friendly, always interested in conversing with Hanna about what each particular piece might be worth, and she willingly shared this information. If these paintings were traded to those who might appreciate them, they would be saved.

Hitler himself stopped by the warehouse one morning for a short visit, as if he had more important business to attend to. He was in a foul mood and barely acknowledged Hanna with a nod, a low, "Frau Fleischmann." He stomped through the building, snorting and coughing, his head jerking about as he examined the art, poor Herr Strasser quivering at his side. "Jewish-Bolshevist subversives," the Führer snarled.

Again she feared not just for the art, but for herself. The man had a very long memory, and was known to hold a grudge. He knew she was the wife of the deceased Jew Moses Fleischmann, an expert on the modern, and Hanna was sure now, after her dinner at Berchtesgaden, that he recalled it was she who'd sent him out of the gallery, portfolio tucked under his arm.

Soon other dealers, those Hanna had known from Berlin, visited the warehouse, and she realized that her suggestion had been passed on to a higher level. Hitler was taking advantage of those who knew the value of a Picasso or Van Gogh. He might despise the art, but he was aware of its worth. The best of the paintings, those that could fetch the greatest prices, would not be destroyed. But what of the others?

CHAPTER TWENTY-SIX

Hanna

Berlin
August–October 1938

"We are installing another location at Schloss Niederschönhausen," Herr Strasser told Hanna one morning. She knew this as a palatial estate on the outskirts of Berlin, and guessed the location would provide a more appealing setting for showing the art and for entertaining guests and buyers. "I would like you to assist in the selection of our inventory to be relocated."

Hanna realized that she was being asked to select those pieces that would survive, those that might be purchased and therefore escape possible destruction. There were so many; how could she choose?

She began, picking not only those that she personally favored, but those she felt would be of interest to buyers. Each day several were loaded onto large trucks to be transported to their new location. Hanna continued entering the information into the records: the official records and her own secret records.

Often she was required to spend her days at Schloss Niederschönhausen, accompanying "clients" who came to examine the art. Foreign dealers could buy just about anything they wanted. Deals were made—always in foreign currency. And always, Hanna was instructed to inform the museum representatives, the gallery owners, and the collectors who came to purchase, that the money would go back to the German museums, that new art would be purchased with the funds.

She was moved from her small dingy hotel to the newly refurbished Schloss Bellevue, which once served as a royal residence and had now been taken over by the Nazis and set up as a hotel for their guests. The hotel was lavishly furnished with damask drapes, velvet furniture with tapestry cushions, marble moldings and banisters, rugs from the Orient, paintings in gilt frames. Meals were served in an elegant dining hall, prepared by one of the finest chefs in Berlin. She sat with dignitaries, government officials, and honored guests. Hanna told herself she was not one of them, that she was here only because she wished to save the art. When she allowed herself to think of her children in America, she wondered if they were better off without her. How would they feel if they knew their mother was working so closely with the Nazis, sharing meals with government officials and men of rank in Hitler's army, men who spoke openly of destroying the Jewish race?

One morning, she was informed that a group of representatives from a museum in Basel would like to examine paintings housed at Schloss Niederschönhausen. One representative was particularly interested in work by artists from *Der Blaue Reiter* of Munich. Since Hanna had an intimate knowledge of these particular artists, she was asked to accompany him through the collection.

Her young assistant—the second who had been assigned to her, the shadow who accompanied her everywhere—escorted her from the hotel and drove her to the facility. He dropped her off and went to park the automobile. She guessed that the young man, a beefy youth named Günter, was also in need of a cigarette, as he no longer smoked in her presence or near her paintings since she had severely reprimanded him for smoking in the galleries.

A group of men stood with Herr Franz Hofmann inside the

entry. He turned and was about to introduce Hanna when her eyes caught those of one of the gentlemen. Her heart pushed up, catching in her throat, and she thought she might faint. No air entered her lungs. She couldn't breathe.

It had been many years since she had seen him. The lines emphasizing his smile had been etched deeper in his face. His mustache was flecked with silver, and his hair had turned a snowy white. But he was still as handsome as the day they met twelve years ago on the ship from America.

"May I introduce Herr Johann Keller from the Kunstmuseum in Basel," Herr Hofmann said. "Our Frau Fleischmann has great knowledge, particularly of *Der Blaue Reiter* in which you have expressed an interest. She would be pleased to escort you through the collection."

Hanna could see that Johann Keller was as stunned as she to meet once more, and they were both without words until Herr Hofmann and his group of clients were well beyond hearing distance.

"Hanna," he said slowly, and the color and tone of her name from his lips sent a surge of heat through her. "I didn't expect this."

"Nor I," she said. The years had been good to him. Hanna knew that she looked very different from when they first met, that she had aged. Perhaps not well. But strangely at this moment she was grateful they had met here rather than at the Köpenickerstrasse location. When she worked at the warehouse she barely bothered to look in the mirror before she left her hotel. When she was to meet with clients at Schloss Niederschönhausen, she styled her hair, put on makeup, and checked her clothing to assure it was clean and pressed. She was grateful for these services that residing at the elegant Schloss Bellevue Hotel now allowed.

"You look well, Hanna," he said, and Hanna wondered if it could possibly be true. She felt as if the hardships of the past years had drained her of any beauty and health she might have once possessed.

"And you also, Johann." They stood silently studying each other and she sensed he wanted to touch her. "You are now employed by the Kunstmuseum in Basel?" she said.

"For the past nine years. And you, Hanna?"

"Here in Berlin, for a short time now . . ."

He waited for her to explain further, but she could think of nothing she might tell him without revealing something that would put her in danger.

"Your business in Munich?" he inquired.

"We closed the gallery, and then . . . Moses passed away shortly after . . . Eventually we had to sell everything." Hanna shivered, thinking of Moses, of Josef, how she never spoke of these losses, how there was no one in her life now who knew or cared.

"Oh, Hanna, I'm so sorry," he said sincerely.

She felt a hard, cold lump in her chest, and then a rough, hot stone of renewed guilt over the betrayal of her husband. "It was difficult to find work, and then this opportunity."

"Willy. He's doing well?" There was caution in his inquiry, as he knew from their long-ago conversations that Willy's health was at times very fragile.

"In America with my sister."

"In America? Yet you remain here in Germany?" His voice was low and there was a softness of color, the soothing timbre of a voice that had comforted her years ago when she feared she might lose her son.

She felt a tear well in her eye, but ordered herself not to cry. Not here, not now. "Life is not always as one might wish," she said. Surely Johann would know it was not by choice that she had been separated from her children. *Her children?* She would not speak of little Isabella. Hanna would not. Could not.

"Herr Keller," she said, her voice rising in volume, "I would be delighted to show you through our collection."

As they started through the gallery, though it was but a more agreeable storage place than the grain warehouse, they spoke nervously, guardedly. He told her that he was on the verge of retirement, but had been asked by the museum to come to Berlin to acquire art that had been removed from the German museums. His sons were doing well. The two eldest were married and Johann now had two grandchildren. The youngest son had just started university. He did not speak of his wife.

"Oh, Hanna, not a day has gone by since we parted that I have not thought of you," he said abruptly, turning to her, reaching for her hand. She stepped back, fearing someone might notice.

"Oh, Johann, please . . ." She could not tell him that she, too, thought of him each day, that she saw his face, his smile, his eyes in their beautiful little daughter. Isabella, now in America, growing up with neither a father nor mother.

"I knew when we parted," he said, "we agreed we would not meet again. But now, is it not fate that has brought us together once more?"

Hanna thought of the last time they were together. At sea, a world between two worlds, existing only for that time and place. She had dreamed of seeing him again, but never imagined it would happen. Now what could she dare ask of him?

"I must see you, Hanna, away from here, away from this business."

She thought of a conversation she had several weeks ago with one of the Berlin dealers. He had implied that it might be possible for someone in a particular position to withhold items for private viewings. Works of particular interest to his clients could be sold without going through the normal channels, and if she could assist . . . He didn't outright ask her to do this, but Hanna understood what he wanted. She was tempted, as additional funds might have helped her find some way out of Germany. Now she realized if she were to meet Johann, even if she could escape her constant escort, questions might arise if they were seen together.

"Herr Hofmann says you are interested in work from *Der Blaue Reiter*," she said, motioning as she walked ahead of Herr Keller.

They passed sculptures displayed on a large table and approached a colorful Kandinsky, a piece Hanna remembered so clearly from the early days of *Der Blaue Reiter* in Munich. A man on a horse, the lines very simple, the colors—red and yellow and blue—pure and vibrant.

"One of your favorites," Johann said as they stood before the painting. "The Russian."

"I've always been fond of this particular artist," she said stiffly, and then with a little smile, "though many might claim him as German."

"And the music?" he asked with his own quick smile. "Do you hear the music?"

She felt a sudden pulse of pleasure at his smile, at the realization of how well he knew her, though they had spent little more than a week together.

"So many years have passed, Hanna."

"And so much has changed."

"And yet, so much remains. Feelings that we were forced to deny. Have these changed?" He touched her now, lightly on the hand, and she did not draw away. And it came back to her—the intensity of the short time they had spent together. They had agreed then that being together would have hurt so many they loved. Why could they not meet under different circumstances, in a world in which they might find each other and be together? Moses was gone, but surely Johann still had his wife. If this were not true, he would have spoken of a similar loss when she told him of her husband's death. Yet, even if Johann was free now, Hanna had no control over any aspect of her life. She was a prisoner in her own country. And she knew she could not tell him of the deception she had lived with for these past many years.

"This painting," she said, pulling her hand away from the heat of his. "Perhaps it might find a home outside of Germany."

"Perhaps," he said, but he was not gazing at the painting. He was staring at Hanna.

She turned quickly and they moved on to another canvas, *Zwei Katzen Blau und Gelb*, two colorful cats curled into a beautiful composition, a lovely piece by Franz Marc.

"Could we meet later?" he asked.

"You speak of fate, Johann. Is it fate that dictates we must meet only when I fear a great loss is imminent?"

"A loss?" he asked, thoughtfully.

She wanted to explain what was happening in Germany. She wanted to explain so much. They were alone, without her usual escort, and she sensed that she might speak more freely, and yet at the same time a never-ceasing fear, her constant companion now, a distrust of everyone, would not release her to speak openly.

"How is it that you came to be here," he asked, "assisting to rid Germany of the modern? This is the very art that you loved, paintings that were identified with the Fleischmann Gallery."

Hanna could not speak. How could she tell him of her personal fears, as well as her fears for the art and for her country?

"Would it be true," he asked, "to say we are not only acquiring art, but rescuing it?" His eyes moved slowly over the colors of Franz Marc, appraising the piece, and then he glanced back at Hanna and she caught something in his eyes that told her he understood she did not support the Nazi government, that she, too, wished only to save the art.

"Oh, Johann," she said, and then, before she could pull them back, the words escaped her mouth, "I fear it might all be destroyed. It must be taken so that it might survive." She felt a sharp, painful stab in her chest.

"The world is not without eyes, without a heart. Perhaps there is more than art that cries out for rescue."

"Indeed there is much in Germany in need of rescue."

"There has been talk," he continued carefully, "that the proceeds might be diverted from the museums to . . ." He hesitated as if he wished Hanna to finish his sentence.

Inwardly she told herself to hold on to some caution. "For Hitler's military efforts?" she said, her voice barely above a whisper. This was the first time she had admitted in words what in the darkest part of her heart she knew was true.

Hitler had recently annexed Austria. Surely the world outside grew uneasy as Germany openly rebuilt its military forces.

They moved on to a Klee done in dark earth tones. Paul Klee, also a member of *Der Blaue Reiter*, was Swiss, as was Johann. Hanna knew he had a particular affection for this artist.

"Your fellow countryman," she said.

"Lovely," he said, "though some might claim him as German or French!" And then, abruptly, with a shift in his tone, "There's talk of an auction in Switzerland early next year or in the spring to offer the remaining pieces. Word is being circulated that it might be conducted by the Fischer Gallery."

Hanna was aware of the ongoing correspondence between Franz Hofmann and Theodor Fischer in Lucerne. Switzerland, a neutral country, had become a refuge for many artists and cultural elites who had fled Germany, and was now becoming a haven for the art. Herr Fischer was one of the few non-Jewish dealers in Switzerland who had the knowledge, the contacts, and the experience to conduct this type of auction.

"When can I see you again?" he whispered.

Hanna glanced back to the gallery entrance and could see her assistant had returned and was walking toward them.

"Oh, Johann," she replied in a quiet, now-quivering voice, as her eyes darted about, "it is difficult . . ."

"When?"

"Not here, not now." Their eyes locked.

"Perhaps, the auction," he said. "We will meet in Lucerne, and . . ." His voice became even softer. "We might speak again of art, and other aspects of finding new homes for—"

They were unable to continue their discussion as Hanna's young assistant approached. Herr Hofmann soon joined them with the other members of his group, who had questions about various works that Herr Hofmann felt Hanna was best qualified to answer.

That evening, each detail of the day replayed continuously in her mind. Over the years she had tried to convince herself that their feelings for each other had been too far removed from the real world to be authentic and true. He had come in a time of need, when she feared she might lose her son. Had he come now to rescue not only the art, but Hanna herself? Or, had she completely lost touch with reality?

Surely Johann understood her dilemma. She had heard nothing of plans for her taking part in the auction or accompanying the art to Switzerland, but now she was infused with a spark of hope. If only she were asked to assist with the paintings in Switzerland.

Late the next morning, Johann Keller and his associates paid another visit to Schloss Niederschönhausen, but he and Hanna had no time alone. Quick glances were exchanged, but no words passed between them.

That following evening, after she had eaten a light supper and was about to retire, Hanna heard a knock on the door. Her heart leapt with a hopeful flutter.

She opened it to find Helene standing before her with hair disheveled, eyes swollen, her face blotched with red.

Glancing quickly down the hall, Hanna saw that all was quiet. Her young assistant, who had taken a room a few doors down, was constantly aware of any comings and goings, though she had yet to have a guest. Hanna motioned her in. "How did you know where to find me?" She could see Helene had come with bad news, her hands twitching and shaking, picking at the hem of her jacket.

It's Jakob, Hanna thought. She invited Helene into the sitting room, ashamed now that she was living in such luxury.

They sat silently for a moment, before Helene said, "I contacted your former employer in Munich, and through him I knew to find you here in Berlin. I hoped perhaps you had been able to go to America, since I had not heard from you, but then I . . ." She looked around the room as if searching for something, and then she began to weep, uncontrollably, unable to continue.

Finally, she whispered, "He's gone."

"Jakob?"

"No, no . . ." She closed her eyes and took in several quick, deep, gasping swallows of air as the tears fell, as she rocked back and forth. "It's Willy."

Hanna did not leave her room the next day, nor the following. Helene and Jakob invited her to stay with them, but she knew she could not. She was given a short leave from her work—though the understanding was that she was ill. Hanna would not speak of her son.

Willy, who had lived much longer than the doctors had predicted, had come down with pneumonia, and his poor body could no longer fight. If she had been there, if Hanna had been with her son, she was sure this would not have happened.

A letter from her sister in America found its way to her. Käthe wrote of Willy's passing. She did not tell Hanna that it had been peaceful, and did not ease her pain by telling her he had not suffered. Isabella, Käthe said, was a bright little girl, doing well in school. The fact that her daughter's letters had become less frequent during Hanna's final days in Munich, and seemed very impersonal, told her that she had not only lost her little boy, she had also lost her daughter.

Hanna returned to her work, to her waiting.

CHAPTER TWENTY-SEVEN

Hanna

Berlin
November 1938–April 1939

On the morning of November 10, 1938, Hanna had breakfast delivered to her room, as she was going early to the warehouse to prepare more art to be transferred to Schloss Niederschönhausen, and didn't want to wait to eat in the dining room. The previous evening she had skipped dinner altogether, as she often did now. She had little appetite.

As she stepped out of the hotel, the air was filled with the unmistakable scent of smoke, and in the distance dark clouds rose.

Günter pulled up in the automobile.

"What is it?" she asked as he ran around to get the door for her.

"Let's find out," he replied with curiosity.

They followed the smoke, which Hanna soon realized was coming from more than one single location. Günter headed toward the nearest plume. The smoke thickened as they got closer, and people ran through the streets in obvious agitation. Sirens sounded in the distance, piercing the air with blistering color.

As they approached the building, Hanna recognized it as the

charred remains of an old synagogue where she knew Jakob
Kaufmann, Helene's husband, had worshipped as a child. Hanna's heart beat rapidly and then seemed to skip a beat. She felt a
throbbing in the back of her neck as they continued slowly past
the building. In the nearby cemetery she could see headstones had
been shoved over and desecrated.

Günter rolled down the window and shouted to a young soldier on the street, "What is this?"

"You've heard about the assassination in Paris?"

Günter shook his head. The scent of fire and smoke intensified
as it came in from the open window. Hanna could barely breathe.

"The Jews are murdering innocent Germans." The man coughed.

"The Jews and their property must be destroyed," another
soldier shouted, raising a fist. A dog barked a deep blue and then
another howled, and again the sirens shrieked.

Günter glanced back at Hanna, and she could see the sympa-
thy in his eyes, and she felt for a moment it was for the Jews, not
the Germans. They continued on slowly, passing more men, some
in civilian clothes, others in uniform, running through the streets,
shouting and waving at one another in a mad attempt to control
the confusion. Some appeared to be directing and encouraging
the chaos.

Hanna saw that buildings had been vandalized, glass broken
out of the windows, shards scattered about in the streets. She
could hear it crunch under the automobile tires.

They passed more young men shouting, throwing rocks, dashing
into damaged buildings. Their car rolled by a scene of building after
building, smoldering, vandalized, windows shattered. It all seemed
to move in slow motion, as if it were not even real, but rather a mor-
bid, gross dream from which Hanna would soon awaken.

They drove on through neighborhoods that Hanna knew were
filled with Jewish businesses. Men were running out of the buildings, hands filled, larger items tucked under their arms, obviously

looting. Günter attempted to turn down a side lane, but it, too, was filled with men dashing about, clogging the street. As they approached a familiar area of exclusive shops, Hanna held her hand to her mouth. She was going to be ill.

She needed to get out of here. She needed to escape.

She grabbed for the door handle, yanked, and gave it a shove. Her hand froze and a putrid stench rose up as she gazed down. The blackened remains of a person lay in the street. The scent of burning flesh.

The entire contents of her breakfast lurched violently from her stomach onto the ground, the car door, the car seat.

She looked up in horror to confirm what she already knew. The sign above the building, covered with black, might have been illegible to one who did not know. But Hanna knew. She knew it was the business of Jakob Kaufmann, jeweler.

She must have fainted. When she woke, Günter was fanning her with a piece of paper clutched in his large hand. His eyes were wide with horror. Moisture glistened on his brow.

Hanna glanced out the window, tinted with soot, and realized they were no longer in the area that had been torched and vandalized, that Günter had managed to get them out. The smell of her own vomit filled the car, though she could see the poor boy had attempted to clean it up.

"What happened?" she asked him.

"You must have fainted," he said.

"No, I mean—"

"I'm sorry. I should not have taken you there."

Hanna didn't have words, but she knew the young man was correct. He should not have taken her there. His duties, as well as hers, were dictated by others. He had no permission to drive off his assigned course and route. He could be severely reprimanded by his superior for not taking her directly to the warehouse this morning.

For a long moment they stared at each other.

Finally, he said, "May I request that you not mention this to anyone?"

Another stretch of silence, and Hanna asked, "May I ask of you one favor?"

He nodded.

"The store, the jeweler's shop. Kaufmann Jewelers. Will you inquire for me—the proprietor?"

Again, he nodded.

Over the next few days, in the dining hall, talk was of nothing other than what had transpired in Germany on the night of November ninth.

"Why should it take an incident such as this?" a thick man in military uniform told another sitting at his table. "This Jewish conspiracy against the Reich should have been put down long ago."

"The Jews should have paid long before the assassination," the man's companion replied with a mouthful of food. "They must pay for what they have done."

Hanna generally took her meals with her assistant, but could always hear the conversations going on around them. Sometimes she was invited to sit with others in the dining hall, which she found repulsive. Often she skipped meals altogether. But she realized this was the only place she could learn what was really going on in Germany.

The Nazi-controlled newspapers, which Hanna often found left behind in the dining room or in the lobby at the hotel, ran stories of a young Jewish man living in Paris. The man had gone to the German embassy to assassinate the ambassador. Finding the man had not yet arrived, he shot another official who died of his wounds two days later.

In retaliation, Jewish businesses and synagogues throughout Germany were torched. Cemeteries and schools were vandalized.

Many Jews murdered. And this was all presented as if it were the logical, correct, just reaction.

From the guests, in bits and pieces of conversation, Hanna learned that the man was disturbed by the forced removal from Germany of all Jews of Polish citizenship. They had been arrested, their property seized. They were all sent back to Poland.

"They are Polish Jews. Not Germans," one of the diners at the hotel complained. "We must make space for the true Germans."

From his companion, as he gulped down a swallow of beer, Hanna heard, "Their own people don't want them. The Poles have even refused these Jews."

A third voice came in, as knife and fork noisily chopped away at a steak. "If Hitler thinks he can get rid of the Jews by forcing them to leave, he may have to reconsider. No one wants them. No one wants this pollution in their own country."

Hanna guessed these Polish Jews were somewhere in limbo, waiting to get into Poland, unable to return to Germany.

Insurance payments to the Jews for the damages were confiscated by the state, and additional fines were imposed. All of this she learned from other guests at the Hotel Bellevue who were quite intent that the Jews must pay.

"Herr Goering insists that the Jews not get their hands on these insurance payments," Hanna heard a man announce one day as he sat enjoying his dessert. "They've stirred up all this trouble and should not be rewarded for it."

Hanna thought of her many encounters with Herr Goering as he examined and then selected the art as if he were a refined gentleman.

"He's imposed a fine for all the damage. If it weren't for the Jews' greediness, none of this would have happened," another replied. "It's only fair that they be held accountable. If it means getting rid of the whole lot, so be it."

Hanna and Günter exchanged looks, and she excused herself and went to her room. Could there be any doubt now of the dangers to the Jews in Hitler's Germany? Was the rest of the world aware of what had happened?

Hanna lay on her bed shivering, praying that she might survive to go to her daughter.

She knew now that many Jews had been arrested and sent to Hitler's camps after the night of November ninth, and feared that Jakob and Helene might be among them. Or were they dead?

The following day, Hanna's assistant informed her, sadly, reluctantly, as they were driving to the warehouse, that he was able to obtain the information she had sought. Jakob Kaufmann was dead, killed in the riots of November 9.

A tear welled in Hanna's eye, but she felt more rage than sadness. "His wife, Helene?" she asked.

"I don't know."

"I must go to her."

The young man nodded. "Tomorrow."

But the following morning, when Hanna went down for breakfast, she learned that Günter had been relieved of his duties, and she had been assigned a new assistant.

Often Hanna took out the photo that Käthe had sent—the children smiling into the camera. Willy a young man, though still a child. Now he was gone, and Isabella was eleven, no longer the little girl in this photo. Hanna knew that, somehow, she had to find her way to her daughter.

Plans for the auction in Switzerland moved forward. It was to take place on June 30, 1939, with previews in both Zurich and Lucerne prior to the sale. Letters were sent to prospective buyers—those who had made the trip to Berlin and purchased work, collectors and dealers who had expressed interest, museum representatives. Many were now reluctant to come to the city. Hanna had little contact with anyone outside, but she believed, after the riots of that November night, now often referred to as *Kristallnacht*—the night of broken glass—the world might finally understand the horrors taking place in her country.

She did not hear from Johann Keller.

One day as she was carefully completing the suggested text for the catalogue, describing the 126 pieces that she herself had recommended for the auction, a list that had been closely scrutinized by Herr Hofmann, Herr Ziegler, Herr Goebbels, even Hitler, Hanna realized that they were coming to the end. After the auction, the work that had been deemed unworthy, work that she herself had been forced to omit from the auction, pieces not picked up by clients in Berlin, would be destroyed.

Over the next few days she considered the possibility of taking some of the smaller pieces out of the warehouse—drawings, watercolors, prints, and graphics. The canvases were too large and bulky. One afternoon, when she had a rare moment alone, she concealed a small print between her skirt and slip and miraculously she managed to smuggle it out with her that evening. Two days later, she was able to take a small watercolor, the next day a drawing. She feared that she would be discovered, but with over 16,000 pieces, it might be some time before the discrepancies were realized. Each evening, she tucked her rescued art beneath her bed, in her bureau, in the closet of her room.

Among those she was able to remove from the inventory was a small Kandinsky done in greens, blues, and golds, taken from the Staatsgalerie in Stuttgart. It still contained a hint of representational art—possibly a horse with rider, a mountain—yet the painting was moving very close to abstract.

She thought back to her first encounter with Kandinsky, the Russian Prince, as she served him dinner in the Fleischmann home shortly after her arrival in Munich. Then an image of the art student at the Academy came to her. The colors of Kandinsky's *Composition II* flashed in her mind, the painting Hanna and Moses had always referred to as Willy's Colors. She pictured Kandinsky leaving the gallery, the door closing behind him as the young artist, A. Hitler, entered. There was something pathetically symbolic in this disturbing reflection.

Hanna had not seen nor spoken with Wassily Kandinsky in more than twenty years, yet it seemed their lives and work were once more intersecting.

Among the art she successfully removed were a tiny Klee with colorful figures of fish, confiscated from the Dresden museum, and an Otto Dix pen-and-ink drawing from the Staatsgalerie in Stuttgart, depicting the horrors of the Great War in black and white. A Max Beckmann from the Mannheim State Gallery— two intertwined figures, surely obscene to Hitler—also made its way out of the warehouse. Somehow she would set these free, though she had no idea when or how. But she was determined that at least these four small pictures would survive.

She wished that she might save more, but soon thousands of pieces that had not been purchased or designated for the auction in Switzerland were removed from the warehouse, which was now almost empty. Hanna knew that they would be destroyed.

On March 20, 1939, much sooner than even she had predicted, Hanna witnessed the burning of 1,004 paintings and 3,825 drawings, watercolors, and graphics—yes, she knew the exact number because she had meticulously inventoried and catalogued each of them. She had saved so few, and she knew this was just the beginning of the final purge. She watched as the flames, the colors bright and glaring in her ears, licked, and slapped, and devoured.

Theodor Fischer, a slender man with thick dark brows hovering above his spectacles, arrived from Lucerne in April to examine the art selected for the auction in Switzerland. It was soon obvious that the man had no love for the art. He saw it as a business and nothing more, so Hanna conducted herself in a business-like manner. They worked easily together.

"May I make a suggestion?" Hanna said boldly.

Herr Fischer looked back from examining a painting by the German artist Emil Nolde. Silently, he nodded.

"Perhaps if we provide the paintings with proper frames, they would appear more appealing to the buyers."

Again Herr Fischer said nothing.

They would never have shown a painting at the Fleischmann Gallery unframed, and Hanna had always selected the materials herself, the colors and textures, as well as the harmony of the sounds, guiding her.

Finally Herr Fischer replied, "I believe your assessment is correct. Speak to your supervisor about supplying the proper materials. Anything we can do to make this rubbish more agreeable."

The day after Theodor Fischer left Berlin, Hanna learned he had asked that she travel to Switzerland and assist with the installation at preview locations in Zurich and Lucerne, as she exhibited an efficiency and dedication that he greatly admired.

Much to her surprise, the arrangements were made. Hanna would be going to Switzerland.

CHAPTER TWENTY-EIGHT

Isabella and Lauren

New York City
August 2009

Isabella picked up the photograph of herself and Willy and carried it to the kitchen. She got a pair of reading glasses—one of many she stashed around the house—and a small screwdriver out of the junk drawer, pulled the wastebasket from under the sink over to the table, and sat.

Willy smiled up at her from behind the cracked glass. The girl stared, the raw pain reaching out to Isabella, who felt oddly both detached from and entwined with her younger self. She'd kept the picture in the bedroom bureau and hadn't looked at it in years. She'd kept the feelings hidden away for a long time, too.

We'll just see if Lauren O'Farrell follows through and brings a new piece of glass tomorrow, Isabella thought, flipping the photo over. As she pried at the metal tab holding it in the frame, the screwdriver slipped, jabbing the base of her thumb, leaving a streak of broken red skin. She felt a flash of pain. Her hands were trembling. She set the frame aside and placed one hand over the other, pressing at the skin around the unsightly scratch.

As she moved her fingers over the blue veins of a spotted hand that looked much older than she felt inside, Isabella was reminded again that she had some serious decisions to make. Once more she asked herself if it had been wise to invite this young woman into her home. She'd concluded, after her call, that Lauren O'Farrell had learned about the Kandinsky painting and she'd come to question the legality of its ownership. Isabella believed she had the proper papers, and some type of authentication needed to be done before she passed on. But could she trust this young woman? After spending the afternoon together, each stepping carefully with their guarded words and revelations, Isabella still wasn't completely sure. She imagined Lauren was entertaining the same thoughts about whether or not she could trust Isabella.

But Isabella was absolutely sure of one thing now—the woman had come to make accusations about her mother. The way Lauren kept pressing for information on Berlin. Yes, she was here to make accusations.

At times Isabella wondered if perhaps her mother *had* collaborated with the Nazis. Or stolen art. What if the money for her education, for Isabella's early life in America, had come from sources other than those her mother claimed? Yet there was the art in their home in Munich and in the gallery—all gone now. She knew the paintings were valuable, though deflated by what was happening in Germany at the time they were sold. But there would have been some family money. The Fleischmanns had been very wealthy.

And, still haunting her thoughts—the fear that what Mr. Keller told her years ago when they met had been nothing but lies. Lies to protect Hanna.

Isabella got up and stepped over to the refrigerator. She felt weak, her stomach empty and queasy at the same time. She should eat something. Opening the vegetable crisper, she took out lettuce, a tomato, broccoli, mushrooms, and fresh green onions. Yes, a nice salad. She'd add some canned tuna. She walked over to the bread-box and pulled out a loaf of French bread. Maybe she'd have a small glass of wine.

As she washed the lettuce, sliced the tomato, she couldn't shake the thought that she had to decide soon, and this whole ordeal with Mrs. O'Farrell had reminded her of the necessity of doing so.

Andrew always told Isabella that it was up to her to decide what to do with the Kandinsky. Legally, and perhaps emotionally, too, the painting belonged to Isabella. It hadn't even been mentioned in Andrew's will. Ownership of the business, Fletcher Enterprises, now being run by a Fletcher nephew, had been divided up among the Fletcher family members, Isabella still retaining majority control. At her death, Isabella's shares would be distributed in the same fashion, and family members knew this would be their sole, though very generous, inheritance. She had a fairly large income each year, and much of it went to charitable causes, including those that supported art and children. These gifts would continue after her death. Several of the older Fletchers knew about the Kandinsky, though none had expressed a love for this type of art and, amazingly, the existence of the painting had not become public knowledge. Because of the many reproductions she owned, visitors had always believed that it, too, was an imitation.

She hadn't displayed it openly in the home since Andrew's death and she'd kept pretty much to herself. Most of her trusted friends were gone, and in all reality she hadn't had many. With so many secrets, she found it hard to confide in others. Andrew had been her best friend. Her only friend, she thought at times.

If she dropped dead today, the painting would most likely have to be sold to pay the estate taxes and would undoubtedly go into a private collection. She knew this wasn't what she wanted. It had been hidden for too many years. Perhaps it was time for Kandinsky's *Composition II* to make itself known to the world.

Isabella got a can of tuna out of the cupboard, half expecting Mittie to come sauntering into the kitchen at the whir of the can opener, the whiff of fish. That fat, old, saucy cat had been her companion for more than twelve years, and she'd lost him just three months ago. She'd considered getting a new cat, but at her age, that would be about as ridiculous as getting a new husband.

Isabella sat alone, eating her salad, sipping her wine, turning one thought and then another over and over in her mind.

On the walk to the subway, Lauren called Patrick and told him she was on her way.

"Should I start dinner?" he asked.

"There's some chicken thawing in the fridge. I can broil it when I get home." She knew if she left it to Patrick, he'd fry it. "You could get started on a salad. Tomatoes on the side." She knew Adam wouldn't eat the tomatoes, and Lauren knew that right now she didn't have the energy to talk him into trying a bite or two. "Maybe a can of peas." Strangely, her son loved those mushy little pale green peas from a can. She'd stop at the bakery a block from home and pick up a loaf of the Kalamata olive ciabatta bread that Patrick loved.

"She actually agreed to see you," he said with some pride in his voice. He'd always thought Lauren had a lot of nerve, as well as courage, in what she was doing. "You learned more about Hanna Fleischmann?"

"You won't believe what I learned," she said, immediately thinking of Mrs. Fletcher's request. She couldn't—wouldn't—share anything about the Kandinsky with Patrick. "I've got another appointment with her tomorrow."

Lauren could hear Adam, talking to his dad in the background, and Patrick said, "*Your* son needs some attention." He laughed. "Can't wait until you get home."

As she hurried down to the subway, Lauren thought of Mrs. Fletcher's uneasiness, her obvious discomfort when she mentioned her mother waiting in Berlin for her papers to go to America. Yet, throughout the afternoon, the woman's emotions had jumped from extreme composure, to anger, to sadness, to exhaustion, and back again. Maybe Lauren was reading something into Isabella's reaction to the mention of Berlin.

Her train arrived; she got on, found a seat, and pulled out her notebook. Flipping past the page on which she'd written the frame's measurements, she jotted down information, dates, and facts that Mrs. Fletcher had revealed to her, underlining those she wanted to verify or research further. Weary, Lauren closed her eyes. Images of Mrs. Fletcher's apartment worked their way into her head—the paintings, the lovely furnishings, the drawing of young Hanna, the photo of Isabella and her brother, Willy. She thought of the stories Isabella had told her. Realizing that their stories—Isabella's and Lauren's—had come together in an obvious but oddly unexpected way, Lauren wondered why she had not considered this possibility earlier.

She'd known from the moment she discovered that Isabella Fletcher was likely the daughter of Hanna Fleischmann that Mrs. Fletcher's father was Jewish. But she'd been unable to get past the fact that Isabella's mother was, at the least, a thief and Nazi collaborator, if not a traitor to her own family. Now Lauren wasn't sure of anything.

The picture of the Fleischmann children morphed in Lauren's mind to a different black-and-white photo, this one taken in the late thirties in London. Lauren's father as a toddler, his five-year-old sister, Mimi, their mother, Miriam Rosenthal. Lauren had discovered it in her father's desk when she was seven. She knew she shouldn't be going through her father's things, but she also knew there were secrets in those drawers. The woman in the photo had a haunted look in her eyes. Like a crazy person.

Lauren knew now that this picture had been taken shortly before the German bombings began to destroy much of London.

Finally, several days later, Lauren got up the nerve to ask her mother.

"Your father, his sister, your grandmother Rosenthal," she said. "Your father says you have your grandmother's eyes." Lauren wondered at the time if she, too, had crazy eyes.

"What happened to them?" she asked.

"They're gone now," her mother replied.

Isabella lifted the cardboard backing off the frame and removed it to expose the back of the photo.

At the top her mother had written—no, it appeared to be Aunt Katie's hand—the date 1936, Isabella's age 9, and Willy's 25.

Below this were several lines in her mother's script, so she knew these had been added later. They appeared to be dates, then initials, names of German cities, German words. Isabella stared down at the letters and numbers, as if reading some sort of code. *St. Galerie. Galerie N. M.* Her heart tightened and contracted, her stomach turned. She gasped.

After several moments, she shook the frame, dropping the shattered glass into the wastebasket. She picked up the glass of wine sitting on the kitchen table next to the empty salad plate. Taking a sip, she stared down at the words her mother had written.

Was this the very information she had been searching for these past many years?

Had her mother known that one day Isabella would find it?

Yet alone it made no sense at all. Unless it was combined with what Mr. Keller had told her.

Lauren sat on her bed, Adam, bathed and pajamaed, cuddled at her side. Her laptop, the notes she jotted down on the way home, along with a stack of art books, lay out on the bedspread.

She'd just gone through the photos on her phone, studying them, wishing she'd had the opportunity to take more. She felt only a trickle of guilt. Mrs. Fletcher had asked that she not take notes and, as Lauren was about to leave, that she share nothing they had spoken of. She'd told Patrick at dinner that she'd promised Isabella she wouldn't disclose what they had talked about. He was disappointed, but understood. Lauren wouldn't show the photos to anyone either, not even Patrick. Not just yet.

One of the art books lay opened to the section on the Expressionists. Adam was especially fond of these paintings—the ones with the *best* colors and blobs, as he called them.

He had gone to his room to retrieve his crayons to do a picture of his own, based on the very Kandinsky that Lauren had been studying—*Composition II.* As he drew, his tongue moving along with his busy hand, he asked his mother to tell him a story about the painting.

It was a little ritual they went through often when Lauren was studying, reading about a particular artist whose work she'd come across in her own work. For those paintings that were representational, the stories often involved the people and the recognizable images in the paintings. Sometimes they were based on true stories, often revised to earn a "G" rating. Sometimes Lauren just made them up. Adam seemed to prefer the made-up stories. He liked stories where the heroes and villains were easily identified. Throw in a monster or two and he was especially delighted.

Lauren started in, "There was once a lovely young woman who heard music in the colors."

"Was she a princess?" Adam asked, looking up at his mother with large, curious blue eyes. He had his father's eyes and cute round nose. His hair was dark, like both Lauren and Patrick, but he had inherited his mother's curls.

Lauren smiled, finding it interesting that Adam made no comment about colors making music. His interest was in whether she was a princess or not.

"Yes," Lauren said, "she was a princess and her name was Hanna."

"Like Hannah at my school?"

"A little bit," Lauren answered, thinking of the beautiful three-year-old, blue-eyed blonde in Adam's preschool. She thought perhaps her son had a little crush on the girl. "She was also very pretty. But this Hanna's hair was bright red."

"No, not red," Adam said with a giggle, shaking his head of bouncy dark curls. They'd had a similar discussion earlier about red hair. To Adam, red was the color of an apple. People didn't have *red* hair.

"Reddish brown," Lauren conceded with a laugh. "Okay—reddish brown." She picked a crayon out of his box labeled Burnt Sienna, though she knew this wasn't right. Too brown. How had Isabella described her mother's hair—*brilliant, showstopping red*? Lauren wondered for a moment if she was betraying her promise to Isabella Fletcher—it was Hanna Schmid Fleischmann she was thinking of as she told Adam the story of the woman who heard music in the colors.

"And then," Adam said dramatically, his hands rising into the air, "a bad man comes and tooks all the colors away. And all the music." He was lately into joining in the storytelling himself, adding his own elements of drama. "All the peoples are very sad."

"Yes, the bad man came and took them away."

"And the kingdom was sad and black and lonely," Adam said. He looked up and grinned at his mother. "What is the bad man's name?"

"Adolf," the word slipped out.

"That's a funny name," he said, nose wrinkling.

"This story takes place in Germany," Lauren replied, at the same time telling herself, *Not yet.*

"What's Germany?"

"A faraway place."

"Across the ocean?"

"Yes."

"Are there castles and monsters?"

Lauren said, "Germany is full of lovely castles."

"Can we go there?"

"Someday. Maybe." She thought of the lovely, magical Neuschwanstein Castle she'd toured years ago in Bavaria. Disneyland's Sleeping Beauty Castle had been modeled after this very castle, which looked like something out of a fairy tale. Adam would love it.

"And then the good guy," the little boy continued, "comes and founds the colors and the music and puts them all back happy on the earth."

"Yes," Lauren said, wondering what was wrong with her that she would tell such a story to a small child, making a fairy tale out of a terrible reality. Soon enough he would learn the truth about the evil man in Germany who had taken away the music, the colors.

"Time for bed, sweetie," Lauren said as she scooped up a handful of crayons and started replacing them one by one in the box. Adam helped her, slowly putting them in, point up, just the way she'd shown him.

"But I want to finish the story," he said. She could see he was being so particular with the crayons in hope of extending his bedtime. "I want you to tell me about the man who rescued all the colors and music."

Lately he was into such big words—*rescued*?

"What makes you think it was a man?" Lauren said with a laugh. "Maybe it was a woman."

"A mom?" Adam asked, an incredulous grin spreading over his face.

"Yes," Lauren replied, sweeping him up off the bed into her

arms. They needed to do a little more gender-equality training at that preschool, she thought. "Yes, a mom," she said emphatically.

As she carried him into his room and settled him into bed, kissed his forehead, and tucked in the covers, she was struck by one of those moments of pure, true love.

She stepped out, and then glanced back as she lingered for a long moment in the doorway, wondering what she would do to protect this child from harm. What she wouldn't do. Send him away if necessary? And what would she do to survive if they were separated? What would she go through to find her way back to him?

CHAPTER TWENTY-NINE

Hanna

Berlin and Weitnau
May 1939

Late one afternoon when she returned to her hotel, Hanna found a letter from her brother Frederick. She wondered how he knew where to find her. She had not been in contact with him for more than a year.

The note was brief, the writing shaky, almost unreadable, and at first Hanna doubted it had come from him. His wife used to write, but she'd been gone for years now, and Hanna didn't recall ever getting a letter from her brother.

Much time has passed since your last stay at the farm, he wrote. *Please come for a visit.*

The brevity, typical of her brother, convinced Hanna it was indeed Frederick's hand. But she found the formality of the words very odd. He must have something to tell her, something he could not write in his letter.

She requested time to visit her family before her departure for Switzerland. She did not believe her request would be granted, though her tasks toward the auction had been completed. The art had been prepared; the proper packing and shipping for transport to Switzerland had been arranged. Hanna was scheduled to leave the following week to arrive for the uncrating and installation at the first exhibition preview. At times she wondered if she would truly be allowed to leave for Switzerland. Hitler had eyes and spies everywhere. Possibly one of them was aware that she wanted desperately to go to America. Yet, she had no money, and she was without the proper papers, even if she could flee from Switzerland.

Surprisingly, she was granted a short leave. Her young assistant, newly assigned—her third—was sent to accompany her.

The day of her arrival, Frederick, Hanna, and her escort, a thin young man named Klaus, sat at the kitchen table drinking coffee.

"The children are well?" Hanna asked.

"*Ja.*" Frederick didn't know that she had lost her own son, but she would not tell him about Willy. Such conversation might lead to talk of Isabella, safe now in America.

Hanna surveyed the room and realized how little their home had changed—the same stove where her mother, Hanna, Käthe, and then their stepmother had prepared meals. The plank floors covered with well-worn rugs where little Peter often curled up for a nap, where Leni played with her dolls, perhaps dreaming of the day she would be a mother.

Then she glanced at young Klaus as he got up to refill his cup for the second time, and Hanna realized how much everything in her own life had changed since she'd left her childhood home.

"The grandchildren?" she asked her brother.

"Visiting with Fritz and his wife, her family, before the harvest." He had lost weight. She knew he was not well, as he held his cup with a shaky hand. She thought of the uneven script of his letter, while Frederick went on to explain that his youngest son and two grandsons were serving in Hitler's army.

"Fritz has been allowed to stay?"

"Hitler believes the farmers are as important as the military in rebuilding the strength of Germany."

Young Klaus sat quietly, gulping his coffee. Again he refilled his cup, and then held up the empty pot. Hanna rose to make more. Klaus paced the floor, gazing out now and then through the window as he waited.

Shortly, after the coffee was ready and Hanna had poured them each another cup, after little conversation had passed, she commenting on the warm weather, the young man excused himself. Perhaps to relieve his boredom, as well as his bladder, Hanna thought.

"I'm going to Switzerland," she told her brother.

Frederick nodded, but he did not inquire about her present employment. Her escort's red-and-white swastika armband left no doubt that she was working for the party or the government, now little distinction between the two. Surely Frederick understood it was not a position she had taken voluntarily.

"Helene visited," he said.

Hanna gasped with surprise. "Oh, thank God she's alive." And not in one of the camps, she reflected with a prayer of gratitude. Her gratitude was accompanied by a sense of relief that Helene had not attempted to contact her or come to her with the sad news of Jakob's death. After the events of November ninth, life had become especially dangerous for any Jew attempting to move about in Hitler's Germany, and Hanna was now living within a nest of Nazis. But why had Helene come to visit Frederick? As far as Hanna knew, she had never come to the farm, had never communicated with Frederick in any way. "You know about Willy?" she whispered, feeling a tear well in her eye.

"*Ja,*" Frederick replied, but his eyes could not meet hers. "I'm sorry, Hanna." He glanced cautiously toward the door.

Hanna knew they would have little time to speak before Klaus returned.

"Why did she come?" Hanna asked softly.

"She has left you some egg money." He smiled, despite what Hanna knew was on both their minds, thoughts they would not speak aloud.

"Egg money?" She realized he meant there was something upstairs in the girls' bedroom, in the bureau in the middle drawer, right between Käthe's and Leni's. She had never suspected her brothers knew where she kept her private treasures. She smiled now, too, thinking how simple it would have been for anyone to know.

"Also, something in the barn," Frederick added in a low voice. "I will keep it safe until you return from Switzerland."

"What is it?" Hanna whispered to Frederick. She did not tell him she would not come back, something she had sensed since arrangements were made for her journey. She did not tell him that her nights were filled with dreams of rescue, dreams of Johann, that these dreams were always overpowered by the nightmares. She did not tell him that after the auction she would have no useful purpose to Hitler, that these terrifying nights were filled with visions of her own death.

"Helene called it 'Willy's Colors,'" he replied.

"A painting?" Hanna asked in shock.

"*Ja.*"

"From Botho von Gamp?"

"I don't know. She said you would understand, because both Willy and you had loved it."

Hanna wanted desperately to go to the barn to look, but soon Klaus returned. She couldn't imagine how Helene had managed to get the Kandinsky. When they parted the last time, she feared that Helene hated her for leaving her son to die in America, for working for Hitler. Had she been wrong?

Later that night, in her private moments in the girls' room, Käthe and Leni now far away, Dora leaving no trace, and Frederick's young daughters long gone to their own husbands, in the old worn dresser, under a stack of bed linens, Hanna found a small pouch. She loosened the string, and spilled the contents out on the bed. Before her eyes they sparkled with the sounds of ice and snow. Diamonds! Helene's gift to Hanna. Perhaps she thought this would provide her with an escape.

At the very bottom of the drawer, she found two papers. Hanna picked up the larger and unfolded it. A bill of sale to Helene from Botho von Gamp for Wassily Kandinsky's *Composition II*! The man had refused to sell it to Hanna, though he was probably aware she had little to offer him. She wondered if he'd come to the realization that the painting might eventually be destroyed or confiscated by the Nazis, and better to rid himself of it now for a price.

And then she read the smaller, a handwritten note from Helene.

Dearest Hanna,

By the time you receive this, I will be dead. I can no longer continue. Please honor us all by finding your way to Isabella.

I am sorry.

My love,
Helene

Hanna sat on the bed, shaking. She could not weep, as if all her tears had dried.

That night she picked at the stitching along the bottom of her skirt, and in the quiet of this room where she had laughed and argued and dreamed with her sisters, Hanna hid Helene's gift along the hem. Then she found needle and thread in a small box in the bottom drawer and sewed the bill of sale, Helene's note tucked inside, into her pocket.

She waited until the middle of the night, then opened her door and tiptoed downstairs, hoping to make her way to the barn. Smelling smoke, she peered around the corner to find her young escort, standing in the hall, cigarette dangling from his mouth. Hanna returned to her room.

Early the next morning, when again she felt they were alone, she asked Frederick to describe the painting.

His eyes blinked nervously. "Hitler," he whispered, "has brought strength back to Germany, but at what price . . . the sacrifice of treating all justly." He shook his head. "Oh, little sister, the world will judge us harshly. I do not agree with Hitler's ways, but this painting . . . Perhaps my ideas of art are much like his. I, too, wish to know what I'm looking at." He went on to describe the painting. "Bright colors, a horse, or perhaps a giraffe, in the center. Women to one side, but not true forms. They are kneading bread, or perhaps washing the laundry on stones." Again he shook his head, his eyes still twitching.

"You find it disagreeable?" she asked.

"Quite," he said with a slow, cautious smile.

"Wouldn't it be lovely if once more we lived in a world where we could disagree? Where each could choose what he or she finds agreeable?"

Frederick's smile remained, but it was now filled with sadness and regret. "*Ja,*" was the only word he could find.

Hanna left the farm, never having had the opportunity to go to the barn to examine the canvas left by Helene. But she knew, from her brother's description, from the bill of sale, that it was *Composition II*, painted by the Russian Wassily Kandinsky.

Back in Berlin she made final preparations for her departure to Switzerland. The night before she was to leave, Hanna carefully removed the lining in each of the two pieces of luggage that would accompany her on her journey. In the larger she inserted the small paintings and drawings that she had rescued from the warehouse. In the smaller bag she placed Helene's bill of sale for the Kandinsky and her own drawing done years ago at the Academy in Munich. Then, using the professional stitch of the tailor that her stepmother, Gerta, had taught her more than forty years ago, she sewed, concealing them inside the lining. As she stitched, Hanna remembered how unkind she had been to Gerta. She could hear her shrill, childish voice insisting that she did not need her stepmother's help, that her own mother had taught her to sew. But she could see now that Gerta's stitches would be undetected if there was any thought that Frau Fleischmann was smuggling art out of the country. Hanna thought of how much she had disliked this woman. She could no longer use the word *hate*, as there was far too much hate in her world now. Hanna said a prayer of thanks for Gerta as she finished.

Carefully she folded her clothes and packed them in her bags, nestling the photograph of Willy and Isabella that Käthe had sent to her from America in this protective softness in the larger bag.

Later that night, unable to sleep, remembering the inventory lists she'd successfully transported in the move from her old hotel and hidden in her room, realizing she couldn't leave them behind, Hanna rose. If she put the lists inside her bag with her clothing, authorities might question her having this information. Could she hide them along with the art in the lining? She glanced out the window, sensing the sun would soon rise, and feared her time was running out, that a hurried job of ripping and sewing might be easily detected. And adding the bulk of these to the hidden art might call attention to the re-sewed lining. Should she destroy the lists? Yet she felt at least the information regarding the pieces she had hidden in her luggage should be saved.

Carefully she lifted the photograph of her children from her bag and removed the frame. On the back of the picture, in the same abbreviated manner she'd used on her lists, she recorded the inventory information pertaining to the concealed art. She replaced the photograph in the frame and then, as quickly as she could, she tore the lists into tiny pieces, flushing some down the toilet, hiding others in the soil of the potted plants in her elegant room in the Hotel Bellevue.

CHAPTER THIRTY

Hanna

Switzerland
May–June 1939

Hanna traveled to Switzerland by train with her young assistant—newly assigned, her fourth—who, along with representatives from the Fischer Gallery, assisted her in setting up the first preview exhibition, which would run for ten days in Zurich. She worked diligently, retreating alone to her room at night. Always she was escorted by her young man, a serious, stern-faced fellow named Helmut, who treated her with the utmost respect. Frau Fleischmann, Hitler's Curator of the Degenerate.

Hanna had not heard from Johann Keller, and again she attempted to dismiss him from her thoughts—the visions of Johann when they first met on the ship, and then the more mature Herr Keller from their meeting in Berlin. Yet hopeful images kept pushing into her head. She would see him again. Hanna knew that he would come to the auction in Lucerne.

One morning, as she was attending to a well-known collector at the preview in Zurich, she turned to retrieve materials from the office set up for them at this site and there he stood—Herr Johann Keller. He was not alone, but with another gentleman, one of those Hanna recognized from the group she had met in Berlin at Schloss Niederschönhausen.

Her eyes locked for a moment with Johann's and a fire Hanna feared was coloring every visible part of her body rushed through her. They were not able to speak at this time, but he nodded as if to say, *I will not let this opportunity slip by. I will find you, Hanna.*

She slept little that night, anticipating what might happen the next day.

The following morning, he appeared again, this time alone. He walked up to Hanna and said, "Frau Fleischmann, we met in Berlin when I came with representatives from the Basel Museum."

"Yes, so nice to see you again, Herr Keller," she replied in her professional dealer's voice, bearing down on her lip to suppress her smile. "I recall you expressed an interest in one of our Franz Marcs. Please, it is on display over here."

She escorted him to the painting, and then after some discussion about the piece, they walked together through the entire collection, Hanna feeling strangely giddy despite what she saw as the seriousness of these days and the sale that would take place the following month in Lucerne.

"Oh, Hanna," he said softly. "I must see you while you are here in Switzerland."

"I could wish for nothing more," she whispered. "It will be difficult. Particularly here in Zurich." She motioned with her head toward the desk where her assistant sat, watching over her like a humorless guardian angel. "Perhaps in Lucerne where there will be more distractions as we prepare for the auction."

"Arrangements could be made," he said in a low voice. "It is your wish to go to America to be with your son?"

Hanna stood, her legs growing weak, saying nothing, feeling as if she could no longer maintain this calm, praying she wouldn't break down into uncontrollable sobs. He did not know that she had lost her precious Willy. This was surely not the time or place to tell him. And he did not know about Isabella. "Yes," she whispered, the word coming out with a scratchy hoarseness. Her throat felt as if it were covered with gauze.

"I see you've found Frau Fleischmann," a representative from the Fischer Gallery said as he approached.

Johann said, "I look forward to seeing you in Lucerne next month, Frau Fleischmann."

"Yes, I hope to see you as well as your colleagues from Basel."

For the remainder of her days in Zurich, the scene played out in her head. She and Johann would go to America to be with their daughter, Isabella. But Hanna could not conjure such images without reminding herself that she had lived in a world of deceit since Johann had come into her life. And now she continued her lies. He didn't know about Isabella. He did not know that Willy was gone. Hanna pushed away the thought that she was also deceiving herself. Johann still had a wife in Switzerland, and he had not suggested he would go with her to America. But clearly he had told her that he would help her escape. And hadn't he expressed his love for her when they met in Berlin?

Hanna knew if she and Johann were to have anything between them again, she must tell him the truth.

At the end of May the paintings and sculptures were moved from Zurich to Lucerne where they were scheduled to preview for a full month leading up to the auction at the Grand Hotel National on Lake Lucerne at the end of June. Hanna was set up in an elegant private room at the hotel. Her assistant took an adjoining room. The door between the two rooms was always locked, but she knew he was keeping a close eye on her.

There was less activity during the early days of the preview than she had expected, fewer dealers, collectors, and foreign gallery and museum representatives coming in and out of the Grand Salon at the hotel than anticipated. Some days she did little, yet each evening when she returned to her room she was exhausted.

Supper was delivered to her and she retired. Her assistant checked on her each night, asking if there was anything she needed.

One morning a photographer showed up, escorted by a Fischer representative. He moved about, taking pictures of a number of the most important pieces, and then asked Hanna for assistance in adjusting one of the larger paintings displayed on an easel. "To get the light correct," he explained. He took several shots, from this angle, then that, asking for Hanna's help in moving the painting against a more neutral background. She felt a small warm spike deep in her chest as she realized he was not only taking photographs of the art, he was clearly aiming the camera directly at her!

Hanna waited, watching each day, her eyes scanning the preview hall, the entryway, searching for Johann Keller.

She knew it would be difficult during the day, as her assistant was always near, but she wondered if she might have some freedom in the evening. One night, after supper, after putting her ear to the adjoining door and hearing no movement, she unlocked the door to her room and entered the hall. All was quiet. If she knew where to find Johann, she could just leave, but then she glanced back and there he was—her young escort. Did he never sleep?

"Is there something you need, Frau Fleischmann?" he asked.

"I was feeling restless," she answered, attempting to steady her voice. "I thought maybe a walk along the lake."

"The hotel is locked each evening," he said with a subtle smile. "For security of the guests."

It was then that Hanna realized she could neither leave nor return at night. She had a key to her own room, though she was escorted to and from it each day. But she did not have a key to get in or out of the hotel at night.

"I will accompany you," he offered, holding up a key.

It was a warm, late-spring evening. They walked together along the lake, not even speaking. She knew the young man's name was Helmut, but she knew little about him other than that he was from

Dresden. She could see there was little point in getting to know these polite young men who were assigned to look after her. Surely she did not want to get into a political discussion, and none of them seemed to know much about art. She wondered if there was a hidden plan to prevent her from befriending her assistants. She thought of Günter, and the drive they had taken that early November morning, of the horrors they had discovered. She wondered where he was now.

After their walk, Hanna was escorted back to her room.

"I will see you in the morning," Helmut said stiffly.

"Yes, tomorrow." She entered her room and locked the door.

The next morning, Hanna stepped out before breakfast had been delivered to her room, and within seconds Helmut's door opened and his uncombed head popped out, the young man rubbing his eyes. It was as though he could hear her coming and going. If Hanna had been given an extra sense in her ability to hear the colors, her assistant had surely been gifted with an extra ear. Even though she had her own room key, he could hear every time she opened the door. She could not come or go without his being aware.

"Oh, there it is," she said innocently as the breakfast cart came rolling down the hall. "I'm so hungry." Hanna held the door for the boy with the cart, and realized that even if she could leave the hotel, there was no point in her running away unless she had a plan of escape. She knew she would have to receive help from someone.

And so, each day she watched for Johann Keller.

During the final week of the preview, a continuous line of prospective buyers paraded through the hall. And always, Frau Fleischmann was required. An additional German representative was to be sent from Berlin by Herr Franz Hofmann to look after things, to take an accounting of what was sold, the purchase price and successful bidder on each piece, but he would not arrive until the day before the auction. It was Hanna who had the greatest knowledge of the collection, the specifics on each of the 126 paintings and sculptures offered. She was in constant demand.

Two days before the auction, she was walking down the hall with her assistant, on her way to the Grand Salon to meet with a buyer, when literally she ran right into Johann Keller. Hanna stopped, as did her heart.

"Herr Keller!" she said, feeling completely out of breath, as if he had just knocked the wind out of her—which in truth he had.

"Frau Fleischmann," he said, taking her arm. "I was on my way to the exhibition hall. May I escort you?"

"Please," she said. Of course, she had her own escort, so the three of them walked together.

As soon as they were inside the hall, Johann requested pen and paper, and Hanna's young man went to fetch them.

"You're staying here at the hotel?" Johann whispered.

"Yes."

"I'll come to you."

"I'm constantly watched," she replied quickly. "You've taken a room here in Lucerne?"

"Yes, here at the hotel."

She tried desperately to hide her smile. She would not have to leave the hotel to see him. If only . . . "I'll come to you," she said swiftly.

"Your pen," the young man said, handing it to Johann. "And paper."

"Thank you," Johann replied. "Now, this lovely piece by Franz Marc . . ."

They continued through the hall, viewing the paintings, Johann scribbling notes. Hanna's heart thumped with anticipation over what might transpire within the next few days. She knew if she were to escape it would have to happen soon.

"Thank you for your assistance, Frau Fleischmann," Johann

said as they stood before the final piece on display. He reached for her hand. Before he released it, he held his left hand over hers and squeezed softly. She felt the folds of paper and clenched tightly until she reached her room. She opened the note and read:

Come to me, my darling. Room 408.

B ut again that evening Hanna was unable to break away, though she and Helmut walked again along the lake. She was determined that she would make her way to Johann the following night. She had to—they were running out of time.

They strolled quietly, without words. The lake was calm, the evening balmy, but in her mind, Hanna engaged in a noisy, frenzied conversation with herself. She *must* tell Johann about Isabella. No, she shouldn't tell him. If he learned she had kept this from him all these years he might be angry and refuse to help her. Yet this knowledge might provide further reason for him to aid her in her escape, to eventually come to her.

As they turned and headed back to the hotel, Hanna realized she could not predict how Johann might react to such news. After she was free and safely in America with Isabella, she would decide if she should tell him. When her mind was clear of all this worry.

Helmut unlocked the hotel door and motioned Hanna inside.

The following day, Herr Keller appeared again. Hanna's chest tightened at the mere sight of him. Her pulse increased as if she were a young girl in love, and she wondered how such feelings could invade her body when the world around her seemed fraught with hate. If she truly loved him, she would tell him the truth. Yes, she must tell him. Johann must know that he had a daughter.

A smile flickered quickly across his face, but his voice, calm and businesslike, betrayed nothing. Again he expressed an interest in acquiring Franz Marc's painting of the two beautiful cats. "I believe lot eighty-eight," he said, referring to the catalogue number, "would be a perfect time for an acquisition."

Hanna noticed the use of the word *time*, and took it hopefully to have another meaning.

She *must* tell him now, she thought.

But again, her assistant, who had been sent off on another errand, appeared. They were unable to continue this discussion. Hanna sensed that Johann's cryptic reference to lot eighty-eight had more to do with her own rescue than the rescue of art.

The representative from Berlin, Dr. Hopf, arrived late that afternoon and Hanna was asked to join him for dinner.

As they ate, she told him of the preparations they had made, of those who had come to preview the art.

"Herr Fischer reports that you have been extremely helpful," he said.

"Thank you," Hanna replied.

"You have served the Führer well. You have served Germany well."

Hanna's shoulders stiffened, her back ached, and her head throbbed. She didn't want to have this conversation. She did not want to be dining with this man, pretending she was one of them, one of Hitler's faithful followers.

Finally, after dessert and coffee, she excused herself. "There is more work ahead of me tomorrow."

"Yes, a memorable day for all of us." Dr. Hopf nodded to Hanna as well as Helmut, who had sat quietly during the meal.

As they approached the door to her room, Hanna stumbled and dropped her bag, the contents of it spilling out. She stooped to pick up a small scrap of paper and a hairpin, as the young man turned for a moment to grab a handkerchief and then chase a lipstick as it rolled across the floor of the hall. Suddenly, a thought came to her. Quickly, Hanna stuffed the paper inside the lock of the door, thinking this might prevent it from clicking as it opened and closed. Thankfully, Helmut didn't seem to notice then or as he graciously handed her the hankie and lipstick and bid her a good night, the door closing quietly between them.

Just after midnight, she inched the door open, glanced into the hall, and then waited a moment. She heard nothing but her own breathing. Quietly, carrying her shoes, she made her way into the corridor leading to the staircase. She climbed one flight of stairs, then another, until she reached the fourth floor. She waited a moment, catching her breath before stepping out into the hall, which seemed impossibly long as she gazed down the stretch of plush carpet. Based on the configuration of rooms on her own floor, she guessed 408 would be the fifth on the right. Shoes still in her hand, she moved quietly past room 400. She heard voices inside. Her heart jumped. She glanced across the hall at 401, then passed 402, and 403, moving cautiously down the hall.

When she arrived at room 408, she tapped on the door, and when his beautiful face came into view as he opened it, she slid into his room and into his arms, and felt safer than she had in many years.

The world outside disappeared. All was right and good and whole, as the horrors of Hitler's world vanished. Here in Johann's embrace this evil could no longer harm her.

She clung to him desperately, hungrily.

"Oh, Hanna," he said. "How I have longed for you."

He took her shoes, which, unaware, she still clutched in her hand. He dropped them to the floor. Then slowly they began to undress each other. Untouched by another for so long, Hanna shivered as though a new and undiscovered pleasure awaited her. His flesh against hers, the sound of his voice, the smooth, soft texture of the pale hair along his arms and legs, felt so natural and yet so unfamiliar. How had she survived without him, and how could she continue if they could not be together?

* * *

Later, as they lay in bed, after having fallen asleep in each other's arms, neither spoke, as though words would break the spell. And Hanna knew they would. They had but this one night before the auction, and she had much to tell him. Yet she could not bring herself to speak of Willy or Isabella. She wanted to hold on to the perfection of this moment as long as possible.

"What will become of us, after tomorrow?" Hanna finally asked.

He tightened his embrace.

"I can't go back," she said.

"I know," he replied.

If she could only stay here with him in Switzerland, though she knew she could not. In Zurich, he had asked if she wished to go to America to be with her son. She had said yes. If he had made arrangements, it would be to escape to America, and she knew it must happen within the next two days. She was scheduled to return to Berlin the day after the auction.

"You will not go back," Johann said firmly. "Papers have been prepared. You will be identified as a Swiss citizen. A driver will be waiting by the lake." He described the automobile and exact location. "Despite the rumors of a boycott," he told her, "there will be a heavy turnout for the auction. With many valuable pieces offered, an opportunity that will not present itself again, a good crowd should appear tomorrow, and I believe the best time for you to escape is during the auction itself when there will be many distractions."

"Lot eighty-eight," Hanna said.

"I was afraid I would have to deliver my plan in code, that it might prove impossible to find time together. Oh, but you are a clever girl," he said, running his fingers across her arm. "I will have one of my assistants approach yours and ask for—let's say a catalogue, something that will divert his attention for a moment."

"Then I will make my way to the car waiting by the lake? He will take me—"

"You'll leave from France."

Again they were silent. She heard a motorcar down on the street. Was it a guest arriving from a late night? Or was it an early-morning traveler leaving the hotel?

"There's been talk of a boycott?" Hanna asked.

"Yes, rumors are rife that funds from the art will go to Hitler's military efforts." He presented this almost as if he wished her to deny it.

Hanna had been cut off from the publicity surrounding the event, though she guessed there were those with concerns about Hitler's intentions for the funds collected from the sale of the art. She had always been instructed to tell buyers the proceeds would be used to purchase new art for the German museums.

"If buyers boycott the auction," she said, "what will become of the art if it is not purchased here? It might return to Germany to be destroyed."

"Would Hitler do such a thing?"

"He is an evil man. Surely you know it is not by choice that I have been assisting with the art. I fear the man. I have no doubt he would destroy whatever is not sold. I also fear that my own usefulness has expired."

She told Johann about her first encounter with Hitler many years ago, about her visit with him at his mountain retreat, about her being invited to the grand opening of the Haus der Deutschen Kunst, and then the exhibition of *Entartete Kunst*, how she'd been ordered to Berlin to help with the inventories. She described the bonfire at the Berlin fire station, the destruction of thousands of pieces of art. She told him of what she had personally witnessed in November, and of Jakob's murder, how she feared that Helene was gone now, too.

The shadows on the wall had shifted, and Hanna knew it was

morning, that the rising sun would soon lighten the sky. Their time had slipped by so quickly. She must return to her room.

"Will I see you again, Johann? Or will fate continue to dictate our future?"

"Hanna, I know that somehow, yes, we will be together, but first we must reunite you with your son."

Hanna felt a surge of heat—ignited surely from her deception—jolt through her. She sensed that Johann felt it, too, as if this current of tension had been conducted from her body to his. His eyes narrowed and the lines fanning out from the corners deepened. She knew if they were ever to have a life together, she must tell him the truth. She must tell him now.

"Oh, Johann . . ." She was shivering. The safety and warmth of his presence could no longer calm her.

"The plan will work, I promise." He pulled her protectively into his arms. "Don't be afraid."

Oh, that she could remain here forever, but she forced herself to break away. She sat, facing him. "Willy is gone."

"Yes, in America." His voice was low, his expression one of grave concern. She could see that he thought she was too frightened to attempt this escape. And then confusion deepened in his eyes as she begged for understanding with her own.

"No," she said. "He—Willy . . . Willy is gone. He was very ill. His body wasn't strong enough to . . ." Her voice trembled. "Oh, Johann, he's . . ." Her lip quivered. "He's dead." Again, he reached for her, but Hanna could not let him hold her until she finished telling him what he had to know.

"When?" he said.

"Helene came to me in Berlin. Shortly after I saw you. She told me that Willy had become very ill in America." Hanna tried desperately not to break down, to keep herself together so she could tell Johann the truth. "We lost him. In America. And I wasn't there. I wasn't there." She was sobbing now, unable to continue.

"Oh, Hanna my darling, I'm so very sorry." He took her in his arms, and she could no longer resist the reassurance of his embrace. "How have you survived such great losses?" he said softly, stroking her hair. Hanna's entire body throbbed as Johann rocked her back and forth.

Finally he said, "We must carry on with our plans. You must not return to Germany. You must go to America. And someday—"

"We might find one another again?" she whispered.

"Oh, Hanna," he started, hesitating. "I—"

"I know, I know," she broke in. "I understand," she said, gulping back her tears. "I don't expect you to leave your family." Hanna couldn't say *your wife*. She just couldn't say that. "I would never hurt my own children."

"Your children?"

"Yes," she said, the word itself coming forth as a confession.

Slowly he released her and stared into her eyes. Hanna could see that he had been crying, too.

She looked down, ashamed. "Oh, Johann. I have . . . I have a daughter." Her eyes rose to his as she said, "We have a daughter."

What she saw in his face now was a mixture of disbelief, anger, sadness. She had never seen this intensity in his eyes, around his tight lips, and she realized her certainty that they knew each other well was perhaps the greatest lie. Had she known only that which one reveals to a lover in the first throes of love, the heat of passion and intimacies of the body suppressing reality and truth? She didn't know the real Johann Keller. He did not know the real Hanna.

He rose from the bed and walked over to the window, gazing down upon the lake and the first morning light.

"Why, Hanna? Why did I not know? Why did you not come to me with this news?"

"We agreed."

"But a daughter," he said, his voice rising. "A child. *My* child." He sat on a chair next to a small table in front of the window.

Morning light slanting into the room brought out the planes and angles of his face, and she thought of the night they met, how she felt he was the most beautiful man she have ever seen. He lowered his head, covering his face with his hands, saying no more for a very long time.

"Tell me," he said quietly, not looking at her. "Tell me about her."

"Her name is Isabella."

"A name I would have chosen," he said with a faint smile. "A lovely name."

"She is a beautiful little girl with long blond hair and soft blue eyes." Hanna was imagining the child of eight she had left in America. She had just turned twelve, and Hanna realized that she couldn't describe how she might look now. "She's very smart," she continued. "Very clever, and so very kind and watchful with her brother." Even now Hanna could not picture Isabella without Willy. "She has a stubborn streak, an inability at times to admit when she is wrong."

"Like her father."

"Yes," she said, but Hanna was thinking of Moses, not Johann. Again she sobbed. She felt so alone. "Please, Johann," she begged, reaching out for him.

He said nothing for many moments, until he stood, walked over, and sat on the bed, his back to her. "You should return to your room, Hanna."

Back in her room, she bathed, thinking this might calm her nerves, which it did not. With anxious fingers, and trembling hands, she dressed for breakfast, but ate little when it arrived. When her escort called for her, she was confident that he was unaware she had spent the night away. She was less confident that she would make her way to America, fearful now that Johann would not continue with their plan. A picture formed in her mind—his back turned to her, staring out the window, and she shivered at the thought that he might desert her here in Switzerland, to be returned to Germany. A greater fear worked its way into her head—now that he knew he had a daughter, he might go to America himself and claim her as his own. What would this do to Isabella if Johann revealed what Hanna had just told him?

She did not hear from Johann or see him that morning, or early that afternoon, but she knew he would be at the auction.

With her assistant, Hanna arrived early at the Grand Salon to help with final preparations. It was Friday, June 30, 1939. The auction was scheduled to commence at 3:00 P.M.

When Herr Hofmann's representative, Dr. Hopf, entered the hall, Hanna greeted him and he asked that she join him. She explained she must be available if Herr Fischer needed her, and he was escorted by a Fischer representative to a seat in the front row.

Hanna stood with Helmut toward the back, surveying the assortment of prospective buyers as they entered—Swiss, French, British, and American collectors, dealers from Paris and New York, museum representatives from Antwerp, Brussels, and Liège. Most of them she recognized, and even knew which particular pieces they had earlier expressed an interest in purchasing. But there were others whom Hanna had never seen, and she assumed they were bidding for clients who wished to remain anonymous.

She waited anxiously for the group from Basel, for Johann Keller.

The hall with crystal chandeliers and arched windows overlooking the peaceful setting of Lake Lucerne was ringed with sculptures to be offered at the auction. The paintings would be presented one by one in the order in which they appeared in the catalogue once the auction began. Pages flipped quietly as buyers studied the offerings and conversed in whispers.

Finally, the Basel contingent arrived, passed by her, moving toward the rows of chairs, settling near the back. From her standing position, Hanna could easily make eye contact with Herr Keller during the auction, and he could signal with a nod, a blink of the eye.

But Johann did not look back at Hanna. He did not even attempt to locate her in the hall as he talked with another member of his group.

There were still several empty chairs toward the front, and just minutes before 3:00 P.M., one of Herr Fischer's assistants escorted the Basel representatives to seats in the first row. As Johann sat, Hanna strained to catch his expression, something confirming they would continue with their plan.

Nothing.

Counting rows and chairs, subtracting for empty seats—and there were many more than she had imagined—Hanna guessed there were about three hundred prospective buyers gathered in the Salon of the Grand Hotel National that day. Had such a sale taken place at a different time, under different circumstances, Hanna knew the room would be unable to hold the crowd. Buyers would be standing in the aisles, against the walls and windows, overflowing out into the hallway. Clearly, many collectors and museum representatives had refused to come to the auction in protest. Yet others, she knew, had arrived with intentions of rescue. Some had come with less noble purpose, fully aware of this opportunity to pick up a true bargain without the competition of those who had chosen to boycott the sale.

Herr Fischer entered the room and stood surveying the crowd. He adjusted his glasses and mounted the podium.

The bidding began with a small painting of flowers called *Chrysanthemen* by Cuno Amiet, estimated to sell for 2,500 Swiss francs, going for a mere 850. This was followed by an Alexander Archipenko sculpture that drew less than half of what had been anticipated.

Hanna wondered if this was how it was to be, and it appeared so as the bidding continued, paintings and sculptures selling for much less than estimated, some not even making the reserves. A Gauguin went to the Musée des Beaux-Arts, Liège, for 50,000 Swiss francs, 13,000 less than estimated. Van Gogh's self-portrait, one of the most eagerly anticipated paintings, was picked up at a bargain price by an American collector. At 175,000 Swiss francs, it sold for the equivalent of just over $40,000.

Saved, she thought each time a painting was successfully purchased. *But what of me?*

Johann made no eye contact, nothing to acknowledge her presence in the hall, as she watched his every move. Was he attempting to hide any sign of their plan? Was he merely trying to protect her? Or had he decided that she was not worthy of rescue?

The Kunstmuseum Basel acquired two Chagalls for half the price they were expected to bring. Each time a bid came from one of Johann's associates, she strained to catch a glimpse of him. He did not look back.

As the bidding continued, Hanna felt both excitement and apprehension twisting and turning deep inside her. She sensed a similar tension within the group—a damp brow being wiped with a handkerchief in the back row, nervous fingers twisting a program near the middle of the room, the anxious flutter of a paddle in the front row. Without the competitive bidding such a sale would normally bring, some of the art was being practically given away.

As lot number 85, *Liegender Hund im Schnee*, Dog Lying in the Snow, the first of eight Franz Marcs to be offered, came on the block, Hanna felt as if she were counting the last moments of her life. Her mind went numb and she did not realize it had sold until the next painting came on the block.

Lot 86. *Eber und Sau*, Boar and Sow.

Herr Fischer started with 1,000 Swiss francs, trying to hold on to the enthusiasm he'd elicited on the last painting, which Hanna now realized had actually gone over the estimated bid. But Herr Fischer could not entice them on this one, and it went unsold.

Lot 87. *Die drei roten Pferde*, Three Red Horses. Hanna was growing warm, as was Fischer, she guessed, from the hint of irritation in his voice, the moisture forming on his brow.

"Five thousand, ten thousand?" he inquired. "Fifteen, twenty?

Surely for this fine Franz Marc, I hear twenty . . ." He glanced around the room, and Hanna felt he was staring at her, as if he knew when the next painting appeared, she herself would disappear. "All done at fifteen," Fischer spat out, as though he himself were ready to be done with it all.

When lot 88, *Zwei Katzen Blau und Gelb*, Two Cats Blue and Yellow, appeared, Hanna was sweating profusely, her hands trembling as she attempted to catch a glimpse of Johann in the front of the room. In profile, Hanna could see him as he whispered to his assistant. And then, for a moment as quick as a blink, he glanced back at her, their eyes met, and he nodded. The young man approached her assistant and asked that he fetch an additional catalogue for the group from Basel. Hanna had carefully made sure that there were none readily available.

As soon as Helmut left her side, she hurried through the back corridor, down the hall, into her room, and grabbed her bags. She glanced into the hall, realizing she could not return the way she had entered. She opened the door to the balcony, stepped out, and carefully dropped one bag, and then the other to the ground. Hiking her skirt, she climbed over the rail and awkwardly tumbled to the ground. She felt her ankle twist as she hit.

Feeling dizzy and wobbly, Hanna stood. She reached for the smaller bag, then the larger as she glanced around. She ducked behind a bush as a couple passed. They did not see her and continued around the building to the hotel entry. She started toward the lake. Her ankle ached. With each step, the bags became heavier and heavier, as if they were filled with stones. Should she leave one? Drop it right here? The larger contained the art she had saved; the smaller, her own drawing and the bill of sale for Kandinsky's *Composition II*, which Frederick would keep for her until she returned. But Hanna wondered if she would ever return, and then she wondered if she would even make it to the car.

Surely by now Helmut was aware she was missing, and perhaps even reporting her disappearance to Dr. Hopf.

As fast as she could move, she hurried down along the lake, her heart pounding, her cheeks burning with anxiety, her ankle throbbing, feeling as if it were now not sturdy enough to support the weight of her body.

Just as she had hoped, the automobile that Johann had described was parked along the lake at the exact location indicated. The driver stood outside, pacing, glancing at his watch with agitation. He looked up, puzzled, as Hanna was now dragging both bags and leg. He ran to meet her, grabbed one bag, then the other, threw them into the backseat, and then took hold of her arm and shoved her inside. It all seemed surreal, everything moving so rapidly, and yet at the same time her life was standing still.

When they were well outside the city, the driver handed her papers. A Swiss passport identified her as Hanna Schmid—her family name—as if she were moving backward in time. Everything was in order, papers for passage to America, leaving from the French port of Bordeaux. Her skin felt prickly and warm. Her ankle throbbed and sweat dripped from her forehead. She stared down at her passport picture and realized it had been taken by the man who'd come to photograph the art, that she was correct in her observation that he had also photographed her. She wondered if these phony papers could get her to America. Was she a fool to attempt this?

They sped through the countryside, arriving at the French border. The inspector studied the papers, looked up at Hanna, down at the photo, up at her again. She swallowed hard, her heart now throbbing in her ears. He motioned them through.

As they drove, Hanna did something she hadn't planned. She took the largest bag, opened it, ripped out the lining, and removed the four small paintings and drawings, the confiscated art. She had backed them with cardboard to protect them and, surprisingly, they were none the worse for wear. Quickly, she ripped the lining completely from the bag and folded it over the drawings. She pulled a ribbon from a nightgown packed in the bag, found pen and paper, and then stuffed everything else back inside. Carefully, she tied the ribbon around the cloth from the lining as if she were wrapping a present. Then she wrote the following note.

My dearest Johann,

Again I must reveal a truth I have kept from you. These are paintings and drawings that I have taken from the confiscated German collections. I fear if I attempt to take them with me I will be discovered. So I have chosen to leave them here with you with the sincere belief that you will safeguard them. Someday I wish that they be returned to their rightful owners, the people of Germany. Someday I hope we might be together with Isabella. But my greatest hope is that someday we will all live in a world in which our lives are not dictated by others. Guard them carefully until my return.

  Please forgive me.

              Hanna

The driver, surely aware of the ripping of fabric, the scratching of her pen, did not look back and he did not question Hanna.

When they arrived at the port of Bordeaux, she handed him the bundle.

"Please, this must be delivered to Herr Johann Keller."

The man nodded, but said nothing.

Suddenly, she thought of the contents hidden in the second smaller bag—her own drawing and the bill of sale for *Composition II*. Traveling from Germany to Switzerland as part of a government-sponsored group, she'd had no trouble, and at the

French border she had crossed without difficulty, but what if the officials at the port ripped through her bags and noticed the matching set no longer matched—that there was a lining in one and not the other? What would they think? Would they become suspicious? Would this prompt them to more carefully scrutinize her papers? Hanna thrust the smaller bag into the driver's arms, her heart beating rapidly. "And this, too," she told him.

Startled, he took it. "Godspeed," he told her.

Hanna's papers were inspected. The official opened her bag and took a quick look inside. The clothes that she had replaced after she removed the lining and art were in disarray, among them the skirt in which Hanna had concealed Helene's diamonds. She prayed he would not examine the clothing, that he would take the disorder to mean the guard at the border had done a thorough check. The port official did not seem to notice that the lining had been removed. He didn't even glance at the photo of Hanna's children. "Fine, fine," he said, motioning her to move along.

Hanna stepped onto the ship, her ankle and now her entire leg throbbing, her body so wet her underclothes felt as if they had melted to her skin. She glanced back. Her driver had already left.

She stood clutching the rail of the deck and watched as the ship pulled away, until the land was but a fine line on the horizon. A breeze, smelling of the sea, blew against her face and through her hair. The warmth of her body had been replaced with a chill. Little bumps rose up along her arms and legs.

Hanna was on her way to America.

CHAPTER THIRTY-ONE

Lauren

New York City
August 2009

The following morning after she'd dropped Adam at preschool, Lauren grabbed a cup of coffee at Starbucks and headed for the frame shop to have a piece of glass cut for Isabella's photograph. She'd have to pick up Adam at eleven thirty, get some lunch— she'd promised him McDonald's—then drop him off at day care. He went three mornings a week to preschool, which he loved, and she tried to arrange her work schedule around this. But often, as yesterday and again today, she had to set up afternoon appointments. Fortunately, there was a spot for him today at the drop-in day care. Adam was not happy about this. He complained that it wasn't fun and they made him take naps and he didn't want to go. Guiltily, she'd used the Happy Meal bribe to avoid an escalating argument with her three-year-old son.

Lauren could use a nap herself. She'd had little sleep last night, her mind jumping with thoughts of what Isabella Fletcher had told her. She kept dozing off, dreaming, waking. The colors and forms of Kandinsky's *Composition* appeared, then vanished—in her dreams or wakeful imaginings, she wasn't sure.

* * *

The previous night, after putting Adam to bed, Lauren had returned to the comfort of her own and settled under her covers, propped up by several pillows. Again, she went over the information she'd scribbled in her notebook, adding additional notes, jotting down descriptions of paintings she'd seen in Isabella Fletcher's home, those that might be authentic and possibly taken from the collection of confiscated, state-owned art in Nazi Germany. She paged through more art books and Internet sites, matching styles to artists. She found evidence that several paintings similar to Isabella's, if not identical, were now in museum collections, and guessed that the woman was telling the truth when she said that most of hers were copies.

As far as Lauren knew, a complete inventory list of paintings held in the Berlin warehouse did not exist. But a reconstruction of the Lucerne auction catalogue did. Complete with photographs of the art, it had been put together from materials in the archives of the Fischer Gallery in Switzerland, as well as several other sources considered reliable. Lauren found no matches with Isabella's art and those pieces from the Lucerne auction now described with a heartbreaking *Present location unknown.*

She knew that the art auctioned off in Lucerne was lost forever to Germany. Postwar rulings concluded that it was legitimately owned and sold by the official German government, and could therefore not be reclaimed. Paintings worth millions, formerly owned by the state, now hung in museums and private collections around the world. Legally purchased art could not be reclaimed, but what of stolen art? Art stolen by the Nazis, stolen once more by Hanna Fleischmann? And there was, of course, the confiscated art that hadn't even made it to Lucerne. Some had been sold earlier, some destroyed, and some lost.

On the Internet, she verified what she knew about the Kandinsky painting, checking the name of the owner of *Composition II*. Botho von Gamp.

"What are you looking for?" Patrick had asked as he slipped into bed beside her. He'd been sitting at the kitchen table all evening, going over a brief for an upcoming case.

"Can't tell you," she said with a weary tease in her voice. "Thanks," she added, "for getting Adam."

"Hey, he's my kid, too. You about finished?"

Lauren shrugged, knowing she was too tired to continue. "I'm not sure what I'm looking for," she told Patrick.

What was she looking for? she asked herself.

A lost Kandinsky painting?

Degenerate art? Confiscated art? Art that rightfully belonged to whom? The people of Germany?

Or was she searching for wealth that might have been gained illegally from the disposal of stolen art? Isabella Fletcher certainly lived in a beautiful home in an area where, even during this economic downturn, apartments were selling for millions. Yet Lauren had to admit this money could have come from completely legitimate sources. Andrew Fletcher's business. His share of the sale of the family farm in Onondaga County. She knew little about either. The business, Fletcher Enterprises, was privately owned and she had no access to financial records.

What exactly had she been looking for all these years? Revenge for Hanna's betrayal?

Lauren set her laptop and BlackBerry on the nightstand and lifted her pile of books off the bed, dropping them carefully to the floor. She turned off the lamp.

"Sweet dreams," Patrick said as he gave her a good-night kiss.

But even then, as she lay staring into the darkness, Lauren knew the dreams were not to be sweet.

* * *

The man at the frame shop was flipping the sign on the door from Closed to Open when she arrived. Gulping the last of her coffee, she tossed the cup in the trash receptacle outside before stepping in.

She gave him the dimensions of the glass and explained it was for a very old photo, a family heirloom, and she wanted to make sure it was the best-quality glass.

"A family heirloom?" he asked. "If you bring it in, I can do the glass and frame, make sure it's properly assembled to protect it."

"It's not my family. It's a friend." *A friend?* she thought. Had she and Isabella Fletcher become friends? "Unfortunately I don't have the picture with me."

"I'll cut the glass for you," the man said, brushing his hands over his apron, "but doing a proper framing would be much better, particularly for an older photograph. Moisture, temperature variations. If it's not properly framed I couldn't guarantee it."

"How long will it take to cut the glass?"

"I've got a job in the backroom to finish up. Say about forty-five minutes to an hour."

Lauren glanced at the digital display on her BlackBerry. She had almost three hours before meeting with Mrs. Fletcher, an hour and a half before picking up Adam. If it took an hour, that would be pushing it.

"Great," she said. "I'll be back in half an hour." She hoped this might encourage him to get to it sooner.

She found a coffee shop down the street, hitting it about break time, and had to wait to order. After searching for an empty seat she found a single chair outdoors and sat, sipping her second coffee, hoping this one would perk her up. She was so tired. She rubbed her eyes, and then attempted to massage the weariness out of her temples. Closing her eyes, she felt dizzy. Colorful after-images flashed in her head.

Then everything seemed colorless, as she thought once more of the black-and-white drawing of young Hanna Schmid. An innocent girl. *Innocent.* This word played through her head.

A taxi horn honked; a group of chatty young people—summer tourists with backpacks slung over their shoulders—walked by on the sidewalk.

Mrs. Fletcher didn't want to talk about what her mother did during the time she was in Berlin, waiting for her papers. Maybe she knew nothing about it. Could this possibly be true?

Lauren glanced at her phone, checking the time.

Isabella's mother, Hanna Fleischmann, had lost her husband, her children were in America with her sister, and even the art she and Moses loved had been taken away—*sold.* No choice—these words kept running through Lauren's head. *No choice. Survival. Escape. Innocent.*

Now Lauren wondered—was Hanna Fleischmann's true story one that had never been told, a story that was very different from the one that Lauren had attempted to write for her?

CHAPTER THIRTY-TWO

Hanna

America
July–August 1939

On July 10, 1939, Hanna arrived in America. She had not sought help on the ship for her ankle, fearing she would be discovered. After spending her first few days wondering if this was a terrible mistake, the swelling went down and she knew it was only a sprain. Nothing was broken, and it seemed to be mending on its own, though her entire leg was black-and-blue.

Despite the summer heat on the morning of her arrival, Hanna put on dark stockings to hide the remaining discoloration. She slipped on her shoe, still a painful undertaking, and walked off the boat, straight and tall, making every effort not to limp, fearing it might cause some concerns with the port officials about her health.

Thankfully, she was able to pass through customs without incident, and then step onto dry land. Her sea legs, intensified by her not-altogether-trustworthy ankle, forced her to walk slowly as she moved through the crowd. Noisy seagulls flapped overhead, their colorful shrieks mixed with the lively chatter of other passengers being greeted by family. Sweaty young men unloaded cargo, passing baggage from hand to hand, stacking trunks and boxes on carts. Hanna had but her one bag, which she had kept with her the entire trip.

The sun, bright and high in the sky, pressed down on her and she held her hand to her eyes to search about for a familiar face, though she sensed she was on her own from here. She had told Johann about her sister and brother-in-law in America, but didn't think he knew enough about them to contact them. She would have to determine how to find her way to Käthe and Hans herself. To Isabella.

Here in New York City, she could find someone to exchange Helene's diamonds for American dollars. Then she could take the train to her sister's.

As she continued to walk, trying to decide where to go from here, she heard a woman's voice call out.

"Hanna."

She turned, and a beautiful, tall, slender blond woman stood before her.

"I'm Elsa," the woman said.

Hanna stared, no words escaping her mouth. She was so obviously Johann's sister.

"You're Hanna?" the woman inquired, her voice soft and kind, the color of pink meadow saffron.

"Yes, I am Hanna." She heard a quiver in her voice, wrapped in a harsh, grating tone as if her vocal cords had rusted from lack of use over the past week and a half.

"I'm Johann Keller's sister," she explained. "I was afraid I wouldn't be able to find you." She let out a relieved breath. "But you are just as Johann described."

Hanna wondered what he had told her. Surely not—

"Just the one bag?" Elsa asked.

As Hanna nodded and the woman took it from her, Hanna thought of the other bag and the contents from the lining of this one. Had the driver delivered her bundle along with the smaller bag to Johann?

"Come." Elsa motioned. "My husband has parked the automobile."

They walked without speaking. When they arrived at the car, the woman introduced her husband as Robert. Hanna, as just Hanna. She guessed that Johann had given them but one name, as if to protect her identity. She also realized that her passport was made out to Hanna Schmid, the name that had been entered into her records as she arrived. She was no longer officially Hanna Fleischmann.

"You had a pleasant journey?" the man asked.

"Yes," Hanna lied.

Elsa, who sat in the backseat with Hanna, turned to her. "You're to join your family in Onondaga County?"

Hanna nodded. Johann knew this much—that her family lived on a dairy farm south of Syracuse. She wondered if they were going to deliver her. It was a good distance, several hours by train.

"They have been notified?" Hanna asked slowly, forming the English words carefully, awkwardly.

"Johann thought it best to wait," she replied.

Hanna wasn't sure what this meant—in the unfortunate event that she not make it?

They drove through traffic, past a landscape of tall buildings intermingled with smaller ones, lines stretched from window to window with laundry hanging to dry in the summer sun. Children playing kickball in the street.

"Would you like something to eat?" Robert glanced back at Hanna.

"No," Hanna replied, "thank you." She was too nervous to eat. "One request, please?"

"What is it?" Robert asked.

"I have no American dollars—"

"We have funds to assist you," Elsa broke in.

"I have"—Hanna hesitated—"I have gems . . . diamonds that I wish to exchange, if you might assist me."

"Robert?" Elsa asked her husband.

"Let's go home, have lunch, and I'll make some calls."

They lived in a nice apartment with large windows overlooking a grassy area that reminded Hanna of the Englischer Garten in Munich, and for a moment she was struck with a longing for home, wondering if she would ever return to Germany. And then she thought of Johann, what it might be like living here in New York City with him in such a lovely apartment. He could work at one of the city's museums or galleries; perhaps she could, too. Isabella could enroll in school here. *Oh, Isabella,* she thought, *will you even know me?*

Elsa presented Hanna with a sandwich of white bread, cheese, and ham on a beautiful floral-patterned china lunch plate, and a small dish of fresh fruit in a matching bowl. Hanna ate slowly as Robert made several calls from a phone in the hallway. He spoke quietly and she could not understand what he said. Elsa put a record on the phonograph, and the two women sat with no need for conversation. The music was soft—violins, Brahms, a lullaby, the colors soothing pastels.

Hanna wondered what Johann had told them about her, and she wondered what the Americans knew about Germany under Nazi rule. She remembered conversations with Käthe and Hans during her last visit. They knew little of Hitler. But that was four years ago. Should she ask Elsa?

But just then, Robert came into the room. "We have an appointment at eight tomorrow morning, which means you cannot leave today, unless you accept our offer to purchase the ticket for you. If you wish, you could stay here tonight and take the train in the morning."

Hanna questioned whether she should just accept the funds, but she doubted there would be any place other than New York City to make this exchange and she wanted to get it done now. She was eager to see Isabella, but . . . "Please, if it is no bother to you, I wish to do the exchange."

The following morning, early, Elsa served her breakfast, wished her well, and Robert drove her into an older part of the city. They pulled up to a tall brick building and took the elevator up to the fourteenth floor, for which Hanna was thankful, as her ankle was still causing her some pain.

A thin, nice-looking man, who reminded Hanna of a younger Jakob Kaufmann, spread the diamonds out on a white sheet of paper. He ran his perfectly manicured fingers over the stones, and then examined each with a jeweler's glass. He did not speak as he carefully placed them one by one on a scale, as if an added word might alter the weight.

"Very nice," he finally said. He did not ask where the diamonds had come from, but made an offer.

Hanna had no idea if it was a fair price, but trusted that this man, as well as Robert, was trying to help her. She did not tell him that she had several more diamonds. She would save them for later. What she needed now was enough to get her to Käthe's, enough to live on until she could decide what to do next.

As they rode back down on the elevator, Hanna asked Robert, "I may send a telegram to my sister?"

"At the train station," he replied.

When they arrived, Hanna purchased her ticket and sent the telegram:

ARRIVE SYRACUSE 3:45 TRAIN FROM NEW YORK CITY.
HANNA

She could only imagine what Käthe might think. It had been almost two years now since she'd written her sister. Unless Leni or Frederick had communicated with her, she knew nothing of what Hanna had been through over the past two years. But even Leni and Frederick didn't know why she was in Berlin, though of course her brother must have understood, when she showed up at the farm with her Nazi escort, that she was working for the government.

Robert sat and waited with Hanna in the busy, noisy station. She tried to picture what Isabella might look like now. Perhaps like a pre-teenage Leni, who was very pretty. Hanna wished she had a gift for her daughter. At a small vendor's cart, stocked with cigarettes, newspapers, and candy, she bought a chocolate Hershey's bar for a nickel, wishing it was chocolate from Germany. As she pulled an American ten-dollar bill from her bag—she had nothing smaller—the vendor said something rapidly that Hanna did not comprehend. Yet she understood by the scowl on his face that he was not happy to make change for such a small purchase. She glanced over at the news rack and then, impulsively, she grabbed a copy of the *New York Times*, then two more Hershey's bars.

Quickly, the vendor counted the change out for her, slapping it into her palm, an exaggerated tone of irritation in his voice. She tucked the chocolate in her pocket, the newspaper under her arm, and walked back to where Robert sat.

"They've announced your train," he said, holding out a hand. "Elsa and I wish you the best of luck."

"Thank you," she replied. "Please tell your wife once more, thank you."

On the train, she scanned the paper, wondering if there was any mention of what was happening in Germany. She devoured two whole bars of chocolate as she attempted to translate an article with the headline, "Chamberlain Bars Any Coup in Danzig; Pledge Is Sweeping."

As she picked out words she understood, the article seemed to confirm what Hanna heard in the chatter at the Hotel Bellevue during her last weeks in Berlin—it was Hitler's intention to take back the free city of Danzig, which had been under the protection of the League of Nations as a provision of the hated Treaty of

Versailles. The British evidently were not willing to accept this. Surely, the world was once more headed toward war. Hanna knew that Hitler was not to be intimidated by the British.

, She attempted to read an article regarding debates in the U.S. Senate over neutrality legislation. Her head throbbed, exhausted from these strained efforts to read the English, worn-out from her travel, from having slept little last night. Her ankle ached. The chocolate turned in her stomach.

Fitfully she slipped in and out of uneasy daytime slumber, her head jerking up every time the train slowed at a new stop. At each station she read the names on the buildings and boards, fearful that she would pass right by her destination, that she would miss it.

When the train finally pulled into Syracuse, Hanna gazed out onto the platform, scanning the clusters of people, some with bags waiting to board, others with eager faces ready to greet incoming travelers.

There they were!

Käthe stood along with Hans and a tall thin girl. If she had not been standing beside her aunt and uncle, Hanna wasn't sure she would have recognized her own daughter. The expected tears of joy did not flow. Hanna was terrified.

She grabbed her bag and moved along with the other passengers, who clogged the aisle, gathering baggage, children, and lunch sacks. Hanna felt so nervous and frightened she thought she might faint. Why should she feel anything other than sheer happiness? she wondered, as a raw panic surged through her.

As she stepped off, Käthe ran toward her, wiping tears with one hand, pulling Isabella with the other. Then Käthe stopped, gently nudging the girl forward.

Isabella held out a bouquet. "Welcome to America, Mother," she said stiffly as she offered Hanna the small bunch of flowers. The color of her voice had deepened.

Hanna grabbed her daughter into an awkward hug, and the

tears gushed from her eyes, her body heaving with emotion, fear turned to joy, to exhilaration.

Time stood still, and then she was embracing Käthe, and then Hans had wrapped his big arms protectively around her.

Once more Hanna held Isabella, and then she stood back, her hands on the girl's shoulders. She was no longer a child, but a young woman of twelve, taller and much thinner than Hanna would have imagined. Much to Hanna's horror, she had cut her hair, which was a darker blond than Hanna remembered, and now barely grazed her shoulders. She wore a pale green summer sundress, sprinkled with yellow tulips, and Hanna could see she was budding little breasts.

Käthe cried, "We thought we might never see you again."

Hanna's brother-in-law had her bag, though she didn't remembering letting go of it. He motioned to them all. "Let's go home," he said with a grin.

As they walked, Hanna flanked by Isabella on one side, their warm moist hands intertwined, Käthe on her other side, she gazed at her daughter and realized how much she resembled the beautiful woman who had greeted her in New York City—Johann's sister.

"You've grown," Hanna said in German.

"It's been four years," Isabella replied in English.

"What a relief to have you here with us," Käthe said. "What a wonderful, wonderful surprise to receive your telegram." She burst into tears again and had to stop to fully embrace her sister once more. Suddenly both sisters were laughing, wiping away more tears.

Hanna glanced at Isabella, who stood rigid, as if she didn't know what to do.

They continued on to the car.

As soon as they were settled in the automobile, Hanna and Isabella in the backseat, Käthe and Hans in the front, Hans said, "Are you hungry? Should we go get something to eat?"

"We've got plenty of food at home," Käthe replied with a laugh. "Didn't you notice I was baking all morning? The children are all coming over to welcome Hanna."

Hans laughed, too, and Hanna remembered how easily and agreeably they teased one another, laughing over each other's missteps like two young lovers.

Hanna turned to Isabella and didn't know where to begin. She gazed down and realized she was still clutching the bouquet her daughter had given her. The delicate flowers, daisies, were starting to wilt. Then she remembered the chocolate, and reached into her pocket. She pulled it out and felt her fingers push into the candy, softened by the summer heat as well as the warmth of her body. Had she removed the outer brown paper wrapper, she might have poured the chocolate out of the foil like syrup from a silver pitcher.

"I bring you a chocolate bar," Hanna said, "but I am sorry it is . . . it is . . ." She searched for the word.

"Melted?" Isabella looked down with a frown, and then said, "We can put it in the icebox when we get home."

"Yes," Hanna said.

They drove on, through the countryside now, passing scenery both familiar and new, fields of summer crops, horses bunching together under the shade of a single tree, a newly painted bright red barn alongside a sun-faded farmhouse.

Finally Hanna said, "What do you study in school?" She spoke slowly, deliberately in English. She was speaking to a stranger, in a foreign language, to a girl she had just met, someone else's child.

"We're on summer vacation now," the girl said.

"What do you enjoy to study," Hanna asked, "when you go to school?"

"English literature and history."

"You like to read?"

"Yes."

"Good," Hanna said. She looked down at the soft bar of

chocolate she still held in her hand. She could think of nothing more to say.

Warm smells from Käthe's kitchen, along with her three eldest daughters, their husbands, and Hans and Käthe's youngest son, Herman, the only one still living at home, greeted Hanna as they arrived. Children of every age and size ran about the house. Some Hanna recognized, others she did not—new grandchildren who had arrived since her last visit.

The table overflowed with *Brotzeitteller*, *Krautschupfnudeln*, *Kartoffelsalat*, *Krautsalat*, *Zwetschgen-Strudel*, and *Dampfnudel*, dishes from home that Käthe had learned to make from their mother, their stepmother, or the cook in Munich.

Käthe's children were much older than Isabella, but several of the granddaughters were close to her age. Hanna watched as she joined the girls, giggling and whispering to one another like sisters. Isabella barely spoke to her mother other than to reintroduce the cousins and bring her a plate of food as if she were an invalid. Käthe, who'd noticed her sister's uneasy step, had asked about her leg on the way home. Hanna told her it was fine; she was just tired.

Isabella appeared to be a polite, thoughtful young girl. Hanna felt she had little to do with this as she sat quietly observing the scene. It was Käthe and Hans who had raised her daughter for the past four years.

A room with two beds had been prepared for Hanna to share with Isabella. After the children and grandchildren left, she was exhausted. Slowly, she climbed the stairs to the bedroom and fell into a deep slumber before Isabella came up.

The next morning, the girl was curled up, fast asleep. Hanna stood and walked over, staring down at her daughter as she had when she was a baby, watching with a tender ache as her back rose and fell with every soft breath. She thought of those first months when Isabella was a new baby, when Hanna herself tossed and turned in her sleep, fretting over what she knew was true—that

Isabella was not Moses' child. And yet, as a gift, she had come to them, the child they had both longed for. And once more, Hanna thought, *I have been blessed.*

She dressed quietly and went down to the kitchen. Käthe was toasting bread, drinking coffee as she worked. Hans sat, newspaper in hand, forking a plate of eggs, potatoes, and ham. He glanced up as if this was just another day.

"*Guten Morgen,*" Käthe said, reaching into the cupboard for a cup.

"Good morning," Hanna replied. She had decided she would speak only English. For her daughter, she would speak English.

Käthe poured coffee and offered it to Hanna, motioning her to sit.

"Did you sleep well?" Hans asked.

Hanna nodded. She must have. She could remember going to the room, putting on her nightgown, slipping into bed, and then it was morning. She had not dreamed.

"The bed was comfortable?" Käthe set a plate of buttered toast and a jar of homemade jam on the table between her husband and sister.

"Yes, very." Hanna added cream to her coffee, a spoonful of sugar. She stirred, took a sip, then another. "Thank you, both, for . . . the party." She owed her sister and Hans much more than a mere thank-you for the welcome party. For the past four years they had kept Isabella safe, caring for her as if she were a member of the family. "Your family has grown. Very good children and grandchildren. Isabella is very good here."

"She's a good girl," Käthe replied.

"I did not know," Hanna said softly, "it would be this difficult." Yet, she knew she should have anticipated this discomfort with her daughter.

Käthe said nothing, though Hanna was sure, as a mother, Käthe knew what she was talking about. She sat and held the plate of toast.

Hanna shook her head, and took a sip of coffee.

"She's been through so much," Käthe finally said. "Her father. Willy."

"Does she blame me?" Hanna asked. "For not being here to care for Willy?"

Käthe pursed her lips, and then said quietly, "I think she probably blames herself."

Hanna remembered the day she had left to go back to Germany to tend Moses. She had told Isabella to look after Willy. What a horrible burden to place upon a child of eight. And Hanna had promised she would make Isabella's father better. How would she ever trust her mother again?

Hanna couldn't stop the tears. She dropped her head and wept into her hands.

"Time," Käthe said simply, placing her hand on her sister's shoulder, and this seemed so unfair to Hanna. She had spent the past six years waiting. Waiting for life to improve in Germany and then waiting to be reunited with Isabella.

"Thank you, Käthe, thank you, Hans, for taking care of my little girl."

Hans nodded, but seemed uncomfortable with this conversation. Shortly, he picked up the newspaper and excused himself.

"May I?" Hanna asked, pointing toward the newspaper.

"Yes, of course," he replied, handing it to her. "You ladies have a good day." He left the kitchen, out the back door, the screen door swinging behind him.

Hanna's eyes ran down the first page of the newspaper and she could see it was the same *New York Times* she'd bought at the train station the day before.

"Would you like a nice big, hearty American breakfast?" Käthe asked, as if attempting to lighten the tone.

Hanna shook her head. "Maybe some toast." She lifted a piece from the plate. She spread jam on it and took a bite. It slid down uneasily. She took a swallow of coffee, then another. She looked

down at the newspaper, remembering the articles she had attempted
to translate the day before. "What do you know in America, about
what happens now in Germany?" she asked her sister.

"We read anything we can find related to Germany. The rest of
America . . ." She waved her hand. "The Depression hit many families very hard, but now life is better and people are just trying to
tend to themselves. Unless it directly affects them, most Americans
don't really care."

"What does Isabella know?"

"We've tried to protect her." Käthe got up and poured herself
more coffee. She walked back to the table and refilled Hanna's cup.
"Hans doesn't leave the newspaper lying around. We don't talk about
it. With you still in Germany, not having heard from you for so long,
we didn't want her to think . . . Well." Käthe walked back to the
stove and set the coffeepot on a burner. "It should be obvious," she
went on, "to anyone who reads the paper or listens to the news
reports on the radio, that Hitler has clear intentions of reclaiming
what was lost in the Great War, that the world is on the verge of
another. Sometimes it's all buried on the second page." She picked up
Hans' plate and carried it to the sink. She turned on the water and
rinsed it off. "But, clearly, for anyone to see what is happening to the
Jews—the events of November ninth did make the front page. Yes, we
know." She stared out the window above the sink for a moment, and
then turned to Hanna. "Yes, the world is aware, but as I've said—"

"Jakob was murdered," Hanna whispered, "on November ninth,
and I fear Helene is gone now, too."

Käthe nodded sadly, then swallowed hard, as if this was something she had already guessed.

"Do you receive letters from Leni?" Hanna asked. "Frederick?"

"Not often. You know Leni." Käthe sat at the table.

Käthe and Leni had never really gotten on.

"Frederick's wife used to write," Käthe said, "but no, he's never
been one to sit down and send off a letter."

Frederick's wife had been gone for more than twenty years now, Hanna reflected. Oh, how the time did move on . . . Her mother had been gone for more than forty years, her father for thirty. She thought of Frederick's letter that found her in Berlin, her visit to the farm, the Kandinsky painting in the barn. The colors and sounds formed in her mind, though she had thought of it very little on her journey to America.

"When will it end?" Hanna asked, and yet she knew there was more to come. She knew from what she had heard at the Hotel Schloss Bellevue where she had sat and taken meals with some of Hitler's most devout followers.

The days continued thus, Hanna visiting with Käthe each morning, whispering in the early hours over the newspaper stories as Hitler moved toward Poland, as Great Britain protested.

Hanna cleaned up in the kitchen. She helped with the laundry and ironing, the housework.

During the days, Isabella helped her aunt Katie, as she now called her, with outdoor chores, feeding the pets, gathering the eggs. She spoke little to her mother, taking off after finishing her tasks, hopping on her bike with barely a word of farewell to Hanna. Sometimes she would ask to ride into town with Hans, to go to the library, to visit friends from church and school. When she was home, she sat quietly, reading a book.

Anything to avoid me, Hanna thought.

Käthe assured her that this was the way with girls of Isabella's age. Their friends were now the most important part of their lives. Käthe had raised five daughters, and surely she knew.

"But we have not seen each other in four years," Hanna protested.

Käthe didn't reply, but Hanna knew that this made it even more difficult.

"Give her some time," Käthe suggested.

* * *

In August a telegram arrived for Hanna. Käthe slipped it into her hand without inquiry, though Hanna saw the tightness in the muscles around her mouth and eyes, the crease across her forehead, and she knew a thousand questions must be racing through her sister's head.

Hanna read silently:

Packages delivered. Isabella must know truth.

Johann Keller

It seemed so terse, yet wasn't this the nature of a telegram—each word increasing the price. Why not a letter? she wondered as she tucked it in her pocket.

He was angry with her for not telling him about their daughter. But he had received the art. He had written *packages*. This surely meant he had received the smaller bag as well as the art bundled in the lining of the larger. Did he realize the drawing and the bill of sale for the Kandinsky were hidden in the bag?

He wanted Isabella to know the truth, but Hanna could not bear what this might do to the girl, who adored Moses, her papa. This truth would completely sever the fragile thread that was now holding Hanna to her daughter. She would be willing to give up anything now to reclaim her. Even Johann Keller.

Yet he knew where she was if he wanted to find her. Robert had helped her send the telegram from the station, then placed her on the train to go to her family. Now Johann had sent a telegram. Yes, he knew where she was.

She had been weak before, but she would not be weak again. Hanna did not send a reply to the telegram.

* * *

O ne day she invited Isabella for ice cream, just the two of them. She wanted to talk to her about getting their own place. If they were together, alone, without so much family always dropping in and out, as Käthe's children and grandchildren tended to do, they could get to know each other better. They needed more time alone. And Hanna needed to go where she couldn't be found.

Hans gave them a ride into town and dropped them off at a drugstore that Käthe said had a wonderful fountain for ice cream and sodas.

Isabella asked to sit at the long counter on the round swivel stools, though Hanna would have preferred a booth. Isabella ordered chocolate ice cream; Hanna got vanilla.

"Koebler ice cream," Hanna said with a smile, pointing up toward the sign.

"Yes," Isabella replied, not bothering to look up.

"You have many friends," Hanna tried again, turning toward her daughter.

"Yes," Isabella replied, looking into the mirror behind the woman in the white apron who had just scooped the ice cream from deep cartons in an open freezer.

If only she could speak to me using more than a yes or a no, Hanna thought with a touch of anger. "I am happy you have friends here in America." She tried not to reveal the frustration in her voice.

"What did you do in Germany?" Isabella asked, stirring her ice cream. She had barely taken a bite.

"Your father and I had an art gallery," Hanna answered, confused.

"No, after Papa died, when you were alone."

"I worked." Hanna stared at the soda glasses and ice cream dishes lined up along the counter below the mirror. Her eyes rose to her own face, to her daughter who gazed down at her ice cream, her spoon moving in a slow circle.

"Where?" Isabella demanded. Her head jerked up. She glared at her mother's image in the mirror.

Hanna hesitated. "At an art gallery."

"Then the art was more important to you than me and Willy." Isabella swiveled in her chair and faced her mother. She was making no attempt to hide her anger. She didn't even offer this as a question, but simply a statement.

"Oh, Isabella," Hanna cried, touching her daughter's hand, which felt as cold as the chilled dish, "I did try to come to you, all that time. I did try desperately to come to you and Willy."

"You're a little late for that," Isabella said, shoving her ice cream away. She bounced down from the stool and stood. "I'm finished. I want to go home."

Hanna slid off the stool and followed Isabella out the door, realizing as she walked briskly to catch up with her daughter that her ankle was completely healed. If only injuries of the mind and heart were so easily mended.

The lack of talk, interspersed with sparse and hesitant conversations, continued in such fashion. Hanna could barely get her daughter to speak to her. When Isabella chose to talk to her mother, she picked at her for bits of information. Hanna attempted to share, though there was much she withheld. She told her daughter that she had lived with Aunt Leni, that the cousins were all well, though Hanna didn't know if this was true. She said she had visited Uncle Frederick on the farm, that she had stayed for a while with Helene and Jakob. She could not tell her daughter that Jakob had been murdered, that Helene was probably dead now, too.

After dinner each evening, the women cleaned up in the kitchen. Hanna washed, Isabella dried, and Käthe cleared the table, put away leftovers, and swept the floor. Hanna decided this was the best time to talk—busy hands, a communal task, provided a casual setting in which the conversations came more naturally, more generously. She asked Isabella about her friends, what they liked to do, trying to keep it light, not too invasive.

"Today Theresa and I were riding bikes and we went by the lake," Isabella offered one evening. "This boy named Andrew Fletcher was showing off with the other boys, doing fancy dives."

"Andrew? The oldest Fletcher boy?" Käthe asked. Hanna was learning much about this little community from dinner table talk, from their evening chats over the dishes. Käthe seemed to know everyone, could tell you who was related to whom. Hanna knew the Fletchers owned one of the largest dairy herds in the county, that the Koeblers were well respected, that Hans' creamery was supporting a good many small dairies in the community.

"Andrew's fourteen," Isabella replied, as she dried a dinner plate. "His sister Mary is in my class."

"Mary is the tall girl with the dark hair?" Hanna asked.

Isabella nodded. "Theresa thinks Andrew is very handsome."

"Do you?" her mother inquired casually.

"Oh, he is rather nice-looking," she said shyly, but it seemed she was on the verge of a grin.

Hanna treasured these little bits of mother-daughter talk. Gradually she would win Isabella back.

But then, just two days later, as they were finishing up, Isabella seemed in one of her moods. The girl could shift from shy, giggly preteen to sullen young woman quicker than Hanna could scrub a dinner plate.

"Why do you refuse to use father's name?" Isabella asked.

The dishwater had cooled. Hanna was about to add some hot water when these unexpected words came out of her daughter's mouth. She felt her body tremble.

"I saw the passport," Isabella said. "You're using your family name, not Fleischmann." She was taking the clean, rinsed dishes from the rack and drying them, not missing a beat as she began this interrogation. Hanna could hardly keep the slippery plates from sliding from her fingers. She continued stacking and rinsing, saying nothing. Isabella picked up another plate, dried it, and shoved it into the cupboard with such force Hanna feared it would break.

Finally Hanna said, "In my drawer?" She heard the harshness in her voice, though it came out in such a way because she was trying to control the tremor.

"Yes," Isabella came back with defiance, not even trying to cover the fact that she was snooping in her mother's personal belongings.

"I was unable to use my name," Hanna replied.

"Because we are Jews?"

But we aren't Jews, Hanna thought. *You don't even have a Jewish father.* This thought made her shudder even more.

"I listen to the radio," Isabella said. "On occasion, I even see a newspaper or a magazine, when Uncle Hans is unable to get them out of the house quick enough. I know that Hitler does not like the Jews."

Though Käthe said they were trying to protect her, Hanna knew that Isabella was curious, that even if her uncle removed all newspapers and magazines from their home, Isabella often went to the library, and perhaps even read or talked about these things when she was in school.

Maybe it was best that her daughter knew. But this personal curiosity frightened Hanna.

"You do not understand, Isabella," she said, "how difficult it was in Germany, how difficult it was to leave. At first Hitler wanted to rid Germany of those he did not like, but then—you say you have read the articles. There are Jews now who are unable to find other homes. They are stuck. They cannot leave."

"So, if Hitler was trying to get rid of the Jews, why didn't you just come to us in America earlier, when you could?"

A vision of Josef murdered at the gallery flashed in Hanna's mind, and she could hear the color of blood, and then she saw herself sifting through the charred papers and art at the gallery, going through Moses' bank accounts, standing in line at the embassy in Berlin. If only she had been able to leave then, just after Moses' death. How could she ever explain to Isabella why she could not get out?

"What were you doing in Switzerland?" Isabella came back.

"It was better that way." Hanna stared out the window above the sink. Patches of yellow grass, scorched by the summer heat, spotted the yard, the mixed colors creating incompatible sounds. A big tabby cat moved slowly, stealthily, across the yard, ready to pounce on a bird that seemed larger than the cat.

Isabella snorted. "I can see there's something you are hiding."

"Bella," Käthe interjected, using the name her American girl-friends called her, "can't you see it is difficult for your mother to talk about it?" She brought the remaining coffee cups and saucers to the sink. "Just leave it at that, child." This was the first time Hanna had heard her sister speak so harshly to Isabella.

"And what about the *packages*? Are you a spy for the Nazis, Mother? And who—though I know you won't answer—is Johann Keller?" Isabella demanded. "What is this truth that you are so reluctant to tell me?" She threw her dish towel on the counter and stomped out.

Hanna stood, her hands still in the sink water. Though it was tepid, she shivered, feeling so cold her teeth chattered. Isabella had seen the telegram in her drawer. Hanna should have destroyed it.

"She doesn't understand." Käthe picked up Isabella's towel and lifted a dish from the rack.

Neither did Käthe, Hanna thought. Even her sister did not know about Johann Keller. She didn't know about the confiscated art in Berlin. How much longer could Hanna bear the burden of these lies and secrets? Maybe she should tell Käthe about Johann, about the art, about Hitler, about the auction. But how could she admit that she had worked so closely with the Nazis, that she had lived comfortably in an elegant hotel in Berlin, sipping wine and eating steak while Jews were being slaughtered in the streets? The heat of this shame washed over her. And what would she say if Isabella asked why she didn't just walk away? Had she been threatened? Were there prison bars on her door and windows? Could she justify what she'd done by claiming she was attempting to save the art? Memories came to her of those days working in the warehouse in Berlin, how she had allowed herself to forget the outside world, Helene and Jakob, her own children.

How important was the art now anyway, when the world was faced with another war? When the Jews in Germany were being sent to camps, and some, like Jakob, being murdered?

Käthe slid the last plate into the cupboard. She put her hand on Hanna's shoulder, and then wrapped her arms around her sister protectively. "We're so happy that you are finally here with us."

"If only Isabella felt the same."

"She will," Käthe assured her once more.

CHAPTER THIRTY-THREE

Hanna

America
August 1939–May 1940

At the end of August, Käthe received a letter from Frederick's daughter-in-law. Frederick had died. He was the last of their brothers. The farm would go to his eldest son. Hanna wondered what would become of the painting in the barn, and if anyone knew it was there. It would be some time before she could return. Maybe never.

Just days later, Hitler's army invaded Poland. Within two days, Britain and France declared war on Germany. The second Great War had begun.

Hanna's sleep, which until now had been oddly without images, was haunted with visions.

She sat at the dinner table with Hitler. He was stuffing his mouth with cake, and then it was not cream-laden torte, but bodies—tiny charred bodies, burned torsos like she had seen on November tenth, that he shoved into his wide mouth. He smacked and snorted, and then he ran his sleeve over his lips, cream clinging to his little square mustache, and said to Hanna, "You, Frau Fleischmann, you are next." His blue eyes bored into her. "You have betrayed me."

Hanna woke, covered with sweat, and it seemed she could smell the man, and then her nostrils were filled with the scent of burned flesh, the smells of November. She ran to the bathroom and the stench now mixed with the putrid smell of her own vomit. She could feel the man's presence. Hitler was intent on taking over the entire world. They would not be safe, even here in America.

Yet America seemed barely aware. She saw how easily they all went about their lives—when she went to the market with Käthe, when she attended church on Sunday with the family, when she stopped with Hans and Käthe for an occasional soda at the drugstore. As her sister had told her, unless they were directly affected, they seemed barely to care. And Hanna thought—is this any different from what she had seen in those early days in Germany?

They watched the war from a distance. While there were articles in the newspaper, questioning whether America could stay out of the war in which Germany seemed to be eating up one country after another, Hanna wondered if anyone, other than those who had family involved overseas, was even reading these stories.

With Helene's diamond money, Hanna bought a used automobile. She wasn't even sure why—perhaps to entice Isabella, who often hounded her uncle Hans to teach her to drive. The boys had been allowed to drive on the farm when they were her age, she reasoned.

Hanna began taking long drives in the country, to have time alone, to think. Often she invited Isabella to go, and one day she said yes. As her daughter jumped into the car, Hanna thought of the very first time she had ridden in an automobile, how giddy and boy-like Moses had been, how happy she had been at the time.

They pulled out of the driveway and started down the road toward the creamery, neither speaking until Isabella said, "You had another bad dream last night."

Hanna was not aware her daughter knew of the nightmares.

"Maybe you should have a room of your own," Hanna suggested. "We could get an apartment with two bedrooms."

"I don't want to move," Isabella said, but there was no defiance in her voice. She sounded very grown-up, as she offered her reasons: "I have my friends here, my school, Aunt Katie, Uncle Hans, all the cousins."

Earlier Hanna had talked about New York City, where she guessed they could easily disappear, but she soon realized from Isabella's reaction that this would never work. She hadn't brought it up again until now.

"Something close," she suggested. "You could go to the same school."

"I'm sorry, Mother. I'm just not ready."

The fact that she was implying, that at some point she might be ready, gave Hanna hope. She would just drop it for now. She was willing to concede that this relationship with her daughter would take time, just as Käthe had told her.

Several days later, after supper, Hanna was driving her daughter into town to go to the library and Isabella asked, "What happened to the art?"

Surprised by her daughter's question—for a quick second she thought she was asking about the confiscated art—Hanna gave the steering wheel an involuntary jerk. Quickly, she straightened the car, though she heard a gasp come from Isabella.

No, Hanna reassured herself, Isabella wouldn't know about that. Käthe still didn't even know. They continued down the road, neither speaking.

"Why did you live with Helene and Jakob, and then with Leni?" Isabella finally asked, though Hanna had not yet replied to her first question. "Were you lonely?"

"Yes," Hanna answered, "but there were other reasons." She stared out the window. The trees were starting to leaf, a pleasant-sounding green tipping the slender branches. The snow had been gone for weeks now. Hanna had been in America for almost ten months. "It was difficult. The business was not doing well."

"Because Father was a Jew?"

"Yes, that made it very difficult." Hanna wondered if Isabella remembered the boycott, which was really the beginning of the end of the business. Then Hanna and the children left for America, Hanna returned, the gallery burned, Josef was murdered. Isabella knew now that Josef, as well as Helene and Jakob, had died, but Hanna had given her no details of the circumstances of their deaths. The girl seemed to finally understand there were things her mother wished not to speak of. Perhaps Käthe had said something to her, which Hanna both appreciated and resented. She wished she might share in such intimacies with her daughter, but she knew she could not speak freely to Isabella of so many things.

"We had to sell the gallery," Hanna explained, "then the house."

"The house?" Isabella asked, as if this had not even occurred to her.

Hanna nodded.

"What of the art from the gallery?"

"All sold," Hanna replied.

"How very sad." Isabella gazed out toward the hillside. Herman called them mountains, which made Hanna laugh. The Alps were mountains. These were hills.

"Your father was able to send some of the proceeds here to Uncle Hans," Hanna explained. "He has invested the money for your education." Shortly after she arrived, Hans had gone over the finances with Hanna. He told her they had put the money Moses sent into a savings account for Isabella.

Neither of them spoke again until they approached the main road into town. "The paintings in our home in Munich?" Isabella asked. "Were you forced to sell all the art to escape?"

This was the first time Isabella had used the word *escape*, though Hanna had shared no details on her rescue.

"Yes," Hanna replied, "we had to sell the paintings."

"Sometimes," Isabella said as she rested her head dreamily on the seat back, "I see it, the painting from the music room. Remember you and Papa called it Willy's Colors?" She turned to her mother and Hanna saw that she was smiling. "Remember how he used to dance to the music of the painting?"

Hanna smiled now, too, as she pictured Willy, prancing about with a big grin on his face. She imagined Isabella was seeing the same vision in her own head. It was good that they could speak of these things, that they shared these memories.

"Who was the artist?" Isabella asked.

"Wassily Kandinsky."

"Not a German artist?"

"Russian."

"You knew Wassily Kandinsky?"

Hanna nodded. She had not yet told her daughter that Helene had purchased the painting, that it was stored at Uncle Frederick's. Her brother was gone now, and Hanna wondered if the painting was, too. Sometimes she dreamed that it was still in the barn, waiting for her to come back home to reclaim it.

"I remember," Isabella spoke softly, "when I was very young, going to the gallery with Papa. He would show me the paintings and name the artists. Some of them I loved—especially the ones with the colorful animals—but some of them I thought were silly and horrible." Isabella smiled. "He always said, 'You don't have to like them all.' One day we were standing before a picture in the gallery," she continued, "and Papa whispered to me, 'I don't really like that one either.'" Isabella laughed and Hanna thought she had never heard such a delightful sound, something she had feared was lost to her daughter forever.

Hanna laughed, too, but she knew Isabella was having a false memory. It was her mother who stood in the gallery and whispered this into her ear.

In May a letter arrived. Käthe handed it to her sister without words, though again, Hanna could see the question in her eyes.

"Thank you," Hanna said, taking the letter, glancing at the outside of the envelope. The address was written in a steady script that she easily recognized, though she had seen it but once—on a small crumpled note slipped into her hand at the Grand Hotel in Lucerne. The return address was Basel, Switzerland.

Hanna stepped outside, feeling Käthe's curious eyes follow her as she walked quickly down past the barn. She caught her breath and opened the letter.

Hanna,

As you know, conditions continue to deteriorate through-out Europe as Hitler's greedy hand extends further and further. I pray that we will once more have peace. I pray also for a personal peace. We must talk of these things which we both hold near to our hearts, both family and art. The art which you saved will be returned to the galleries from which they were taken, but events over which we have no control will dictate when we might accomplish this. Though both my country and the country of your new home remain neutral, travel is now impossible. We must meet once more after this terrible war. I do not wish to harm you, only to meet Isabella. Please write to let me know you are well.

Johann

Hanna knew she must destroy the letter. How could she explain if Isabella discovered it? She trembled as she made her way back toward the barn. She found a match on the window ledge and struck it on the old barrel that Hans used on the farm as an incinerator. She put the letter to the flame and watched the charred paper fall bit by bit into the barrel.

As she walked back to the house, she looked up and saw Isabella staring down at her from the upstairs bedroom window. Their eyes locked for a moment, and even from the distance she could see her daughter's eyes narrow, her mouth tighten. Isabella turned and walked back into the room.

CHAPTER THIRTY-FOUR

Hanna

America
December 1941–October 1942

"It's a long one down to around the three-yard line," the announcer's voice blared from the radio in Hans and Käthe's living room.

Hanna and Isabella had dropped by after Mass as they did
every Sunday since moving into their own apartment. Isabella
was in the living room with the men and cousins, listening to a
football game, a strange American sport that Hanna did not understand. She sat with Käthe and two of her daughters in the kitchen,
drinking coffee.

It was December 7, 1941.

"Up to the twenty-five and now he's hit and hit hard," the
announcer's voice grew loud with excitement.

"Can you turn that down?" Käthe called out.

"That a boy!" One of the cousins let out a loud whoop from
the living room.

"Hit 'em hard!" another joined in.

Käthe shook her head and started to get up.

"We interrupt this broadcast," an announcer broke in, "to bring
this important bulletin from United Press."

Hanna and Käthe exchanged glances.

"Flash . . . Washington . . . The White House announces Japanese attack on Pearl Harbor."

The women rushed into the living room.

Hans held up a hand, palm out. A finger rose to his lips. Käthe and Hanna stood paralyzed. The younger women dropped to the floor in front of the radio.

The announcer said something about a Navy base at Pearl Harbor, but the words were coming to Hanna in stops and starts, in a confusion of tones and colors, jerking with the same rhythm as her heartbeat.

"Pearl Harbor?" Herman asked. "Where's Pearl Harbor?"

Isabella jumped up and hurried to the bookcase.

By the time she returned with an atlas, the announcer had gone back to the football game, as if nothing had happened, with little information offered other than that the United States had been attacked. Hanna wondered for a moment if this *had* really happened, if she had heard correctly. She glanced around the room at the faces of her nieces and nephews, eyes wide, faces ashen, blank stares, as if they were all in shock. No one said a word.

Hans flipped to the atlas index. The football announcer droned on.

"Pearl Harbor?" Hans wondered, his voice barely audible.

Hanna didn't know where Pearl Harbor was either. But she knew that Japan was aligned with Germany in this war that now engaged every major world power, save for the United States. She studied Herman as he sat next to his father, the boy's finger moving along the page of the open atlas. Herman was twenty, with a sprinkle of freckles across his face. He looked so young, so much like Hanna's brother Peter, who had not lived to twenty-one. The others gathered, looking over Hans' shoulder.

"It's on an island in the Pacific Ocean," one of the girls said.

"Part of the Hawaiian Islands," Herman added.

Visions entered Hanna's head of her two younger brothers,

Peter and Karl, both killed in the war. With a quick glance, she knew Käthe was thinking the same thing. Would her own son be called to fight for America, the country of his birth, and might he meet his German cousins on the battlefield?

The next day America declared war on Japan. The following day, Herman enlisted. Two weeks before Christmas, Germany and Italy declared war on the United States.

Hanna's nightmares grew more intense. She could not close her eyes without seeing images of Hitler. He was the greedy glutton of her earlier dreams, and then he was a wild beast, preying on every other living creature of the forest and jungle. One night he appeared as the figure in the painting of Saturn by Goya, a monster consuming his own son.

Germany had taken France and was assaulting Great Britain by air. Aligned with Japan and Italy, Hanna feared Hitler would take over the world.

The mood of the nation had shifted. Families sent young sons off to foreign lands. The government issued war bonds. Aircraft and munitions plants employed thousands, many women taking the place of the absent men. Citizens donated blood, recycled rubber, volunteered as airplane spotters.

Isabella was now in high school. Her teachers told Hanna that she needed more challenges, that she was gifted, particularly in language, and their small school didn't offer the variety of classes she needed. Hanna had sent for information on several private schools in New York City, though Isabella resisted.

But that summer, after America had entered the war, Isabella began to talk as if she were ready for a move.

"I'd like to take more language classes," she told her mother. "I speak better French than Mr. Raymond. Maybe in a larger school I'd be able to take art history as an elective. The city might provide more opportunities for you, too, Mother. You could find work in a gallery in New York City."

Hanna understood her daughter's change of heart was unrelated to the reasons she had outlined with such thoughtful consideration and detail. She knew Isabella would never admit that she wished simply to disappear. The girl was embarrassed by her mother's accent, by how easily she could be identified as a German.

Isabella had no accent, no outward sign that she was anything but a true American. But everyone at her school knew. She was part of the big Koebler family, and they had come from Germany. Hanna suspected there might be taunting at school, unkind words toward the German families, though Isabella did not speak of it. But in New York City she could start over again at a new school. No one would know.

Käthe begged them to stay. "If we are attacked, they'll hit the larger cities like New York. We're all safer here in the country. Please don't go."

Hanna thought of family back home—particularly Leni and her family in Munich. She knew Frederick's son and his family would probably be safer in the country. For a moment the colors of the Kandinsky painting flickered in her head, and she felt ashamed that her thoughts had turned to the safety of a painting. And then, unbidden, an image of Johann came to her, and then the small drawings and paintings which he held safely in Switzerland, still neutral, unlike the United States. Would she ever see any of them—family, painting, Johann Keller—again?

In New York City, Hanna attempted to find a job. She enrolled Isabella in a private Catholic girls' school, registering her under the name of Isabella Smith. She told her they were Americans now, and her daughter did not object. Hanna sold her car and cashed in additional diamonds for tuition. But she needed to earn her own money for general living expenses. She wouldn't touch the money Moses had sent from the paintings. It was for Isabella's university education.

She went to a small gallery, reluctant to present her resume. How could she explain that she worked in an art gallery in Munich? She filled out the form using the name Hanna Smith.

"You are German?" the proprietor asked.

Hanna didn't reply, but she knew her silence answered the question.

"I don't believe we have an opening."

How stupid of me, Hanna thought as she left and walked down the street. *"Dummkopf,"* she scolded herself. No one would hire a German immigrant, even if she called herself Mrs. Smith.

At the following interviews, she said, "I am Swiss." And didn't she have the passport to prove it? Yet this provided her no experience working in a gallery. She could add an additional lie. She could say she worked in a museum or gallery in Switzerland, perhaps the Kunstmuseum in Basel.

But even her lies produced no results. She had an accent.

Finally she found a job doing alterations for a dry-cleaning store. She worked out of the apartment on a used machine she had purchased at a pawnshop. The work was sporadic, and she barely made enough to cover rent and groceries. She found the city much more expensive than the country. But, she would not dip into the money set aside for Isabella's education.

Isabella brought no friends home from school. Sadly, Hanna wondered if she had any.

"Do you miss the music?" Isabella asked one evening as they finished supper, a meager meal of soup and bread. With the rationing that began in the spring, Hanna had become proficient at stretching a small piece of meat through the week. The vegetables came from the Victory Garden the superintendent's wife had planted on the rooftop. She'd befriended Isabella, who often helped with the garden after school.

The girl blew lightly on a spoonful of hot soup. "The music, do you miss it?" she asked again.

"The paintings?" Hanna asked. The colors and sounds had been coming to her in her dreams, SS officers in dark uniforms and shiny black boots and helmets, slashing the canvases, kicking holes in them, or setting them on fire. She shook the thought from her head, realizing this probably wasn't what her daughter was asking.

"The piano?" Isabella clarified. "I remember how beautifully you played the piano."

At the farm, Käthe and Hans had an old piano in their parlor, but no one played. Hanna imagined it had been purchased for the children. All had now moved out and lost interest. Perhaps someday one of the grandchildren would want it. Once, when they were still at the farm, Hanna sat and attempted to play. The piano was terribly out of tune. She'd actually laughed, not without bitterness, she reflected now. At the time it seemed her entire life was out of tune.

"Maybe someday we could get a piano," Hanna said. "Would you like to learn to play?"

"Oh, I don't think I have your talent, Mother. But I'd love to hear you play again."

Oddly, Hanna felt some small peace, though the entire world was engaged in a war. Together, alone, she and Isabella spoke to each other. In this forced yet voluntary isolation, she was reclaiming her daughter.

"You miss the paintings, don't you?" Isabella said, carrying her empty bowl to the sink.

"Yes," Hanna answered, "I do."

"Maybe we could go to the Metropolitan Museum of Art," Isabella offered. "My class is going. Someday we could go together."

"I'd like that," her mother said with a smile.

Isabella enjoyed her new school, particularly the variety of classes in which she was now able to enroll. She was taking an art history course, which delighted Hanna.

After school one afternoon, Isabella spoke with enthusiasm. "I asked Sister Mary Luke if we would study modern art, the abstract art, and she said not until second semester. She said if I was interested she could bring in some books."

The following day, Isabella returned home in an exceptionally good mood. Hanna was pulling out the hem of a skirt by hand. She set it aside. "Would you like something to eat?" she asked her daughter, following Isabella into the small kitchen.

Isabella unfastened her school bag and pulled out two large books. She opened one, flipped to where she'd inserted a slip of paper, and placed it on the table.

"Look at this," she said.

Hanna stood over her daughter, looking down at a painting by Cézanne.

"Didn't we have a painting by this artist in our home in Munich?"

Hanna nodded as Isabella flipped another page.

"I saw one similar to this . . ." Isabella stared down at a Picasso reproduction of a group of women done in the Cubists' style. "I think maybe it was at the gallery."

"Yes, a small painting by this artist also hung in the upstairs hallway."

"Sometimes as I'm studying the art, I think of Papa. I'm so excited to start second semester."

Hanna poured a glass of milk for her daughter and placed several cookies on a plate. She had adjusted the recipe because of the shortage of sugar and butter, thinking fondly of the rich desserts they had enjoyed in Munich during the good times. She sat down at the table and leafed through the book with Isabella.

"I would never say, *That's an artist my father personally knew.*" Isabella looked up at her mother. "I would never say, *That artist had a painting hanging in our home in Germany. That artist hung in the gallery in Munich.* Why, that would be bragging, wouldn't it?"

Hanna knew that most of the students at Isabella's school came from wealthy families, and many likely had a valuable painting or two hanging on the wall at home. But yes, it would probably shock them to learn that Isabella had known the work of these artists personally, that her parents had such paintings hanging in their gallery and in their home.

"No one would believe me anyway," Isabella added, and Hanna felt a small tug at her heart. Perhaps it would make Isabella feel more like the others if they knew she had once lived in a grand home on one of the finest avenues in Munich. But Hanna knew her daughter would never share any of this. Hanna doubted any of the girls at her new school knew that she had been born in Germany. That her mother, who sat alone at home over her secondhand sewing machine, had escaped less than three years ago.

"These are good memories," Isabella said, "thinking about the paintings."

Hanna wondered how much Isabella remembered. She was six when they closed the gallery, eight when she came to America, certainly old enough to retain some memory, but it had been almost seven years now.

Isabella nibbled a cookie. "Thank you for sending me here to America when the bad memories had not yet started."

Hanna was touched that Isabella seemed to understand. She was now fifteen, and in many ways she seemed much older. She had never asked again about Johann Keller or pushed her mother to reveal details of what she had done before she came to America. And yet, when Hanna offered a small glimpse into her life in Germany, Isabella grew quiet and listened as if she were recording every word in her head.

Isabella spoke only of good memories of Munich, of Germany. Sometimes she spoke of the fun they had on the farm with Uncle Frederick and the cousins, of outings with Leni and her family, visits to the Marienplatz, picnics in the park with Willy and Sasha.

Hanna wondered if Isabella remembered the day she chased the butterflies, and proclaimed loudly for the entire world to hear that, like her father, she was a Jew.

"The large painting in the music room," Isabella said, "it was by Wassily Kandinsky." She looked down at her book and studied a painting by the Russian, one of his colorful *Compositions*. "You sold the painting?" Again she glanced at her mother. "Do you know who bought it? Maybe we can buy it back after the war."

"This is one of a series the artist called his *Compositions*," Hanna said, slowly moving her fingers over the bright colors. Cautiously, she weighed the words that were now forming in her head. Should she share another small piece of the truth with her daughter? "There is something I want to tell you, Isabella," she said slowly.

Isabella's head jerked up.

"Before I came to America, we did sell this painting you speak of now. It was sold to a man in Berlin. But . . . just before she died, Helene purchased it. To protect it from Hitler—for Hitler hated the modern paintings." Hanna realized she was speaking of the man in the past tense. "She took it to Uncle Frederick on the farm. To keep it safe."

"But what happened to it?" Isabella's eyes lit up with surprise, with hope. "Why didn't you tell me this before?" There was a sudden shift in her tone, and Hanna wondered if Isabella saw this as a betrayal, her mother telling her only part of this story until now.

"I was afraid . . . maybe it is no longer . . ." The words came out with a rough, unsure rhythm. "Uncle Frederick is gone now, but the farm . . . hopefully it is still in the family. I don't know."

"After the war, we could go back to the farm." Excitement tinged Isabella's voice. "We could go find it. Willy's Colors."

Hanna touched her daughter's face, brushing away a small crumb of cookie on the corner of her mouth. "Would you want to do that? After the war? Go back to Germany?"

Isabella picked up another cookie and dipped it into her milk. "For a visit, maybe. But no, not to live again. Papa is gone, Helene, Jakob, and Willy. Our home is gone. Not to live, but yes, for a visit. I would like to see Munich again before I die."

Here she was, just fifteen, and Isabella was speaking of death. This saddened Hanna greatly, but at the same time she felt for the first time that this war would end, that they would survive.

Later, as she lay in bed, once more unable to sleep, fearing the return of the nightmares as she did each night, Hanna wondered if she should tell Isabella about the art she had saved from Hitler's purge. Maybe she should just tell her daughter the truth about what she had done. Surely Isabella, who had displayed a greater maturity since the war started, was old enough to understand that her mother had done what she had to do. But might she ask where the art was now? And this would bring up the subject of Johann Keller, Isabella's father, the man who now safeguarded the rescued art.

CHAPTER THIRTY-FIVE

Lauren and Isabella

New York City
Day Two, August 2009

"She never explained how she eventually made her way to America," Isabella told Lauren, "though I'm aware she traveled on a Swiss passport, using her maiden name. Shortly after she arrived, the war started in Europe, then the Americans joined the Allies. My mother was evasive and guarded when asked about those years she'd spent alone in Germany. I know so very little about that time in her life. We moved to New York City, where I could enroll in a private school. My mother took in work doing mending and alterations. Can you imagine? This beautiful, intelligent German woman who had once lived in a lovely home in Munich with Picassos, Cézannes, Van Goghs, and Kandinskys hanging on the walls?"

Lauren shook her head—she couldn't imagine.

But she could imagine a German woman wanting to rid herself of a Jewish-sounding name. A German-American woman wanting to rid herself of a German name.

Today, Isabella Fletcher wore a mint green suit, diamond drop earrings, and a diamond pendant on a platinum chain. Lauren guessed the diamond had to be near a carat. Next to her, Lauren felt quite underdressed, though she'd worn a skirt and blouse today, not the slacks she was used to wearing. She pulled the edge of her skirt down a bit to cover her knees. She was sitting again on the sofa, Isabella in the wingback chair.

"But truthfully," Mrs. Fletcher said, "we were happy to be together. We talked."

Today she was serving iced tea, having made a comment about the warm weather, though it was no warmer than yesterday. Isabella picked up her glass and took a sip.

"Recalling the years I spent with my aunt and uncle and the Koebler cousins brings up conflicting memories. It was a lovely, peaceful setting. Very much like being with my cousins on the Bavarian farm in Germany. As a small child, we often visited Uncle Frederick. Though the American farm wasn't nearly as pretty," she said in a low voice as if someone might be offended. "Yet my mother was not there. She went back to Germany for my father. He never made it to America."

They were treading over familiar memories, things Isabella had shared with Lauren yesterday. Again she considered how she might move the conversation along without offending Mrs. Fletcher.

Lauren glanced down at the table at the Bubble-Wrapped glass she'd had cut for the frame. She had presented it to Isabella as soon as she arrived at the apartment this afternoon. Mrs. Fletcher had said, "Thank you," but nothing more. Lauren wanted to offer to help her put it in the frame, but decided to wait.

There was also a large manila envelope on the table. It had been sitting there when Lauren arrived. She sensed it was something important, as Isabella kept eyeing it as they spoke. More photographs? Lauren wondered. Or more art?

"Did you talk about Germany?" she finally asked. "Did you and your mother talk about Germany when you were reunited in America?"

"Yes," Isabella replied with a half smile, "we talked, but only about the good memories, never the bad. But as I've told you, my memories of life in Munich were all good. As a child I really had no idea how horrible life had become. But then, of course, Papa died, then Willy."

She said this without feeling. Yesterday during the latter part of their conversation Lauren was very much aware of how emotional the old woman had become, but today, even through a retelling of her brother's death, the woman had remained composed.

Lauren thought of the many heartaches Isabella had gone through during her life. As a child, she had been separated from her parents, lost her father, and then watched as her brother died a painful death from pneumonia, all the while wondering why her mother was not there. How could Lauren possibly suggest that Hanna Fleischmann had aided the Nazis, filling her own pockets along the way? Again, she considered that maybe Isabella didn't know. This was a true possibility. Maybe the old woman didn't know about her mother's activities in Berlin and in Lucerne. But . . . she knew about the Swiss passport.

Lauren glanced around the room, mentally separating those pictures she knew to be copies from those she suspected were originals. Then her mind wandered down the hall, past the dining room, and into the powder room, adding additional images. Just a few small pieces were possibly authentic, and according to what Isabella told her yesterday, she possessed documentation to show they had all been purchased legitimately. Maybe none of these had anything to do with the Nazi-confiscated art.

"I finally had to accept that there were things that Mother just *wasn't* going to share with me," Isabella explained. There was something in her tone and then in the way she looked at Lauren with an even gaze and pursed lips that seemed to say, *And there are things that I'm not going to tell you either.*

She knows, Lauren thought.

"Eventually," Isabella said, "Mother told me that Helene had purchased the Kandinsky painting in Berlin and that she had taken it to Uncle Frederick's farm to hide it."

"Because of this Nazi censorship?" Lauren asked.

"Partially, yes. I think she just wanted Mother to have it. It really was her painting, hers and Willy's. It was a showpiece in our home in Munich. In the music room." Isabella shook her head dismissively. "Yes, I believe I told you that yesterday."

Lauren nodded. *And where is it now?* she was tempted to ask. But instead she said, "Then after the war it was sent to your mother in America?"

"Yes. Well, no, that's not exactly how it happened. But, as you can see, yes, it was eventually returned to our family."

As you can see? Lauren wondered. She had yet to see any evidence that Isabella Fletcher possessed such a painting.

CHAPTER THIRTY-SIX

Hanna

America
September 1945–June 1946

On the first day of September of 1945, Hanna woke with terrible cramps and discovered the bedsheets soaked with blood. She had stopped her monthly periods years ago, though sporadically had these cramps and bleeding. This was much heavier. She got up, went into the bathroom, and took out one of the pads Isabella had left in the medicine cabinet. Isabella had been gone for a week, leaving early to start work at the school library. She had been accepted to Vassar, a prestigious all-women's college in Upstate New York.

Hanna stripped the bed and put the sheets in the bathtub to soak. She'd haul them down to the apartment house washroom later that morning. She made coffee, the one cup she allowed herself each morning, got the newspaper, and sat down to read.

According to headlines on the first page, the war in the Pacific was all but over. The Japanese had yet to surrender, but this past month, in August, Japan had been devastated when the United States dropped atomic bombs on Hiroshima and Nagasaki, something so horrible Hanna could not imagine. The world knew that the war in Asia was about to end, again with the triumph of the Allies, though Hanna could see no triumph in war.

The war in Europe had ended in May when Germany surrendered. Hitler, as it turned out, had not lived to surrender.

Hanna remembered clearly the first day of May. It was cold and rainy, the gray colors and tones carrying no trace of spring. She had finished a batch of sewing and was taking the subway to deliver it to the dry-cleaning store and pick up more work. With the rationing and the lack of merchandise available, including clothing, she was very busy now and had a large bundle to return. She made her way to the subway, fighting the wind, package in hand, struggling with her umbrella, attempting to close it as she approached the entrance tunnel. An elderly man, sopping wet from the rain, but grinning like a lunatic, stopped to help her. Since America had entered the war, it seemed everyone was working together, strangers and family alike. Suddenly he started dancing a jig, and then he shouted to everyone within hearing distance, "He's dead! Hitler's dead!"

"It's over, then? The war is over?" a mother clutching two small children asked.

"I'll believe it when I see the body," a teenage boy replied. "If this is coming from those lying Germans, I won't believe it 'til I see the corpse."

Hanna got off at her stop, still wondering if it was true. The war had produced one crazy rumor after another. Hitler had died at least a dozen times already.

The manager at the dry cleaner's had heard the same, and on the way home, Hanna picked up a late-edition newspaper. Germany had indeed announced Hitler's death. The Führer, according to German radio reports, had gone down fighting to the end.

Hanna felt numb. Strangely, she did not rejoice at this man's demise.

The articles that appeared in the following days confirmed Hitler's death, but it came about in a much more cowardly way— he had committed suicide in a bunker in Berlin.

Hanna folded her newspaper and rose to rinse out her cup. She felt dizzy. She should get something to eat, she told herself. She sat down again. The phone rang.

"Mother," Isabella said, "it's over. The war is over. The Japanese have surrendered."

Intense heat invaded Hanna's body. Blood rushed to her head, pounding like two hammers at the base of her skull. And then she felt herself drop to the floor.

The next thing she knew, she was being hauled out on a gurney. Mrs. Semple, the building superintendent's wife, stood beside her as they loaded Hanna into an ambulance. She knew she had soaked through the pad, through the cover on the gurney. She could smell the blood. Mrs. Semple's concerned look told her that something was terribly wrong.

"Isabella call," Mrs. Semple told her. "She say she talking to you on the phone. Suddenly you not there anymore. So, I go up to the apartment and . . . These nice young men take you to the hospital. I call Isabella."

"The war is over," Hanna said.

"Yes," Mrs. Semple replied, "good news."

The news from the doctor who saw Hanna at the hospital was not.

"I have some concerns," he said after Hanna explained that, yes, she had these irregular bleedings, but nothing this bad before.

"I thought it was just part of the change," she said, aware of the defensive tone in her voice. She should have known.

"I'm sending you to a women's specialist," he said without a great deal of emotion. He scribbled the information down on a pad.

When Isabella called, frantic, saying she was on her way home,

Hanna told her she had simply fainted, overwhelmed that finally, this terrible war was over.

In November, as she did each year, Hanna traveled from New York to the farm to celebrate Thanksgiving with Käthe, Hans, and the family. Isabella would meet her there. She'd set up an appointment to see the specialist, but she'd decided it could wait until after Thanksgiving. She didn't want to worry anyone.

On Wednesday evening, the day of her arrival, Hanna helped Käthe get the good china and crystal out in preparation for dinner the following day. The house had been filled with activity earlier in the afternoon, Käthe's daughters buzzing about the kitchen. They'd all be back for Thanksgiving dinner. The two out-of-state girls and their families would be arriving later that night.

After helping with pies, Isabella had gone off to visit the Fletchers. She'd been writing Andrew Fletcher since he'd enlisted, and Hanna guessed there would be talk of marriage when he returned. The girl was just eighteen. Hanna hoped they would wait until she finished college.

"A letter arrived for you this week," Käthe said. She'd already told Hanna on the drive from the train station that there was a letter for her from Frederick's daughter-in-law, Anna Schmid. It had come shortly after Käthe received a letter herself, Anna writing of the loss of their two sons in the war.

"Yes, from Anna?" Hanna asked, perplexed. Käthe stood on a stool, handing dinner plates down to her. Hanna assumed Anna's letter contained the same sad news as Käthe's, and she was in no hurry to read it. "You said it was up on my bed. Didn't you?"

"A second letter. This one from Switzerland." Käthe's reply came with the intonation of a question. "I put them both on your bed upstairs."

Hans had taken her bag up earlier. Had Isabella been upstairs? Hanna set the dishes on the kitchen table, rushed up to her room, and hurried to the bed. She picked up the letters propped against the pillow. The first was from Anna, and beneath it—a letter from Johann Keller.

Hanna stared down at her own name, written in his distinct script. She felt light-headed. Her chest constricted. She sat on the bed, rearranging the letters in her hands, shuffling them like a two-card deck. She placed Anna's letter on top, and then, slowly, she opened it.

Dearest Hanna,

Before Father Frederick passed away he told us there was a painting in the barn for you. We were not aware until recently that you were in America with Käthe. Frederick knew we could not return it then, but he was adamant that you know it is here. I have sad news. Both of our sons died in the war. Eventually we will probably sell the farm. Fritz has not the will to continue. There is much healing to be done here in Germany. The painting has been removed from the stretchers and could be shipped to you. Please let us know what you want us to do.

Anna Schmid

Hanna knew that again Germany would have to rebuild itself, that many young men had been lost. She was barely encouraged by the fact that the painting had survived. She set the letter aside and picked up the one from Johann. Again she studied the outside of the envelope. The return address was the same he had used in Basel on the letter she'd received over five years ago. Much in her life had changed since then. She opened the letter.

Dearest Hanna,

Finally it is over. I have begun my attempts to return the art, but it may prove to be more difficult than anticipated. Germany has suffered enormous losses. There is no order. The channels through which I would normally conduct this return no longer exist. I will be coming to New York in the summer to visit my sister. I would like to meet with you and return your drawing as well as the bill of sale for your Kandinsky painting. I hope that I might meet Isabella. I realize that she is now eighteen. Please, Hanna, write to me. I have gone too many years with no word from you. At times I can accept that you do not want Isabella to know that I, not Moses, am her father. You have both suffered too much. Perhaps it is selfish on my part to want this daughter who I had no part in raising, but it is not by my choice that this is how it all came to be. Please write to me. I do not wish to harm you or Isabella. I want to talk about what we are to do now. Perhaps the end to this terrible war might provide a new beginning for all of us.

Johann

Hanna returned the letter to the envelope, stood, and slipped it into her pocket.

The morning after Thanksgiving, Hanna sat with Käthe, drinking coffee, eating leftover pie for breakfast. Hans had already gone out, along with young Herman, who had returned home safely from Europe. Everyone else was still sleeping. They talked about the end of the war, about the family losses in Germany. Hanna felt exhausted, as if she had fought this war herself. She thought about young Andrew Fletcher, grateful that he, too, had survived, unlike many of the young men who had gone off to war.

"I hope Isabella and Andrew will wait," Hanna said. "She's too young."

"She's in love," Käthe said with a quiet laugh.

"Sometimes love must wait," Hanna said.

Morning light played in a soft pattern along the wall, creating a quiet, muted melody. Hanna gazed out the window. When she turned, she could see Käthe's eyes were on her. Hanna got up to refill the coffee. She sat down.

"The letters from this man in Switzerland?" Käthe asked.

"A man I knew . . . after . . . before . . . " Hanna stumbled over her words. "Before I came to America."

"You deserve some happiness," Käthe said, looking directly into Hanna's eyes. Her sister had guessed that she and Johann were lovers, Hanna realized. Perhaps that was all Käthe needed to know.

"I have known much happiness," Hanna said. "Our childhood in Bavaria before Mother died, the life I lived with Moses in Munich, being witness to such wonderful creativity in Germany, being so close to that, knowing the artists, and the many places we visited, the beautiful art we discovered. Willy, sweet Willy, and my precious Isabella. I have known happiness, dear Käthe."

Footsteps upstairs, a flush of the toilet, the shower running, told them the others were stirring.

"Hanna," Käthe said. She placed her hand over her sister's. "You've lost weight."

"This rationing," Hanna said lightly.

"You are not well," Käthe replied.

Hanna said nothing.

"You've seen a doctor?"

"Yes. I have an appointment with a specialist in New York City."

"Does Isabella know?" Käthe asked.

"I'll wait. I have to see the doctor first. There's nothing to tell her yet. No need to worry her now." Hanna heard small footsteps coming down the steps, high-pitched grandchildren's voices.

"Sounds like the little ones are headed down," Käthe said with a half smile as she stood.

Hanna reached for her. "He must never know," she said, lowering her voice. "Johann must never know where Isabella and I are. Please."

Käthe nodded.

"If there are things you need to get in order," the doctor advised, "I suggest you do them soon."

"How long?" Hanna asked.

"Six months . . . maybe a year."

Hanna took a cab home. She sat in her kitchen, looking around the small apartment. Everything was neat and tidy. The mismatched pots and pans Käthe had given them when they moved to the city were put away in the drawers and under the stove. The china service for four—though she needed only two—was carefully stacked in the cupboards. Three canisters with sugar, flour, and coffee sat on the counter. She stood and walked into the living room. There were no pictures on the walls. Hanna went to the Metropolitan when she wanted to see paintings. There were no books on the tables; she borrowed from the library when she wanted to read. She moved slowly into the bedroom and sat on the bed. The closet was tiny; she had few clothes. The doctor said she must get things in order, and Hanna realized how little she had to get in order. She pulled pen and paper out of the bottom drawer of her nightstand, returned to the kitchen table, and wrote:

My dearest Johann,

*Isabella and I have made a life for ourselves in America. I
beg you to accept this. Please forgive me, but I wish no further communications with you. Please return the art to the
German museums as conditions improve. I have enclosed a
list with a description of each piece and the museums which
owned them before the war. I wish, if possible, this be done
anonymously. I am eternally grateful. You will not hear
from me again. I have instructed my sister that she is to
destroy any further correspondence.*

Yours sincerely,
Hanna

She wrote up the list, remembering clearly every detail of the
four small pieces of art. She tucked it inside the letter and sealed
the envelope. She would mail it when she went to the farm for
Christmas.

Hanna knew she was dying, yet her daughter wrote as if her
mother still had a whole life ahead of her. If Isabella had
noticed her declining health over the Thanksgiving holidays,
she'd given no hint of this in her letters, which were always cheerful. No need to worry her daughter now. She would tell her later,
after the holidays.

She and Isabella had been talking openly about the Kandinsky painting, and wrote about going to Bavaria to reclaim it. But
Hanna knew, even if she were well, it would be difficult traveling
to Germany. There had been so much destruction. She didn't want
to see this. She didn't want Isabella to see this.

The day after Christmas at Käthe's, Isabella said to Hanna, "I would like to go, Mother. We will go together to the farm in Bavaria to reclaim the Kandinsky painting, then to Munich."

"Is this before or after the wedding?" Hanna asked. Andrew, having arrived home two days before Christmas, had given her a ring on Christmas Eve, but they had not yet set a date. "Before or after you get your degree?"

"We're both going to finish school, Mother. I already explained that." She gazed down at the shiny diamond on her left hand, and then looked up at her mother. "Maybe Andrew can go with us."

But Hanna knew she would never return to Germany.

"Yes," she said, reaching for her daughter's hand. "Yes, we'll go back together."

A rim of tears hung on Isabella's pale blue eyes. Of course, Hanna realized, the girl knew her mother was not well, but neither one of them wanted to talk about it, as if the plans for their return to Germany to claim the Kandinsky painting would keep her alive.

In June, Hanna knew the end was near. She was admitted to the hospital. Isabella was home for her summer break, tending her mother, both preparing for the inevitable.

"You have to get better," Isabella said, her voice quivering, her lip trembling. Surely, Hanna thought, her daughter, who'd spoken often with the doctor, knew that she would not get better. "We have to go pick up the Kandinsky."

"*Ja*, we'll go home," Hanna told her, though she had already made arrangements for the painting to be shipped to Isabella in care of Hans Koebler. She should tell Isabella, but everything was growing dark, hazy. Her mind unclear. Sometimes she thought she was only imagining that the painting had survived the war, that it would be sent to her in America. That the war was even over. "*Ja*, we'll go home," Hanna said again.

That night Hanna returned. She was with her brothers and sisters in the green pastures under the protective shadow of the snow-covered mountains. She ran toward the house, and her mother and father stood in the doorway to greet her. She smelled the geraniums that flowed from the window baskets, the cattle grazing on green grass, the scent of her mother as she stroked Hanna's hair. The sound and color of her voice, the music of her childhood. And then in Munich she sat with the lovely golden Helene at the bedroom window, overlooking the city. Helene poured warm tea and offered her sweet-smelling bread. Then she stood with Moses before the Cézanne, his deep voice comforting her as they each held Willy by one hand. And then they were all smiling down upon this beautiful child. Isabella, this gift who had come so unexpectedly to them all.

She heard Isabella's voice. "I love you, Mama. It's okay now. Let go, Mama. Let go. I love you."

CHAPTER THIRTY-SEVEN

Lauren and Isabella

New York City
August 2009

"Your mother didn't live to see the Kandinsky returned to your family?" Lauren asked.

"No," Isabella replied. "By the time it arrived in New York from my aunt in Germany, everyone in my family had died—Papa, Willy, Mother." She picked up her tea. The ice was melting, but the small cubes still made a tinkling sound against the side of the glass. "I was in college at the time. I had nowhere to hang it." She set the glass down on the table. "I'm not sure I would have put it up at that time anyway. So many memories were attached to that painting . . .

"Andrew and I married. I finished college and then taught at an all-girls' high school while Andrew got his degree. We returned to his father's farm, which he eventually inherited along with his siblings. Andrew being the eldest, we lived for a while at the farm. He suggested we hang the Kandinsky in the dining room, though he used to say that modern painting on the wall of the old farmhouse looked about as out of place as a hula skirt on a Holstein." She laughed and glanced over at the photo of her husband. "It had been dismantled and rolled for transport from Europe and later

Andrew enlisted a couple of the farmhands to help him stretch the canvas and mount it back on the wooden frame. That was rather a comical scene, those men attempting to figure out what the heck that picture was all about. One of them—Ralph, I believe, was his name—thought it was a fine picture. Henry said he couldn't see for the life of him what that artist was thinking." Isabella laughed again and Lauren couldn't help but smile as she visualized a couple of overall-clad farmworkers stretching a Kandinsky.

She asked, "How long have you been here in New York City?"

"We bought the apartment back in the seventies, but we rented earlier. Andrew always knew I was more comfortable in the city. After Mother and I made the move to New York, then after the war, everything seemed different. I'd been close to several of my cousins—actually my cousins' children, my second cousins, as my Koebler cousins were much older than I. And I had other friends, but . . . Well, you know how sometimes those friendships of your youth . . . People move on, they change . . ."

Lauren nodded in agreement.

"Andrew always explained to anyone who asked that it was his laziness that financed our move to the city. He said he was darned tired of milking all those cows! He developed a number of machines that made it more efficient and less time-consuming, and others that are still used in the processing of milk and dairy products. He did quite well. Andrew's sister's son is now president of the business, Fletcher Enterprises, and the family sold the dairy farm years ago. A large corporation came in and bought Koebler Creamery, along with most of the small family-owned farms in the area that supplied milk for the production of dairy products. There haven't been any Koeblers involved for years now, although the company still uses the recipes that originated years and years ago. And, of course, the family name."

Lauren was aware that the company hadn't been owned by the Koebler family in many years. She thought back to several

months ago when she went to Onondaga County to look for some
trace of Hanna, how she had found very few in the community
who had any recollection of the original Koeblers. The only ones
she talked to who might have possibly known Isabella Fleischmann Smith Fletcher were an elderly couple. The wife seemed to
recall a Koebler cousin who married that Fletcher boy. Though
the husband, who appeared to be several years older than the
wife, said he was sure that Andrew Fletcher had married one of
the Koebler sisters.

Eventually this did lead Lauren to New York City and to Mrs.
Andrew Fletcher.

Isabella shook her head. "It's hard to believe we are now so
many generations removed from the original families who founded
the business in America. That happens at my age—by the time
you turn eighty the world has changed hands so many times.
Franklin D. Roosevelt was president when I arrived in America.
Most people think of that as ancient history. I've lived through a
dozen American presidents. Do you know there are young people
now who barely have an understanding of what happened during
World War II? It's hard for me to believe that."

Again Lauren agreed. She had studied history, and along with
that the history of art, but it did surprise her how many people her
age and younger saw no value in learning more about the past.

"Did you ever return for a visit to Germany?" Lauren asked.

"Oh, Andrew and I talked about it . . . but so much had
changed. Our home was gone, the gallery. No, I never returned."

Neither said anything for some time, and Lauren sensed that
Isabella's story was about to end—and, thus, Hanna's also. Then
Mrs. Fletcher reached for the envelope on the table and handed it
to the younger woman.

Their eyes met and Isabella nodded as if she was giving Lauren permission to open it.

On the top she found several documents, obviously bills of sale for the original artwork that hung in the Fletcher home. Lauren examined each carefully, matching the information with pictures she'd seen on Isabella's walls. She recognized the names of galleries in New York, one in Chicago, one in Los Angeles. There were documents for several pieces that she hadn't seen, but she hadn't made it into the master bedroom, and perhaps there was even a third bedroom. All of the papers looked official and listed provenance—dates, previous owners, and galleries where they once hung.

The large envelope also contained a smaller manila envelope. Again Isabella gestured for her to open it.

The first document was a letter from an Anna Schmid. It was in German. Though not fluent, Lauren had a reading knowledge of the language. Anna wrote that a painting, which had been left at the farm for Hanna, was being sent to her in America. The letter was dated September 1945, the handwritten message in faded ink. The envelope, addressed in the same hand, was attached with a paper clip and was obviously authentic—proper stamp and postmark. Lauren had no doubt that the letter was sent from Germany more than sixty years ago, shortly after the end of World War II.

The second document was a shipping bill of lading with a detailed description of the item to be shipped: a very large painting, the size stated in centimeters, which would easily match the purported size of Kandinsky's original *Composition II*.

A third document was a bill of sale from Botho von Gamp to Helene Kaufmann for one painting by Wassily Kandinsky entitled *Composition II*. It was dated March 15, 1939. Lauren ran her fingers over the inked signature. It appeared to be authentic. The original, not a copy.

"I think you'll find everything in order," Isabella Fletcher stated. "Everything sufficiently documented to verify that all of the originals here in our home are legitimate purchases. The documents for the Kandinsky should prove sufficient, too, if there are any questions as to its proper ownership. Helene Kaufmann was my half sister, and there are no other heirs. I don't believe anyone would challenge that I am the rightful owner." Isabella cleared her throat and then she said, "Being an expert on this type of thing, I thought perhaps you could write a report or whatever it is you do to verify all of this. I would pay you, of course." She smiled. "After I'm gone . . . Well, it's important that this be taken care of now."

This is why I am here, Lauren thought. *As simple as that, this is why Isabella Fletcher invited me into her home.*

"I'd have to see the painting," Lauren said.

Isabella let out a small chuckle. "Well, yes, I believe that is a legitimate request." The woman stood. Lauren followed her down the hall, past the dining room, the bathroom, another closed door, and then another. Isabella reached into the pocket of her mint green suit jacket, pulled out a key, and unlocked the door.

They entered the room, much larger than the bedroom Lauren had peered into yesterday. The master. Above the king-sized bed hung a large colorful painting, covering a good part of the entire, high-ceilinged wall.

Kandinsky's *Composition II.*

Breathless and stunned, Lauren approached the painting and studied it carefully. The colors, still bright, the pigments in yellows, blues, greens, reds, outlined in black. The leaping animal-like figures. The vaguely human forms. A signature ran across the lower left corner: KANDINSKY in block letters, the lower portion of the *S* sweeping long and low like the tail of a snake. It was dated 1910. She was sure it was an original Kandinsky.

For several moments, the room was very quiet.

Finally Isabella said, "You will verify that everything I have shared with you is true?"

"You've had it appraised? For insurance purposes?" Lauren asked as she turned back to Isabella. Lauren couldn't imagine how Isabella had kept this painting a secret for all these years.

The old woman's face flushed with embarrassment.

"It's not insured?" Lauren asked incredulously.

"At first when it arrived from Germany, such a thought never even crossed our minds. Andrew was an astute businessman, and yes, eventually he told me we should have it insured. Particularly as the value of paintings by such artists continued to climb. I suppose it was foolish, but I didn't want anyone to know we had it. It just seemed . . ." Isabella shook her head, obviously aware that such a painting, a piece of history, should be protected. She didn't look at Lauren but stared up at the painting. "I don't know. Andrew and I argued about it now and then. He'd say something like, *What if a thief came in and stole it?* and I'd say, *No one knows it's here, but if we have it appraised and insured, word would surely get out.* And then he'd say, *What if the building burned down?* and I'd reply, *I've lost this painting before, and what would we get if it was destroyed? Money?*"

She turned and looked directly at Lauren. "I've been rich. I've been poor. And then wealthy again. What does money mean?" Isabella fingered the diamond pendant and laughed quietly. "Well, I must confess I enjoy nice things, but when I look back on my life— Mother and I were happy in New York when we had nothing, and my best times with Andrew were probably those first years of our marriage when we had so little. No, money isn't everything. And what would I do with money? Have a long-dead artist paint another picture? If I had children perhaps I would feel differently."

"I'd suggest you have it insured," Lauren said, attempting to keep anything Isabella might consider judgmental out of her tone.

"Yes, I suppose you are right. You could help me with that. You must work with insurance companies that specialize in such policies."

"Yes, I could give you some names."

Isabella gestured toward the door and they returned to the living room.

"I trust you've received what you came for," Isabella said as they sat and she carefully arranged the items back in the envelope and placed them once more on the table. She drained the last of her tea and Lauren realized, by the finality in the way she said this and then placed the tea glass back on the tray, that their conversation had come to an end.

And just as it had begun, it would end with Isabella Fleischmann Fletcher calling the shots.

Lauren felt as drained as the tea glass. She took out her notebook and wrote down a couple of possible insurers for Isabella, aware that there were few that even wrote such policies. "They will suggest an appraiser you might contact," she told Isabella as she handed her the names.

"But can't you do that?" she asked. "Appraise the painting?"

"That's really not my area of expertise."

"But you'll verify that the papers are all here?"

"Let's have an appraiser come in, verify the authenticity and value for insurance purposes, then we'll go from there."

"Yes, that sounds right," Mrs. Fletcher said. "Thank you." She rose as if about to escort Lauren to the door.

Lauren stood and glanced down at the envelope and then at the Bubble-Wrapped glass.

"Are you sure I can't help you put the glass in the frame?" she asked again. She just couldn't leave yet. Too much of Hanna's story had yet to be told.

"No, that's fine," Mrs. Fletcher replied. "I'm sure I can take care of it. Thank you."

Neither spoke, yet neither moved. Lauren knew she couldn't let go.

"Yesterday when I came," she finally said, her voice low and controlled, "you said you wanted to tell the true story of your mother."

Isabella said nothing. A tight, composed smile spread over her face, and Lauren guessed that she'd share nothing more about Hanna Fleischmann. The old woman was done.

"The truth," Isabella replied after a long hesitation, "and you said you weren't afraid of the truth."

"Yes."

Now Isabella stared down at the table. She looked up at Lauren again and something had changed, something around her eyes. It was not that confident, controlled facade that Lauren saw now, but an expression that held a hint of relief.

"Perhaps you could," Isabella said, "yes, perhaps you could help me."

She went back to the bedroom and returned with the photograph of Isabella and Willy. Lauren noticed she had removed the broken glass and placed the picture back in the frame, unprotected. Isabella set it on the table beside the wrapped glass and studied it for several quiet moments before she said, "You do know there is more to this story. My mother's story." Her eyes were still on the photo.

"Yes," Lauren replied.

"After my mother died, after I cleaned out the apartment in New York that summer, I returned to my aunt and uncle's farm, and"—she looked up at Lauren—"there was a phone call."

CHAPTER THIRTY-EIGHT

Isabella

New York State
August 1946

After going through Hanna's things in the apartment in New York, Isabella realized how little her mother had left—nothing for her daughter to hold on to, no memories of their life in Germany. A few letters. One photograph, taken in America—a smiling Willy and a young Isabella, staring into the camera with an uncertain look. A few worn dresses and skirts. Hanna had come to America with one small suitcase, and she had left this world with little more.

The last week of August, Isabella was sitting in the kitchen at the farm with Käthe when the phone rang. Aunt Katie got up to answer it.

"No," she said tentatively, "my sister passed away in June."

Käthe nodded as she listened for several moments. She said nothing, though Isabella detected a tension in the way she ran her fingers up and down the telephone cord. Her back stiffened as she turned away from her niece. She glanced over her shoulder at Isabella. "Yes," she finally said. She held the phone out for Isabella. A hesitant look had settled on her face. "A gentleman wishes to speak with Isabella Fleischmann."

Isabella took the phone. "Yes," she said, "this is Isabella Fleischmann." She hadn't used her real name for several years now and it seemed strange, yet comfortable.

There was no reply, and for a moment she thought whoever was on the other end would hang up. The line was silent, though not dead.

"I'm sorry," he finally said, "for the loss of your mother."

His voice, oddly, sounded very much like Isabella's father, Moses Fleischmann. He spoke English with an accent. It was a beautiful, comforting voice. "To whom am I speaking?" she asked.

Even before he said, "My name is Johann Keller," Isabella knew. She had always known that one day she would speak with Johann Keller. As if this man were the key to unlock the mystery. Everything about her mother would finally make sense.

"Your mother and I were friends," he said, his voice cracking. "Friends in . . ." Again, silence. "I have something I would like you to have, something I believe your mother would like you to have. If you will let me know—"

"I'd like to meet," Isabella broke in.

"I'm staying here in New York with my sister . . . We could—"

"There's a coffee shop near the Metropolitan Museum," she said, thinking instantly of one of her mother's favorite places. "Tomorrow. I can be there by tomorrow morning."

"You are at university?" the man asked.

"Yes," Isabella replied. He had come in carrying an official-looking briefcase, ten minutes early, and she guessed he had intended to be there waiting for her. But she had arrived fifteen minutes before the agreed time. When he entered the coffee shop, he did not glance about searching for her, but walked over without hesitation and said, "Isabella."

He was a handsome man, tall and thin. She took him to be in his early sixties. His hair was white, his eyes very blue. There was something reassuring and confident in his looks, as there had been in his voice when she spoke to him on the phone. Would this man reveal to Isabella the truth Hanna had kept from her daughter? Was this man a Nazi? And then another question worked its way into her mind: *Were my mother and Johann Keller lovers?*

"What are you studying?" he asked thoughtfully. "At university?"

"I've just finished first year," she answered, wondering if they would make small talk as they warmed up to speak of why he was really here. "I haven't decided on my major just yet. I've always had a knack for language."

"Yes," he said, as if he knew this about her.

He glanced at her left hand. "You're married?" His pale eyebrows rose. Did he think she was too young?

"Engaged," she said. "I promised Mother I would finish school."

He nodded in agreement.

The waiter appeared with the coffee they had ordered.

"American coffee," Mr. Keller said with a smile, shaking his head in mock horror. He added cream and sugar, and picked up his spoon to stir. His eyes moved around the room. Reproductions of art from the Metropolitan hung on the walls. "You like art?" he asked.

"Yes, as did my mother. We often came here. She loved going to the Met."

Again he nodded and she could see this pleased him. He commented no further on the place she had chosen for this meeting.

Isabella regarded her coffee, but her stomach turned with nerves, and she knew she could not drink any.

Finally he said, "I don't know how much your mother told you." He stirred his coffee, and once more Isabella thought how comforting she found his voice.

"There were things she couldn't," Isabella said, "*wouldn't* talk about. In many ways I had accepted this, that there were parts of her life . . ." Isabella looked directly into Mr. Keller's eyes. He did not blink. He was studying her as she had studied him. Did he see something of Hanna in Isabella? "After the war," she continued, "after the soldiers discovered what had taken place in the camps, the murder of so many Jews, she seemed even more reticent." *She knew she was dying,* Isabella thought, *and even this she did not tell me. Did she think she could protect me from the reality of death?* "I knew she had suffered, that she had escaped. We lost my father, then Helene, his older daughter—my half sister—and her husband, Jakob." Somehow she sensed that this man knew of these people, that he knew more about her life than she knew herself.

Yet now he seemed hesitant to speak—they sat quietly.

After several more moments, he lifted his briefcase from the floor and took out a sheet of paper. He handed it to Isabella.

She unfolded it on the table. It was written in German. Her eyes moved quickly down the page. It was a bill of sale for the Kandinsky *Composition II*, made out to Helene Kaufmann from Botho von Gamp, dated March 15, 1939, Berlin, Germany.

"How did you get this?" she snapped. She had recently received correspondence from Anna Schmid outlining the arrangements Hanna had made to have the painting shipped to New York.

"Your mother told you nothing?"

"Very little. She told me about the painting, how Helene had purchased it, how it was being hidden on the farm in Bavaria. But no, she told me very little. Why are you now in possession of this document?" Her tone remained sharp.

With composure, Mr. Keller produced a rolled paper and handed it to Isabella. She unrolled it, securing the paper with one hand, Mr. Keller placing his hand on the opposite end to allow it to lie flat. It was a drawing of a young woman.

Slowly, as she studied the figure, the fullness of the breasts, the thick hair, plaited and pinned up, wayward curls falling to her shoulders, Isabella realized this was a drawing of her mother, a very young Hanna. Had she been a model in her youth, and was this just one of her secrets?

"Where did you get this?" she asked again, perplexed, the harshness now gone from her voice, replaced with curiosity. Her eyes rose to Mr. Keller's.

"When your mother left Germany, knowing she would not return," he started in, "she carried with her several items that were very important to her. She was afraid they would be found as she passed through the port authorities, that she might be discovered."

"Because she was traveling on false documents?" Again she regarded the drawing.

"Yes. So she sent these items back to me."

"To you?" Isabella's head jerked up. Mr. Keller said nothing. "Did you know my mother when she was a model?"

"No, no," he said. "This particular drawing came as a gift from your father. It was one of the only pieces she still had when she was forced to flee."

"She was a model." Isabella spoke more to herself than to Mr. Keller as she considered the drawing once more. "She looks so young, and so . . . I don't know—shy, in a way—but at the same time very brave and confident. The way she sits on the chair, shoulders back, hands folded in her lap. She looks like she could take on the world. Nothing between herself and the . . ." Isabella laughed, and felt herself blush. She was sitting here with a stranger, discussing a nude portrait of her mother. She looked up at Mr. Keller. "Do you know how I think of my mother?"

"Tell me," he said.

"Not like this." She touched the drawing with her free hand, running her fingers slowly along the curve of the young woman's shoulder. "Guarded and frightened. That's how I see her."

"The war," he said, as if this should be obvious.

"She lived through two."

"As did many," Mr. Keller replied.

"So many losses—Father, Willy, Helene, Jakob, Josef . . ." *And more we probably don't even know of yet,* Isabella thought. "She told me that they had to sell the art to survive in Nazi Germany, to escape." Isabella searched Johann Keller's face, and for a brief moment it seemed she was looking into her own eyes. Into the eyes of someone who had suffered a great loss. She gazed down again, fearing she might burst into tears.

"She told you nothing about her escape?" Mr. Keller asked.

"No." Isabella shook her head and released the paper. Mr. Keller rolled the drawing back up.

"Nothing about the work she did in Berlin?" he asked.

"Nothing."

"The auction in Lucerne?"

"No."

Mr. Keller hesitated, as if carefully considering his words. She could see a tightness about his thin lips, about his eyes.

"Please," Isabella said, "I want to know."

"Before the war," he said slowly, adding more cream to his coffee.

"Yes," she said with cautious encouragement.

"Hitler abhorred anything in art that was modern."

Isabella nodded.

"Anything declared distasteful—based on his own determinations—was confiscated from the state museums." Mr. Keller took in a deep breath, still contemplating, Isabella was fully aware, how much of this she should know. "After your father died . . . your mother was very knowledgeable, particularly with the modern artists that Hitler found so vile. She was brilliant, in fact," he said with a smile. "I've never known such a woman . . ." He hesitated. "A woman who could hear the colors."

His words startled her. Her mother had shared this with so few, and now it was as if she had slipped in between them, right here in the coffee shop, and said to her daughter, *I trust this man, and so must you.*

Yes, Isabella thought once more, they were lovers. Strangely, this did not bother her. How lonely her mother must have been after her father died. If this man had brought her comfort, why should this be denied?

But why had he not come to Hanna? Was it because of the war? Had her mother given up this—the man she loved—to come to her daughter?

"Hitler saw it, too," Mr. Keller continued. "There was value in what this woman knew. Value in the art which he claimed to detest. Hitler took advantage of everyone and everything, taking what he wanted to further his cause, discarding anything else. He used your mother. She was forced to work at his facility in Berlin to identify the art, to catalogue, to compile lists."

Isabella gasped. Was this the secret her mother had been hiding from her all these years?

Her shame? She had aided Hitler?

Mr. Keller went on. "She also took part in an auction in Lucerne to sell this confiscated art."

But why, Isabella wondered, couldn't she trust that her daughter would understand? That she would accept that her mother had no choice. "Hitler detested the art," she said, "yet he knew it might be valuable in increasing the Reich's wealth?"

"Yes," Mr. Keller replied.

"Many years ago," Isabella said, "I saw a telegram you sent to my mother." Then, boldly, she recited the exact words, " 'Packages delivered. Isabella must know truth.' "

Mr. Keller blinked once, and then again, and Isabella could see his composure slipping away, if but for a mere second.

"Is this the truth she wished to hide?" Isabella asked. "That she aided the Nazis?"

Again his lips tightened and a tension passed over his face. He lifted his cup, but Isabella knew it was empty. She had yet to take a drink of hers. The waiter came over, refilled his cup, and asked Isabella if she'd like hers warmed. She shook her head.

"She was able, during her time in Berlin," Mr. Keller said, "to hide, to save, several pieces of art. You are aware many were destroyed in a fire in Berlin?"

"No," Isabella replied hurriedly, wishing Mr. Keller to continue.

Again he seemed to consider his words, and then he said, "She feared this would be the fate of the art that was not chosen to go to the auction in Switzerland. That it, too, would be destroyed. She left this rescued art with me, and I am now in the process of returning it to the proper German museums. When she traveled from Berlin to Switzerland for the auction, she concealed them in her suitcase lining, along with these items." His thin hand swept across the rolled drawing and the document on the table, which Isabella had placed protectively under her own.

"Diamonds, too," Isabella said, and noticed another shift in the facade of his face. He was surprised. She guessed that between the two of them, the story of Hanna might be revealed. "From Helene. Mother hid them in the hem of her skirt. She sent me to private school on Helene and Jakob's diamonds."

"Did you make good use of your mother's sacrifice?"

"Are you asking if I'm a good student?"

He nodded.

"Yes, I am."

"Your parents would be very proud of you," he said with a smile.

"Thank you," she replied softly, fearing again that she might cry.

"I feel you should know what your mother did," Mr. Keller said, "because at some point her name might be linked with the art trade in Germany, and there might be accusations that she, as other German dealers, took advantage and gained personal wealth through their dealings. As the history unfolds, I believe it will be revealed that much art was stolen, looted, hidden, some regretfully destroyed, before, during, and even now after the war. The story has yet to be told. When it is, the story of Hanna Fleischmann must be told correctly."

"Thank you," Isabella said, "for sharing this with me."

"The art will be returned. It was your mother's wish that this be done anonymously. But your mother's story must not die with her death."

"It won't," she assured him. "Will you keep me informed of the developments in the return?"

"Yes, of course."

They sat for several moments, guardedly considering each other, exchanging no further words. Mr. Keller drained his cup for a second time. He reached for his briefcase. Isabella did not want this conversation to end. She needed more.

"Mr. Keller." She reached out and touched his arm. She felt him tense. "When did you meet my mother?" she asked.

Again, she sensed the caution, his grip tightening on the briefcase. "I was working for a gallery in Basel," he said, slowly returning the briefcase to the floor. "I came to Berlin where your mother was working."

"You're Swiss?"

"Yes."

"Please, go on," she said.

"I represented the Kunstmuseum in Basel. We wanted to purchase some of the art. A rescue, we believed, though the pieces were eagerly received into our collection. We met again in Switzerland at the auction. It was there that arrangements were made for your mother to come to America."

In her mind's eye, Isabella could see the portrait of her mother as if it were still spread out before her, this young woman she would never know.

"She was a wonderful, brave woman." Johann Keller removed a handkerchief from the pocket of his jacket and dabbed at a spot of moisture on his upper lip. He folded it carefully and returned it to his pocket. "That is why you must know the truth. Your mother was a good, brave woman. A remarkable woman. Her story must not be lost."

CHAPTER THIRTY-NINE

Lauren and Isabella

New York City
August 2009

"The art was returned to the German museums?" Lauren asked.

"Honestly, Mrs. O'Farrell, I'm not sure."

"You never heard from Mr. Keller again?"

"Never. Several years later I sent him a letter addressed to the museum in Basel where he said he worked, asking if there had been any developments regarding the conversation we'd had in New York."

"But he didn't answer?"

"I received a reply from the museum director. He informed me that Johann Keller had passed away a year earlier, that he could help me if the matter was related to business. If it was personal, I might contact his widow."

"His widow?"

"Yes, he was married. It seems my mother was having an affair with a married man."

Lauren said nothing for several moments. What do you say to an eighty-two-year-old woman who's just admitted her mother had an affair over seventy years ago? A comment, she decided, was neither necessary nor appropriate. Finally she said, "Did you ever try contacting some of the museums to determine if any of this government confiscated art was returned?"

"Really, Lauren, do you know how many museums there are in Germany and how many paintings, drawings, and other pieces of art were stored at that warehouse in Berlin?"

This was the first time Mrs. Fletcher had referred to Lauren by her given name. "Between sixteen and seventeen thousand," she replied.

Isabella smiled. "I suppose someone in your line of work would know these facts."

"Yes." Lauren smiled, too.

"Let me show you something," Isabella said. Her tone remained calm, yet at the same time tinged with a sense of discovery. Was that final protective layer of distrust being lifted?

Slowly Isabella took the photo out of the frame and removed the cardboard backing.

"What is it?" Lauren asked, staring down.

"I think it is a list. I believe it is a description of the art that my mother saved from the warehouse."

"Wow." This was the only word Lauren could come up with. She studied the handwritten script. Dates, German cities, German words—some obviously names of museums, initials she thought might be artists. "She's written the descriptions, the artists, the museums in Germany from which the art was originally taken?"

"Yes, I believe so."

"Maybe he *did* return it," Lauren thought, realizing she'd said the words aloud, realizing that her own caution and misgivings were dissipating along with Isabella's.

"With this information," Isabella said, "we might be able to track down the art." Again there was a hint of tension in her voice, a slight hesitation. "For years I've pushed this aside, knowing that my mother had indeed worked for the Nazis, knowing what Mr. Keller told me, yet wondering if he was withholding something, always sensing there was more to the story. I felt he was attempting to protect my mother, perhaps even lying. It was so obvious that he had loved her. And I continued to wonder about the fate of the art. If it was never returned, this wouldn't exactly clear my mother's name if she were accused of crimes against Germany. When I met with Mr. Keller, he said that at some point accusations would be made. I believe he was leaving it to me to defend her. Yet, I felt he had withheld important facts that were essential for me to do this. Then, for more than sixty years, I waited. No one came forth with allegations of theft or Nazi collaboration, and I felt as if it would never happen, that I would not be required to speak of any of this. So, I set it all aside. But then you came . . ." Isabella stared at Lauren, as if asking, *Where do we go from here?*

"I'd like to help," Lauren said.

"We could write to these museums," Isabella replied cautiously, "and ask if these particular paintings were returned." Lauren could see she was putting it all on the line. She wished to move forward.

"We could," Lauren replied. "But I've got an idea that might be a lot easier, and a lot quicker. At least to get us started. Using this list, the names of the museums, the cities, the artists . . . Yes, let's start with the names of the museums. Many of them list inventories on their websites, along with contacts and phone numbers. Still fluent in German?"

"Yes, of course," Isabella replied.

Lauren reached down into her bag and pulled out her Black-Berry. "Well, let's get started checking this out."

CHAPTER FORTY

Lauren

New York City
Two Years Later

"I wish Mrs. Fletcher could be there," Lauren said as Patrick turned onto Fifth Avenue.

"I'm sure she'll be there in spirit," he replied. "If her health would allow, she'd come."

And Hanna, Lauren thought, *I wish she could be here, too. I think she'd be pleased.* She glanced in the backseat at the two children, the baby strapped securely in the infant safety seat, Adam in his booster. Five-month-old Melanie sucked away on her pacifier, her plump little chin resting against the bib Lauren had put on her to protect the new dress, at least until they got to the museum. It was a beautiful fall day, trees in the city just beginning to turn. An Indian summer, the sun bright, the sky blue. Lauren couldn't have ordered a more perfect day, though the presentation would be held inside.

Lauren had been asked to speak. She was wearing a new suit— slender black skirt and tapestry-like jacket with more color than she was used to wearing. She'd gone over and over her notes, wanting to get every word exactly right. For the past week she'd sat daily with Isabella, adding and deleting as Mrs. Fletcher gave her approval with a nod, her disapproval with a shake of the head. Sometimes a verbal suggestion was offered, though the woman struggled at times to express herself. She'd been released from the rehabilitation facility just four months ago and, according to the therapist, she was doing wonderfully. Isabella might not agree with that assessment.

During the months following her initial meetings with Mrs. Fletcher just over two years ago, Lauren and Isabella had worked together using the information Hanna had written on the back of the photograph of Isabella and Willy. They'd determined that each piece of art Hanna had taken from Berlin was returned many years ago to its rightful home. This had been done anony-mously. Lauren learned through a director of one of the museums that a Swiss man, a noted scholar on early twentieth-century art, named Peter Keller—oddly a source Lauren had used in one of her undergraduate papers—had assisted his father in returning the art. He was almost ninety years old now, and an acquain-tance of the director. Peter Keller's father, Johann Keller, had passed away before the final piece had been returned, and his son never knew the identity of the woman who had taken the art from the warehouse in Berlin and asked that Johann return each to the German museum from which it had been taken.

After they had completed their project, Lauren was satisfied that Hanna had taken nothing for herself and that her family had benefited in no way. Her careful tending of the art had, in fact, saved some that might have otherwise been destroyed.

Lauren continued to drop by now and then to see Isabella, but as the months passed, the visits were less frequent.

About a year later, she received a call from an attorney who left a message stating that he would like to set up a meeting to discuss a matter relating to Mrs. Andrew Fletcher. Lauren's heart dropped as she recognized the name of the firm as one that had assisted her Goldman grandparents in their estate planning. Her initial thought was that Isabella had died. Relief flooded through her when she returned the call and the attorney said they would be meeting with Mrs. Fletcher at her home.

"We're here," Patrick announced as they pulled into the museum parking garage. "You ready?"

"Yes," Lauren replied with an anxious smile.

Isabella had wanted Lauren to be present at the family meeting, which consisted of the attorney, Mrs. Fletcher, and her nephew, Richard Barber, who had just recently retired from Fletcher Enterprises, the business now being run by Isabella's grandnephew. It was obvious from the items discussed that Andrew and Isabella had been very good to the remaining members of the Fletcher family. Isabella sat without words as the terms of her will and her wishes for the disbursement of her property were explained. The art was being gifted to various museums throughout the city. The attorney described each piece and Isabella's intended recipient.

"One pencil drawing," he read off the list, "nude woman in chair. Eighteen by twenty-four inches on paper. Circa 1900 to 1910. Artist unknown. To Lauren O'Farrell."

Lauren glanced at Mrs. Fletcher, realizing it was the drawing of Hanna. What a wonderful gift, and how truly touched she was to be considered worthy of this. She nodded a thank-you to a completely controlled Isabella as Lauren herself fought back the tears, as the attorney continued to read.

Kandinsky's *Composition* would be donated to the Metropolitan Museum of Art, this gift to be made as soon as possible. Lauren, because of her knowledge of the painting's history, was being asked to coordinate this effort.

Richard Barber appeared unemotional about all of this, and Lauren guessed that he'd been informed of his aunt's wishes earlier, that this meeting was really for Lauren.

As Patrick parked the car, she glimpsed at her notes again,

though she knew every word of her speech by heart. Every word had been approved by Isabella. She slipped her note cards into her small bag. Patrick was helping Adam. Lauren lifted Melanie out of the car seat. She'd fallen asleep during the drive. Maybe she'd nap through the presentation and reception. The baby's blue eyes popped open wide.

"You'll be a good girl while Mommy talks?" Lauren asked. She'd considered getting a sitter, but decided this day was too important. History was being made and Lauren wanted the children to be present, even if they would have no memory of the event. As she exchanged a look with Patrick, she felt the heavy pounding of her heart and that annoying little twitch behind her left eye. She must be crazy, bringing a baby and five-year-old to such an important art museum presentation.

"We're fine," he said, reassuringly. "Too late to reconsider now. If she gets fussy, I'll take her out."

"I'll take her out, too," Adam offered.

"Thanks, sweetie." Lauren took her son's hand. "You've got the camera?" she asked Patrick.

He pulled it out of his pocket and snapped a picture of Lauren with Melanie balanced on her hip, Adam holding her hand.

"You look great," Patrick said.

"Thank you." She felt good about having chosen a colorful outfit, something that both Hanna and Wassily Kandinsky would, no doubt, find quite fitting for the occasion.

As they entered the gallery, Patrick took Melanie and reached for Adam's hand. Lauren's eyes were drawn immediately to the Kandinsky *Composition*. Here in the museum, under a lighting system designed specifically for the painting, the colors were stunning. A group had already gathered. The director headed toward Lauren, but was stopped by a woman she recognized as one of the museum's most generous donors. Lauren's eyes swept the room to see if maybe Isabella had changed her mind.

When Lauren called last evening, she'd replied with a definite *no*. Lauren guessed that the woman had too much pride to show up in such a physically deteriorated condition. One side of her body was partially paralyzed, and though she was beautifully dressed when Lauren visited—thanks to a home health-care worker—it had become even more tedious and difficult for her to leave her home. During the time they'd spent together, Lauren had learned that Isabella was proud, but maybe a little shy, too. Even before the stroke, Lauren guessed that she seldom went out. Groceries were delivered; a woman came in to clean each week. Isabella never spoke of leaving the apartment, and one day when Lauren invited her for lunch, the woman said, "Oh, I'm just more comfortable here at home."

Lauren spotted the mayor of New York, and then the governor. Several stories had appeared in the *Times* about this donation. It was big news. She wondered if any of Isabella's relatives would appear. Richard Barber was the only one she would recognize, and she didn't see him.

She shot Patrick a disappointed look, and then she turned, shocked, as her mom, her dad, her brother, his wife, and their daughter and son entered the room.

"What a nice surprise!" Lauren exclaimed, rushing over to them, kissing her mom on the cheek, giving her dad a hug, then taking the others into a group hug as her heart pounded with both excitement and nerves.

"Oh, look at you!" her mother squealed, taking the baby from Patrick. "Look how big you are."

"And me, too," Adam said.

"Yes, you are getting so grown-up," his grandmother replied as Lauren's father gave the boy's hair a little ruffle.

"What are you, fifteen now?" he said with a tease in his voice. Adam giggled, and Lauren observed, not for the first time, that her dad was so much more lighthearted and affectionate with the grandchildren than he'd ever been with Lauren and her brother.

"We're very proud of you," her mother said as her father nodded. That was about as much as she'd get from him, and it was enough. They were here.

They'd flown in from California last night, her mom explained, and were staying at their usual hotel. They never stayed with Lauren and Patrick even when the trip was planned well in advance. Her mother's constant refrain: "You know we old folks need a bit of privacy, and your father, he's up at least half a dozen times a night."

As the director approached, Lauren introduced her family, even as her eyes darted around the room again. Still no Isabella. No one to represent the family other than Lauren.

The program began with the director introducing several dignitaries and donors and acknowledging a number of others in the room. He invited everyone to a reception in the Patron's Lounge following the presentation, and expressed his sincere thanks for the generosity of Mrs. Isabella Fletcher in the gift of the Kandinsky *Composition II*, one of the greatest art revelations of the century.

Then he introduced Lauren as a representative speaking for Mrs. Fletcher, whose health did not allow her to attend.

"As with any painting," Lauren began, looking out over the gathering, "there is always a history—the history of the artist, the time and place in which it was created, and a history of those who have enjoyed and owned the painting throughout its lifetime." Lauren steadied her hand on the lectern. She was feeling especially jittery now that her parents were here. She glanced down at her notes. When her eyes rose, there she was in the back of the room, one arm looped through her nephew's, one hand on her cane. She wore a lovely fall suit of rust-colored wool. A woman Lauren took to be Richard's wife stood to his left; a young couple, most likely the grandnephew and his wife, followed closely behind.

Isabella lifted her head proudly, a half smile on her lips, and then she rolled her eyes toward the nephew, indicating, Lauren had no doubt, that *he*, not Isabella, was the reason for their tardiness.

Lauren smiled at Isabella, so very pleased that she was here, feeling now as if the day had suddenly become whole. Knowing she would not want to be introduced or cause any interruption, Lauren paused for only a brief moment as the little group settled into seats in the back.

"I would like to tell you the story of a young woman," Lauren continued, "who in 1900 at the age of sixteen left the family farm in Bavaria and set out for Munich. Perhaps she was looking for an adventure and some excitement, but I'm sure at the time she had no idea what was to come. She found work in the home of a distinguished art dealer and a love was sparked—for this man who would eventually become her husband, and for the art." Lauren met Isabella's eyes once more and she could see a subtle flash of approval, which helped calm her unsteady hands and voice. "A passion that would remain for a lifetime and which would eventually throw Hanna, involuntarily, into a world where every step, every thought, was controlled." Lauren paused for a moment, taking a deep breath. "This woman was Hanna Fleischmann, Isabella Fletcher's mother. The art dealer was Mrs. Fletcher's father, Moses Fleischmann."

Isabella nodded. Again Lauren looked out over the crowd: Patrick, Adam—thankfully, being very well behaved—her brother, sister-in-law, and their children. Her mother held the baby on her knee with a gentle bounce. Both stared out at full attention, Melanie obviously recognizing her own mother's voice.

"This painting"—Lauren turned and motioned toward the Kandinsky *Composition*—"would not be hanging before us today if not for Hanna, her family, and their heroic efforts." Lauren explained how the painting was originally purchased by Moses Fleischmann as a gift for his wife to celebrate the birth of their son, how it was reluctantly sold, and then reclaimed. She shared the story of how it was hidden away at a family farm in Bavaria during the destructive years of World War II.

"But the story goes much beyond this single painting."

She spoke of Hitler's censorship and artistic purge, of Hanna's being enlisted to help with the cataloguing in Berlin, of her separation from her children, of rescuing and secretly concealing the art taken from the warehouse.

"Hanna felt that the right of artistic expression," Lauren said, "which Kandinsky himself believed originated in the soul, was as essential and as important as the right to life itself." She went on to tell of how this saved art was eventually returned to the German museums. "Though these pieces might be considered less significant than the Kandinsky painting before us, each was important to Hanna, who risked much to save them, and this must be remembered as we tell her story."

Lauren turned again toward the large painting. "Wassily Kandinsky's *Composition II* has meant so much to Mrs. Fletcher over the years, as it did to her mother, Hanna Fleischmann, her father, Moses Fleischmann, and her brother, Wilhelm. It is with some sadness, yet with joy, that she presents it to the Metropolitan Museum of Art."

Once more Lauren's eyes met Isabella's. Not a tear to be seen. But Lauren could feel it—the great joy and satisfaction in Isabella's eyes, finally knowing the truth in what her mother had done, in having Hanna's story told here today, sharing her courage with the world. Then Lauren caught her father's eye, and she was sure that she detected a glisten.

"Not only does this painting represent Isabella Fleischmann Fletcher's childhood in Munich and the happiness of her family, but it represents her mother Hanna's struggle, her survival. Perhaps even more important," Lauren said, "this painting represents the freedom of creativity itself, and Isabella has asked that I express how greatly pleased her mother, Hanna, would be to share this with all of you." Again she glanced to the back of the room. Isabella's thin lips quivered as they formed the words *Thank you*. Lauren nodded, took in another deep breath to keep her own emotions in check, exhaled, and continued. "Return someday with your families and friends, and as you view this painting, share with them the story of Hanna Fleischmann."

Lauren turned and gazed at Kandinsky's *Composition II*. The memories that Isabella had shared flashed in her mind, and she felt as if she could actually see the painting hanging in the music room in Munich, and then, for a very brief moment, she felt as if she could hear it—the vibrant, triumphant sounds of the colors.

ACKNOWLEDGMENTS

Many thanks to these friends and writers for reading early drafts and chapters: Renie Hays, Paul Van Dam, Joyce Davis, Judy Frederick, Coston Frederick, Maria Eschen, and Pat Koleini. I'd like to extend a special note of gratitude to Linda Kahn for a rush reading as we approached the end.

Thank you to Margrit Robertson and Coston Frederick for sharing memories and observations of life in Germany and America in the years leading up to and during World War II. Thanks to my Berkley editor, Kate Seaver, with an extra thank-you from my greatest-generation and baby-boomer readers for the larger-sized print. Much gratitude to editorial assistant Katherine Pelz for her technical support in getting me through the frustrations of those final edits.

As always, I am grateful for my wonderful agent, Julie Barer, who, even after reading draft after draft, did not give up on the story. To my husband, Jim, once more, thank you for your support through this lengthy process and for handling the baggage on our research field trips to Munich and Berlin.

I have relied on information from numerous sources and publications to frame Hanna's story in the proper historical context. Among these are: *The Rise and Fall of the Third Reich*, William L. Shirer, Simon & Schuster, New York, 1960; *Prelude to War*, Robert T. Elson and the editors of Time-Life Books, Time-Life Books Inc., Alexandria, VA, 1976, 1977; *The Rape of Europa: The Fate of*

Europe's Treasures in the Third Reich and the Second World War, Lynn H. Nicholas, Alfred A. Knopf, Inc., New York, 1994. Two books published in conjunction with art exhibitions have been extremely helpful. *"Degenerate Art": The Fate of the Avant-Garde in Nazi Germany* by Stephanie Barron was copublished in 1991 by the Los Angeles County Museum of Art and Harry N. Abrams, Inc., for an exhibition that later traveled to the Art Institute of Chicago. *Kandinsky: The Path to Abstraction* was published in 2006 by Tate Publishing, a division of Tate Enterprises Ltd., Millbank, London, on the occasion of an exhibition organized through the collaborative efforts of Tate Modern, London, and the Kunstmuseum Basel. I had the opportunity to view the Kandinsky exhibition at the Kunstmuseum in October 2006.

READERS GUIDE

FOR

The Woman Who Heard Color

DISCUSSION QUESTIONS

1. What opportunities open up for Hanna when she becomes an employee in the Fleischmann home? How do these allow her to choose a different path from the one she might have taken had she stayed on the farm? Do you believe Hanna is a woman ahead of her times? What role do Hanna's own choices and her early fearlessness play in determining her future?

2. Were you initially suspicious of Isabella's story, and were you surprised by how it all unfolded? Did you find her memories to be a reliable source of information?

3. What was life like for a Jewish citizen in Germany prior to World War II? What was restricted and what were the human costs as Hitler took power? What do you think it was like for Hanna, a Christian with a Jewish husband? How did her marriage affect her relationships with her own family members, particularly her sister Leni?

4. How do you think Hanna felt as a child when she discovered that others did not hear color? Does this condition make her more empathetic with those who might be considered odd or different? Isabella describes her mother's synesthesia as a gift rather than a liability. Do you believe Hanna came to see her blending of the senses as an asset, too?

5. What role should the government play in determining what is acceptable art? Who should decide what type of art is shown in publicly supported museums? Should certain types of art be subject to government censorship?

6. How would you describe Hanna's role in cataloguing the confiscated art? Why does she agree to work with the Nazis in this endeavor, and how does she reconcile her complicity with her feelings of disgust? Does she have a choice? What are the consequences of her decision?

7. Though Hanna leaves Germany in 1939, before the start of World War II, do you see anything in her story, particularly relating to her involvement with the art, that might foreshadow the historical events that follow?

8. Some of those purchasing art at the auction in Lucerne come to save it, others to pick up a bargain. Do you believe these buyers realized the funds would be diverted from the museums to build up Hitler's military strength? Should they have avoided the auction in protest? Why or why not? Do you believe the German museums should be able to reclaim this art?

9. Why is Hanna's legacy so important to Isabella as an adult? How does Lauren play a critical part in preserving Hanna's story and allowing her heroics to live on?

10. At one point in the story, Isabella says, "So much family history is lost just because no one listens . . . Or when it's never even told." Lauren agrees yet has always been reluctant to ask her father about his own history. Do you think Lauren will eventually encourage her father to share more about his childhood and her grandparents' lives? Do you have family stories that have been told through the generations? Has family history been lost? What is the effect of untold wartime histories disappearing as the World War II generation passes away? What lessons and stories must not be forgotten?

NOTES